TINDERBOX UNDER WINTER STARS

Book Two in The Tinderbox Tales

EMMA STERNER-RADLEY

Heartsome Publishing

SIGN UP

Firstly, thank you for purchasing Tinderbox Under Winter Stars.

I frequently hold flash sales, competitions, giveaways and lots more.

To find out more about these great deals you will need to sign up to my mailing list by clicking on the link below:

http://tiny.cc/matb

I sincerely hope you will enjoy reading Tinderbox Under Winter Stars.

If you did, I would greatly appreciate a short review on your favourite book website.

Reviews are crucial for any author, and even just a line or two can make a huge difference.

Dedicated to Heimdal.
(Because he was always my favourite Norse god and seemed the right being to dedicate a Nordic themed book to.)

ACKNOWLEDGMENTS

As always, I didn't create this story alone. First, I had the lovely writer Em Stevens to beta read for me and Helen Clarke to do a sensitivity read for the character of Anja. Then the paid professionals swooped in and performed heroics, thank you to my editor Jessica Hatch and my proofreader Cheri Fuller – my knights in shining Track Changes.

This was a long and sometimes painful project and I'm so very grateful to my wife, Amanda Radley, for her patience and understanding.

As always, thanks to my supportive family back in Sweden and in memory of:

Malin Sterner
1973-2011
Du fattas mig.

AUTHOR'S NOTE

Unlike Making a Tinderbox, this book didn't get a full introduction. I'm sure a clever reader like yourself knows the drill by now. This book's theme of a gaslamp fantasy world inspired by real events, countries, and creeds is the same as in Making a Tinderbox. The difference is that this story's faux-Victorian setting borrows from the Scandinavian countries with hints from Russia and Britain.

Squint and you might see inspiration from the Sami people, the KGB, the War of the Roses, Freemasons and… you'll find characters with Swedish names. (Don't worry, I've picked names that English speakers should be able to pronounce/read.) You'll find a map and glossary at the end of the book.

Thank you for picking up this book. Now, make yourself a hot drink, and sit back to learn what awaits Nessa and Elise.

CHAPTER 1
SILVER HOLLOW CASTLE

The Queen of Arclid's high heels beat the stone floor into submission as she headed for her brother's room. The corridor reeked of mould and the gas from the ill-kept gaslamps lining the walls. She grimaced as she saw a gloomy painting of her ancestor, Albertus the Third. His overspending and habit of strangling his lovers after copulation had started one of the many revolts against the Royal House of Hargraves. She did not need to be reminded of such things. This morning's ride through the village of Ground Hollow had shown her that there were, as always, people protesting the Hargraves monarchy. She couldn't think why. It wasn't as if *she* strangled lovers. She might be on her way to strangle her brother, though.

A minute later, she flung open the doors to Prince Macray's bedroom, revealing her brother busy tying the laces at the waist of his britches. In the bed was a pretty, blond youngling, his strong body fully exposed, and through a smug smile, showing yellow, crooked teeth.

A peasant. How vile. They are simply everywhere!

Ignoring the naked man, she addressed her brother. "Are you quite done, Macray? You were meant to meet me in the throne room fifteen minutes ago. Not that I would call that little broom closet a throne room. This castle is as minuscule as it is old-fashioned. I cannot see why you remain here."

He pulled on a linen shirt. "Because, dearest sister, you will not have me at Highmere and the two castles in the Highlands are not much better than this one. We need more gold to bring them up to a suitable standard."

"Last month we substantially raised taxes to gather coin for your wedding and the trimmings, we cannot raise them even more. Not if we want to keep the snotty Nobles and quibbling commoners happy. Although, I see you are doing your best to please the commoners," she said with a nod to the blond in the bed.

Macray smirked, his chinless face annoying her more than ever. "I do what I can. Besides, we cannot all sit around pining for little runaways."

She gave him the glare she usually reserved for traitors and assassins awaiting punishment. He took a step back but kept his unappealing smirk in place.

"Get rid of your shaft-glove over there, and we can discuss what exactly it is you are implying," she hissed.

Without looking over at his bedfellow, Macray barked the word, "Out." The handsome blond obeyed, pausing only to grab a tatty set of clothes before sauntering out. She had to congratulate him on his decision to get dressed in the hallway. He was clearly well-trained.

She drew herself up to her full height, aware that this made her a little taller than her younger brother. "Now that we are alone… care to explain what your slip of the tongue there was in regard to?"

"No slip of the tongue, dear sister. You spending the last month and a half running around my castle, scowling at everyone and everything is tiresome. I can only deduce that you are pining over that little harlot, Elisandrine Falk." He snorted. "To think that you nearly married her to me, only so you could visit and bed her when you fancied. You could have at least told me of your plan. Or married her yourself."

"Do not be absurd. You know the rules; Nobles must take partners of the opposite gender to reproduce. Besides, I am not *pining*. I am seething. No one turns me down. And no one makes a fool out of me, especially in a tavern full of commoners, half of them thugs and the other pleasure-sellers no doubt. She will pay."

Macray buttoned up his shirt buttons. "Yes, but your efforts to find her have been fruitless. You have had the two creatures who were seen leaving with Elise and her peasant girl locked up for days. Trying to scare them into giving up their friends, to no avail. You will have to let them go soon before they are missed." He paused on the top button. "Actually, how *will* you keep them from telling everyone about your embarrassment? Not to mention your desperate hunt. Kill them, perhaps?"

The Queen hummed. "I considered that. However, both this Cai and this Fyhre have people who would make noise about their absence. It is bad enough that Nightport knows how I was snubbed and thwarted. I do not need the news to spread further. What I shall do is both threaten *and* bribe them to ensure they do not open their pretty mouths. Discretion is key."

"Then let the firestarter disappear into oblivion, sister. Elise is long gone by now. Hidden in some hole somewhere. That is surely punishment enough? Everyone has forgotten about her but you."

"I do not forget so easily."

"I know. That is the problem," he said, rolling his eyes.

"Do not take that tone with me. You might be my blood, but I am still your Queen."

His hands fell and he sighed. "Marianna…"

She twitched at the rare use of her given name but did not cease glaring.

"…We have the wedding next week. I shall marry that skinny simpleton you chose for me, and Arclid will love us again. I will beget the royal brats that you refuse to carry yourself. But, Marianna…" He took a step closer to her. "You must stop making everyone's lives miserable for the sake of a *woman*. Let the little sleep-around scurry off to the ends of the Orb. You have Arclid to rule, a brother to support in his new marriage, and tricky trade relations with the other continents to uphold. Not to mention unruly subjects to keep happy."

She crossed her arms over her chest, pursing her lips.

He advanced a little more. "Lest we forget, Storsund is closing in on us, trying to gain control on this side of the sea. You know whom I mean by that, the people who are *actually* pulling the strings. Not just in the Storsund Trading Company, but the government of their wretched nation."

"Yes, yes. The blasted *Joiners Square*. Starting off as a union and then growing to covertly overtake a nation," Marianna intoned. "Absurd."

Macray looked up from fiddling with his cufflinks. "That is why you are spurning their suggestions to share their superior steam technology, is it not? To keep them from gaining a foothold here?"

Marianna put her hands on her hips. "Well, imagine the nerve. Claiming that they only want to help us lay train tracks in the Highlands to improve our trade. Phah! Besides, our people do not need all these newfangled things." She looked out the window to the village of Ground Hollow in the distance. "They only need to keep their heads down; plough the land, produce the items we use and trade. And pay their taxes to the crown, of course. I do not care if trains would raise the manufacturing speed and trade. It would also spread knowledge and coin throughout the land. Which is the last thing we need." She turned back to her brother. "Arclidians are unruly and likely to rebel enough as it is. If they can use trains to further their causes and communicate, disaster awaits. They will start *unions* – just as in Storsund!"

"Exactly. So, you must focus on that. On the direction Arclid is, or is not, going. Not on Lady Falk and her farm wench."

Gods, he nags worse than mother did.

"I want my tinderbox-maker punished, Macray."

He ran his hand through his hair. "Punished how? Exile is clearly not enough for you."

"I have a plan. Which is none of your business."

Macray's brow furrowed. "As you say. I know my role is not to question."

"Precisely, brother dear. I can do whatever I wish. No one and nothing can stop me if I have made my mind up. I will burn the land and, quite literally, bleed my people dry if that is what it takes to get what I want."

He swallowed visibly. "Yes, growing up with you taught me that lesson more than once. Still, your reaction seems somewhat extreme for someone who has been spurned. Not even *your* pride is that big. Take a deep breath and think this through."

She squinted at him.

What is he hinting at? Deeper feelings for my past lady of court? Mental instability? Weakness? She shook her head at the ludicrous thought. *How dare that little rat question me? I was the firstborn Hargraves. The throne, and absolute power, is mine alone. No one may question me.*

Marianna lifted her chin, looking down her nose at her brother. "I shall not take any deep breaths. My breathing is perfectly adequate. I shall have my pet back and then move on to dealing with Joiners Square. Both are things I can do while having to sit through tedious meetings about your wedding. Thank the gods those will be over soon."

He sighed, reaching for his cravat on the table. "Whatever you say... my Queen."

CHAPTER 2
SNOW AND SEA WINDS

essa Clay squinted beyond the ship's bow. Was that land ahead? She pulled her worn, ox-leather coat tighter against the snowflakes peppering her from above. Yes, that must be Storsund in the distance. The vast northern continent.

Her chin trembled. This place seemed so different. So unsafe. Still, it would hopefully be out of the Queen's grasp, which was all that mattered. If she *was* hunting them, surely she wouldn't know that this was where they had gone. No one in their right mind would come to Storsund with winter on its way.

A man coughed behind her, and her shoulders slumped.

Well, no one except the Lindberg family, I suppose. But then, they're going home and apparently love the cold.

Mr Lindberg had expounded on that subject night after night on this ship. He had gone on and on about the light when the ground was covered in snow, the bracing effects of cold, the pleasures of big roaring fires, and a hot, bitter Storsund drink called coffee.

The man coughed again as he approached Nessa. "There

you are, silly girl. I've been looking for you. You cannot hide from me, yes?" His Storsund accent was as broad as his waistline.

"Hello, Mr Lindberg. I mean *Albert*," she corrected herself. Throughout the past six weeks he, his wife Eleonora, and their obnoxious but adorable little daughter, Sonja, had been their constant companions, quickly forcing Nessa and Elise to call them by their first names.

Luckily, Nessa and Elise had spent most of their time in their cabin, making love and talking. But they had to come up on deck for food eventually, and, the instant they did, there was the Lindberg family.

It was all Elise's fault. The gods bless her good intentions but curse her skill at socialising. Elise had taken the advice of their friend and guide back in Nightport, Hunter Smith, and asked someone who looked well-packed if they would sell them some winter clothes. It had turned out to be the Lindberg family. After the transaction, Elise had begun chatting with them and made friends.

Of course, Elise didn't reveal that the reason they were embarking on a long trip between continents, without more than one change of clothes, was that they had to escape in a hurry, as they were hunted by a monarch wishing to keep Elise as a mix of court jester and courtesan. Imagine thinking one could own Elise's quick temper, hunger for bedplay, and her tendency to cause trouble, "make her surroundings a tinderbox" as the Queen called it, as a source of amusement.

Nessa balled her hands into fists. Elise was not a plaything. And she was never going to be dragged back to court to serve that… bloodsucker. No, Elise had told the Lindbergs that they had left on a whim. That they were travellers who just up and left when the fancy took them. Something which was as far from Nessa's careful and anxious style of living as it could be.

But the Lindbergs had bought it. They bought anything Elise told them.

"Hm. Am I disturbing you? You seem to be thinking about things, yes?" Albert said.

"What? Oh, sorry. What were you saying?"

"You must listen. You're so distracted around me. I said that I've been looking for you, Mrs Glass."

Mrs Glass. Nessa was still not used to the new alias. Nor pretending to be married. Lying about something as sacred as marriage made her worry they were jinxing themselves somehow. She had grown up seeing a hale and enriching marriage between her parents and knew what a beautiful thing it could be.

When I do marry, I wonder if I can live up to the standard they have set. Can I fulfil their expectations in any part of my life?

"I see. Well, you found me," she replied, trying to sound happy about that. She pulled up her trousers, ones that used to be Albert's.

Perhaps I should've sprung for one of Eleonora's dresses. At least it would've fitted better.

The Lindbergs were an interesting couple; he was as short as his wife was tall and his skin as milky-white as hers was umber-brown. Most of all, Eleonora was incredibly slim while Albert looked like a caterpillar who had swallowed a marble, short and stout with a large clump of fat in the middle. If marble-eating caterpillars could have trimmed blond beards and definitely untrimmed blond eyebrows.

"Is that land?" He squinted so much it looked like his huge eyebrows had swallowed his eyes.

"I believe so."

"Aw. Surely that doesn't mark the end of our bibbing friendship?"

"*Budding* friendship," Nessa corrected with a smile.

"Yes, yes. Brimming friendship. You must come stay in Charlottenberg. In our house."

Nessa brushed away the strands of her almond-brown hair which the wind blew in her face. "I fear we can't. We're travelling on to Skarhult, remember?"

"Mm. Yes. You say this several times. I don't know why. Frightful place. All city and factories. No sea view like in Charlottenberg."

It also has also no Lindbergs. And unlike Charlottenberg, it's not the first town the Queen would search if she came looking for us.

"All the same, it's where we are going. A friend from Nightport will probably come visit us there, so it would be awful of us to settle anywhere else."

"Ah, yes. This Hunter Smith? I'm still sad not to have met such a, how do you say, extravagant person. We went to Arclid for adventure but only ended up paying too much for lodgings, drinking too much, and getting food poisoning."

"Well, Nightport can be exciting, but it can also be dangerous. Having seen tavern fights, powder abuse, and... *other things* there I can attest to that. You'd be better off bored than in danger."

"If you think that, you should stay in Charlottenberg! Yes, it is a harbour city like Nightport, but it is a safe one. Smaller, richer, and better guarded."

"Didn't you say that Skarhult is richer and better guarded than Nightport, too? I thought it was a Storsund trait?"

He squirmed. "Well, yes, true. But Charlottenberg is prettier, yes? And smaller. Small is safe."

"If you had seen where I grew up, you'd know that I've had my share of 'smaller,' but thanks all the same," Nessa said, smiling to take the sting out of her words.

He ran his hand over his beard. "I see. I cannot convince

you to accept our hospitality, yes? Shame, you and your exotic tales have made this journey for us."

She kept up her smile, but her cheeks were starting to hurt a little.

The sound of heeled boots was heard on the deck. "There you are, my cherished," Elise said before wrapping her arm around Nessa's waist.

Nessa blew out a long-held breath. Elise was here. She would deal with the social interaction, leaving Nessa to her agonising about the Queen and acclimatising to a new and frightening place.

"Albert, pardon the intrusion, but I fear I must steal Nessa away to discuss plans. The captain just told me we should make port tomorrow."

Albert's mouth fell open. "Really? Captain Levi said that?"

Elise inclined her head. "Yes, go ask him yourself if you like. He is below decks."

"Aha! I shall find him. Excuse me, ladies."

When he had waddled off, Nessa breathed out a thank-you.

"You are most welcome. So, what was that little save worth to you?" Elise asked with a smirk.

A woman of action rather than words, Nessa went straight for what they both wanted, a long and heartfelt kiss.

After a while, Elise pulled away, smiling with her eyes closed. "Mm. Quite the reward."

"Anything for my hero."

"You do not require saving, my cherished," Elise said with a laugh.

Nessa looked out at the near-black waves being cascaded by flecks of white. "Are you sure?"

"What do you mean?"

"Well, we're running away from someone dangerous," Nessa murmured.

"We cannot be certain the Queen is hunting us, you know that."

Nessa kept her eyes on the sea. "Still. I feel like she must be. There's an unease… deep in my bones."

Elise kissed her cheek. "Pardon me for saying it, but unease is eternally buried in your bones. You always find something to fret about. On the run as we might be, we must try to live our lives and not constantly look over our shoulders."

Nessa surveyed Elise's seemingly carefree face. "But if she finds you—"

"Then we shall find a solution," Elise interrupted. "I fear her too, but we cannot let that fear take over our minds. Or our hearts."

Nessa looked about herself, first ahead to Storsund and then back to whence they'd come. Arclid. Led by the unrelenting, coldhearted monarch who was probably baying for their blood. Nessa hummed noncommittally in response to her beloved.

"Oh heartling," Elise said, taking her hand. "Come away. Let us go find you something to eat. We can sooth your stomach, if not your mind."

Nessa let herself be led away. That unease still tapping like distant drums.

CHAPTER 3
CHARLOTTENBERG

E lise was back on dry land, snow-clad as it was. She was also finally away from the noisy and eerily named Hangman's Dock, and could now take in the city of Charlottenberg, which unfurled in front of her in the morning light.

She reached into the pocket of her coat, producing a cherry-red leather notebook. When she had purchased some of Eleonora Lindberg's spare clothes, she had also bought the notebook from little Sonja. The girl had drawn what she explained to Elise was a swarm of lux beetles on the first page. Otherwise the notebook was empty. The girl was not fond of drawing and had gladly parted with the book and its accompanying pencil.

Elise planned to use it to jot down the architectural highlights of the places she visited. She had already filled in the details of Silverton where she was born, Highmere where she had been a lady-in-waiting to the Queen, Ground Hollow where she had met Nessa, and Nightport, the city where her destiny had been shaped and she had fallen in love.

She hadn't mentioned to anyone that she was jotting it

down in letter form, as if she was writing home to her father, the royal architect. As if the red pox hadn't taken him from her when she was a child. That was only for her to know. She swallowed the lump in her throat and began to write down what she could see.

Papa, Charlottenberg has mainly two- and three-storey buildings made of sandstone, with wooden roofs. The houses are painted in muted, soft colours. Some of the roofs are New Dawning – I never would have guessed that the style you worked on in Arclid reached other continents. I wish you could see it.

"And what about your family's farm? You planted things in dirt, yes? With your hands?" Elise overheard Eleonora asking Nessa.

"Something like that," Nessa mumbled.

Elise had to intervene before Nessa's politeness waned. Six weeks in close proximity to the Lindberg family had taken its toll on the shy woman Elise loved. She walked over and placed herself between them.

"Eleonora, may I ask you or Albert about the big building over there? The one with the gilded letters on it."

"Elise! There you are. Yes, of course," Albert said. "It's the city hall. Grand, yes?"

"It is, indeed. I thought it might be a church?"

"No, Storsund isn't as religious as Arclid. Here in the south of the country, called Sund, we save our faith for our great leaders," Eleonora replied. "They do not want prayers, only our hard work and a part of our coin. To keep our great nation growing, yes? In the north, however, the people called 'the Viss' pray to old guardians of lakes, winds, and such. Silly superstition, yes?"

Nessa was ignoring the biased comment, busy inspecting the building with the big, golden lettering. "Are you sure we'll be all right despite not knowing the language?"

"Yes, yes. Most people in Storsund know some Arclidian.

At least down here in the Sund area. And you'll stay with us civilised people down south," Albert said cheerfully.

Nessa began grumbling about bigotry, so Elise decided to change the subject. "Where could I and Nessa procure a nice meal and perhaps a bath before we travel on to Skarhult?"

"Many places, sweet Elise. Farther down this road is a famous inn. If I talk to the landlady, she will be impressed because I have impressive job. I shall get you a deal for a bath and food, but without renting a room, yes? Wait here," Albert said.

He walked off, his speed, as always, hampered by his gut.

"Wait for me," Sonja said and rushed after her father. She nearly got in the way of a woman on a pedal cycle, making Eleonora gasp and run after her wild six-year-old.

"Alone at last," Elise whispered in Nessa's ear, before giving the earlobe a quick kiss.

Nessa smiled, the first genuine smile she had worn since Elise woke her by caressing her thigh this morning.

How I love that wide, beautiful smile.

"Finally. Tell me, do you think the Lindbergs intend to follow us all the way onto the train to Skarhult?"

Elise laughed. "Quite possibly. Will you be nice?"

Nessa's forehead wrinkled. "Yes, of course. They mean well and like us."

"Yes. Nonetheless, I shall find a way to get rid of them as soon as a chance arises."

"Oh, thank the gods," Nessa said with a sigh of relief.

Elise laughed again, until she saw Nessa's smile fading as she peered at the foreign city. She caressed Nessa's pale cheek.

"Heartling, you must try to calm your nerves. I know you like your safety and that this place is new, but you will wear a hole in your stomach with all the fretting."

Nessa leaned into the caress. "I know. I just don't know

how to stop constantly feeling… small and helpless. It's pitiful. *I'm* pitiful."

"No. It is merely that you—"

Elise was interrupted by a shout from behind them.

"Stop him!"

They both spun around to see a man with a scarf over his mouth barrelling towards them. Behind him was a woman in a black leather coat with fur trim. She was running almost as fast as him but breathing harder. When they got closer, Elise noted that she was perhaps not young enough to be chasing after masked men. The man was holding a bag in his hand. He ran right for them and, in one swift move, snatched the satchel that hung off Nessa's shoulder, and ran down a side road to their right. Before Elise knew what was happening, Nessa was rushing after him, almost slipping in the top layer of snow.

A lifetime of farm work and the heavy lifting of a glass-blower's apprentice had given Nessa stamina if not speed, and Elise was sure she'd catch up to the thief. What worried her was what might happen when she did. Elise began to run after them, only to find that there was no point. The thief, Nessa, and the older woman were all coming back to the road Elise was on. And behind them was what looked like a group of soldiers or guards.

Someone shouted behind Elise. She didn't understand what they said, but she saw them point to the two men and the woman in grey uniforms who chased the thief.

As Elise watched, the thief turned to look at his pursuers. That was when Nessa threw herself forwards, knocking them both to the ground. They tussled as Elise reached them. Her heart beat frantically as she saw the thief push Nessa to the ground and struggle to get back up. Just then, the other victim hit him with her arm. Elise saw his eyes roll back in his head, and then he collapsed onto the cobbles with an unhealthy bang.

It made no sense to Elise that a blow from a woman's forearm could made such a loud noise, nor that it could knock him unconscious. Still, she was glad it had. Elise's rage had been rising to the surface, and if no one else had subdued the man, she wasn't sure what she would've done.

There was a mass of shouted orders and hubbub. The people in uniform were upon the thief and clasping his wrists in handcuffs. One of them checked on Nessa, understood that she was a foreigner, and brusquely asked for her story in Arclidian. When she said she had been robbed and caught the thief, his tone lightened.

The older woman who had knocked the robber out answered his questions in their shared language. Or did they have more than one? Elise remembered that the continent of Obeha had four languages, so perhaps Storsund had more than one as well. Elise listened to them, as she kneeled next to Nessa and checked her for injuries. Nessa was looking up at them, too, a frown on her features.

Dash it. If she was unsettled before, gods only know what she will be like now. I wish I knew how to grow her confidence.

She kissed Nessa's temple and whispered, "It is all right, heartling. You were so brave. Foolish, but brave."

Nessa mumbled a distracted thanks, her focus still on the foreign conversation. The man who had questioned them pointed to the thief's head and then to the older woman's arm. With an annoyed grunt, she took off her fur-lined coat, showing an athletic figure beneath. She pulled up her sleeve, revealing an arm that shone in a way skin did not. It looked like porcelain painted a colour similar to the woman's tanned skin.

Elise had seen a leg that looked like that once, it had belonged to a rich merchant who dined with the Queen. He had shown his wooden leg which he had just gotten covered with fashionable painted enamel. Like this woman's arm, it

27

was very detailed. Her manufactured arm was equipped with an elbow, a tapered wrist, and a perfect copy of a hand. There were cracks in the enamel between the fingers and the hand, and the woman showed that if she squeezed her lower arm up against her bicep, the fingers moved into a clumsy fist.

Extraordinary. How is that done? Clockwork?

The uniform-wearer blushed furiously and looked down, as if the woman had pulled her trousers down instead of her sleeve up. He waved dismissively, and she tugged her sleeve back down and put her coat on.

Another of the three in uniform turned back to Nessa, and in a heavy accent asked her for a more detailed account than she had given before. As she stood up, she elaborated as much as she could.

He nodded curtly. "Thank you, madam. This man will be judged this afternoon. With your testimony and that of Miss Ahlgren here, he'll be sent to prison. For a long time, yes? This man is known to us but has never been caught. Well done. Next time, wait for us. Do not take risks, yes?"

"Yes? Uh, I mean, I will w-wait for the city guard next time, yes. Th-thank you," Nessa panted.

"Not city guard, madam. We work for the city and the government of Storsund, but we are with Joiners Square." He moved his fur cloak aside and pointed to a silver and cream-yellow emblem on the chest of his grey uniform.

Elise knew that Nessa had as little idea as she did about what "Joiners Square" was, but Nessa nodded anyway.

The man barked something to his colleagues, who then dragged the now struggling, jostling thief away. The female capturer kicked him in the shins when he began shouting.

Elise was brushing down Nessa's leather coat. It was straining over her three layers of clothes. They would have to buy real winter coats soon. Their thin Arclid outerwear would only keep so much of the cold out. Elise had noted that coats here were either large fur ones or leather ones with fur lining and trim, much like the woman in front of them wore. She was busy checking the bag that the thief had taken from her.

Nessa blew out a breath. "So much for 'smaller being safer.' I'd like to be the one to tell Albert that he seems to be wrong about his secure harbour town," she said, still a little breathless.

"It *is* safe. Compared to some places, yes? But it has poor people, who will do what they must to survive," the woman said.

What was it they called her? Miss Argren? Ahlgren?

Elise observed her. She was hard to age. Somewhere in her fifties, perhaps? The weathered face seemed to say as much, as did the grey streaks in her jet-black hair. Nevertheless, her bright green eyes and her movements were those of a younger woman. Her face was striking in its clear, symmetrical features. She was the sort of woman you couldn't take your eyes off.

Satisfied that the contents of her bag were all accounted for, she turned to Nessa. "I thank you, young lady," she said.

"No need to mention it. If I had not caught him, those soldiers, or whatever they are, would have done."

The Storsund woman snorted. "Joiners Square would have caught him, yes. But probably too late and doubtless sacrificing me and my belongings to do it. They don't care about you unless you are part of their organisation. Or paying them, yes?"

"Their organisation?" Elise asked.

The woman gave her a curious look. "You foreigners do not know of them? Curious." She widened her stance, standing more comfortably. "They're everywhere here. They started as a union. A group of joiners were tired of being mistreated at work. In Storsund we work hard and long hours, yes?" She waited for them to nod before she carried on. "It got too much for them when they barely had time to eat and sleep. The union bought a house in a bad part of town. They called it

Joiners House and started to meet as a group to deal with their employers. Thus far, an excellent idea as unions have saved our people. This one, however, was different." She paused, probably looking for the best way to tell the story. Or maybe translating the words in her head.

"After a while, more joiners wanted to take part. They gave what little coin they had to the organisation, which was still nameless. Soon they had enough coin, and need for space, to purchase all the broken buildings around an old square. They began calling it Joiners Square and named themselves after it, yes? I will not tell you all. Not here and now."

"Please tell us. We're new here, and this sounds like something we need to know," Nessa whispered.

The stranger looked around, focusing especially on a young woman with strawberry blonde hair who kept glancing over. Their new acquaintance lowered her voice. "Fine. In short, their organisation grew until workers of all kinds joined them. Then they grew even more and started something like a mix of an army and a religion. Their highest ranks are all former Storsund military. They give their grand marshals and high captains an almost godlike status, yes?"

"How so?" Elise asked.

The woman scowled. "They make them seem mystical and all-knowing. Secret rituals and stealthy ways to succeed in business and such silly things. Soon, Storsund's rich wanted to join, too. That was when it really grew. It was not long before they controlled our government. Now not only are they our military, but transport, trade, and medical care all have Joiners Square's silver and yellow emblem stuck on them. At least here in the south." She shook her head. "They're everywhere. Their spies and their soldiers surround us. Only a small number question them, and they're all forced into hiding. I should stop talking now, you'll learn more about them if you stay here for a while, yes?"

Elise and Nessa glanced at each other. Elise took her lover's hand and squeezed it reassuringly.

"Yes, we're staying for a while, I think," Nessa said.

The older woman brushed her sleeve off. "Good. Enough about Joiners Square for now, then. I should like to buy you a coffee as a thank-you for your help."

Elise looked at Nessa, who nodded.

"That sounds lovely. I think Nessa here would most of all like a hearty second breakfast and to be away from a family we met on our travels. Is there a quiet place nearby where we can get some food?"

"Yes. Down that street is a cafe. It has coffee and pastries and some... what do you call them? Sandwiches, yes?"

Nessa's face lit up. "That'd do nicely. Thank you."

"You two go ahead, I shall go bid the Lindbergs farewell. And discuss meeting up in the future," Elise said.

The stranger inclined her head. "Of course. We'll be in that cafe down there. Blue sign, white letters."

Elise kissed Nessa's cheek. "I shall meet you there soon."

With that she walked into the inn where the Lindbergs had gone. Guilt ate at her for giving them the brushoff, but they'd been glued to her and Nessa these past weeks, annoying Nessa and sometimes testing Elise's short temper. She had exploded at them a dozen times, something they didn't seem to mind. As long as she spoke to them and occasionally asked questions, they were happy with whatever mood she was in.

Which is why they struggled with Nessa's silences and need for solitude, I suppose, she considered, as she looked out over the street. *Never mind that. Buck up. This will surely not be the last I see of the Lindberg family.*

She hurried her steps to the inn, fastening a smile to her face.

CHAPTER 4
NEW EXPERIENCES

Nessa shivered as she followed the woman to the cafe. The adrenaline had left her system now, leaving her cold and tired. And starving as a marrow-oxen.

The stranger stopped outside the cafe. Nessa wanted to ask her name, but in her social ineptitude, she was unsure how. Should she just introduce herself?

"Here we are," the woman was saying. "Good food for good price, yes? Much of it served warm. Plenty of strong coffee, too."

She pointed to a tall chalkboard next to the cafe's door. Written in small letters was what Nessa assumed was the menu.

Her cheeks burned. "I can't read that. I'm sorry."

"Ah, of course. Under sandwiches it says, 'bread choices', yes? You have rye, oat, or wheat. Then the fillings. Pork and soured cream, reindeer and herbal butter, venison and strong cheese, egg and smoked —"

"Sorry to interrupt. Would you mind if we go inside to

decide? My nose is about to freeze off, I think," Elise said as she joined them.

There it was, the warmth which always appeared in Nessa's chest when Elise was next to her. She took Elise's hand and felt safer.

"Good idea," the stranger said and opened the door for them.

They were faced with a steep set of stairs. As they climbed them, they saw a bright locale with birch floor and beige walls. Dainty tables with white linen cloths and elegant menus. It was pretty, but so... *foreign*. The unease in Nessa's stomach was replaced by a loud growling.

A smile twitched at the corners of the stranger's mouth. "Sounds like we need food quick, yes? Pick a table. I'll order coffee and cheeses while we choose what to eat. Be back soon."

Elise chose a table by a window. The warm room had misted the window glass with condensation. Nessa sat down next to her and picked up the menu. She was relieved to see that it had Arclidian translations of the dishes on one side.

Elise whispered. "Coffee and cheese? I would understand a drink and some bread before the meal. But *coffee* and... *cheese*?"

"A new continent, new ways, I suppose. I just hope I can eat and drink it," Nessa murmured.

She chewed her lower lip until Elise reached out a finger and pulled the lip out from under the teeth. "It will be fine. If you cannot stand it, I will order you something plain."

Nessa smiled a little, the shame of her own fearfulness making her cheeks burn again.

The stranger walked back with big, confident steps. She placed a tray on the table. On it were cups and saucers, objects Nessa had only seen in the windows of Nightport's finest taverns. There, they had been chipped and plain. These cups and saucers were bright white with blue flowers around the thin rim. Nessa worried she'd break her cup.

In them was something so darkly brown it was almost black. It smelled strong, like a mix of nuts and alcohol, perhaps? Steam danced on the air above the dark liquid.

The tray also contained a plate with little cubes of cheese. Most of them were the buttery yellow of the cheese Nessa had grown up with, but a few were white with streaks of blue or green through them. She tried to hide her scepticism. Those white cubes looked like the fruit of some poisonous mushroom.

Nessa's stomach growled again. Elise picked up one of the yellow cubes of cheese, sniffed it, and smiled.

"Time to feed the monster in your stomach, heartling," Elise said with a wink. She still hadn't mastered winking, so both her eyes briefly closed.

She brought the cube to Nessa's mouth, pressing it against her lips. Nessa took the cheese and kissed the fingers, playing along with the pretence that it was flirtation and not Elise saving her the embarrassment of asking for the plainest, safest food.

Nessa chewed and swallowed. "Mm, that was nice. Creamy!"

"Yes, we take pride in our dairy," the stranger said while picking up one of the cups.

Nessa ate another piece of cheese and eyed her coffee, wondering how hot it was.

Their hostess cleared her throat. "I must thank you again. Thank you for catching the… um, wrongdoer?"

"The thief?" Elise offered.

"Yes. The thief. Thank you. My Arclidian is rusty, yes? It will come back to me as we speak."

Elise held up her hands. "Your Arclidian is splendid. We do not even speak your language at all."

"*Languages.* There are two, Sundish and Vissian. I speak both but mainly Sundish, which is the language of the south. So, it is used here as well as in my native Skarhult and the other big cities of Storsund."

Nessa and Elise looked at each other.

"Skarhult?" Elise asked.

"Yes. One of the biggest cities in Storsund, only a train ride away."

Nessa smiled and nodded. "We know that much, I'm happy to say. We were only asking because that is where we're heading."

"What a coincidence," the woman said.

Elise clapped her hand on the table. "How silly! I just realised that we have not introduced ourselves yet. I am Elise Glass, and this is my wife, Nessa Glass."

Nessa did a double-take. Being called Elise's wife was still startling. But it did have a nice ring to it.

"Well met. I'm Anja Ahlgren. Welcome to Storsund. Although, perhaps I should welcome *you* home?" she said, looking at Elise.

Elise's forehead furrowed. "Pardon?"

"You... are not a Wayfarer?"

The furrows grew deeper. "As in that I travel?"

Anja shook her head. "I mean a Wayfarer as in the creed. No? My mistake. I thought you were born here. Your darker skin, black hair, and light eyes... you look like my kind."

Elise tilted her head. "Your kind? I thought Storsund folk were fair-skinned blondes interspersed with people who had immigrated from the other continents."

"No. Our continent, like yours, is split into sections. Arclid has the Highlands, Midlands, and the Lowlands, yes? We have the north, Vitevall, snow, pine trees, and mountains, mainly. And the south, Sund, where most of the cities and leafy forests are. And, these days, where most of the railways and factories are located."

Elise's eyes lit up. "Is this Wite... Vit... *Vitevall* where your folk come from?"

Anja gave a brusque shake of the head. All her movements seemed rough. "The proud Viss live up in Vitevall. Lightest of blonde hair and skin so white you can see the blue veins under it. Flat noses and sparkling dark eyes. They live apart, not fond of the south's noise and... What is the word..." She drummed her fingers on the table. "Oh yes, *commercialism*. You have the Sundes here in the south, more mixed appearances but often pale with red or blonde hair. Then you have my people, the Wayfarers. Dark hair, light eyes, tan skin. We and the Viss tend to be more muscular than the Sundes, something that Joiners Square hates. They want their Sund soldiers to fill out those strict uniforms of theirs, and not with fat."

"No immigration?" Elise asked.

"Other people have started braving our shores, and most of us are happy about that. Soon we will be a melting pot of all traits and colourings, like Arclid. Not a day too soon. We need change, yes? The separation of the three creeds on this conti-nent is horrible."

Nessa ate another cube of yellow cheese. Elise, however, seemed to have forgotten all about the food and drink. She sat forward on her chair. "I see. Fascinating! You are very knowl-edgeable, I must say."

Anja blew on her coffee. "About this? Anyone from Stor-sund knows this. I might be a little more interested as I'm a historian."

Elise bounced forward in her seat. "Are you? Do you school children?"

"No. I used to. A few years ago, I left to write down some of our history. Especially that of the Wayfarers. I am two-thirds into the book. Writing it day and night, yes? But the typing became slowed after this happened," she said, lifting her right arm so that the hand's enamel glittered in the light from the window.

"I am so exceedingly sorry to hear that. Would it be rude to ask how that happened?" Elise broke in.

Nessa closed her eyes. Why did her ladylove never think before she spoke? "That's inappropriate," she whispered.

Anja smiled. "That's all right. You may ask. I don't mind. What I mind is when people stare without daring to ask questions, yes? Don't treat me differently."

She handed them both their cups and saucers, seeming to plan her words. Nessa wondered if it was to translate them or because it was a hard subject to speak of.

"I was skiing in the mountains with two friends. Below our peak, workers were laying railroad tracks, yes? To transport the north's raw materials, timber, stone, and blocks of ice, to the rest of the country. And then returning with luxury goods form the south. Important work."

"But not without danger?" Elise suggested.

"Exactly. Their work set off an avalanche. As I and my friends tried to get away from the oncoming snow, we crashed down the mountain side. My arm got—" she paused, tapping the table again. "Fastened? Wedged? Yes, *wedged* between rocks that came tumbling down. One of my friends only got big bruises. The other, Matthias, got a bad head wound and died."

Nessa didn't know what to say. Even Elise seemed to struggle until she managed to whisper, "I am so sorry for your loss."

"Matthias was the loss. The arm, it was one of those things that happens. Those things that life sends to test you. I do not cry and moan. I still write, but I'm bad with my left hand. Anyway, let us speak of nicer things. Try your coffee, yes? I want to see what you make of it."

Elise tried hers first. She blew on it, like Anja had, and

then took the daintiest sip. The face she made was as if she had filled her mouth with ash.

Anja laughed, deep and heartily. "You can soften the taste with milk if you like. Or sharpen it with vodka. Have you tried vodka?"

As Elise was busy eating cheese to remove the taste of the coffee, Nessa replied. "Yes, that made it over the sea to Arclid. I had it in a cocktail. Strong stuff. I'd like to try it on its own."

"That can be arranged, yes? Try your coffee first."

Nessa tasted it with trepidation.

Remember that Elise made a face when she tried the ale in the Goblin's Tavern, too. She's a former lady-in-waiting and almost became a princess. She's got a spoiled palate.

The taste was strange. It changed in her mouth, from bitter to rich, from harsh to nutty sweetness. It somehow tasted as hot as its temperature.

"I... don't *not* like it," Nessa settled on.

"That's how it starts. A few cups and you'll love it," Anja said with a smile.

Elise tilted her cup so that the dark liquid sloshed. "Do you usually have this with cheese? The Lindbergs, the family on the ship over here, said it is drunk near constantly."

"We drink it with every meal and usually in between them, too. Keeps you warm, yes? Not simply because it is hot, but because it makes your heart race. Also wakes up the brain," Anja said between sips.

A waiter came over, and Nessa dove into her menu. She ordered a rye sandwich with pork and soured cream. Elise hadn't paid attention to the menu and began scrabbling through the Arclidian translations of the dishes.

"Take your time. I can order next," Anja said. She turned to the waiter and offered him a short sentence. The words sounded complicated. He wrote it down, as he had Nessa's order. Elise was still staring at the menu as if she wanted it to give up its secrets. Her finger was running along the words, and her eyes looked panicked.

"Want help, yes?" Anja asked kindly.

Elise seemed to hesitate. "I am looking for something with less... meat. And maybe a vegetable?"

Both Anja and the waiter chortled. Nessa stiffened, ready to pounce if Elise was being mocked.

Anja clicked her tongue. "Sorry. We eat sweet fruits to last us between meals, but vegetables are only survival food. Beetroots, parsnips, turnips... they are for soups when there is no meat or bread, yes? I think there is a sandwich with breaded ice-eel and green cabbage, yes? That is lighter."

The waiter broke in. "True. You can even order it without the eel? Will take a little longer. But, is possible, yes?"

"Oh, I do not wish to be any bother. I shall order it with the eel. I like seafood," Elise said, looking more confident than Nessa guessed she was.

"Please also bring three glasses of honeyed almond milk and another pot of coffee," Anja added.

The waiter replied in their language and left.

"That was Sundish?" Elise asked.

Anja drank down the last of her coffee and refilled her cup. "Yes."

Elise watched her keenly. "Is that what you are writing your book in?"

"No. It is currently in Arclidian, which I write better than I speak it. I will make translations for the other languages later. The book was meant to be sent abroad, you see. To inform you other continents that we are not only snow and railroads."

"And a few coal mines," Elise added.

Nessa slapped her leg under the table. She didn't think Anja was easily upset, but Elise's tendency to cause trouble, her so-called 'fire-starting', had to be kept under a watchful eye.

Anja blew on her coffee. "Yes, we have many coal mines

out in the west. They're the lifeblood of our vast factories and impressive trains."

They all quieted for a moment as a large family walked in, chatting and shouting their way to a table in the opposite corner.

Nessa snatched a piece of blue-veined cheese and popped it in her mouth. It tasted strange, almost like it had gone off. She had some coffee to swallow it down.

Elise was slowly running her finger around the rim of her coffee cup, watching Anja. "So, you are from Skarhult? What brings you to Charlottenberg?"

Anja put her coffee cup down. "Collecting my coin. I have shares in the Storsund Trading Company. Their head office is here, so I like to stop by and see what the whispers are and get my earnings. Then I took a walk, and got robbed, while waiting for my train to Skarhult."

"Oh! Can I ask when it leaves? We need to find a train there, too. It'd be nice to travel with someone who knows how the ticketing system works," Nessa said, fidgeting with her cup. She wasn't sure about this woman, but she was tired of the sinking feeling in her stomach. Being so unsure of everything since they left Arclid was draining.

Anja, up until now the perfect hostess, looked doubtful. "There are many trains. Mine is in forty minutes. But there will be another soon after that."

"Nessa is right. We could use a guide. And we have been told that we are exceedingly entertaining travel companions," Elise said.

Anja said nothing, but the lines on her forehead increased.

Nessa put her hand over Elise's on the table. "I'm not sure we should impose further. Anja wanted to thank us for our help with the thief, and she has now done that. After we finish our meal, we should let her get on with her day in peace."

Elise pouted. Anja busied herself with her cup, drinking the coffee faster than was probably pleasant.

The waiter interrupted the awkward silence to bring them their drinks and sandwiches. When he left, Anja poured herself some more coffee and they all began eating. Out of the corner of her eye, Nessa saw Elise swallow down most of her food with generous helpings of her honeyed milk.

There was a wet thump on the plate as Anja slammed her half-eaten sandwich down. "That was rude. I am a loner, not used to company, yes? Of course you should take my train. I will show you where to get tickets and good places to sit."

"Are you sure?" Nessa asked, unable to help the excitement creeping into her voice. "I know about not being comfortable with unwanted company and would hate to bother you."

"I am sure. I wish to help you."

"Oh, thank the gods. Trains are new to us, and, while I am happy to charge in and try new things, this worries even me," Elise said with a chuckle.

"It is decided, then. We travel together," Anja said, pointing to them with her coffee cup.

Nessa raised her own cup. "I'll toast to that."

Elise lifted her glass of almond milk, realised it was empty and stole Nessa's to toast with. Flooded with relief at not having to journey alone, Nessa didn't even mention the milk theft. They would be safer now that they had a guide and a plan.

A thought, long buried, surfaced. *As long as this country isn't filled with the Queen's spies.*

Swiftly, Nessa's stomach soured. And she knew it had nothing to do with the coffee.

CHAPTER 5
DINNER AND DECISIONS

Queen Marianna Hargraves stifled a yawn. The wedding ceremony was finally over. Macray had married Kelene, the skinny former lady-in-waiting who had happily taken Elise's place as future princess.

Now they were all seated in the dining hall of Silver Hollow Castle. Macray was making a toast to his new bride, thanking all the gods individually and mentioning the glory of the Queen and the royal family at every possible juncture.

Marianna marvelled at her brother's acting skills. It was impossible to tell that he was miserable because his life of bedding every commoner within reach was over. After all, Nobles lived in mixed-sex relationships, and cheating brought dishonour.

That was one reason she would not marry. The other was that she would never share her power.

Her Queen's aide, Adaire, was as close to having a partner as Marianna would ever get. She considered her decision to ask Adaire to stay in Highmere and keep an eye on court, despite almost all of the scrounging Noble courtiers travelling down to

Silver Hollow Castle for the wedding. Perhaps she should have invited one of Adaire's cousins? After all, the Aldershires were the second oldest and most distinguished Noble bloodline after the Hargraves.

Oh well, too late to reconsider now. Besides, what do I care about who people think I should have invited? I am the Queen, my opinion is law.

Macray finished his speech and bowed to the beaming Kelene. The two hundred or so guests all toasted with their glasses of sunberry essence. Marianna swallowed all of hers down and signalled to a servant for a refill. When she came over with the decanter, the Queen noted that the wench was quite fetching.

Has Macray only employed pretty commoners to work for him? Of course he has. Thinking with his trouser snake as always.

The girl bowed and stepped away with the decanter. Marianna gave her a charitable smile before unashamedly staring at the young woman's cleavage. Tempting. But no. She preferred lovers with Noble blood. You never knew if a commoner shared your bed because they wanted to or because they felt like they had to. Marianna expected to be desired by her lovers.

Her thoughts went unbidden to Elise Falk. Where was the pretty fire-starter now? The Royal Guards had lost track of her after that fateful night at the White Raven, but there had been a recent sighting. The new information did not come from the tight-lipped Cai or the rebellious Fyhre, who, after being released, seemed to have vanished into thin air. Instead, it came from a fisherman stumbling from a tavern to the docks to sleep the drink off in his boat. He had seen two women matching the description of Elise and Nessa Clay on the night of their departure, in the company of a coquettish young man dressed head to toe in cobalt blue.

Marianna scoffed under her breath.

Not a colour in which one can stay inconspicuous.

The young man had been located, apparently being somewhat infamous in Nightport, and was now down in the Silver Hollow dungeons, below their feet, being asked questions. Nicely. However, as Marianna's frustration grew, she considered throwing her past caution to the wind and asking with the aid of fists.

If Elise and the farm wench had been going to the docks, that only meant one thing. They had, as suspected, boarded a ship and left. However, one of the first things the Royal Guards had done after the disappearance was check the rosters for the ships leaving Nightport. There was no Falk or Clay on any of them. Marianna had even double-checked the passenger lists for the ships to Obeha herself. It was the only other continent that Elise was familiar with and had a lovely, warm climate even in winter. It was also vast enough for the runaways to easily hide. It would be the natural choice for Elise.

Still, there had been no names that matched. Not that this meant anything; all the rosters had a few occasions of two women travelling together. Elisandrine and her farmer could have taken any names and safely sailed away.

Unless that peacock in the dungeon speaks, I have to decide if I command my Arclidian spies on other continents to seek information on passengers arriving around the time of the travel to the continent in question. Around seven weeks to Western Isles. Six to Storsund. Ten to eleven weeks to Obeha. How long ago was night in the White Raven now… around two months ago?

Marianna winced. So much time had been lost during the planning of the wedding and while her guards searched Arclid for the two escapees. She ignored the cheers and toasts around her and consider her second option.

OR, do I contact the authorities on those continents and ask them to help me root out a traitor to the crown of Arclid? That would be more effective, but it would lead to more questions. Especially from the blasted, nosey Joiners Square.

The need for secrecy infuriated her. It would have been so much simpler if she could command every citizen of the orb to look for Elise. Nevertheless, she had to keep herself away from humiliation and from the Arclidians' disgusting habit of rebelling when they felt their fellow commoners were being mistreated.

That settled it, it would be more furtive to stick to her own spies. They were all in place, awaiting orders. As soon as she was back in Highmere, she would have Adaire send the orders on the smaller steamers, which were built for speed and not comfort. These ships carried letters and missives as their cargo, not passengers, and therefore shaved a week or two off the journey. Marianna sipped her drink.

Where is that tinderbox maker of mine? I want her here. And then I want to see the light die in those peculiar, pretty eyes as I follow through with my plan.

"Your Majesty?"

Marianna was shaken out of her reverie.

"Are you all right, my Queen?"

It was the fop next to her. What was his name? He was a younger son of one of the Highland Nobles. Winthrop? Winterson? Ah, what did it matter?

She sniffed. "I am very well, thank you. Pondering matters of state. Have all the dessert courses been brought in?"

"I believe so, your Majesty. I heard them announce cream cakes, custard-filled cherry buns, honeyed winterberry tarts, and gooseberry pies with sugar pumpkin sauce. I am not certain what the large things on silver platters are."

Marianna thought back to the wasted weeks of wedding plans. "They are large Saint Maria cakes with ginger wafers and candied Fletcher-plums as decoration. Kelene's choice. Clearly an incorrect one."

"Oh. Ah. Yes, of course, my Queen. They seem…" He seemed to be grappling. "…not sweet enough?"

She gave a curt nod. "Also, complicated, and foreign. This is the main dish of the dessert course at an Arclidian royal wedding. It should be a thoroughly Arclidian dish."

He nodded rapidly and mechanically, like a clockwork doll wound too tightly, in his relief at having said the right thing.

Exceedingly dull. No one ever surprised her. Not anymore.

Those spies better work fast and find me Elisandrine Falk. Before I die of boredom and frustration.

Everyone was raising their glasses in another toast. They would all be drunk out of their skulls before the desserts were devoured. Marianna lifted her glass. She intended to be the drunkest person there and then have an early night. Gods curse them all and their carefree cavorting!

CHAPTER 6

STORSUND'S TRAINS, ELISE'S NOTES, AND NESSA'S FEAR

Excitement roiled Elise's stomach, making her regret that breaded eel. The snow crunched under her boots as they walked towards the railway station. Soon she would see trains and after that... she would actually be on one. Imagining anything moving that fast and over such great distances made her dizzy.

Are we there yet? How far away can this station be?

Nessa and Anja were ahead of her, discussing train seats. It amused Elise that they both walked so similarly, straight-backed and with hands in their pockets.

"I have a minor class ticket. That is the cheapest. Those train carriages are crowded and with few seats, yes? I think I will add some coin to get a better journey. You should do the same. First time on a train should be a pleasure, not a chore," Anja said.

Nessa nodded. "Whatever you think best. Am I right in thinking there are seats by the window?"

"Yes. But if we all wish to sit next to each other, we can't all sit by the window. We'll see what spaces are free when we buy tickets."

47

Elise looked around. The crowds had changed. It was no longer people busying about their morning errands or on their way to work. There were ladies in the most elegant outerwear ambling about and men pushing prams with babies. It was so civilised and composed, it reminded her of Highmere. Only the freezing cold, which seemed to bite her cheeks and ice the breath in her nostrils, showed her she was far from home.

Good, sunny Highmere has the Queen in it. She is like a cat lapping up every ray of sunshine but, at the very idea of a place as cold as this, stays in her warm bed of silks and satin.

Elise noted and then buried a vein of shame-filled arousal running through her hate for that woman. The Queen was her hunter, thinking her a pet to tame or a trophy to claim. Elise clenched her jaw. She would run for a lifetime if she needed to, she was never going back to the Queen.

Besides, all arousal for others was inconsequential. Elise was no longer someone who bedded people at the drop of a hat. She shared only Nessa's bed. That was all she needed.

The thought warmed and refocused her. "Anja, is it far to the train station now?"

Anja turned to look back at her. "No. We will be there soon."

Elise smiled. "Splendid."

"Where do we buy the tickets?" Nessa asked.

Elise didn't hear the reply. She was busy wondering how it would feel to be on the train as it whooshed along the track. Far, far away from the Queen.

When she next looked up, she saw a building made of sandstone, like the rest of the town, but this one stood much taller. It commanded attention. There were gilded birds of prey on the tips of the tall roof and a large sign painted right on the sandstone in burnt orange.

She had to get her notebook out and write this down.

"Wait a moment," she said to her companions and began taking notes.

She heard Anja whisper, "What is she doing?"

"She makes notes on architecture," Nessa answered in equally hushed tones.

Out of the corner of her eye, Elise noted Anja inspecting her.

"Does she do that a lot? Just stop in the middle of everything to write things down?"

"Only when we see some new architecture or design," Nessa replied.

Elise wrapped up her notes quicker than she would have liked to. Discomfort niggled her whenever people talked about her as if she couldn't hear them.

"My apologies for the delay. Shall we go in?" Elise said with forced energy.

"Yes. You will find this building disappointing inside. It does not match the pretty outside. But Skarhult station, that is... how do you say... grandiose."

Elise put her notebook back into her carpet bag. "I look forward to seeing it."

"Me too," Nessa said, placing an arm around Elise's waist.

Anja turned and strode towards the imposing doors. They hurried after her. It mattered little if the station's interior was pretty or not. Elise only wanted to behold a train.

As they walked through the doors, a wall of sound hit them. Inside the large building were sights, sounds, and smells in a bewildering but exciting mass. It was an invigorating tonic to Elise.

"Awful, isn't it?" Anja muttered.

"It's... very crowded. But exciting to those of us who are new to it," Nessa replied.

Elise ignored Anja's disdain and Nessa's diplomacy. "It is

49

an absolute wonder! Look at all the paintings on the walls, as beautiful as all the finely dressed people!"

Anja let out something between a hum and a scoff and walked them towards an archway to their left.

They ventured through the arch and into a canopy of glass and steel. It must have been obscured by the high-tipped ceiling they had seen from the front. There were several sets of train tracks with walking platforms between them. And on about half of them – vast, colourful beasts of metal that stopped the breath in Elise's chest.

Beside every train stood a person in uniform with a sign that had place names and times. Anja was walking them towards the one which read *Skarhult*. An emerald green train stood there waiting. The imposing contraption huffed and puffed loudly, as if it were in a foul mood. Smoke billowed out of its chimney.

Is chimney the right word? How marvellous to find something so new that my language does not have words for it!

Anja stopped and grunted. "Ah, I forgot. You need tickets, and I need to pay extra to change mine from a minor class ticket to a major one. We need to go back inside."

"All right. Lead the way. Thank you for upgrading your ticket, by the way. We can pay the difference," Nessa offered.

Anja shook her head curtly as she walked. "No need. I have coin enough. I inherited a modest amount from my uncle. That was when I decided to stop working at the school and begin writing."

Elise was loath to leave the trains, and judging by Nessa's constant glances back to them, so was she. But like dutiful children, they followed Anja back inside. She pushed through the crowd to what looked like a small window at the far wall.

Anja strode up to it and said something to the man inside, handing over a small piece of white card. He replied in clipped words that rung out in the same complicated melody. Then he stamped her card and took some coins from her.

Anja turned back to them. "You're all right with me ordering two major class tickets for you, yes?"

"Yes, please," Nessa replied.

Her voice sounded small. Elise forced her focus out of her own excitement and into her beloved's discomfort at the situation. She took Nessa's hand and whispered, "All is well. We have a guide now, and everyone has seemed safe and trustworthy so far. Well, besides the thief. Other than him, people here seem more civilized than back in Nightport."

Nessa whispered back, "Yes, but at least I knew the language there. And I could always walk back to Ground Hollow."

Elise had no reply to that. She merely squeezed the calloused but gentle hand that lay limp in her own. "I promise to let no harm come to you. We are going to have a wonderful adventure."

Nessa nodded hastily. Elise doubted the truth behind her agreement.

While they had been talking, Anja had apparently purchased their tickets.

"That will be six coppers each," she said to them.

"Oh. Th-that is a lot," Nessa said, paling even further.

"Yes. Major tickets are costly. Minor class is only two coppers, but as I say, have very bad conditions."

"We shall gladly pay the major class price. At least for this, our first trip," Elise said.

She reached into the satchel on Nessa's shoulder and took out their coin purse. She counted out twelve coppers and handed them to Anja. Looking around to see that no thieves had seen where the coin purse was, she returned it to the satchel.

Anja gave the man in the window the coin and got two pieces of white card in return. The text on them was the same burnt orange as on the sign outside of the building. Elise wondered if others would have noticed that or if it was merely her being her father's daughter.

They took their tickets and headed back to the tracks. As they walked, Anja said, "By the way, almost everyone in the south speaks some Arclidian. You could easily have gotten your tickets in your language, yes? I merely thought it would be faster in Sundish as my Arclidian is, as I said, rusty."

"It's absolutely fine. Actually, I think it's improving," Nessa said with an encouraging smile.

Elise had to agree with that. Anja's sentences were getting longer, her vocabulary increasing, and not every sentence ended with "yes?" Still, the charming accent remained.

They were back out by the trains again. The air smelled of smoke. Not the smoke of Nightport, which had been from fireplaces and factories, but a foreign smell, not unpleasant, but cleaner and mechanical.

"Ready to board?" Anja said.

"Yes," Elise said, a little too eager.

Anja smiled at her. A rare thing with this woman, wasn't it?

They walked to the man with the Skarhult sign. Anja showed him her ticket, and Nessa and Elise followed suit. He nodded to them all and indicated the first door of the long train.

They got on, and at once, Elise marvelled at the interior of this metal contraption. The walls were the same emerald green as the outside. There were windows with red velvet curtains and seats covered in plush cushioning of the same colour. The seats were two and two with little tables between them. On the tables were oil lamps and ornate tinderboxes to light them with, still allowing space for the train rider to put their items down.

Elise started at the sight of the tinderbox.

Anja peered at her. "Everything all right?"

Elise swallowed. "Yes, I was merely… pondering the fire risk."

"Ah. Fires are rare, but they do have pump bottles of water in every compartment just in case. This is but one of the luxuries you find here but not in minor class. In those carriages, you'd be packed in like animals. Rarely any seats, and where there are seats, they have no… softness?"

"Cushioning?" Elise suggested.

Anja grunted. "That's it. No cushioning."

"Where can we sit?" Nessa asked.

"Your ticket will have a number on it."

Elise looked at her piece of card, her *ticket*, she corrected herself. It said 5B. She looked over at Nessa's and saw that she was in 5A. Anja pointed at the numbers on the train walls above the seats.

"I am in seat 4A, the window seat here. So, I will sit opposite you, yes? Unless you both want a window seat, in which case we switch, and I sit in 5B," she said.

"I d-don't know," Nessa said, looking in panic to Elise.

Elise smiled reassuringly at her. "I think we will sit as our tickets say at first. Then we can switch later if we wish. Will someone sit in 4B?"

"Possibly," Anja replied.

"Shame. I was going to suggest that our bags could be in that spot," Elise said.

Anja shook her head. "There is a place for luggage, not that you two have much of that. You travel surprisingly light. Anyway, at the back of this carriage are what we call luggage racks."

So, she noticed that we arrived without real luggage. Curses.

"Perfect. I'll put our bags there," Elise said while relieving Nessa of her satchel.

"Thank you," Anja said, handing over her own bag.

Elise quashed the impulse to have a quick glance into it. Her curiosity for the stoic older woman shouldn't make her forget her manners and common decency.

She put the bags on the top shelf, noting that she or Anja would have to get them down as the shorter Nessa couldn't reach. Then she went back to their seats.

Anja was leaning her head back, eyes closed. A perfect opposite to Nessa, who sat stiff and stared out the window as if she expected the gods to appear on the platform with burning spears and judgement.

Elise sat down next to her and kissed her temple. "Exciting, is it not?"

Nessa blew out a long breath. "I suppose."

Elise leaned in to whisper right into Nessa's ear. "Heartling, when we get to whatever rooms we hire, I intend to settle between those legs of yours and relax you. And I do not want you distracted by the muscle knots you are creating now. Try to get those shoulders away from your ears."

Nessa sniggered, lowering her shoulders as requested. Elise gave her temple another kiss.

The train hissed loudly, and a thrumming noise began. The man with the sign outside shouted something in Sundish and then, in Arclidian, bellowed, "Departure is now, ladies and gentlemen. Take your seats on the train to Skarhult."

Five or six people came in and sat down, leaving the carriage still half-empty. But from what Eleonora Lindberg had told Elise, the train stopped often and took on more people while only a few left.

The train seemed to be vibrating now. Elise's heart was working overtime and her blood humming with excitement.

Nessa took her hand and shakily whispered, "Here we go."

The train began to move, and Elise was filled with a lightness, as if she were flying across the land. She bit her lip, holding back an elated laugh. It made no sense that Arclid had fought against the trains for so long. This was magic! She closed her eyes and squeezed Nessa's slightly damp hand.

"Yes, my heartling. Here we go!"

CHAPTER 7
TO SKARHULT

S ome time later, Nessa asked how far along they were and was told they were about a third of the way.

"At least I believe so," Anja said with a shrug. "I never timed the journey. I only go to Charlottenberg when not working, and then I do not let my timepiece control my days."

Elise's golden eyes went wide. "You have a timepiece?"

Anja opened her coat and pulled out a pocket watch. "Don't you have these?"

Nessa chuckled. "Well yes, Arclidians have them, but *we* don't. Only the Nobles can afford them. Oh, and the church timekeepers, who get timepieces to keep church clocks working. All commoners tell time by them. And the movements of the sun, of course."

"I had one," Elise said quietly, gazing out the window. "I was given a golden pocket watch when I was at—"

"Which you didn't get to keep when you left your employer, right?" Nessa interrupted. She had to stop Elise before she slipped up and said *at court*. They might not be in Arclid anymore and were not sure that the Queen was really hunting them, but they were still laying low.

Elisandrine shook herself out of her reverie. "Right. Quite so. I had to leave it behind as it was… a gift that came with my profession."

"I see," Anja said. "It must have been a high-paid job then, if timepieces come at such a premium, yes?"

Elise didn't hesitate, fully in control now. "I was a companion to a rich and powerful Noble. A lady at court."

"Sounds rather tedious," Anja muttered.

Nessa worried Elise would become defensive at the rudeness, maybe even have that temper of hers flare up.

Instead, Elise laughed. "It was at times, although the court intrigues forced my mind to be alert. You had to be one step ahead of the closest plotting lady who wanted whatever favour you had just managed to get. The court of Arclid is like a flock of starved vultures. Wanting treasure, power, and attention rather than meat."

Nessa's jaws tightened with jealousy at Elise's sudden patience. She wished Anja was a man, thereby ensuring that "Only-Women-Thanks Elise" would not have any physical interest.

Stop it. Elise's roving days are over, flirting is just her way. Quell your insecurities, Clay.

Massaging her jaw, Nessa focused back on the discussion of the pocket watch. Anja's was not as gilded and gaudy as the one she had seen Prince Macray peer at during town celebrations. This was a functional yet elegant open-faced timepiece which turned out to have a pattern of an ice bear on the back. The silver was so darkened with time and use that it might as well be tin.

"Lovely. Are they expensive here?" Elise asked.

"No. We have a lot of people who work with watchmaking and clockwork. Time belongs to all in Storsund, not just to the rich and powerful."

Elise and Nessa glanced at each other. Such a thought

wouldn't go down well in Arclid. Especially not at the court in Highmere.

Elise began asking how the watch worked, something which Nessa found she couldn't focus on in her fatigue. Her mind seemed to have been filled to the brim with new things and threatened to spill over.

The view outside the window took her attention instead. Gone were the pastel buildings of Charlottenberg. Now she saw only occasional wooden houses flanked with dense forest. Grey clouds filled the sky, making it appear like dusk even though it was only early afternoon. As the sky got darker and darker, promising thunderstorms, the ground got lighter. There was more snow here. The light, dirty dusting on the ground in Charlottenberg was replaced with a shimmering white blanket.

The train was warm, seeming to thaw the cold which had set in her bones during the six-week sea voyage. Seeing that Anja had taken her coat off, Nessa took hers off, too. She was growing sleepy. For a long time, she watched the layer of snow growing thicker as they travelled, covering every house and tree.

Her reverie was interrupted by Elise's hand on her thigh. "Nessa? Did you hear my idea?"

"What? No. Sorry. I was watching the snow."

"I just asked if perhaps we could stay with Anja for a few days?"

Nessa looked over at Anja and saw what she interpreted as hesitance.

"Heartling, we've only just met her. Perhaps we shouldn't simply invite ourselves into her home?"

Elise pursed her red lips. "But it would be most beneficial to all of us! I could even help Anja by taking dictation."

"Take what now?" Anja asked with a frown on her clear features.

"Dictation is when you say out loud what you want written and someone writes it for you. I enjoy history and would love to be of use to you. Not that I doubt your ability to manage on your own," Elise hastened to say. She smiled apologetically before adding, "In return, we would only ask for a roof over our heads. Then Nessa can look for an apprentice position with a local glassblower, and when she finds one, we can rent some rooms in town."

Anja ran a hand over her unruly hair. "I... don't live in the centre of Skarhult, only in an industrial area farther out. You seem like a city woman, you would not like my little hovel."

Elise laughed her silver bell laughter. "Oh, hush. I am sure it is not a hovel!"

Nessa was about to apologise for Elise's impetuousness when they were interrupted by a man in a railway uniform clearing his throat. In front of him was a silver cart which held a pot of coffee and a stack of cups, matching saucers, and a small glass bottle filled with milk. At least Nessa assumed it was milk. Who knew in this peculiar place?

"Pardon, ladies. Coffee?" the man said, his ginger moustache twitching with his nervous smile.

Anja whispered, "A cup is included in your ticket. Take one even if you don't want it and I'll have it."

"Yes, please," Nessa said, unsure if she was keeping the cup or handing it over.

Elise nodded with her nose scrunched up. They all knew she wasn't drinking hers.

Anja accepted her cup and saucer, her bright eyes seeming to twinkle when the black liquid was poured.

When the ginger-haired man moved on, Nessa said, "You really do love this stuff, don't you?"

"Love it and need it. If you have it everyday, you are likely to become addicted," Anja replied and took a long slurp.

Elise pushed her coffee over to Anja, looking sheepish.

Nessa blew on hers, watching her lover.

Is that look because you forced the houseguest idea or because you spurned her favourite drink?

Anja put her cup down with a satisfied sigh. "We are lucky to have such a good trade deal with the Western Isles."

"Is that where you get the coffee?" Nessa asked.

"Yes. There are frequent ships between our southwest coast and the closest of their islands. We get coffee, and in return, they receive sturdy timber and grains that do not grow in their warm lands."

"Speaking of warmth. There is a lot of snow out there and our boots aren't made for it. We'll need to buy boots and other winter wear when we alight in Skarhult," Nessa said to Elise.

Anja nodded gravely. "Yes, you will. And woollen underwear which covers arms and legs, yes? It'll keep you alive."

"Thank you for the suggestion. We shall make that a priority," Elise said, still looking cowed.

Anja blew out a breath and sat back. "Now, Elise, returning to your question. As I mentioned before, I'm a loner, while you two are strangers I met only this morning. Why should I house you?"

Some of the energy returned to Elise's features. "Because we can be of use to you. I can help with the writing, as I said. Nessa is strong and capable and can assist around the house. You cannot be sure we are not thieves or murderers, but we cannot be sure you are not one of those, either. *We* are, however, willing to trust *you*."

The defiance in Elise's voice threatened to morph into anger, so Nessa interrupted. "Anja, I know this must seem hasty to you. We've had to live our lives taking chances and trusting strangers lately, but you have not. Perhaps there is a compromise? Why don't we come stay with you for only a day or two? Then we'll know if we get along and if anyone is planning any attacks with a bread knife?"

Anja stood up. "Perhaps. I will think about it. I need to stretch my legs."

She walked down the carriage and began striding back and forth.

When she was out of earshot, Nessa turned to Elise. "Heartling, you can't just rush things along like that. You must be patient."

Elise huffed.

Nessa tried again. "I know your style of pushing and being bold worked well for us in Nightport, and I'm grateful. However, here we might have to wait longer to get jobs and lodging. We might just have to make do and prepare for discomfort."

Elise jutted her chin out and stared out the window.

"Really, Elise? You're not going to reply?" Nessa softened her tone. "Just… don't push so fast. I know I've said it before, but not everyone is as flexible and free as you, heartling."

Elise busied herself with brushing down her coat. "Fine. I will endeavour to be patient."

"Thank you. I'm sure your plan will come to fruition anyway. It always does. Just use a subtler, gentler touch."

"Yes, yes. I get it."

"Great. Now, speak plainly… on a scale from one to ten, how much do you loathe coffee?"

"Eleven," Elise drawled before pursing her lips.

Nessa laughed, prompting Elise to sigh and put her head on her shoulder.

"I do so adore it when you laugh. How quick you are to laugh was one of the first things I fell for."

Nessa kissed her hair. "Really? What were the other first things?"

"Fishing for compliments, are we?"

"Merely passing the time until we get to Skarhult," Nessa replied stiffly while picking up her coffee cup.

"Aha. Hmm. I would say that the first things were your honesty, your shyness, your beauty, and how eager you were to help. Even a complete stranger, like I was then."

"My beauty?"

Elise adjusted her head on Nessa's shoulder. "Yes."

"You... find me beautiful?"

"Of course, silly. I cannot take my eyes, *or my hands*, off of you."

Nessa sipped the last of the coffee. "I-I thought that was just because you love me."

"Oh, come now, even the Queen had to admit that you are attractive. Even if she did so in her unpleasant way."

"Don't mention *her*. I'm trying not to think about her," Nessa hissed. She looked down at her hands and mumbled, "Trying to shake the feeling that she's right behind us, scheming to take you away from me."

"Sorry. I can find other examples. What about your best friend's wife, who had a colossal crush on you? Or even Hunter Smith, who in all his disinterest in the pleasures of the flesh, could not resist flirting his head off when he saw you."

Nessa scoffed. "Hunter flirts with everyone. It's how he hides that he doesn't want to bed them."

"True. But when he flirted with you, he pointed out that you have a natural, obvious beauty. One that does not require cosmetics, like mine does. Or require a certain taste in looks, like, well, like Anja's appearance does."

Nessa stiffened, hoping that Elise hadn't felt it. "You find her attractive?"

"Mm. I suppose I do. In an austere, handsome sort of way. She has a certain... presence and such striking eyes."

"No, *you* have striking eyes."

Elise gave a hollow laugh. "I have peculiar eyes, my treasure. It is not the same thing."

"Peculiar? No! The way your eyes look is like," she paused. "Like morning sunlight. Golden yellow, all bright and warm."

Elise moved her head off Nessa's shoulder and faced her. "You say the sweetest things."

Nessa was going to answer, but something in the way her lover looked at her made her stop. Elise's gaze moved from her eyes and down to her lips. There was a shiver of pleasure working its way down Nessa's spine to settle between her legs.

Annoyingly, it was interrupted by Anja coming back to sit down.

"The next stop will be Skarhult," she said, peeking into Nessa's cup and scowling when she found it empty.

How does she not need to relieve herself every two minutes if she drinks that much?

The train slowed to a halt. Anja and Nessa put their coats on while Elise, who had kept hers on, merely stretched and yawned. The fresh, cold air outside would be good for them all.

Nessa's wakeup call came as her right foot sank into a patch of untouched snow. It was the only part she could see that wasn't trodden in or otherwise disturbed.

The only two times in her life when there had been snow in Ground Hollow, it had been untouched when she first saw it. A thin film of fragile white covering the farm, like lace over a dress. Then she and the other children had played in it, quickly ruining it, leaving only traces in the middle of the fields, where their parents wouldn't let them play for fear of injuring the crops.

She looked along the platform and saw that the snow here was trampled and packed into a dense crust. But the snow at the end of the platform, where there were no trains or passengers, looked like it would be ankle deep. The train tracks were clear. Did someone shovel them every time snow fell? If not, would they be stuck here? Warily, Nessa searched the sky.

There was no sign of snow, but the gloomy clouds, with the reflection from the white snow and the city, appeared darkly purplish. Did that mean there was snow in them?

She shivered and cast a glance over at Anja. Should she bother Anja with a prompt to take them to a shop where they could buy winter clothes? And then maybe lunch? Maybe even food before the shopping? It must be past lunchtime now, and the energy of Nessa's sandwich at the cafe had been burned through.

Anja gazed ahead at the city beyond the station, a severe look on her face. Her pepper-and-salt hair blew across her eyes, and she shook her head violently to clear her vision. She appeared to have a million things on her mind. Nevertheless, it was Nessa's role in her relationship with Elise to be the practical one. They needed winter clothes, and if this was a large city, they needed a guide. Nessa geared up to ask, to be the whiny, nagging one once more.

Before she could speak, Anja began putting her gloves on, struggling when she used her prosthetic hand. "Now then. Proper boots and thicker coats, yes? As I said, more covering underwear will come in handy too. Ready to go?"

With that, she strode down the platform. Nessa's breathing calmed. Elise had once again found someone to guide them. She had to learn to trust her heartling with these things.

CHAPTER 8

THE QUEEN AT COURT

Marianna drew in deep lungfuls of the air. That overpowering scent of roses and lavender meant she was home. The rose scent came from the specially cultivated rosebushes that bloomed year-round all over court. They were bred to be purple to match the rosebush on the Hargraves crest. The lavender was her own perfume, concocted of purified alcohol, stronger than even sunberry essence, and dried lavender. She made sure it was sprayed all around court, since, unlike the Hargraves roses, the lavender refused to be cultivated to bloom year-round. She liked that about lavender. Uncompromising. Unyielding. Powerful.

She squinted as the winter sun's brightness reflected off her white- and pink-streaked home. It was said that the amount of sun hours in the city of Highmere was the reason the Hargraves had founded their court here. They had built this stunning castle in Centurian marble, the priciest building material on the orb, because of how it would reflect the sun.

Marianna puffed out her chest. *Highmere only grew to become Arclid's capital because the other Noble families imitated us, building big Centurian marble houses here, making this city a gleaming pearl in the sun.*

And yet, the peasants complained about the cost of Highmere, claiming that they wanted that coin for their tawdry huts and dull crops. She sneered. They didn't understand that it was worth some sacrifice to have such a stunning court and surrounding city.

Especially if we are going to impress the Storsund envoy, or rather, Joiners Square envoy. Was that this week? I shall have to ask Adaire.

Marianna strode into her castle, guards on her heels throughout every corridor and staircase until she got to her bedchamber, when they respectfully positioned themselves on either side of the door.

She found Adaire by the desk in the chamber, her long fingers rifling through a mass of papers. Seeing to any and all paperwork was one of her duties as Queen's Aide. Adaire was part advisor, part secretary, and full-on-lover to Marianna.

In a fit of rare nostalgia, she remembered when she had informed Elise of that. Telling the young and newly arrived Lady Falk that Adaire came from the second oldest and most prestigious Noble family, the Aldershires. Explaining how, together with the imbecilic Macray and the high priest and priestess, Adaire formed the inner circle at court. Then, of course, the council of advisors, all over-educated people with no guts or spine. After that, the ladies in waiting; bored Noble ladies pawned off on Marianna by proud Noble parents.

Elise. She could have been yet another of those bored and boring ladies in waiting. But it took one day before she, in a fit of rage, threw her bedsheets at a footman who had been insolent.

Ah, memories. Her mirth faded. How those memories soured when Elise left. And how she would pay.

"Are you quite well, my Queen?"

"Yes," she replied, "merely fatigued from the journey."

"I see. I shall be with you shortly, your Highness. I need to locate this proclamation for you to sign later."

Adaire returned to rifling through the papers. Her Adaire. The only one who understood her. Well, to a point. Adaire was logical and calculating. She had never seen the fascination with Lady Elisandrine Falk. She could not see how Marianna could become obsessed with someone so impulsive, carefree, and emotional.

Shame. If she had been a little more like Elise, especially between the sheets, I might not need any other lover in my life.

Marianna could control almost everything, but she could not quench her need for drama and spark. She needed fire-starters like Elise to brighten her accountable, solemn life as regent. That was why all her concubines were impulsive, vibrant, highly sexual, and utterly... *alive*. Not to mention stunningly beautiful. Elise could have been one of them. Those lucky people who spent their days playing games, reading books, engaging in sports, and hunting. And their evenings in their Queen's bed. All taking turns, or sometimes coming in packages of three or four.

Unless it was one of the nights when Adaire shared her bed. Even a Queen needed affection and meticulous skill sometimes, and that was what Adaire provided. Both in and out of the bedchamber.

Adaire looked up with the proclamation in her hand, the sunlight fading her eyes from midnight blue to ultramarine.

"There. Apologies for the wait, my Queen. Such a pleasant surprise that you have returned earlier than expected. How was your sojourn down to the lowlands?"

Marianna rolled her eyes. "My cretin of a brother is safely married and ready to produce the next heirs to the throne. Taking that pressure off of me, at least. I knew he would be good for something eventually. How have things been here?"

"Everything has been, as my letters informed Your Grace, quiet and under control."

Adaire placed the proclamation back on the desk and strode towards her, quietly and gracefully. How did she move so silently? Sure, her trim figure did not put much weight on the marble floors, but she still had a woman's ample curves and incredibly long legs, making her even taller than Marianna.

She stood in front of her queen, close enough to touch but not taking the initiative. She knew her place. It was up to Marianna to choose if they were to touch or not, but her sudden proximity showed that Adaire was willing. The Queen's aide could always keep her distance without any repercussions.

Marianna watched her for a moment, savouring the cold beauty of her muted taupe skin, eyes so midnight blue they were almost black, and those pale lips. She found her heartbeat picking up. She grabbed Adaire's neck and pulled her into a rough kiss. It was answered with fervour immediately. Adaire pushed her body against the Queen's. Her grip on Marianna's waist was tight.

You would never admit it and show how weak you are for me, but I can feel how much you have missed me.

Marianna stopped the kiss as quickly as she had instigated it. "I would order you to take your clothes off and spread your legs for me, but I am wearied after my trip and require a hot bath and a rest. After that, I want a light meal, and then... I want you."

A quick smile danced on Adaire's pale lips until she supressed it.

"As you wish, my Queen. There is the proclamation and some matters of state that need attention, but I suppose they can wait."

"Yes, they can," Marianna said pointedly.

Adaire nodded and began helping her with the laces at the

back of her dress. As the tight laces opened more and more, Marianna relished in the deep breaths now possible.

"Is there anything you wish for me to attend to while you have your bath and rest?" Adaire asked.

A vein in Marianna's left temple pulsated, as it always did when her temper faltered. She made her tone stern. "Yes. However, only if you can follow my command without questions or judgement."

Done with the laces, Adaire gently tugged the tight, heavy dress off Marianna's shoulders and down her body. "I do as my Queen bids, you know that."

Her voice gave nothing away, perfectly professional as always.

Marianna sighed. "Naturally. Still, what I require of you is… something I know you disapprove of."

"Oh?"

"Yes," Marianna said wearily, stepping out of the dress which was now bunched around her heeled boots.

Adaire gathered up the dress. While hanging it by the door for the servants, she called over her shoulder, "Disapprove or not. If it is something you want me to take care of, I shall see to it. You must, however, explain what it is, my Queen."

"I know," Marianna clipped. She lifted her chin. "I want you to send out orders to my spies on the other continents. Tell them to put aside their usual tasks and focus all efforts on finding Elisandrine Falk."

Adaire turned but did not speak. Marianna continued. "Give physical descriptions of Elise and Nessa Clay along with whatever else we can pass on. The farm wench was apprenticing with a glassblower and will probably search out a new master. While Elise has no talents or ambitions, she does have a distinct Highmere accent. And manners which will stick out anywhere other than a royal court."

There was a weighted silence. "Your Majesty, are you certain you want your spies to devote all their time on this search? What about their examinations of the other governments?"

Marianna found herself growling. "The game of politics can play itself out for a few weeks. The Storsund envoy is coming here soon, is he not?"

"In four days, Your Majesty."

"Excellent. That is one government in hand, then. And our trade arrangement and friendly relationship with Obeha is dependable. For as long as we are of use to each other, that is. The Western Isles, well, they tend to keep to themselves. With their weak military and weaker arsenal, they are hardly a threat."

Adaire looked sad, or was it disappointed? Marianna couldn't tell.

"Pardon me for speaking plainly, my Queen. But if I do not, no one will. Broadening your search for Lady Falk increases the risk of people finding out what happened that night. Are you ready for Nobles and commoners to know that you are spending so much time and coin on a woman who has committed no crime other than spurning your brother's hand in marriage?"

"Adaire. This discussion is exactly what I wanted to avoid. I am no fool. I know what is at stake here. Now, obey my orders without irritating me further."

Adaire stiffened, but she held her gaze. "As you wish, my Queen." She sniffed and crouched to take off her mistress' boots.

Marianna ground her teeth. "I want her back, Adaire. I want her to pay."

"With her life?" Adaire asked coolly.

Marianna peered down at her. "What do you think?"

Adaire tilted her head in thought, showing off her long, graceful neck. "If you wanted to kill her, you would have your spies do that and send you her head in a box. And we both know that you do not bed anyone against their will."

Marianna huffed. "Of course not. What sort of failure would resort to something so monstrous? Sometimes it takes some work, but in the end, my lovers all come begging for me. Like you did." Marianna paused at a memory before adding, "I may have told Elise that I would have my other courtesans all *initiate her* at the same time when she came back to court, but that was only because I know that she normally enjoys that sort of thing."

Adaire raised her eyebrows. *That sort of thing* was exactly what Marianna liked too, but not what Adaire enjoyed at all.

Was that disapproval or jealousy in those midnight blue eyes? Those intelligent eyes, how Marianna loved them. It was why her stationery, wrapping paper, and even bedding all came in that particular shade. Of course, she would never tell Adaire that. She would never give anyone that sort of power over her.

Adaire adjusted her crouching position. "What does that leave us with? Do you want her back to torture her? To make her apologise? Grovel?"

"Oh, much cleverer than that, my treasure. Never mind that now, I am tired and do not intend to discuss it further."

Adaire looked up, her thin lips squeezed so tight they made a straight line. "As you wish, Your Majesty."

Marianna rolled her eyes. "I know what you are thinking. You think Elise an unhealthy obsession of mine."

"With all due respect, my Queen, no, you do not know. We grew up together. I was raised in this castle to be your aide, as my mother was king's aide to your father. In all that time, you have seemed many things, but never confused. Your plans and wishes for Lady Falk seem… irrational," Adaire stated.

Marianna was about to argue when Adaire continued. "She has angered you, therefore you should want her punished and out of your sight. However, you also want her by your side, and there is a light on your features when you speak of her. I cannot help but wonder how much of this is about Lady Falk and how much is about your pride and need for conquest."

Marianna had the sudden urge to kick her foot out and push the crouching woman over. She quelled the impulse. "I think that is your jealousy speaking more than your sense, Adaire. You wish my face lit up that way when I spoke of you. Stop being ridiculous and be grateful that you are my confidant and favourite lover."

Adaire looked affronted.

Marianna pointed down at her. "And no more arguments! Do as you are told and send out the orders when we are done here. Quickly and meticulously. I want everyone with any form of discretion in their bones to be out searching for that light-eyed harlot," she said through gritted teeth.

"Yes, my Queen. I shall see to it while you have your bath."

"No. Later. Now, *you* will give me my bath."

Adaire stood up, boots held in her hands. "Pardon?"

Her confusion was understandable. Servants assisted during royal baths, not someone with the clout of a queen's aide.

"I do not wish to wait with bedding you. You will give me my bath and then follow me to bed and *welcome me home* properly. Let us put an end to our disagreement. Unless you do not want that?"

The disapproval that had come into Adaire's thin face faded away. The pale lips drew into a smile which made her even more attractive.

"A splendid idea, my Queen."

Marianna reached out a hand to stroke Adaire's dress-clad chest. "Good. Afterwards, you will see to the next step in my hunt for my tinderbox-maker."

As Marianna gripped and squeezed a firm breast, Adaire dropped the boots and moaned, "Yes, my Queen."

CHAPTER 9
A FAWN FRETTING OVER WOLVES

Elise looked around as they headed for what must be Skarhult Station. The snow made everything look magical.

She had loved snow as a child. Growing up in Silverton, on the border between Arclid's Highlands and Midlands, she had seen plenty of it. She had played in the white drifts with her father and her cousins. Snow was fun and adventure. It was playing games until you couldn't feel your nose or fingers anymore and adults forced you in to thaw by the fire. Eating honey cakes and drinking warm milk. The winters of snow and childish fun had ended when they moved to Highmere. Then it had been schooling with other Noble youth. Endless social gatherings. Being forced to speak to Noble ladies and gentlemen while her mother plotted what to do with a daughter who had those peculiar eyes, those odd, light eyes which did not belong on a Noble.

Then the red pox hit and took her father. That had been their first winter in Highmere. There had been no snow, just rain and freezing winds. All she remembered from that winter was everlasting damp and everlasting grief.

Seeing snow again was a bittersweet balm on those wounds. She breathed in and out slowly, until the breaths were no longer shaky. Then she turned to Nessa, who was scanning her surroundings, like a fawn fretting over wolves.

My sweet Nessa. She could do with taking some deep breaths, too.

Elise sought her eye and grinned, getting only a wan attempt at a smile back. There was nothing to calm Nessa now, nothing but time to adjust to this new place.

Elise shivered and looked up at the cold sky. It wasn't snowing.

She recalled her grandmother explaining to an impatient granddaughter, "It cannot snow if it is too warm or too cold, my sweetest one. You must wait."

They walked into the station, following in the efficient footsteps of Anja. The station had such high ceilings. Shadows played on them, thrown by gas-lit chandeliers. The ceiling, the floors, the walls, all blindingly white, whiter than even the snow outside.

Another recollection pricked up at the sight. Her mind seemed to use this quietness to take stock. This memory was of the white-washed walls of the White Raven in Nightport. Elise could almost smell the stale alcohol, smoke, and the chemical odour of the illegal powders sold there. And… the mix of purified alcohol and lavender which was the Queen's perfume. For a moment, she was back there that night when the Queen met Nessa. She hadn't really thought about how close to disaster they had come.

And now is not the time.

She cleared her throat and asked Nessa, "Is this not completely marvellous?"

"Yes, but so… bright."

Anja gave a curt nod. "Far too bright. Stupid Skarhult prides itself on its white buildings, despite the need to repaint.

The smoke from the trains and the dirt carried by the snow stick to the white and then... time to paint again."

Without further explanation, Anja took off walking again. To her surprise, Elise found herself missing the chatty Lindberg family. They had been clingy and nosey, but at least they were good for a long talk.

"Nessa, button your coat. We are going outside again."

"Look at you, being the sensible one for once," Nessa joked. She did, however, button her coat up. As soon as her hands were free, they were on their way to their usual resting place, the pockets of her leather coat. Elise stopped the one closest to her and took it.

"I was putting my hands in my pockets to keep them warm, but this is better," Nessa cooed.

"We're going to a used clothing shop two streets away," Anja said over her shoulder. "You'll buy gloves, yes?"

"She hears everything but only replies to what she wishes," Elise whispered with laughter in her tone. "Part of her stoic style, I suppose."

Nessa smiled. "Stoic or grumpy?"

Elise was about to answer but was distracted as her vision filled with the white city. She blinked at its vastness. Almost every building was three floors or higher, but not like in Nightport where they had just slapped on an extra floor when the population grew. These houses looked like their builders long ago took pride in their work, crowning their structures in the strange minty green of aged copper.

As she got her notebook out to make notes, Elise remembered her father explaining that copper started off the usual reddish-brown but out in the elements, it would turn green in fifteen to twenty years. She looked back up again and realised that she now had a guide to age the structures. The roofs of these houses were almost all made of copper. Domed like onions, or like piped droplets of thick ganache. All but a handful of them were a pale green. Elise swallowed a lump in her throat. It seemed that, in her knowledge and in her memories, her father lived on.

Nessa sniffed in the cold, so Elise hurried up with her notes.

"There, I am done. Thank you both for waiting. Time to go purchase warmer clothes?"

She put the notebook away and, once more, followed Anja who had marched off to the left. Her strides led them down a broad street, lined with benches which stood abandoned in the cold afternoon.

It was still dark with heavy clouds that threatened rain. Elise wondered how this white and copper city, with all these ornate streetlights, painted white with copper details, of course, would look in moonlight.

She was becoming winded trying to follow Anja's pace, but she wasn't going to complain and risk annoying her. Perhaps Nessa had been right, she had pushed too much too fast.

Nevertheless, it *was* a perfect solution. They needed a place to stay while Nessa looked for an apprenticeship and she sought work. Meanwhile, Anja needed someone to help with the book. If they worked well together, surely Anja would need to dictate more books and allow Elise to assist her?

She chewed her cold lower lip. She needed to learn the languages of the Western Isles and Obeha to help with the translations. Maybe she should start with Sundish? Either way, she could be of help, and they could get an instant home. It was perfect. Why were people always so hesitant? She stomped through the snow, taking her frustrations out on the white stuff. She took a few calming breaths, watched them come out as smoke.

It didn't matter, she reminded herself. They'd find jobs and lodgings soon enough.

It's just that I am responsible for Nessa. I made her come here, leaving Arclid and her family and friends. Now she is homesick, worried about her day-to-day needs, and possibly hunted by the Queen.

Elise sighed, then shrugged the worries away for the moment.

This was good, as Anja had stopped abruptly, pointing to a shop. "Here we are. They're said to have cheap, warm clothes."

"Um. *Said to?* You've never shopped here?" Nessa asked, eyeing the building.

"No. I buy my clothes in the smaller second-hand shops at the edge of town, closer to home. This place is bigger, though. More choices for you."

Elise couldn't understand why in the name of the gods they were standing outside debating. "Right, my hands and shins are covered in icicles. I am going in to buy gloves and trousers."

She strode in and was faced with a large shop. Clothes on rails hung along every wall. Elise was used to tailors' shops and the few second-hand shops she had frequented in Nightport. All of them had been considerably smaller than this place.

"Yes. *Plenty* of choice," Nessa said as she joined her.

At the counter stood a finely dressed woman with a vacant look and a long, shining, strawberry-blonde braid. Elise couldn't help but adjust her own hair, making it curl inwards to her chin. Anja did nothing to smooth her own black-and-grey tangle. Nessa, as always, wore a braid, whose almond-brown tresses were making their escape.

Not that Nessa seemed bothered. She was scowling at the clothes as if trying to pick out which fruits might be ripe and which were rotting at a market stall. Her seriousness warmed Elise's heart. As always.

The cashier was looking at Nessa, too. "Welcome. I did hear you speak Arclidian, yes?"

Nessa started. "Ah, yes. That's right. Th-Thank you."

"You're welcome. You ask if you need help, yes?"

"We will," Elise replied with a polite smile, saving Nessa the trouble of gathering her speech.

The cashier didn't acknowledge the comment but simply returned to folding scarves.

Anja waved for Elise's attention. "This is a good coat. Thick fur on the inside. Nice, warming fur is another thing we have plenty of, now that the railroads connect the north and the south," she said proudly.

Elise assessed the coat, making sure it wasn't just warm, but also her size and not… *ugly*. It wasn't. It did however smell faintly of animal, and Elise tried very hard not to think about the animals who had died to provide her with warmth. But, there was no other option, unless she wanted to wear nine layers of cloth. Elise took the coat and hung it over her arm.

After a short while of browsing, they had two pairs of shirts and trousers each for Nessa and Elise. Giving up dresses hurt Elise's vanity, but it would be worth it for warm legs. Anja wouldn't let them avoid the all-covering underwear made of thick imported cotton. She thrust four pairs each at Elise, who vowed to rewash them at the first opportunity, bad at laundry as she was.

When it was time to get a coat for Nessa, she shook her head. "I've treasured this leather coat since I got it for my eighteenth birthday. I'd prefer not to part with it. Is there any way I can still wear it? Maybe if I add more layers underneath?"

Anja scowled. "Layers are good, but they cannot solve everything."

Elise was just about to make a quip about 'mottos to live your life by' when Anja added, "I suppose you could buy a fur shoulder cape. One like Joiners Square soldiers have over their uniforms."

Nessa's face lit up. "I'll do that then."

"As you wish," Anja said. Her expression hinted at a lack of faith in Nessa's intelligence. "Seems odd to be attached to an impractical piece of clothing. But then so many things people do seem odd to me," she muttered before ladening Elise down further with a large pile of woollen socks.

Nessa appeared to bounce with joy at keeping her coat. "I'm going to go find a fur cloak. Or was it cape? Never mind, I'll find one."

She relieved Elise of some of the bigger items of clothing and disappeared farther into the shop. Elise adjusted the remaining garments in her arms and asked, "Do we have everything we need now?"

"No," Anja said and piled two pairs of black gloves and a couple of matching scarves on top of the socks in Elise's arms. "You still need boots. I will not have you getting wet, cold feet. But we get them from bootmakers later. What about your head? Hmm? Have you even thought about your head?"

"You mean we need hats?" Elise suggested.

Anja was the perfect blend of unimpressed and impatient. "Yes. Hats! Something to keep your brain from turning to ice."

"I saw women with some sort of fur-lined bonnet at the station. Warm but still ladylike. Do they sell those here? White fur would look nice with my black hair," Elise enthused.

Anja rubbed her brow. "They're not practi… oh, for snow's sake. Fine! There are some on the wall behind the counter. We'll look at them when we pay."

Nessa was walking back to them with her a fur cape proudly perched on top of her pile of clothes.

"Pick up something to wear on your head!" Anja shouted over.

Nessa beamed. "I've got that! I took it off a mannequin next to the cape-cloak-things. Look!"

Elise lifted the cloak and drew out a small-brimmed, scruffy cavalier hat.

Nessa nodded empathetically. "That's it! I thought it might be just for men, but it fits my head."

Elise looked at the hat from all angles. "I am certain it does, my cherished. But is that a reason to wear it?" Elise looked back up at Nessa. "It looks like it might have fleas."

Nessa bristled. "Well, it doesn't. I like it and will look dashing in it. Stop grimacing, your face might stay like that."

Anja just said, "Won't warm your ears, but have it your way. Can we go get *Madam Ladylike's* bonnet now and leave? I'm hungry."

They went to pay, and Elise hurried over to enquire about bonnets. She was struggling to get the stylish cashier to make eye contact.

Look at me so I know I can speak with you. She felt like waving a hand in the woman's face, but even she wasn't that ill-mannered. *Strange. It is like she cannot see me.*

The cashier gave Nessa a forced smile instead and asked if she wanted to purchase a carpet bag for the items. Nessa, wary of expenses, asked for the cheapest bag they had.

Abandoning her attempts to get the cashier's attention, Elise surveyed the bonnets on the wall and found one she liked. "May I please have a closer look at that white one there?"

Once more the cashier didn't look at her, but she did take the bonnet down and hand it over. It was soft and fitted perfectly.

"Splendid. Add that to our tally, please," Elise said and handed it back.

The woman didn't reply now either but tallied the items and informed Nessa of the cost. With a grunt, Nessa counted out the coin and handed it over. To their surprise, Anja had already begun packing their clothing away in the carpet bag. To further confuse them, the cashier immediately left.

"What is going on here? Why was she behaving like that?" Elise whispered.

Anja scoffed. "You mean not talking to you and me but referring all questions to the lighter-haired person, yes? The one who *doesn't look like a Wayfarer*?"

Suddenly, Elise's stomach ached in the same way it had when the children at school teased her about her light eyes or their parents made crude jokes about her parentage.

Nessa's mouth grew thin. She turned in the direction where the cashier had gone, but Anja caught her arm before she could do anything rash.

"No. People like her claim that Wayfarers cause trouble wherever we go and that we don't like to pay for things. You picking a fight with her, or us returning the goods we just bought, would prove her bigoted assumptions."

"So we're just going to let her get away with that? With treating people like this?" Nessa bellowed.

"There is nothing you can do or say to change her mind. She wore a Joiners Square pin on her lapel. They're Sund-centric, believing that the Viss and the Wayfarers should not be part of Storsund," Anja muttered. "They say we're 'holding progress back' and 'refusing to be contributing parts of society.' I've screamed myself hoarse in defence of my people, but they just say that my loud complaining proves that my kind are trouble."

"Can nothing be done?" Elise asked, clenching her fists so tight that her nails dug into her palms.

Anja grunted. "There'll always be people who don't have empathy and need someone to blame for everything that goes wrong in their life. Joiners Square preys on that and makes these people feel like they are allowed to hate others." She put a hand on Elise's arm. "There *are* people who are fighting the injustice, yes? The Viss, many of the Wayfarers, and the anti-Joiners Square Sund underground movement. But change is slow. And that is a good word for the woman we just met... Slow," she said with disgust.

With that she turned and marched out, their bag in her hand. They had no choice but to follow her.

As they did, Nessa put her arm around Elise's shoulders. "Are you all right, heartling?"

"No."

"I can see why not. You know, I'm impressed that you managed to hold your temper. The Lady Elisandrine Falk I first met would've bitten her head off. And rightly so."

Elise slowed her pace, letting her feet move of their own accord. "I have yet to reach that stage of anger, I suppose." She ran her hand over her eyes. "That brought back a lot of childhood memories. You know, if those children and their cruel parents had known there was a disliked group of people who looked like me here in Storsund, they would have had a name to call me. They would have said my mother slept with a Wayfarer. Humans are horrible."

Nessa kissed her cheek. "Yes. We can be. But humans can be rather wonderful, too. You're proof of that."

"Hm. Young love – sweet even when faced with bigoted oxen-shit," Anja said over her shoulder.

Nessa chuckled. "I was right. Your Arclidian is definitely improving with practice."

Elise watched them.

How can they joke and banter right now? How are they not burning with this injustice?

A couple of steps away from the shop's door, two finely dressed women, one blonde and one ginger, walked past. It was a balm on Elise's wounds to see them politely greet *all three* of them. Right as the women were about to step into the shop, Elise had a thought.

"Excuse me, ladies."

One of them turned, giving a bemused smile. "Yes?"

"I should not frequent this shop if I were you. Not only does the cashier discriminate against customers of different creeds than herself. There are also…" she stepped closer to them and conspiratorially whispered, "rats."

The women both gasped, and the blonde choked out the word, "Really?"

"Yes, really. We observed several of them running across the floor, did we not?" Elise asked Nessa and Anja.

Anja just stared, while Nessa, used to going along with whatever her lover said, nodded emphatically. "Yes. And the clothes. There was… um… something wrong with them, too."

"Yes, thank you, Nessa. I almost forgot about that. We think there might have been moths in the clothes. If you buy anything from here, you risk bringing home moth eggs. They might hatch in your wardrobes and eat away at all your clothes."

The two women gaped. The ginger one even covered her mouth with her gloved hand.

Encouraged, Elise carried on. "If I were you, I would completely cease shopping here. At least until the place has been sanitised and all the clothes replaced. I suggest you warn your friends, too."

The blonde spoke up. "I will. We have had these problems with cheaper shops, yes? But this one, it's so *reputable*."

Elise hummed her agreement. "Shocking, is it not? I can only think that they got too confident in their own success and stopped cleaning properly. That is how you end up with vermin and such. And when they bed in, it is hard to get them out."

"I suppose you're right. This is most upsetting," the ginger-haired woman said. "Thank you for the warning. We will spread the word loud and wide, yes?"

Elise took her hand and tried to look concerned. "Yes, do! You are most welcome. I wish you better shopping elsewhere."

The two women hurried off, whispering in disgusted voices. As they watched them go, Nessa leaned closer to Elise and whispered, "No burst of anger, but still with a clever revenge. Impressive."

Anja clapped Elise on the back, nearly sending her reeling. "You're a great liar."

"Hm. Thank you, I think. Now, shall we go get some food? I can hear Nessa's stomach growling."

Anja held out their bag. "Yes. Then you need proper boots. I will not have you dropping frost-rotting toes all over my floor."

Nessa took the bag, her button nose scrunching up as far as it could go. "That's disgusting. You should've said the shop had those instead of rats, Elise."

"I shall keep that in mind for next time. Now, where do we go to get something proper to eat? No eels, please."

～

An hour later, with their bellies full and new, stiff boots on their feet, they were in no state to walk to Anja's house in the outskirts of town. Nessa reluctantly suggested they splurge on a taxi, so Anja halted a two-horse carriage for them.

Elise sat watching the city pass outside the window. Much of it reminded her of Nightport, the bustle, the noises, and the foul-smelling smoke coming from factory chimneys, although she was finding more differences than likenesses. The cold meant there were no flower girls selling posies on the street corners and no scantily-clad pleasure sellers on opposite corners. They were all probably around, just indoors.

People paced the streets in a hurry to get inside. Some with their heads bowed against the wind, probably wishing the walk would magically shorten, others talking and laughing with each other to distract from the cold. There were a few street vendors, but they were all safely ensconced in little huts of white-painted wood.

The houses and shops grew fewer and farther apart, while there was an increase in factories and stables. A couple more streets and they pulled up by a modest house in the shadow of a huge factory building. Anja let them in, and Elise thanked her with her warmest smile, getting only a nod in return.

How do I charm this woman enough to make her employ me?

After taking her outerwear off, Anja strode over to an oil lamp and lit it. Elise saw oak floors and walls painted moss green. The decor was sparse, as she had assumed. She hadn't expected the cat, though. A large black cat sat on a chair and stared, evaluating the newcomers. Nessa hurried over to it, like she did with most animals.

"Hello there, pretty. Oh, you only have one eye. Lost the other one brawling?"

It meowed as if replying. Anja translated while lighting a fire in the grate. "No. Svarte was born one-eyed. Because of that, the awful owner wanted to drown him. Couldn't sell him like the other kittens in his litter. But Orla, our big river, had frozen that day. The owner was trying to punch a hole in the ice to drop Svarte in when I walked past. I said I'd take him."

"Good choice," Nessa said, reaching out so that the cat could sniff her hand.

"You should have given the owner what he was giving the river, a punch," Elise growled.

"It was a close thing," Anja admitted. She stood as the fire took hold.

It couldn't start warming the room soon enough for Elise, who shivered the moment she took her coat and boots off. She sat down on the plain sofa, bouncing a little on it to see if it would do for sleeping. She stopped when she caught Anja looking at her.

"I'm having a glass of wine to warm my bones. Anyone else?"

"Yes, please," Elise said.

"If you have some to spare," Nessa agreed while stroking Svarte.

"I do. It's good wine. It… might be nice to share it with someone," she said, leaving the room.

"Would you like some help?" Elise asked.

"No. My kitchen is small, and I don't want anyone underfoot."

"As you wish." Elise could quash her curiosity no longer. "Anja? May I look around? I have never been in a Storsund house."

"Fine. Downstairs is the main room, the kitchen, and the washroom. Upstairs is my bedroom, a storage closet, and the library, which has my books and the desk at which I write my book," she shouted from the kitchen. "Do you want some cakes with the wine?"

Nessa finally dragged her attention from the cat to holler back. "Yes to cakes. But wait, did you say you had a washroom? You have a commode and wash basin *indoors*?"

"Yes. Our inventors prioritised getting those into all houses a few years ago. If you think Skarhult is cold now at the start of winter, imagining going out to empty your bladder in the night at midwinter, yes? Lots of chamber pots were used. Which we think is how disease and foul odours spread. Don't you have indoor facilities?"

"Not usually. It is a luxury," Elise replied.

"I should like to start by seeing the washroom," Nessa said, finally pulling her coat and boots off.

The tentative relief on her face made Elise guess she wasn't merely going to *see* them.

Elise ventured upstairs. She found the library occupied with a bare desk and shelves filled with serious looking books in Sundish. There were no letters or ornaments. The bedroom only contained a single bed with washed-out white bedding. She saw no paintings, no splashes of colour anywhere. Elise shivered at the overwhelming sense of loneliness.

Descending the stairs again, she saw Anja head towards Nessa with a tray containing three glasses of dark liquid. There was also a plate filled with strangely shaped pieces of cake in all sizes and degrees of flatness.

"I'm not good at baking. Nor cutting the cake when I finally baked it," Anja explained.

Elise looked at the cakes. "Is that because of your prosthesis?"

Nessa gasped. "Elise Fa… I mean Elise Glass, you can't ask that!"

Anja shrugged. "It's all right, Nessa. That might be part of the problem, but I was always a terrible baker. Anyway, they're flavourful and drenched in honey, so no matter if they look like they were made by a child."

"They look fine," Elise lied.

"I bet they'll taste wonderful to someone who's freezing and tired. All I seem to do today is eat vast amounts and yet I go from cold to colder," Nessa said before stuffing one of the smaller pieces of cake into her mouth.

Elise picked up one of the glasses, looking forward to the alcohol heating her blood. She noticed that the liquid didn't move as much as she'd expect, nor glimmer red in the firelight. It stayed black and thick as treacle.

"May I ask what sort of wine this is? Not normal red wine, I take it?"

Anja chuckled. "No. We do not drink that vinegar of yours. This is black wine. Grapes don't grow well here, so it's made with blackberries and ebony root. We mix lots of honey into it to sweeten it."

Elise observed the liquid again. "Interesting! Is that why it is thicker?"

Anja took a gulp from her own glass. "That and the ebony root. You should try it, yes?"

"Yes, go on, heartling. Try it," Nessa said, licking crumbs off her fingers.

Elise took a sip. She was expecting something vile. Like the coffee, the veined cheese, and of course that breaded eel sandwich. Consequently, it stunned her how delicious the wine was.

Anja smiled. "I guess from the look on your face that you like it, yes?"

"It is lovely! Sweet, thick, and bursting with blackberry flavour. I can barely taste the alcohol."

"That is the honey doing its job. There is more alcohol in this than your acrid grape wines. Drink carefully, yes?"

"And have some cake. It's delicious," Nessa said, handing her a piece.

Elise nibbled on it, aware of what her mother would say about chasing down honey cake with honeyed wine. Not beneficial to her figure.

No, I shall not listen to her unhelpful advice anymore! Besides, fighting off the cold will take all the energy I can put in.

She ate the whole piece of cake and complimented the baker. Svarte jumped up on the sofa and began sniffing Anja's piece of cake.

"Silly cat. I feed him better than I do myself, and he still thinks all food belongs to him."

"Sounds like Nessa," Elise quipped.

Nessa shot her a glare before returning to her wine.

Anja leaned back. "The night is young, but I still wish to go to bed. Your travel weariness must be contagious."

"I must confess to not being averse to an early night," Elise said, suppressing a yawn.

Anja stretched. "Well, I do have a book on Viss folklore I'd like to continue reading."

"So, y-you're all right with us staying here, then? For at least a night," Nessa stuttered. Elise peered at the dark outside and understood her anxious tone.

"I think so. I wasn't sure how I would feel about having you in my house." Anja rubbed her lower lip, staring into space. "It's not bad. I'm still not convinced I can trust you... but I trust my gut, which says you're safe and not terrible company."

Elise braided her fingers in her lap. "Are you certain you do not want to ask us some questions? About our background?"

Anja met her gaze, squinting so that new lines framed her bright eyes. There seemed to be too much knowledge in that look, it made Elise fidget.

But Anja sniffed and picked some cat hair off her trousers. "Why would I do that? We all deserve to keep our secrets. I doubt your past is... what's the word... relevant."

"That is a charming but peculiar notion," Elise admitted. "What if our secrets are dangerous?"

Anja interlocked her hands behind her head. "Well, you're on the run, considering your small amount of luggage. However, though you look around as if searching for your hunters, you do so with a straight back. There is no guilt in either your behaviour or body language."

"What if we're so unscrupulous that we don't feel guilt?" Nessa asked.

"Ha! Do you really think Svarte and I are such bad judges of characters that we could not pick out that sort of monster?" She regarded the roaring fire. "I've not survived this long alone in this vast city by being naive. I'll lock my bedroom door, in which I have a knife the size of your arm, by the way. Oh, and there's nothing of real worth to steal here. Unless you take the firewood."

Having done her duty in asking, Elise shrugged the weight off her shoulders. Anja put more thought into her decisions than she had realised.

"Splendid. I suppose one of us can sleep on this sofa. Is there anything else to serve as a bed or do we need to share it?"

Anja belly-laughed. "If you share it, you'll fall off. I have a metal bedframe upstairs. My brother bought it when he used to come south to stay with me. Now he has a family and is too busy to bother. The frame folds up and then you can put a mattress on it. I warn you, though, it's unstable and it, um, makes noise?"

"Squeaks?" Nessa suggested.

"Yes. That. But that's your problem, not mine. I'll fetch it."

Nessa stepped forward, an insecure look in her eyes. "Do you… need help?"

Anja hesitated. "I suppose three people carrying is better than one. You can take the bed, Nessa, while you carry the pillows and blankets, Elise. I'll bring the mattress."

They fetched the bedding from the storage closet upstairs. Elise noted that the pillows were flat as floor tiles and almost as hard. Still, she was not about to complain.

When it was all set up, Anja stood by the stairs, observing them. "That should be all you need. Only one blanket each, I fear. However, they're big and thick and will do for just a couple of days, yes?"

"Yes," Nessa and Elise replied simultaneously.

"Good. Then I wish you good night."

She marched up the stairs while Nessa and Elise called good night after her.

"You know what? I wager I can stretch 'just a couple of days' into a very long time," Elise whispered with a wink.

I almost managed to keep one eye open that time!

"We'll see, heartling," Nessa said. "Right, I'll go wash up.

Since we no longer have your herb and alcohol tonic, my breath will be foul in the morning."

"No fouler than mine. We must endeavour not to breathe on each other," Elise joked.

"That'll be hard when I come to claim my good morning kiss," Nessa replied.

Elise ran a finger along Nessa's sharp jawline. "We shall have to make do."

Instead of an answer, Nessa tugged her into a kiss, one Elise immediately deepened. Minutes passed in kisses and frenzied caresses until Elise reluctantly broke away. "Sorry, but I am freezing. Where are our new full-length underwear? They will do well as sleepwear, I think."

Nessa gave her lips a peck. "Good idea. The bag with the clothes is over there." She pointed to the bag by her coat, before heading towards the washroom, stretching and yawning.

"I shall take the squeaky bed as I toss and turn less than you," she said to Nessa's retreating form.

"Sure," Nessa whispered before shutting the washroom door.

As Elise got changed, she thought about the turns her life had taken. Everything was such a tangle, and yet she found it hard to regret her choices. Through the window she saw winter stars twinkle at her. The same stars but in a new land.

She bit her lip with excitement and crawled into bed.

CHAPTER 10
THE FIRST NIGHT IN SKARHULT

Having washed and prepared for bed, Nessa came out of the washroom to find Elise in her thick, new underwear. They made her look utterly adorable.

With a happy sigh, Nessa sat down on the sofa to watch Elise get ready. Her feigned-wife combed out her short hair and rubbed some sugar pumpkin oil over her hands while mumbling about the cold ruining her skin. Nessa's joy faltered as she saw the jar of sugar pumpkin oil. Her mother had made that oil for her. Breath caught in her suddenly tight chest.

Mum. What are you doing right now? Are you happy? Have you and Dad prepared properly for winter? Is Layden checking in on you?

Nessa realised that she didn't just miss her parents and her best friend, she missed the little safe things inherent to life in Ground Hollow. Working at the farm, eating meals together in satisfied silence, harvest feasts with Layden's family and her own. And, of course, staying up with her mother to press dammon nuts into oil, infusing it with dried pieces of sugar pumpkin. Later, straining it and pouring it into those little glass jars.

93

Her hands balled into fists almost as tight as her chest. Still, she kept all the turmoil inside. This would pass. She was seeing those times through rose-coloured glasses, forgetting how trapped and out of place she had felt there. No matter how much she wanted to stay for her parents' sake, that life had been slowly strangling her. This new life might be terrifying, but at least she was herself and was heading somewhere. That freedom and purpose were worth the panic and fear.

Her hands relaxed out of the fists. She would become a glassblower and make those little jars for her mother. They would have to serve as a peace offering since Nessa could not be there herself.

Elise put down the pillow she had been fluffing up. "Heartling? Are you all right? You look pale."

Nessa pushed her thoughts down. "Shh. Whisper so you don't wake Anja. I'm fine. It's… been a long day."

"A lifetime," Elise said with a muted laugh.

"I'll sleep like the dead tonight. Although not having you close will take some getting used to," Nessa said.

Elise smoothed the sheet she had put over the mattress. "I know. I never considered that we might not sleep in the same bed. I suppose that was silly of me."

Nessa padded barefoot over the cold floor. She pulled Elise close by her hips and brushed her nose against her neck. The warm skin smelling of sweet cream and lemon water was… home. An undercurrent of safety in this frightening new world. "You're never silly, my cherished," Nessa replied. "Thinking about it, I really don't like having distance between us. I want to share my sleep with you. Can't we push the bed and the sofa together?"

"I wish we could, but the bed is much lower than the sofa," Elise whispered.

She took Nessa's hands and slid them from her hips over to explore her curves. Nessa didn't need convincing, she began caressing everything she could reach while still nuzzling the soft spot under Elise's jawbone.

She noticed Elise's pulse pick up. Her own heart was racing right along. Then they were kissing. Everything but the taste and texture of Elise's mouth disappeared. The tension building in Nessa's shoulders all day melted away as the kiss deepened. They had started making love yesterday, but she had been too tired and distracted to climax, so they had stopped. She could climax these days, but still struggled when circumstances weren't just right. They were more than right now. She craved Elise like food or air. Embarrassed, she heard herself moan as, with quick fingers, Elise undressed her. She managed to just barely stifle the next moan as Elise repeated the action with her own underwear.

Gods, how addicted Nessa was to that sand-coloured skin, those subtle curves, that triangular thatch of black covering the best thing in the world. She fell to her knees and buried her face in the mass of soft, dampening curls.

"No," Elise breathed out.

Nessa stopped immediately. "Don't you want to?"

"Of course I do. I pretty much always want to. But we are in a stranger's house."

Nessa groaned as sense poured back into her mind. "Right. She might come down to use the commode or fetch a glass of water." She groaned again, more heartfelt this time. "Not only would it be embarrassing, it would be rude."

"Exactly. We do not know Anja's feelings about her guests being intimate in her home. We should show respect by showing restraint," Elise replied, though there was a whine to her voice.

Nessa looked up at her, heart still racing. "Yes. And still, my body doesn't care. It's been a long, frightening day. I need the comfort of your embrace and of your pleasure," she said before placing a soft kiss on the black curls on Elise's mound.

Elise whimpered. "Heartling… *you* are usually the sensible one stopping *my* impulses. You know this is a bad idea."

"I know. I just… I'll be quick. Please?" Nessa asked, breathily placing another kiss deeper into the curls.

Elise squeezed her eyes closed. "All right. Make haste and be quiet."

Nessa stood up, tugging Elise into a rough kiss. Elise replied in kind, feverishly pawing Nessa's body. They fell onto the bed, making it squeak in a way which could have awoken the dead.

They both froze, waiting to hear if they had roused Anja. As they lay there, stiff and staring toward the stairs, Nessa felt Elise's heart beat so hard that it felt like it was knocking on her own chest, begging asylum from this situation.

They waited, and time trickled on.

"We did not wake her. Or perhaps she does not want to investigate the noise. Tomorrow I will tell her that I tripped over the cat and fell onto the bed," Elise said quietly, nodding towards Svarte who was sitting on the stairs.

"Splendid idea," Nessa whispered.

Those were the last words spoken. Everything else was in the language of their bodies and their desire for each other. As quietly as the bed springs would allow.

Around an hour later, if Nessa's internal clock was correct, Elise ran her hands up her back and then shook her shoulders gently. She whispered, "Heartling. Do not fall asleep. You must put your sleepwear on and return to the sofa. Anja cannot find us like this in the morning."

"Hm? What? Right. Sorry."

Nessa drowsily clambered off her lover and searched through the room for their undergarments in the light of the dying fire. She found them and threw the taller set to Elise. Then she looked down at the apex of her thighs. "I cannot be bothered to clean up. I'll just wash the underwear tomorrow. And have a thorough bath."

Elise interrupted her yawn to whisper, "Yes. Good idea."

They put their garments back on and both got under their blankets. Even with the effort and rushing blood of lovemaking, Nessa was starting to feel cold. She considered putting another few logs on the fire's dying embers.

Ah well. Should have thought of that before.

She curled up under the blanket and thought back to her earlier sadness and worry, knowing that, for now, Elise had quelled the waves. The successful lovemaking and the sweet intimacy afterwards had worked its particular magic.

Thank the gods for Elisandrine Falk. I couldn't make it through without her.

The last things Nessa heard before sleep took her were Elise's deep breaths and the crackling from the embers. Not a bad first night in Skarhult, after all.

CHAPTER 11
SETTLING IN

Elise dreamt of endless hallways. Elegant corridors where everything was cold, hard marble. From every direction came the Queen's cutting laughter, followed by the smell of lavender and alcohol, which surrounded Elise as she scrambled for a way out. There was an echo of drums. Or was that her heartbeat? It seemed as if her heart was about to betray her, to burst out of her chest.

"Eli-i-ise," the Queen cooed, "come out, come out wherever you are. You cannot hide from me, naughty little tinderbox-maker. I know your secrets. Your past, your fears, and even your darkest, most secret desires. I shall find you and I will bind you to me so that you can *never run away again.*"

Elise jolted awake, shivering from the nightmare and the chill in the room. She wasn't sure what had woken her, but she was painfully grateful that it had. She tried to focus her muddled mind on something other than her dream. There was a thud and a clinking coming from somewhere. She blinked her eyes open and saw wintry light bathing the stark room.

The noises. They are coming from the kitchen, I think?

She looked over and saw Nessa on the sofa, still asleep with her face half-buried in her pillow.

Must be Anja. Oh, something smells lovely. Something cooked?

Elise got up, wrapping her blanket around herself like a cape. The floor was freezing under her bare feet. She searched for her socks and managed find them and to pull them on without her bulky blanket slipping off.

"Ah, you're awake," a voice said from the doorway. "I thought I heard scrambling in here."

Elise wanted to shush Anja so that Nessa could keep sleeping but that seemed rude. She made her point by whispering her reply. "Good morning. I was coming to help you with breakfast."

"No need. I'm almost done. I know you don't like coffee, but it is all I have to warm you and wake you. You can swallow it down with the fried bread I've made, yes?"

"Gladly," Elise said. She adjusted the blanket so it wouldn't fall off and followed Anja back into the kitchen.

Elise watched her get the plates and cups out with practised grace. She wanted to help every time she saw Anja hold something against her prosthetic hand, but something told her not to. Perhaps it was the proud posture of the woman, or the set of her jaw. Either way, Anja clearly did not require help. Elise left her to it and went over to the stove to look at the bread which was making the kitchen smell marvellous. It was golden brown and the seeds in it glistened with cooking fat. Suddenly her stomach felt like a barrel scraped empty.

"It's nearly ready," Anja said, not turning. "Go wash up and get dressed. And wake your ladylove."

Elise obeyed. Soon they were all washed, dressed, and swallowing down large bites of fried bread slathered in winterberry jam with gulps of hot coffee.

Anja put her mug down. "Today we should go to the bath-house. You both need to wash your hair."

"That sounds superb," Elise said around a bite of bread. She couldn't imagine anything lovelier right now than a long, hot bath with plenty of scented soap.

"It's cold. Did either of you light the fire in the main grate before breakfasting?"

Elise and Nessa looked at each other. "No, we didn't," Nessa confessed, tucking her unbraided hair behind her ear.

Anja gave a curt nod. "I'll do it after we have eaten, then. Tomorrow morning, see that you light it before you come into the kitchen."

And just like that, it was settled that they were staying another day.

~

The next morning, Nessa had awoken before Elise. It was she who gently kissed Elise's cheek and said, "Wake up, heartling. You need to see this."

Elise rubbed sleep from her eyes and got up. She had slept in her socks last night, learning the lesson about the cold floors. There were noises coming from the kitchen, indicating that Anja was making breakfast. Elise thought she could smell porridge.

Nessa was lighting the fire in the main grate, the one in the room where they slept.

"Come here. Look what Anja gave me to light the fire with. I watched as she used it on the kitchen grate."

Elise walked over and crouched by the grate. In Nessa's hand was a box with little sticks of wood in it. Their tips seemed to be coated in something.

"Good morning, Elise," Anja said from the doorway. "They're matches. No need for fiddly tinderboxes anymore."

Nessa and Elise made furtive eye contact at the last words. Simply the word *tinderbox* made Elise uneasy.

She took the box of matches from Nessa. "Incredible. So small and unassuming! How do they work?"

Anja came in and showed them. "You two should light *all* the fires tomorrow. Speed things up, yes? I'll wake you when it is time to light the fire in the kitchen."

Elise opened her mouth to speak but closed it again. She had worried all day yesterday that Anja would ask them to leave. It almost ruined the pleasure of her bath and of exploring the Arclidian books in Anja's library. It seemed she needn't have worried.

"All right. Wake me. I'm of more use to you in the morning than Elise is," Nessa said.

Elise smacked her on the arm but didn't argue the obvious truth.

Anja handed over the box of matches. "I'll wake you tomorrow morning, then. What about the plans for the day? Is there anything else you need? We have to buy you your own soap. I didn't mind you using mine in the bathhouse yesterday, but it will run out."

Elise gathered her tongue. She had been thinking about that yesterday. "If acceptable, I should like to stop somewhere to buy some kohl, rouge, and a tonic for fresh breath. Oh, and some oil for hair and skin. Vain I know, but I fear I am used to these comforts."

"We could just buy ingredients to make our own oil. It's cheaper," Nessa suggested.

Anja brushed cat fur off her trousers. "It's decided, then. We'll go buy you these things and then search for glassblowers seeking an apprentice. But now, breakfast. Porridge with honey and dried cherries."

She walked into the kitchen. Elise leaned in close to Nessa. "Do you think she wants to find you an apprenticeship to get rid of us, or is she preparing for us to stay a while?"

Nessa shook her head before whispering, "I can't tell. For

someone so reluctant to have us stay, she seems to have gotten used to us quickly. Your plan to convince her to let us stay longer seems to have come to fruition without you having to lift a finger."

"Mm. We should go have breakfast and see if she mentions anything about it. If not, should I ask?"

"No. She doesn't seem to want to talk about it. Or anything else, really. I can't read her." Nessa bit her lip before continuing. "I think we have to play it by ear and be prepared to move whenever she tires of us. Maybe look around for possible places to rent as we go buying your items later today?"

"Good thinking. Come on, that coffee you seem to be enjoying so much is probably growing cold."

"It really is tastier each time you drink it. I barely grimace at all now. Unlike you," Nessa said and gave Elise a playful bite on the shoulder.

Bickering and giggling like children they came into the kitchen and joined Anja at the table.

Elise's mouth watered at the smell of the porridge. In her old life at court, she would never have dreamt of eating such a thing. Now, its hunger-quelling warmth was a treat.

⁓

The third morning, Elise dreamed she was in a lush bed, lounging naked in soft, warm sheets. A hand had run up her thigh and made her shiver with pleasure and need. She heard herself moan.

"Do not pretend to not have missed my touch. You are nothing without me desiring you, wanton little fire-starter," the Queen had purred in her ear.

A sound had mercifully awoken Elise at that point, making her sit up and shield herself with her arms.

Is this cold sweat due to dread or shame?

She realised that the sound which woke her had been Nessa fumbling with the matches.

Nessa was grumbling under her breath, "Anja made it look so easy. Why won't this work?"

It was colder than the other mornings, and Elise was certain that Nessa's fingers must be shivering with the cold. Nessa cursed under her breath, and Elise laid back down again.

I am certainly not telling her about my nightmares now. Poor thing is in a foul mood.

No wonder, yesterday's search for an apprenticeship had been unsuccessful. It clearly weighed on Nessa. While blinking away sleep grit, Elise contemplated that it weighed almost as much on her. That night in the warehouse on the Nightport docks, she had promised Nessa that she would get her a new apprenticeship and secure her future in her dream profession, thus making up for the fact that they had to run and leave Nessa's old apprenticeship.

However, it seemed they would have to accept that they weren't going to be as lucky in Skarhult as they had been in Nightport. Elise glanced through the door, spotting Anja who was making them breakfast and, for the first time, whistling as she did so. A purring Svarte climbed up on Elise's legs just as Nessa managed to get the matches to work. Elise smiled as she petted the cat.

Maybe there are different sorts of luck.

They had their breakfast and went out to look for glassblowers. This meant trudging down bitterly cold streets for hours, reading signs over every shop and workshop. Anja asked people in shops but only got the names of glassblowers they had already spoken to, ones who had been clear that they did not want apprentices now or in the near future.

A butcher they asked even laughed. "There are glassblowers, yes, but not many. Skarhult is made for sturdy cups, not pretty glasses. You should go into pottery instead, yes?"

When they had thanked him and left, Nessa gave a brave smile. "Well, we're getting nowhere, and it's too cold today to be out on foot. We should go back and try again this afternoon if it warms up. If not, I'll go out on my own tomorrow."

Anja pulled down the scarf which had been covering her chin and mouth. "No. You're staying with me because you need a guide. I promised to help so I will help. You can't read the signs."

"That's not true. I've learned the Sundish word for glass-blower," Nessa muttered, putting her hands in her coat pockets.

"There might be other words on the sign. Or you may need to speak to someone who doesn't speak Arclidian," Anja argued. "You're right about one thing, though. We should stop searching now and go warm up. Tomorrow I'll come out with you and we'll have better luck. The weather will improve as well, I feel it in my bones."

Elise put her arm around Nessa. "I agree with Anja. We are coming with you tomorrow. For now, I think we should head back and light a fire before we freeze to icicles."

They hurried home. Elise watched her breath come out like smoke as she stayed on the lookout for any passing carriages for hire. The cold seemed to pierce right through all her layers of clothes. "I cannot feel my nose anymore," she said, conversationally.

Anja hummed into her scarf. "Just wait until midwinter comes. Then you won't be able to take a walk as long as this without losing sensation in every single body part."

When they were home, Nessa and Elise went around lighting all the fires in the house, while Anja made coffee. They had an early lunch, more to warm up than to quench hunger.

Last bite swallowed, Anja stood up. "I shall go up and try to write. You can clean this up, yes?"

"Of course," Nessa said.

Elise hesitated. "Would you like… never mind. Good luck with the writing."

"Thank you," Anja mumbled as she headed for the stairs. She seemed halfway into her world of history and writing already. Elise was glad she hadn't tried to push her assistance on Anja again. She glanced at Nessa.

There has been enough rejection for our family today.

As they cleared the plates, Nessa kept her eyes down and her shoulders slumped. Elise tucked a few stray strands behind Nessa's ear, caressing her neck as she did so.

"Would you like to do something other than clean and read this afternoon, heartling?"

Nessa gave her a faint smile. "Like what?"

"Hm, what can we do?" Elise pulled the collar of her shirt close for warmth and a faint waft of sugar pumpkin came from her wrist. "Oh, I know! The sugar pumpkin oil."

Nessa knitted her brows. "What about it?"

"We are almost out of it, but we can make new scented oils. I was going to talk to you about this yesterday, but I forgot. Anja has some dammon nut oil in the cabinet here. When I saw that, I asked if she had any small jars."

Nessa's brow smoothed. "And does she?"

"Yes, she has a bunch of empty spice jars we can use! I also saved our two empty sugar pumpkin oil jars. We can reuse them now and buy more later. Not too many, though. We must save our coin until we find employment."

The cloud which had left Nessa's face returned. Elise could have kicked herself.

"Which is currently not an issue," she quickly added. "If it becomes one, I shall go out and get the first job I can lay my hands on. Please do not fret about that, my cherished. Focus on teaching me how to make these oils."

Nessa cleared her throat. "Sure. As we already have the basic oil, it's just a matter of letting the oil infuse with something aromatic in a warm environment, straining it, and then pouring it into the bottles. We need something dried or crushed, something which won't split when mixed with the oil."

Elise looked around. "What about these?" she said as she opened a kitchen cabinet and pointed to jars of herbs.

Nessa tilted her head, surveying the jars with their foreign labels. "Yes. I suppose that would work. But you'll have to be patient. It takes many days for the oil to really blend with whatever you have to give scent."

"All the more reason to start mixing it today."

"True."

Nessa took down the herb jars and began to sniff their contents.

Elise placed a kiss on her cheek. "I shall go get the empty oil jars from my bag. I will be right back."

She found them in her bag and looked at them, then glanced over to Nessa in the kitchen. Then back to the two jars in her hands. They were so small. It seemed unfair to ask such little things to mend such sizeable sadness.

When Elise came back, Nessa smiled unconvincingly. "Good. Now, while the oil infuses with the aromatic compounds, we'll keep them in the covered bowls close to the stove. Then we can strain the liquid and pour it into all these jars. Let's get mixing."

Elise swallowed down her guilt. "Yes, heartling."

An hour later, they had three warm bowls filled with oil and the aromatic components. In the first bowl, lemongrass leaves were already making the oil a tiny bit greener. In the second bowl, sticks of meadowsweet buds floated. And in the third, watermint was spreading the scent of summer.

Elise wished they had more exotic scents, but this would do for now. One day, they'd be able to afford dried flowers and rare spices to mix the oil with, and pretty bottles to decant them into.

Hands washed and dried, Elise wracked her mind for something to do. She saw Nessa blow on her hands and rub them together, so she took them and placed them underneath her blazer and shirt. She almost managed not to flinch as Nessa's cold hands lay against her own warm back.

She looked into the grey eyes of the woman she loved. "Perhaps we should go sit by the fire? I should like to hold you for a while. To make up for not being able to hold you as we sleep?"

Nessa leaned her forehead against Elise's and mumbled, "Yes, please."

Elise stepped away, feeling bereft when Nessa's hands left her skin. It wasn't long before they were cosy on the rug in front of the fire and those hands returned, now to play with Elise's hair and to caress her cheeks. Elise kissed the fingertips when they got close to her mouth, then she enveloped Nessa in her arms and whispered into her hair, "We have some things to discuss."

"What we have is laundry to do. We should do it soon, everything dries so slow in this cold."

"Stop being sensible for two heartbeats, Nessa. That can wait until we have warmed up and talked."

"All right. What did you want to talk about?"

"Well, Anja is letting us stay yet another day and has not mentioned us leaving. So, we must decide, do we want to remain here? I know I championed it, simply because it made such sense on paper. However, if we do not wish to stay, there is nothing keeping us here."

"Well," Nessa began. "We told Hunter we'd be in Skarhult

under the name of Glass, in case he needed to reach us. We should probably stay here."

"All right. But 'here' does not have to be in Anja's house. We could hire a room in a lodging house, like we did in Nightport."

She felt Nessa shrug against her. "I don't mind staying here. You were right, it's a comfort to have a guide in a foreign country. And it's nice to be in a real home."

"Good. Then we shall stay here. Warm and safe."

"Huh. You wanting something safe? That doesn't sound like Lady Elisandrine Falk?"

Elise watched the flames dance. "Things change. I am not alone anymore. Before, if I failed or was in danger, I paid the price. Now we both pay the price, and you are more precious to me than I am."

"I know that feeling," Nessa said quietly.

They sat looking at the fire for a while, Nessa still playing with Elise's hair.

A few minutes later, Nessa asked, "Do you think the Queen is hunting us? Be honest."

Elise didn't have to consider the question. It had been in the back of her head for weeks. "No. But then I said that last time as well, did I not? And then there she was, beating you at cards."

"Excuse me, I was beating her."

"Obviously, my cherished. You are better than her at everything."

Svarte walked in and settled down by their feet, drawing warmth from them and the fire. Nessa tickled him under the chin, and his one green eye closed as he began to purr.

Elise gathered up her courage. "Why did you ask about the Queen? Do you want to go back to Arclid? Do you miss your family too much?"

Nessa hummed noncommittally while scratching the cat's

chin. "Sure, I miss my parents. And Layden. Nevertheless, I made the decision to leave them and live my own life long before you and the Queen came along."

"Yes, but you planned to live in Nightport, where you could return and visit them. From here, it would take a month and a half to go back. Not to mention the steep price. Not that this should stop you," she was quick to add. "If you wish to go back, I will give you your half of our savings and help you book the ticket."

Nessa cuddled in closer and placed her face in the groove of Elise's neck. "Only if you came with me."

"I am the one who is probably hunted, Nessa. I cannot go back."

"That settles it. My home is with you. Besides, I would miss our adventures. We belong together, travelling and exploring."

Elise swallowed the lump in her throat. "But you are sad."

"Life makes you sad sometimes. No matter where you are. That doesn't mean you should break your back to change everything. Sometimes sadness simply has to be endured until it passes, I think."

"If you say so. Still, *promise* you will tell me if it gets too much. The sadness, I mean. Then we will both go back. The Queen be damned."

Nessa's nose rubbed against the skin on her neck. "I promise. Do you… ever miss your mother?"

"No," Elise snapped.

"I suppose you wouldn't. How could anyone treat someone as sweet and wonderful as you so badly? She's your mother. She should love and protect you. I don't understand."

"I do not wish to talk about her. Or even think about her," Elise whispered before burying her face in Nessa's hair.

"Of course. I'm sorry."

Elise kissed Nessa's hair, making love drown out the pain

and rejection.

A few more minutes passed while the fire crackled and the cat purred. Elise breathed in the scent of Nessa, closing her eyes and pretending the outside world did not exist.

That only worked for so long. Elise gave up and voiced her thoughts. "Do you think I should simply go out and get a job? Would they hire someone who does not speak their languages in any of the shops? Or maybe in the factories?"

"Bad idea," Nessa said softly.

"Why?"

"I'm not sure you're built for factory work, mentally or physically. Mentally, neither am I. We haven't seen any other available jobs while we've been out either." Nessa took her hand. "Besides, I still think I'll find an apprenticeship and you'll either convince Anja to dictate to you or find a profession that inspires you. We shouldn't give up yet. Our costs are low right now. We should aim for our dreams, and if the coin starts to dwindle, then we'll settle for any old job."

"You are right. Still. I think I am going to borrow a few of Anja's books and try to pick up some Sundish or maybe some Viss. Maybe Anja would give me lessons, too."

"Maybe. Let's not ask for too much. She already helps us and houses us, only asking us to pay for half of the food and kindling."

Elise hummed her agreement, and they sat in silence again. Lost in their own thoughts, embracing each other tighter for comfort and warmth.

"Elise?"

"Yes?"

"I'd like to make love now," Nessa whispered.

"Me too. However, Anja could be down any moment."

"Hm. Perhaps hiring a room would be a good idea."

Elise laughed before whispering, "Seems I am not the only one who needs to learn patience."

~

A couple of weeks passed in the same way. They ate their meals together, usually in silence unless Nessa or Elise made an effort to keep up conversation. Only Skarhult history could entice Anja to speak at any length. More and more rarely did they go out looking for glassblowers. Their only hope now were the glassblowers that had been out, probably selling their wares or sourcing materials, during the search. The railroads seemed to make manufacturing a lot more ambulatory here than in Arclid.

After lunch, Anja tried to write. She always used that word "try," complaining about how bad she still was at writing with her left hand. Every time, Elise bit her tongue, wondering if she should suggest dictation again.

While Anja wrote, Nessa and Elise cleaned the house, took long walks, or read books. Nessa read for enjoyment and Elise in the attempt to teach herself some Sundish. The rest of the time, they made more scented oils, using whatever dried fruit and herbs they could find around the house.

Elise coveted nicer-smelling flowers and herbs, but their funds were dwindling with paying for their own supplies as well as half of all the food and fire wood. Often this fact drove her to opt for taking any job anywhere. She calmed herself, they had coin for a couple of more weeks. She had to work on that patience.

Instead, Elisandrine threw herself into making the scented oils. It would do wonders for their winter-chafed skin and hair. Besides, she was starting to enjoy it.

~

One day, when Nessa seemed near giving up, luck struck. After breakfast, they had gone out for a walk, following strange tracks in the road. Elise wanted to ask what they were, but Anja and Nessa were deeply engaged in a conversation about Joiners Square's latest grab at power: trying to control Storsund's many farms.

Elise left them to it while watching the tracks disappear into a big, closed building. A man in a Joiners Square uniform stood outside the building, staring at her. Inspecting her? Something about the way he looked at her made the little hairs on Elise's neck stand on end. She shook it off, he probably just reminded her of the Queen's Royal Guards.

Five cold, long streets away from Anja's house, they came across a glassblower's workshop they had visited two weeks ago. The neighbour had then informed them that the glassblower was traveling north and that she didn't know when he'd be back. Today they all stopped dead as a tall man in thick furs unloaded crates from a cart and carried them into the now open workshop.

Nessa self-consciously pulled up her trousers. Despite them being hemmed up and tied with a belt, they were still too big.

If she gets an apprenticeship, I will buy her ones that fit. If she does not, I shall get a cursed job and buy her some anyway.

"Excuse me, sir?" Nessa said in her clearest voice.

He turned, a crate cradled in his arms. It was hard to tell under his furs, but judging from his angular face and sunken cheeks, he must be quite thin. Not a great idea for someone living in this cold, surely? He jutted his pointy chin out as he looked at Nessa. Elise felt an almost maternal wish to stop him from staring at Nessa with that sceptical air.

"Hello. Who are you, Arclidian lady?" he said in a neutral voice.

Nessa shifted her footing, Elise wished she could send her some confidence through the cold air. "My n-name is Nessa Glass. I'm a glassblower's a-apprentice. Well, I was until I had

to had to leave Arclid. Now I'm looking f-for another apprenticeship here. Are you the glassblower who owns this
workshop?"

He put the crate on the ground. "Yes. Are you really a
glassblower's apprentice with a name like Glass? That's funny,
yes? Is it a joke?"

Elise saw Anja blow out a long breath. Clearly she had also
thought the man would merely dismiss Nessa and walk away.

"Uh, yes, it is funny, and no, it's not a joke. It's my name,"
Nessa said in a strained voice.

The glassblower took out a woollen hat from his coat
pocket and put it on. "I have been up to Vitevall to sell my
wares. I am known for making sturdy yet pretty glass, yes? I
make glass you can use for years. They like that up there."

"I see. That makes sense. I grew up on a f-farm. We had no
time for things that weren't sturdy, either."

"Good. Very good. Shame I do not need an apprentice,"
he said, leaning back on the side of his cart.

There was a moment of silence. Elise was just about to fill
it by stepping up and singing Nessa's praises, but stopped
when Nessa said, "I see. Well, neither did my old masters.
They took me on for a short trial and were soon very satisfied
with my work. I work hard and long while asking for little. I
simply love glass and want to work with it and earn enough
coin to keep myself in bread and firewood."

The man jutted his chin out again and stared at Nessa for a
painfully long time. Elise's pulse picked up so much she heard
it rush in her ears.

*It has been weeks of bad news. Please employ her. She is a
proud woman and needs a purpose. And something secure to latch
onto. Please.*

Next to Elise, Anja crossed her arms over her chest, the
wrinkles by her eyes deeper than usual as she squinted at
the man.

He picked the crate back up. "Hm. Do you wish to talk about this inside, Arclidian? No point in freezing our faces off out here, yes?"

Nessa nodded mechanically, then turned around. "Elise and Anja. Why don't you go back? I'll be home soon and then I'll let you know what happened."

Elise found herself gaping before whispering, "What? No. I wish to stay. I am good at promoting you, we both know that."

Nessa hesitated. "Yes. But heartling, I need to do this on my own."

Elise was about to argue again, but Anja took her arm. "Nessa is right. We should go home. We have reindeer meat to prepare and mince."

"Reindeer meat? But... I want to..." Elise trailed off as she saw Nessa's face. There was that wounded pride she had been seeing lately. It was even more raw now. Win or lose, Nessa needed to do this herself.

Whining, Elise gave her a peck on the cheek. "Fine. All right. Be careful, come right back home afterwards and... good luck, my cherished."

"Thank you. I'll see you both soon," Nessa said with a shaky smile Elise knew was for her benefit.

Then she hurried after the glassblower.

It was nearly an hour later when Elise helped Anja mince the dark reindeer meat in a grinder. Restlessness made her irritable and resentful of every insignificant task Anja wanted her to do.

"Are you sure I cannot be of better use in some other capacity?"

Anja didn't spare her a glance. "What capacity would that be? We must prepare and cook this meat before it goes off."

"I... do not know. I should be doing something *useful*."

Elise wrung her hands. "Nessa is fighting tooth and nail for her apprenticeship. You research and write. I... only exist, busying myself about scented oils and applying rouge. Merely a drain on resources."

"Nonsense. You keep me and Nessa sane and happy. Not an easy task." Anja examined the mince before speaking again. "What had you planned to do when you came to Storsund?"

Elise groaned, beginning to pace the small kitchen. "I am not sure. Look after Nessa, make amends for disrupting her life. Perhaps get work where I could use my schooling. Preferably where I would not dislike my employer, as I did when I worked for a printer in Nightport."

Anja hummed while getting a bowl for the mince. "Yes, liking who you work with is important."

Frantically, Elise watched her, searching for clues in her body language. "True. That is why helping you with your work would be so worthwhile. Your passion and knowledge captivate me."

Anja stopped. "Ah. So *that* is where this is leading?"

"It was not 'leading' anywhere," Elise protested. "It was simply my honest thoughts. When we met, I thought assisting you in return for a roof over our heads was a perfect solution. I still do."

"Yes. But I provided the roof over your heads without you having to... help me. I never asked for anything, especially not some form of charity. People see me and assume I'm just scraping by. I'm not, I do fine on my own."

"That is what I was getting at, Anja. I said I thought you could use my help when we met that day in Charlottenberg. Now, I know it is more the other way around. I need your help. The roof over our head is wonderful, but not enough. Our funds are dwindling. Clothes, food, bathhouse visits, firewood... it all costs."

Elise paused to rub her forehead, trying to word the

discomfort that had been spreading through her over the past weeks. "I need employment. But where to look? Everything outside this house is cold and impenetrable to me. When we go into Skarhult, I see people rushing inside, buried under coats and hats. They hasten past without a glance and do gods know what in their perfect white houses." She rubbed her skin harder with her growing panic. "I have no knowledge of the language, no recommendations, and no special skills. I have never actually searched for employment, so I would not know how to go about it. My job in Nightport and the one at cou – I mean, in Highmere – were all but handed to me!"

Anja, done with the mince, washed her hands. "Calm down. No need to shout. If you want me to try and search out a job for you, I can. But I need to know in what sort of profession."

Elise tried for a mirthless laugh, but it came out hysterical. "And, once again, have a job handed to me? I do not even have an inkling of what position I am suited for." She slammed her palm onto the worktop. "And… and… I worry that anywhere I find a position, they will ask me a lot of questions!"

There it was. The truth had, as always, popped out of her mouth, bypassing her brain. Elise growled, wanting to hit herself instead of the worktop.

When will you learn to think before you speak? When will you learn to hide and to keep secrets, you ridiculous fool?

Anja sighed. "Mm. Not everyone will trust your open face and weighted silences like I have."

Elise put her hand on her arm. "Please let me help you for a few days, as a trial. You only need pay me enough to cover Nessa's and my part of the food and kindling. It would be such a tidy solution. If I am of no use to you, I shall not take it personally when you tell me so."

"I'm not sure."

"I know. That is why I am saying you should try it out

before you commit. For what it is worth, I no longer see you as someone who needs help. You clean, cook, mend things, and manage to write. All more than I can do. And done with your left hand, which as I understand you never used for these things before?"

"No. I was right-handed," Anja muttered.

"Consequently, you do not *need* help. However, I can perhaps speed up your writing process. To allow you to you finish this book of Storsund's history sooner, telling the true nature of Wayfarers and how they are treated. All while you help me, a young woman who is not as capable as you. Or as calm in the face of adversity."

Anja chuckled. "You're just young and impatient. And to make things harder for yourself, you've taken on the responsibility for Nessa's happiness. Out of guilt, I imagine." She peered at Elise, green eyes shining. "One day you'll have to tell me why you both had to run and leave her family and work behind. Not today, though. Today, we clean the kitchen. Then…" Anja put a hand on Elise's shoulder. "Then we'll go up and start your dictation trial period. After that, Nessa will be home with news, and I will make us meatloaf. Sound good, yes?"

A sudden warmth rushed through Elise. "Yes. That sounds splendid. Thank you."

Anja said what sounded like a long word with harsh consonants.

"Pardon?"

"That was Sundish for 'you're welcome.' It's just one word in our language," Anja explained.

As she picked up a cloth and began to wipe down the kitchen, Elise practised that word, rolling it around her mouth, amending it when Anja explained how to shape her lips and tongue. By the time they went upstairs to try the dictation, Elise could say it perfectly.

CHAPTER 12
THE GLASSBLOWER'S TEST

Nessa forced herself to breathe slowly and evenly. Panicking would lead to more stuttering. Or worse, to clamping her jaws tight so she couldn't answer questions. That would surely ruin any chances she had of convincing the glassblower to employ her. She pushed her shoulders down and her chin up, trying to at least *look* confident and competent.

"Ah, blessed warm, yes? Well, warmer than outside at least," the glassblower said. "I came home this morning, and before I could even begin to carry in my..." He snapped his fingers as if looking for a word. "My, uh... *new things in crates*, I had to light the furnace. Only now is it starting to warm up in here."

"Y-yes. The warmth is a relief. I know how hot a glassblower's workshop, I mean a hot shop, can become. Sweating was a problem when I apprenticed b-back in Arclid. Now, however, I'd welcome the heat from the furnace all day."

He took off his leather gloves, blowing on his hands. "All day is good. I wish mine would not go out. We both know a glassblower's furnace should always be lit, yes? But when I go away for long periods… what can I do?"

"Employ an apprentice to keep the fire burning? Or to travel away for you?" Nessa said, so eager to get the words out that they were barely audible in their speed.

He laughed. "Good thinking, yes? The problem is, as always, coin. Skarhult is not a good place for glassblowers, not much business, you know? That is why I trade up north. Paying an apprentice? Big, unnecessary cost. Most apprentices would work for free in return for lodgings and learning a profession."

"Yes, I would do so too if I lived alone. I have a wife to consider, Mr… I'm sorry, I didn't catch your name."

He laughed, his cheeks sinking in even further as he did so. "I didn't give it, I think. Forgive me, travel has rubbed away my manners. My name is Fabian Smedstorp. And yours is Glass. Ha! No one could forget that."

Feeling her cheeks burn, she mumbled, "Nessa will do."

"Not with a fitting name like Glass, I think." He peered at her, his eyes twinkling. "So. You wish to learn from me?"

Nessa straightened her back again, unsure when it had slumped. "Yes."

"As I said, an apprentice is a big cost. I *do* need the help, glassblowing is hard to do on your own, as I'm sure you know. But it is a big… how do you say… investment?"

"I know. I believe it will be worth it for you, though. I'm diligent, strong, enthusiastic, and quick to learn. I can start at the slightest wage. Even work for free at first." Relief at not having stuttered flooded through her.

He rubbed his unshaven chin, making a rasping sound. "Hm. Strong?" He looked her up and down. Nessa wished that she wasn't so short and that her layers of clothes didn't hide her muscles.

He sucked his teeth. "Why don't I give you a test? Through

that you can show me what your body can do and how much this apprenticeship would mean to you. If you pass, you become my apprentice. If you fail, you go home and leave me to my work, yes?"

He smirked, and the careful part of Nessa's mind sounded an alarm. "What sort of test? As I said, I am a married woman." The fake marriage slipped into conversation so easily now that Nessa had almost forgotten it was a lie. "I'm eager for an apprenticeship but certainly not desperate enough for something... unseemly."

Her cheeks were burning even more now, but she stood tall. She might have been raised in a small village, but she knew the ways people tried to take advantage of those in need. How often the desperate ended up taking their clothes off.

For the first time, the mirth left the glassblower's face. "No. Not that. Never that."

Nessa bit her cheek. "Right. Of course not. I apologise. I only wanted to be sure."

"You were right to make that clear. Many ogres might ask that of a young, beautiful would-be-apprentice, yes? I would never. In fact, if anyone asks you for something like that, I'll lend you my blowpipe for you to shove up their a... I mean, their kitchen entrance."

The tension in her shoulders lessened. "Good. Thank you for clarifying."

"No need to mention it."

He sat down on a large crate and lit his pipe. The smoke smelled like hay and salt, unlike any pipe smoke Nessa had ever smelled. She shouldn't have been surprised, Anja had said that folk put whatever they could find in their pipes if nothing pleasant had been shipped in from the warmer continents.

When the smoke came readily, Fabian sat back and surveyed Nessa again. He had a way of looking at a person like he was waiting for the next thing you were going to say, convinced it was going to be something funny.

"So, a test. A wholesome but tricky test. Yes?"

Nessa clasped her hands behind her back. "If you'd like."

"I need to know your strength and your... what is the word... commitment. If I'm to spend my small amount of coin and time on you, I need to know that you'll work your heart out for me. For this hot shop. I need you to love this place and the glass that is made here, yes?"

"That makes sense," Nessa replied.

"Good. Now, what to make the test? I need to know three things, I think. That you're strong, dedicated, and that you know at least something about glassblowing."

Nessa nodded, despite suspecting that he was asking himself.

"So, the test should be split then, yes? One for the mind and one for the body. Together they will test your commitment."

"Whatever you think best," Nessa replied.

"How to test your knowledge of our trade is easy, I will ask you about our tools and what to do with them and expect you to answer correctly, yes?"

"Of course."

He sucked on his pipe. "Strength and determination on the other hand. Hmm. I'll find something to test this, yes? First, let's see how much glassblowing is in your mind and heart. Come to the furnace."

Thus, they began. With the workshop warming up, both Nessa and Fabian took their outerwear off. Still smoking his pipe, Fabian held up the tools of the trade and Nessa named them and their uses. His smile grew as she answered quickly, assertively, and correctly.

"Well done, Mrs Glass."

"Please, do call me Nessa."

"I tell you, I cannot. Not with such a fitting surname. If I'm to have an apprentice called *Glass* I shall call her that."

Nessa couldn't help but roll her eyes, something which didn't seem to bother Fabian, who merely laughed.

"Now, let's see if you are to become my apprentice. Determination of the mind and strength of the body... What do you call that last one in Arclidian?"

Nessa frowned. "Endurance? Or physical strength?"

"Let's test that, Mrs Glass."

Nessa took a deep, readying breath, flexing the muscles in her arms and shoulders. A childhood of farm work in rain, wind, and every temperature known to man should have prepared her for whatever was coming. She hoped.

Fabian ran his hand over his bristled, pointy chin again. "You spoke of our Storsund cold and of the heat by the furnace. I think the test should be about hot and cold."

He looked around the workshop. "The crates I carried in and put over there. Move them over to that corner. Without removing any of your thick clothes, yes? Then, when you are done, go outside without your coat and unbridle my horse. Then pull the carriage into the shed next door."

Nessa swallowed hard. "Pull the cart without the horse?"

"It is not impossibly heavy, but it will be a test to do it out in the cold, after moving all these crates in the heat in here, yes? Take as long as you want, don't hurry and end up fainting. But I want to see the strength of your body and your... eh, what is the word..."

"Resolve?" Nessa croaked.

He nodded, his expression grave. "Stop if it is too much. Don't die. I'm sure you can find another glassblower to apprentice you. But if you *can* do this, I'll take you on and teach you right away. Even pay you nice amount of coin, yes? I live, sweat, and bleed for this hot shop and for the glass. Show me that you will do the same."

Nessa stood tall again, not acknowledging the anxious tension thrumming through her body.

"I'll try. No, I'll do more than try. I'll manage it. Even if it takes me all day."

He looked suddenly paternal. "That's the spirit, Mrs Glass."

He sat down on a chair by the furnace and puffed at his pipe. The dancing light from the furnace made his angular, pale, and suddenly solemn face look almost sickly.

Nessa inspected the three layers of clothing on her torso, the two layers on her lower body, and the long, fur-lined leather boots which hid her woollen socks. Deciding to keep her Arclid leather coat and just wear more layers underneath to keep warm might be her downfall today.

If you're not careful, exhausting yourself and sweating in the cold will make you the one who is sickly.

Still, she had been through worse. Harvesting the barley alone, because her father and mother were ill, on a rain-soaked day after her first boyfriend had left her. *That* had been a test. And she had come through it with flying colours. Long after nightfall, she had finally finished and dragged her soaked, aching body, and the accompanying aching heart, into her bed. She had slept like that, soaked and dirty, for nearly fourteen hours. Then she had gotten up the next day to do the chores and get back to work.

If she could do that, she could do this.

She rolled her shoulders and bent to test the weight of the first crate. Rather heavy, but manageable. As she bent at the knees and picked it up, she tried not to think about the weight of the carriage outside.

A while later, all the crates had been moved from where Fabian had plonked them to orderly lines in the corner of the work-shop. Nessa took deep breaths to stop panting and wiped her eyes, which stung from the sweat that had poured from her hairline. Her clothes were growing heavy with sweat. Every-thing was heavy, including her arms. She locked them, willing them to stay strong for the test yet to come.

Fabian stood. His pipe had gone out a long time ago, but it still hung limply between his lips.

"Well done, Mrs Glass," he said quietly as he left the room.

Nessa, bewildered at his departure, took the chance to stretch and grimace freely.

He returned with a large tin cup. "Here. Water with grains of salt in it. You need it after losing so much sweat. I added some coffee grounds for taste and energy. It will taste foul, yes? But help you with the rest of your test."

"Thank you!"

She downed it, not tasting the disgusting mix until the liquid was gone, leaving salty, bitter sludge on her tongue. She tried not to make a face. She planned to give an impression of strength and control. She would show Fabian Smedstorp what Ground Hollow women were made of.

She looked him dead in the eye. "I'm ready to go outside."

He tapped his lips with his index finger. "Mm. I suppose the test wouldn't be real if you wait until you've recovered and dried." He pointed his pipe at her. "As I said before, take your time moving the carriage. I'm in no hurry, yes? I don't want to explain your death to that yellow-eyed, lovesick woman you came here with."

"They're golden. Possibly light amber."

His forehead wrinkled. "Excuse me?"

"Uh. Her eyes. They're not exactly yellow. They're—"

He smirked. "Golden or light member?"

"Amber," she corrected, wondering if he was messing with her.

"Your wife, yes?"

"Luckily for me, yes," Nessa said.

This time the lie slipped out without Nessa's mind painting pictures of what her parents might think about her lying over something as sacred as marriage.

His smirk grew to a beaming smile. "You both did well there, I think. Now, let's see if you do well with that carriage, yes?" The smile disappeared. "I'll unbridle Annika, my horse, and lead her to the stable. You focus on trying to lift, push, or shove the carriage to the shed next to it."

"Thank you," Nessa said, keeping her voice confident.

In silence, they went outside. Fabian pulled his outerwear on. Nessa barely managed to walk away from her beloved leather coat. She shivered the second her hot, sweaty face hit the cold air.

As Fabian walked the horse to the small stable, Nessa looked into the open shed next to it. There was plenty of room for the cart; if she could only get it there. It was far from the biggest cart she had ever seen, certainly small enough to be lifted and rolled by someone strong and using the right lifting technique. The problem was that while she was strong enough to do it when she was rested, fed, and not boiling with sweat, she wasn't sure she would be in this state. With a tired arm, she wiped sweat from her brow, wondering if the droplets might actually freeze soon.

Fabian was putting his fur hat on. "I'd suggest starting. Don't stand there and get frozen, you will catch... um, you know, diseases of the chest."

She was too anxious and uncomfortable to find words for him now. Instead she flexed her fingers to keep them from stiffening in the cold. She bent at the knees and took the grips of the cart. The wood was cold and they were set wide apart to fit a horse, but she could hold them if she widened her reach. She began lifting, achieving barely anything. The muscles in her arms, shoulders, and chest seemed to remember every single crate she had just moved.

Don't think it impossible. If you do, your body shall believe it. Imagine yourself lifting it enough to push it along. No need to take care, there is no cargo. Just get it to the shed any old way you can.

She tried again, pushing up with her legs and back. She got the front of it to lift somewhat and the wheels to move in their tracks in the snow. Then it became too much for her weary muscles. With an enraged shout, she put it back down. She paced back and forth, staring at the cart, wondering if there was another way.

"May I use tools?"

Fabian sighed, more with sympathy than impatience, it seemed. "No, I think that would defeat the purpose, yes? I know that you're smart and capable from our last test. This is about brute strength and the power of your... um... *determination*. I believe you can do this, I wouldn't have given you the task otherwise."

"Right," Nessa said.

She gritted her teeth. Then she stopped in front of the grips and grabbed them again. Putting all her strength into it, she didn't try to lift this time, but instead pushed it. It moved a little. She screamed and kept pushing, feeling throbbing in her temples. It moved a little farther. The snow, slush, and ice were stopping the wheels, though. She needed to lift it if she was to move it all the way. If she got it rolling, it would all be easier. She chuckled mirthlessly to herself. Easier? It would be easier if her arms, shoulders, and back weren't exhausted by those cursed crates.

I can't do this. I can't do anything on my own.

But there was no one who could help her now. Not her parents, not Layden, not Elise, not Hunter. Not even Anja. She let out a shaky breath and wiped her brow again.

Stop complaining. One step at a time. You've moved it. You passed the knowledge test, you finished all the crate lifting. All that is left now is this damn cart and getting it into that cursed shed!

Nessa considered praying but didn't know which of the gods might hear her prayers. Arclid had no gods of winter. Or cart-pushing. She shivered. She couldn't keep standing still like this, she'd freeze. It was time to try lifting the grips again.

She stood before them, staring them down. Their cold wood glared back at her, unyielding. She grabbed them, bent at the knees again, and tensed her muscles. With a few deep breaths, Nessa tried to harness the rage she had for this gods-cursed cart and the snow underneath its wheels. She added thoughts of the Queen, who had wanted to own Elise and didn't care who she hurt to do it. She relived the pain of missing her family and turned that into rage, too.

Then, with an almighty scream and eyes closed, she hoisted the cart. It only lifted a little, but it was a start. After that she had no concept of how she was doing. All she was aware of was her pained muscles and the iron determination to use every fibre of her being to push the cart. She could only hope she was still heading towards the shed.

Suddenly there was a jolt, and she felt cold against her face. She had lost her footing and fallen into the snow. Nessa lay there for a moment, cursing every god she could think of. As she stood and wiped away the snow, her arms shaking and her muscles burning, she saw that the cart was almost halfway to the shed! She could have wept with joy.

Sobering, she heard her father's voice in her head. "No time for all of that, my girl. Wait with such things until the work is done. Everything waits until the work is done."

Nessa grunted victoriously through gritted teeth and bent to take the grips again. She began lifting, but her hands slipped. She wasn't sure if it was because they were frozen stiff, slippery with sweat and condensation on the grips, or because her muscles were so weak they had lost their gripping power.

Probably all of the above. She tried again, this time locking her hands so tight around the grips she heard her knuckles cracking.

Sweat once more poured down her face and her nose began to run, but she lifted the cart again. A muscle in her thigh shot spasms of pain through her leg and up her back. She ignored it. That would have to be dealt with later. She had work to do.

She screamed again and pushed forward. Her vision went hazy, her mind was too busy focusing on the ache and determination to have time for sight. She squeezed her useless eyes shut, hearing her scream turn to pained whining. Her throat was sore now, too. Her feet moved and seemed to find purchase, she must be moving the cart. Yes, it was rolling. And now there was a tiny bit of slope to the ground. It wasn't much, but it gave her the push she needed to keep the wheels rolling on the packed snow.

Don't stop. Do it. Do it... for Elise. Make her proud. Push through the pain. You can do it. Do it for Elise!

Nessa repeated the mantra in her head. The pain in her muscles wasn't as obvious now. It was still there, but somewhere deep inside her. At the front of her mind was just a haze where everything blurred except one thing: she had to keep going.

"No! Be careful!"

Fabian's shout rang out too late. Nessa had hit something. The crashing noise was enough to wake her out of her internally focused state. She opened her eyes and saw the cart against the corner of the shed. She let go of the grips and dropped onto her rump in the snow.

The shed and the cart appeared undamaged. Nessa, however, knew that her strength was spent. Her body refused to move. If someone had told her she was on fire, she wasn't even sure she'd have the power in her limbs to roll the flames away in the snow. She squeezed her eyes closed, trying so hard not to cry. She had failed. It was no surprise to her that she couldn't do this alone, but the defeat still shamed her. Letting Fabian down was bad, but worse than that, was letting Elise down. Seeing the pity and worry in those beautiful golden eyes; Nessa couldn't stand the idea. How would she even tell her?

She heard footsteps in the snow and opened her eyes. Through the mist of tears, she saw Fabian scrutinising her.

He cleared his throat. "You know, I should've mentioned that the snow has more ice under it. And is more densely packed by the shed. You couldn't have known that, yes? Besides, Arclidians know nothing about snow. I should've thought about that. It was unfair of me."

Nessa blinked away her tears and looked at him.

What does that matter? Is that meant to make me feel better? I failed, no matter what the reason. No apprenticeship for me. No good news to tell Elise.

He was waiting for her to answer, his mirthful features now showing only empathy.

"I should've had my eyes open. Then I would've seen when I started to veer to the right," Nessa said, sniffing.

"Well, you'll see where you're going when you get up and do the last part," he said with a big smile.

"I can't. My body won't even move to get me out of this cold, white oxen-shit," she said listlessly.

His smile faded. "Hm. You need coffee. Wipe away your tears, sweat, and snow. Clear your mind. I'll go get coffee, yes?"

Nessa gave a hollow laugh, even that taking more energy than she could spare. "Coffee won't be enough."

"Maybe not for you, but it will be for me. I'm cold, and if I'm going to help you get that thing in the shed, I need warmth in my belly."

He turned and walked away.

"What do you mean by 'help,' Mr Smedstorp?" Nessa shouted hoarsely at his retreating form.

He looked over his shoulder, smiling. "As I said, it was my fault for not telling you about the packed snow and ice by the shed, yes? So, I'll help you move the cart back a little and then into the shed."

Nessa's heart sank even further. "I see. Well, if you just want your cart put away, get the horse to do it. Or do it yourself. It would be quicker than getting my weak arms to help."

"If I do that, you'll fail your task. No, Mrs Glass. You *will* get that cart into the shed and earn your apprenticeship, yes? You'll simply do it with a little help, to make up for me not warning you." He adjusted his hat. "Now, let me get you the coffee so you can warm up. I don't want you getting ill just as you're starting to work for me," he shouted back before walking inside.

Nessa laughed incredulously. She still had a chance at the apprenticeship? He was going to help her complete the test and then be her master? She was going to be a glassblower!

She wiped her tears and sweat, her arms aching even with that small motion. The pain wasn't that important now. What was important was that she hadn't disappointed herself. It wasn't over. She hadn't let her parents, who had instilled determination and hard work into her, down. And yes, she could go home and hold her head up high as she told her heartling that she managed to get the position. Would she have preferred to do it without help? Yes. But what mattered was that against all odds, she was going to achieve it.

With slow, hampered movements, she got to her feet. She leaned against the cart and smiled through tears. When she heard Fabian's steps, she dried her cheeks again and stood as straight as she could.

"Here is your coffee. I put milk in it. For energy and

muscle fuel, yes? Drink up," he said, handing her the cup she had drunk from before.

The liquid was hot, but the cold outside and the milk in it were cooling it quickly. Nessa drank it as fast as she could. She wasn't sure if it was the heat from the drink, or the new hope, that woke her spirits, but she felt almost reborn.

Fabian sipped his coffee, too, peering at her over the rim of the cup. When she had gulped hers down, he took one last sip and put his half-empty cup down in the snow next to hers.

"Now then. Let's get this cart to its home. Just one last push, Mrs Glass."

Nessa tried to clear the emotion out of her throat. "Yes, Mr Smedstorp."

He chuckled while putting a pair of gloves on. "Oh, I think you can call me master, now. Don't you?"

She smiled but shook her head. "Not until I have passed the test. Not until the work is done and I have earned it."

He clapped her on the back, and she tried not to wince at the pain. "A real workhorse. I didn't expect that of you soft Arclidians with your green grass and balmy weather. You'll make a good apprentice. Ready now, yes?"

As a reply, she dragged her body over to the cart and took one of the grips. He took the other and said, "Lift!"

They did, and the front of the cart was up from the snow with its wheels freed. They pulled it back from the corner it had crashed into and managed to manhandle it back a bit. After a moment, the cart was on the right track again. Now all Nessa had to do was push the last bit into the shed.

Fabian walked back to his abandoned coffee, calling out, "All yours now, Mrs Glass. Finish the test with one last shove. Then go home and rest."

No matter how it hurt and how tired her body was, the idea of resting and telling Elise the good news strengthened her. She took the grips for the last time and bellowed as she clumsily shoved it past the shed doors and let it down to the floor. Nessa went down after it, sitting down in a way which looked a lot like falling.

"You all right?" Fabian asked.

She smiled up at him, winded and dizzy. "Yes. Just tired."

He toasted her with his coffee cup. "I'll bridle Annika to the cart again then. We'll drive you home as you're in no state to walk, yes? Well done for passing the test! You're worthy of my teachings, time, and coin."

"Thank you," she panted in a cracked voice.

"It's the truth. Now, I'll put the coffee cups inside and fetch your coat, gloves, and hat for you. You stay here. Rest."

She was only too happy to obey. As he left, she wiped at her cold-numbed face with floppy arms. She wondered how dreadful she must look, but didn't much care. She did it! She was a glassblower's apprentice again. Slowly, she stood up, wincing at the pain and creaking of her body.

Fabian came back, handing over her outerwear. While he bridled the horse to the hated cart, Nessa tried to put the garments on. She gave up on the gloves and stuck them in her pockets. Her fingers were too numb and swollen for them to fit.

"Done," Fabian said. "Jump up and we'll speed you home, yes?"

He helped her up, where she slumped into the back of the cart and muttered the name of Anja's street.

The drive home was so peaceful. She thrummed with fatigue, and yet she was utterly blissful. She looked up at the grey clouds as the cart bumped along snow-packed roads. Her mind was blank and barely registered when snowflakes began to fall on her face. She smiled at them, feeling as if they were a thousand congratulatory kisses.

CHAPTER 13
FIRST SNOW OF WINTER

It was growing dark and had begun to snow when Elise finally saw Nessa return. She was laying at the back of a cart, making Elise fear she might be injured.

Sweet gods, please do not tell me she fell on the ice. Or burned herself on the furnace.

The glassblower walked up to them, his angular face barely visible between his snow-covered hat and pulled-up collar.

"I return to you one Nessa Glass. A woman as strong as an ox, determined as a spider making webs, and clever as a cat planning its hunt. And, also, now a glassblower's apprentice," he said with a big smile.

Elise ran to congratulate and check on her beloved. Nessa was covered in snow, and her face was red-cheeked and puffy.

Elise stopped mid-step. "Heartling," she said on an exhale. "Are you quite all right?"

Nessa sat up, with some apparent difficulty. "Yes. Only bone-tired. I need to sleep. Then eat. Then visit the bathhouse. Then sleep more."

Elise tucked snowy strands of hair behind Nessa's ear. "Of

course. You will have whatever you need. What has… what has happened?"

The glassblower pulled his collar down so more of his face was visible. Elise realised she didn't even know his name.

He beamed. "As I said, your lady is a glassblower's apprentice now. I gave her a test to try her commitment and ability to work. She passed! I shall now be kind, yes? Let her take two days to recover. Then, I expect to see her at the workshop, ready to learn and work."

Nessa dragged herself off the cart. "Yes. I'll be there. Thank you again, Master Smedstorp." She stood in front of him on wobbly legs and gave a little bow and a smile.

He returned her smile but with more gusto. Then he waved, spurred his horse on, and disappeared into the snowy evening.

Anja clapped Nessa on the shoulder. "Well done. By the looks of you, that wasn't easy."

Nessa chuckled and in a slightly hoarse voice said, "No. It wasn't. But worth it."

Elise kissed her cheek. "Come inside. I will help you wash off the worst with a cloth, then dress you in warm, dry clothes and let you sleep for a few hours. Then a spot of dinner, and after that, a trip to the bathhouse, I think. If it is still open, Anja?"

Anja opened the front door. "Yes. It's always open. Skarhult has many bakers and manufacturers who work unusual hours."

"Sounds wonderful," Nessa said, leaning on Elise as she hobbled forward.

When they got in, Elise kissed her wet hair, smelling the snow and fresh sweat on it. "Good. Then we can celebrate tomorrow?"

Nessa nodded. "Why not? Maybe travel into town for a nice supper? After all, we'll have some coin coming in soon."

Elise almost jumped on the spot. "Yes! Magnificent idea."

Anja muttered, "Why must you go *out* to celebrate? It's cold. And full of people. And now also snow. What's wrong with staying in with some good food, wine, and a fascinating book?"

At their feet, Svarte meowed as if he agreed.

Elise hesitated. "Those things are lovely, indeed. Nevertheless, I think it would do us good to get out of the house."

"We do get out. We go for walks. We search for her glassblowers and your tooth tonics."

Elise tried again. "Yes, but to go out at night, for merriment. If it gets too cold, we simply return home. We can go without you if you do not wish to join us?"

Anja sighed. "Well, I suppose it is the first snow of winter, meaning the frost faire opens."

With a yawn, Nessa looked out the window. "This is the first snow of winter? What about all that substance on the ground? That's snow, too."

"The calendar tells us that the week that has now begun is the first week of winter. This is the first snow of that week. Thus, *first snow of winter*," Anja stated, looking at them as if they were ignorant children.

"I see. And that is when the frost faire starts? On the River Orla? Hunter told us about that. He said it was a remarkable and magical spectacle," Elise said, trying not to swallow her tongue with excitement.

Anja hummed while checking her pocket watch. "Oh, it's the same every year. Big wild cats who have been tamed and do tricks, overpriced exotic food, a noisy carousel, furs and silks being sold, and chaotic performances of all kinds."

Elise propped the increasingly heavy Nessa against the wall. "Performances? What performances?"

Something which looked like it could grow into a smile tugged at Anja's lips. "Look at your little ears prick up. You know, *performances*. Jugglers, magic tricks, musicians, plays, dancers with as few clothes as they can have on without becoming part of the river ice," Anja said, chuckling at her own joke.

"Ah, I should love to see the dancers, and the play! Oh, and to go on the carousel."

Anja scoffed. "It'll be filled with sappy couples and excited children. All those painted wooden horses covered in children's sugar-sticky fingerprints."

Elise bit her lower lip. "What about the ice? Will we slip? Do we need skates?"

"You can skate there, but skates aren't necessary. The ice is generally so scratched and gritted that you can walk on it without falling on your arse."

"Not to be a bother. But I still need to sleep, eat, and a have a bath," Nessa mumbled.

Elise looked at Nessa, who was yawning right in her face.

"Naturally, heartling. Let me wash you up and get you into something warm."

"No time. Sleep now," Nessa muttered. She stumbled over to the metal bed and dragged herself onto it. It looked like she was asleep the moment her head hit the pillow.

Anja caught Elise's eyes and whispered, "Let her sleep. I'll tell you more about the faire in the kitchen over some berries and coffee, yes? It looks like dinner will wait a few hours until the glassblower's apprentice wakes up." She pointed to Elise. "Then you'll have to clean those muddy sheets."

～

When Elise asked to look at Anja's timepiece she realised it had been three hours since Nessa had gone to sleep.

"Should we wake her?"

Anja put away the towel she'd been using to dry the dishes. "Why? Are you hungry?"

Elise shrugged, hunger not being something she noticed until she was lightheaded.

Anja looked her over. "Of course not, look at the size of you. You're thin like a sparrow at a health retreat and eat like one as well. I, on the other hand, need food." She glanced out of the kitchen. "Nessa is likely to be ravished when she wakes, not to mention thirsty. Let's get the reindeer meatloaf in the oven. Do you want that task, or do you want to cut the radishes?"

"I think I will stick to what I know and cut the radishes. I cannot recall ever even seeing a meatloaf."

Anja gave her a brief smile. "It's good to know your limitations, although I know you could learn to make this. Just as you learned to assist me earlier today."

Elise laid a hand over her heart. "Does that mean you were happy dictating to me?"

Anja put the meatloaf in the oven. "You write fast and accurate."

Elise wished she'd look at her. Or give away more of her feelings regarding their new arrangement.

"I see. So, do you wish to try dictation tomorrow as well? In the daytime, naturally, as we are going to the faire in the evening."

"Yes, yes. I haven't forgotten about the faire," Anja said. "And yes. I'd like to dictate again tomorrow. Speeds up the process and looks neater than writing with my left hand."

It wasn't glowing praise, but Elise tingled with the sense of achievement just the same. "Splendid! I am so glad to have been of assistance."

Anja opened the cupboard which held plates. "It's fine, it's not like I cannot afford to pay you, despite being prudent with my inheritance to make it last. If I get the book out there, it can start making me some income too. So yes, a good invest-ment, I guess."

"Oh, do try to not sound so overly enthusiastic," Elise said with a quirked eyebrow and hands on her hips.

Anja stopped taking plates out and faced Elise. Whatever facetious or cranky comment she'd expected, the look on Anja's face suggested it wasn't coming.

"I… apologise. I'm not good with these things. I rely on myself and myself alone. And I don't… enthuse as much as you do. The few times when I have, life seems to have punished me for it."

Elise's hands fell to her sides as she sought for something to say. "No need to apologise. I would not want you to alter the way you are just because two strangers burst into your home."

Anja gave a curt nod, and Elise smiled at her, almost drawing out a return smile from her hostess. She took the plates from Anja and placed them around the table.

Anja picked up cutlery and glasses. "There. Now it's all ready for when the meatloaf is baked, which should be a little less than an hour. Wait, no, you never cut those radishes. Get to it, young lady!"

"Yes, Mother," Elise joked, getting a light smack on the shoulder for her troubles. She decided that as soon as she had cut the radishes, she would wake Nessa. She looked forward to hearing all about the glassblower's test at dinner. Later, at the bathhouse, she would tell Nessa all about the dictation. She figured they were making a real friend in Anja, something which the older woman seemed to need as much as they did.

She sang as she cut the radishes, marvelling that their life in Skarhult was finally on track.

CHAPTER 14
THE MAGIC LANTERN SHOW

In front of the Queen and the chosen crowd of courtiers and dignitaries, the colours and light of the magic lantern show transformed into pictures on the wall.

She sat forward on her chair, back straight. It was her natural way of sitting, certainly not to show off her powerful shoulders and the bosom which her corset pushed up. Certainly not.

Marianna wondered what people said about the fact that she wore a corset. The garment had gone out of fashion in the past decade, but she had kept hers. She told her tailor that it was expected of royalty. But the truth was... she enjoyed the restriction. She took pride in the fact that she could endure the torture without ever letting it show and relished knowing that if anyone else restricted her in any way, she'd have their veins pulled out of their body and made into a latticework. Through the corset's tightness, she felt a glow of pride at this sheer power over the most powerful being she knew: herself.

The slide changed, and the next scene of the magic lantern show filled the white wall in front of her. The main character, an elegant banker, suffered a near-fatal wound. The small crowd gasped.

Well, most did. In the darkness behind her, Marianna felt the presence of a man who was not the type to gasp. He wouldn't spare the tiniest reaction for something so frivolous as entertainment. Magic lantern shows were all the rage throughout the orb, and yet, this man seemed about as diverted as if a rat had skittered across his steel-booted feet.

High Captain Nordhall of the Joiners Square stood to attention. She couldn't see the Storsundian dignitary because of the dimmed lights and the fact that he was behind her. She still knew that he would be standing to attention, in his strict and medal-decked uniform. Back even straighter than her own, strong chest pushed forward and hands clasped behind his back. Ice blue eyes fixed ahead and immaculate blond moustache laying tight against his upper lip. That damned Northman and his infuriating disapproval of everything at her court.

Why did Joiners Square, I mean the Storsund authorities, she mentally corrected herself, pretending even in her thoughts that there was a difference. *Why did they send this man? Why not someone charming and interesting? If they wish to win my favour, why not send me someone I might like? Someone who would revere me as they should?*

She moved on the edge of her seat, annoyed that while she hated the stoic man, she also wished to bed him. Of course, that was only to see him unravel as she forced him to come for her and lose all his meticulous control.

Still, he held great influence in Storsund. And she needed the northern continent on her side. Once more, there had been riots in the villages around Highmere and whispers of a nationwide revolt. She kept telling Adaire not to fret too much over it, that this always ended in the same old song and dance. Either the people tried to get another Noble family on the throne, leading to infights between the Nobles, or they tried another form of government, only to realise they did not know how to rule or what they wanted instead of a monarchy.

Due to being half-witted, uneducated peasants.

Marianna smiled to herself. The Hargraves traditionally helped these failures along by sowing discontent among the Nobles and undermining the idea of other forms of government.

Nevertheless, if Marianna could avoid another rebellion now, she should. They took effort, time, and coin to quell and clean up. She had two choices, align Arclid with the powerful, rich Storsund, while keeping the Northmen from colonising Arclid. Or take a husband and breed little royal brats for the peasants to coo over.

Consequently, here she was, entertaining Option A in a frantic attempt to avoid Option B. She was not for marrying and certainly not for breeding. She sought control, wickedness, and entertainment. Nothing so disgustingly wholesome as a *family*.

By the door stood Adaire. Aloof and patient, as always. Awaiting command. Marianna beckoned her over and the queen's aide strode, elegant and almost ghostly on silent feet, towards her mistress. That flawless taupe skin glowing in the light of the magic lantern show. Marianna raked her gaze over her. Her languid feminine beauty stood in direct contrast to the stiff High Captain Nordhall in his grey, high-collared uniform and the dusty fur across his shoulders. Those Joiners Square uniforms were impressive and handsome, yet Marianna preferred resting her eyes on a lavish dress or nicely cut smoking jacket any day.

Adaire caught her appreciative gaze and smirked. The smirk was there one moment and gone the next. Adaire was professional again, standing by her side like a lieutenant awaiting orders. Marianna sighed and return her gaze to the show, where the protagonist had recovered from his wound and met the love of his life. The woman telling the story depicted in the projected pictures had a droning, tedious voice.

Marianna caressed the cool hand which now rested on her shoulder. "Adaire. Have the narrator thrown out after this show. Her voice bores me terribly."

"As you wish, my Queen."

Marianna turned her head to the other side. "High Captain Nordhall. What do you think of the narrator's voice?"

The man took one loud step forwards. "I think she can hear you and that you have ruined her day, yes? Other than that, I find her performance adequate, but not stirring."

Marianna grit her teeth at his chastising. As if it mattered if the wretched narrator heard her. "I see. What are your thoughts of the show in general? Does it amuse you?"

"Amuse is a strong word. It passes the time. I find no 'magic' in it, despite the name. An oil lamp's light being shone through painted glass to show pictures on the wall... Not real magic, yes?"

Marianna was glad he was still behind her and that the room was dark. Otherwise he would surely have taken offence at the face she was making. "Magic. It always comes down to magic with you Northmen. Your hunt for it will be your downfall. Why are Joiners Square so obsessed with magic?"

Marianna felt Adaire's hand on her shoulder squeeze a little. A warning.

Nordhall cleared his throat. "Joiners Square, or rather, the Storsund government, does not become obsessed. That is a vice you find more in the three other continents, yes? We're merely... what is the word... tenacious? Surviving the long winters and brief summers will do that to a people."

Marianna rolled her eyes. "I am sure you are right. You are a very drivel-filled, oh, I mean to say, *driven* people. Still, you did not answer my question. Why this focus on magic?"

"We are a people of science, yes? Most new inventions come from our vast lands. However, science is not all there is. Tales of magic have always existed in our world. We all thought them bedtime stories, yes? But as our scientists find more and more things they cannot explain, we've come to believe that magic might exist. Either way, we want a definitive answer."

"And you are here because you believe you can get that from me."

He spluttered, making her laugh. They were drawing attention from the audience, but no one dared hush the Queen and the Storsund envoy.

She turned her head again, almost gifting him with her eye contact. "I hear your shock. Had you expected me not to know? Did you think you leading the conversation from magic lantern shows into real magic was clever?" Marianna cackled. "Silly ice-dweller! I am Queen Marianna Hargraves of Arclid. Part of a family line who have ruled this continent for four hundred years. I know more than you can ever imagine."

He coughed. "Of course, your Royal Highness."

She smiled as he used her title, something he did only when he was forced to.

"Now, answer the question before the show is over and we are once more surrounded by eavesdropping ears," she drawled.

"Magic would bridge the gap between nature and science – offering complete power. Together, your nation and ours can have that power."

Marianna clicked her long fingernails against the arm of her chair. "That. Did. Not. Answer. My. Question," she said through gritted teeth.

He coughed again, sounding equally fake as before. "Pardon. What was that? It is hard to hear over the narrator and the clicking of the changing glass slides, yes?"

Adaire stepped in. "I believe you heard her, High Captain. She requests that you answer the question."

Was that a sigh I hear coming from our blond ice-dweller?

He sniffed. "Fine. We have reason to believe that your bloodline has always known about magic but kept it secret, yes? Only using it yourselves when you absolutely had to, like during revolts and wars when your reign was challenged. At other times, we believe the Hargraves have done everything to ensure everyone thought magic was a fairy tale."

Marianna leaned back in her chair, caressing Adaire's hand leisurely. "Interesting little theory. When it comes to your offer to make our nations the two most powerful, I am not convinced. It seems to me that Storsund has quite enough power."

She paused, pretending to watch the show, just to make him wait.

"Joiners Square – oh, I mean *Storsund* – are starting to treat other countries as supply larders, taking your fancy steamships over to raid what natural resources you want in the name of the Storsund Trading Company. Power seems to be making you gluttonous," she concluded.

Adaire hummed. "Some even say that you are enslaving your own people in the north to work in coal mines and the forestry industry. Power seems to be making villains of your nation. My Queen is right. You do not seem to need more of it."

There was a pregnant pause.

"Your Majesty," Nordhall said, ignoring Adaire's addition, "do you truly wish to be the one to decide when we have had enough power and how it affects us? Do you not worry that fighting our claim of power might lead to war?"

She turned to face him, whip fast. "Are you threatening me, you moustachioed cretin?"

He bristled. "Of course not. Joiners Square do not

threaten. We do, however, do whatever is in our glorious union's best interest, yes? The possible existence of magic is a question that cannot stay unanswered."

"Oh. It cannot? Well, we shall see about that." The Queen turned to her aide. "We should leave, Adaire. I have matters of state to tend to. Actual business of *ruling*, not crazed schemes or time-wasting dreams."

She stood to leave, and everyone shifted their gaze from the pictures on the wall to their monarch. Even the narrator paused.

High Captain Nordhall held up a hand. "Wait. I believe I was hasty. Apologies for my ill temper, Your Majesty. Naturally, you should keep your family secrets. I am a mere soldier, not versed in diplomacy, yes? I meant no offence."

He stiffly bowed his head, and Marianna sat back down. The narrator droned on.

"If I were you, I should not make assumptions about any 'family secrets'. However, I do accept your apology," the Queen said.

But only because Arclid and I need Storsund and your damned Joiners Square.

She clicked her nails against the arm of the chair again. "Perhaps I would be more likely to speak of my family's discoveries through history if Joiners Square were to demonstrate some... helpfulness."

He took a step closer. "I'm sure something could be arranged, yes? We want to preserve the thriving relationship between our nations. Was there anything you had in mind?"

A hum of satisfaction spread through her. "As a matter of fact, I do have a favour to ask. Mind you, I make no promises that I will give Joiners Square what it wants. However, I would be more likely to do so if I knew they were my true allies."

"I see."

Was that a hint of curiosity in his voice? Marianna pressed

on. "I have… associates in Obeha, the Western Isles, and on your *charming* continent. They are currently searching for someone. A traitor that I need to get hold of." She sniffed. "It is not a matter of life or death, do not mistake me for someone desperate. I do, however, wish to find this person, a woman in her twenties, travelling with another woman of the same age."

"Storsund is large, yes?" Nordhall said. "Much bigger than Arclid. Nevertheless, I can set my best people on finding these women. We do not tend to fail our missions. What do they look like?"

Marianna began describing in a whisper inaudible to the crowd. Elise was easy, with her striking prettiness, those unique eyes, and measurements which Marianna knew intimately. Adaire chimed in, pointing out that the witness at the docks had mentioned Elise's hair was shorter now.

Nessa was more of a challenge, but Marianna had peered quite closely at the woman when they played cards, trying to see what it was Elise found so attractive. All she perceived was a heap of ordinary, dull, drab, and frightfully common! Nice curves were the only saving grace for that dreadful creature who had swept in and ruined Marianna's fun. If the farm wench was brought back with Elise… well, now, she could just as well be killed or tortured. As long as she was out of Elise's life and Marianna's sight for good.

Nordhall made notes in a tiny notebook before returning it to his breast pocket. When he had finished, he dragged a finger across his moustache and quietly asked, "If we do you this favour, find this Elisandrine Falk, you will be more likely to speak of magic, yes?"

Marianna batted her lashes at him. "Yes, I should be much more likely to discuss the existence or nonexistence of magic if I knew this matter was in hand."

He clicked his heels together. "Then you will excuse me as

I go order letters to be sent to Joiners Square headquarters immediately." With that, he bowed and left.

"He should wait for me to give him permission to leave," Marianna muttered.

Adaire shrugged. "The High Captain is a Northman, what do you expect?"

"You do have a point. So, what do you think of my clever idea? Making Joiners Square beg and do tricks for me, even fetching my toys? All just to have a conversation during which I am not obligated to tell the truth."

Adaire did not look as amused as her queen would have liked.

Typical.

Marianna huffed out a breath and said, "All right, Adaire. Out with it, but whisper so the others do not hear."

Adaire leaned in, as close as she could without kissing Marianna's ear, and whispered, "This seems a big favour to waste on finding a… pet. Fates of nations are at stake here. Are you certain that your main focus should be on finding Lady Falk, my Queen?"

Marianna scoffed. "There is that jealously again, methinks. Do not dare intimate that I am not minding affairs of state. I am. That is why I am showing my control over Joiners Square. Demonstrating that if they help me with any whim I may have, I might be kind to them. I am putting myself in a position of power, instead of having them believe I need them."

"Yes, until they notice your eagerness and uncover that it is a lover, not a traitor, you search for. Then they could use her for blackmail or bait," Adaire whispered. "Either way, I do not think letting your biggest opponent know of your weakness is a good idea, my Queen. Nor to make the delicate relationship between Arclid and this strange organisation of theirs hang on something as trivial as revenge."

Marianna's good mood from her victory against Nordhall

was waning, along with her patience for her aide's negativity. "One more word against my plan, and I will make you learn to hold your tongue. Do you understand me, Adaire?"

Adaire dipped her head. "It is your prerogative and responsibility to make any decisions regarding foreign affairs."

"Precisely. Now, keep talking. I am bored with this magic lantern show. It is about as magical as my toes. I prefer your conversation, my cherished."

Adaire seemed to scramble for subjects for a while. Or perhaps she was weighing the ones that were safe?

"You have not said what you plan to do with Elise," she finally settled on. "Some form of torture?"

Marianna waved off the suggestion. "Nothing so gruesome. I want her brought back to me. Then I shall keep her around until she remembers how much she used to admire me, used to worship me. I want to push on that, charm her to the fullest. Then, when she is fully infatuated, nay *addicted*, I intend to break her heart in the cruellest way I can, leaving her devastated and in withdrawal." She sniggered. "Then I shall spread the rumour that she has bedding diseases and vile urges. Humiliate her and make her undesirable to other lovers. In short – make her live out her days alone, heartbroken, and without her much desired satisfaction."

Adaire stared at her in silence for a few beats. "That seems an extreme and rather complicated punishment for leaving you, my Queen."

"It is the punishment Elise deserves."

"You know that you cannot make people love you."

Marianna drilled her gaze into Adaire's. "Do I really have to warn you again, woman? Remember. Your. Place."

Adaire bowed her head, but when it came back up, her face kept its calm mask of disapproval. "I can only give my opinion. The final decision is, as always, yours, and I do not wish to overstep or cause offence. But I beg you, *Marianna*, to give this more thought, especially your dealings with Joiners Square."

It was rare that Adaire used her first name. Their parents had made them stop that when they were no longer girls playing in pigtails but women growing curves and learning about their places in life. Marianna was the ruler of Arclid, her family had won that right four hundred years ago. Adaire was an Aldershire, and therefore the ruler's right hand, but never her equal.

Despite all this, the fact that Adaire used her name now didn't have the effect the aide had probably hoped for. It didn't throw Marianna or make her soften. Instead, it made her realise how weak she would look if she surrendered now. Now, both High Captain Nordhall and Adaire would be aware of any change in her plans. She risked looking flighty and irresolute in Nordhall's eyes and in Adaire's... Marianna might look as if she was bending to her aide's wishes.

Any chance of quitting the hunt evaporated. She set her jaw.

"*Beg* as much as you wish, Adaire. But I know what is right, what I want, and that I shall have it. I also know that your services as a lover will not be needed in the upcoming weeks. Please fetch a selection of my courtesans for me to choose from tonight."

Adaire looked away and intoned, "As you command, my Queen."

CHAPTER 15
THE FROST FAIRE

The next day dawned, and Nessa knew that if Anja hadn't woken her, the pain in her body would have. It was as if she had glass fragments flowing through her blood, digging into her every time she moved. Her shoulders and back were the worst. They had felt better at the hot baths last night, but now they were almost worse than when she had undergone the test.

Anja sucked in air between her teeth as Nessa stretched and winced. "Steady there, lass. I have something for the pain. Ground-up gullveig root. Tastes horrible and might make you a bit drunk. But it removes most of the pain."

"Then I'll gladly accept it."

"Good. Come with me to the kitchen. Elise can start the fires. You should swallow the gullveig root powder down with coffee and porridge."

Nessa began the procedure of dragging herself up to sitting. "Anja. Would you mind awfully if we had fried bread today instead? After Master Smedstorp's challenge, I'm famished."

Her hostess turned and surveyed her. A smile of surprising

warmth made lines by her full lips. "Of course. We'll have some fried bread, some winterberry jam, and even milk to go with your coffee if you'd like?"

Nessa stood, attempting not to wince and cause more pity. "Why not? Any energy is welcome."

"I have no cow's milk. You know how expensive that can be here. But I trust you're used to goat's milk by now, yes?"

Nessa nodded and smiled.

"Good. I'll prepare the powder for you. Wake your wife and tell her to light the fires."

Nessa obeyed and then hobbled to the washroom and after that into the kitchen. She noticed the warmth of pride still in her chest. She had procured another apprenticeship. The Queen had not won by chasing Nessa's dream job away from her.

And you did it yourself this time. Elise didn't arrange it for you.

There was a pride in that, too, even if Nessa would never tell Elise as much.

In the kitchen, she swallowed the foul powder which Anja had mixed into a spoonful of winterberry jam. Then she stumbled about trying to help make breakfast until their hostess glared at her.

"You're in the way. Sit down and let the powder take effect. No need to try and be a hero, especially not as your ladylove isn't even watching."

"What am I not watching?"

Elise walked in. Like Nessa, she was wearing her long underwear and a blanket over her shoulders. Such a contrast to Anja, who was dressed and cleaned as if she had been up for hours. Her grey-streaked hair laid in perfect waves for once, and her skin had been scrubbed to a healthy glow.

She put the fried bread, butter, jam, and coffee on the table. Nessa took a bite-sized chunk of bread, blew on it until it wouldn't scald her tongue, and chewed with happy moans. Anja looked at the table, muttering that it was a shame she had no juice. Then she groaned and said something Nessa couldn't make out.

"Sundish curse words. She taught me those exact words yesterday when she dropped an ink pot," Elise whispered.

Anya switched to Arclidian. "We're out of milk."

Nessa swallowed her bite of bread. "Never mind then. We don't need it."

"Nonsense. I'll walk down the road to where old Nilsson sneaks his fat goats in to graze on the grass behind the dye works." She buttoned her smoking jacket. "He'll be glad to part with some extra milk for coin. Nilsson will do anything for payment. I'm convinced he reports gossip and rumours to Joiners Square for an extra silver a month." She scowled. "Traitor. Anyway, I shan't be a moment."

Nessa watched her waltz out of the kitchen, grab her coat, and merrily slam the door behind her.

"Heartling?"

"Yes?" Elise replied between dainty sips of coffee. She barely grimaced at the drink these days. She'd surely never grow to love it as Nessa had, but she was trying to get used to it, if only to ward off the cold.

"Do you think the fact that you help Anja with her writing is why she seems… cheerier?"

Elise peered into her cup as if the coffee had the answers. "Hm. No, I think she was perking up even before that. Still, I hope my help will bring her some joy. We have a good setup here, do we not?"

Nessa swallowed down her second piece of bread and sighed a happy "yes."

"Splendid. Now, will you at any point partake of any of the other food Anja has provided or are you going to marry that bowl of fried bread?"

"Is that your way of indicating that you want some?"

Elise put her coffee cup down and leaned in to teasingly nip at Nessa's lower lip. "Oh, yes. I certainly want some," she purred with a smirk.

Nessa grinned at her. "Just let my body heal up a bit and the next night I'll sneak over to your sofa."

"I think it is my turn to sneak over to your side of the room. Let me know when your body hurts less. Or when you do not mind a little sting in exchange for the pleasure."

"Gods above, woman, how can you make everything sound so naughty?"

Elise shrugged, looking pleased. "Simply one of my many talents, my cherished."

"Well, as much as you're getting me in the mood, you shan't get any amorous activity tonight. Unless I can have more of this gullveig root. It's beginning to kick in and is not unlike eating honey cake and swallowing it down with a bottle of brandy."

Elise raised her eyebrows. "Sounds potent. Anyway, no bedplay tonight. We shall undoubtedly be home exceedingly late. We are going to the faire to celebrate your apprenticeship and my dictation for Anja, remember?"

"Ah, right."

Elise beamed. "Two incomes, however meagre they might be right now, is something that should be celebrated with debauchery and entertainment. I cannot wait!"

Nessa slathered her next bite of fried bread with jam. "Perhaps we'd be better off staying home and thanking the gods for it?"

"Heartling, the gods stayed in Arclid with the rain and the sugar pumpkins. You got your apprenticeship through hard work and pain. I got my position as Anja's assistant through gentle coaxing and *weeks* of patience. We deserve some fun, some sweet treats, and plenty of strong drink."

"Sounds like someone is not sticking to black wine tonight?"

"Correct. Next station for this train – excess!" Elise shouted and waved a piece of bread exultantly.

Nessa laughed, feeling an overwhelming urge to kiss Elise. She never got the chance as Elise sat forward, wide-eyed, and said, "Do you want me to tell you everything about the faire? Anja was reluctant, but I dragged every detail I could out of her during your nap yesterday."

Nessa took her hand over the table. "No, thank you, heartling. I think I'd like to be surprised. Like I was when we found Core Street in Nightport."

"Oh, this will make Core Street look like a skitter-beetle trying to compete with a fully lit lux beetle. Nevertheless, I shall honour your decision to go there unprepared. I cannot wait to see your face."

"My face? You can't wait to see *the faire.*"

"Both can be true," Elise said, pursing her lips.

Nessa laughed again, reaching across the table to kiss those red lips. They were interrupted by the return of Anja, milk in tow, and the breakfast resumed.

When night finally fell, it was time to get ready for the celebrations.

"I cannot believe we are having our supper at the actual frost faire!" Elise yelped.

Anja shook her head. "Wonderful. Saffron spiced rat and spider-vodka for dinner, then."

Nessa took a step back. "Ew. Surely it can't be that bad?"

"Not quite that bad," Anja grudgingly agreed while putting on a second pair of socks. "We'll find something edible. Everyone should put on all their outerwear. It'll be colder than an icicle's buttocks."

Elise raised her eyebrows at the expression, but Anja ignored her, too busy putting on her outerwear. "It should stop snowing soon," she said. "The real cold is setting in. Which means less snow and more thick ice on the river. That is good, if we're going to be sharing it with all of Skarhult tonight," Anja said with a frown. She stalked out the door and left Nessa and Elise beaming at each other.

"Frost faire," Elise whispered reverently.

Nessa nodded at her, a burst of love heating her from the heart and out. They rushed to get their clothes on and then hurried after Anja.

The snow no longer crunched but instead creaked under Nessa's feet, having lost its powdery softness and been crisped with ice. They were on their way to the centre of Skarhult. Anja was, as Nessa, a firm believer in walking to things. However, as her body still ached, Nessa had asked if they could hire a carriage. Anja had pursed her lips but agreed that they shouldn't walk.

As they strode away from the house, Nessa couldn't remember seeing carriages taking fares on this road. Anja marched on for a couple of streets, until she came to a metal sign depicting what looked like some form of a long carriage. There she stopped and looked ahead.

"May I ask why we are stopping here?" Elise asked.

Anja planted her feet and sniffed in the cold air. "This is where the cable car picks up passengers."

Nessa stopped adjusting her gloves. "The what?"

"The cable car. You've been here for weeks and you haven't noticed one? Large vehicles that take passengers for a fee and run on those tracks in the middle of the road, the ones that have been swept of snow there. See them?" Anja said, pointing out into the road.

Nessa looked down, and in the light of the gas streetlights, she saw the tracks. Not as big and sturdy as railroad tracks, but undoubtedly there.

"Yes, I see them!"

"Good. I'm glad to see they've been cleared. When they get snowed over or frozen solid – no cable cars. But, of course, they clear them perfectly for the first night of frost faire," Anja muttered.

Nessa bit her lip as a memory popped up. "Wait. I think I remember seeing large vehicles coming down these streets when Master Smedstorp carted me home after my test. I thought it was one of those omnibuses you said they have in Highmere, Elise."

Elise shook her head. "Not if it ran on tracks. The omnibuses are just larger horse-driven carriages, holding ten to twenty people. These tracks are something else. I saw them when we were traipsing around looking for glassblowers but did not know what they were."

"They're for cable cars," Anja reiterated. "They're run by cables in the ground, all powered by a huge steam engine in town. There's only two lines, but they cross large parts of Skarhult. I settled out here because houses were cheap but close to the eastern line. I trust steam and cables far more than I do horses."

"Oh, I see," Elise said while staring at the tracks, which had been uncovered like buried treasure after the snow had been cleared off. The excitement radiated off Elisandrine.

She always did adore anything new and thrilling.

Nessa surveyed the tracks, too. She envied that, excitement instead of all of her own fear and worry. There was an unease in her stomach, not unlike the one she'd felt seeing the train for the first time. The tracks, with their moving rope, looked almost ominous.

There was a peculiar sound, like a loud underground whirring, and Nessa looked to Anja.

"A car is approaching," Anja explained. "We'll get on it, I'll pay, and you'll try to get a seat, yes?"

With a nod, Nessa turned to peer down the track. Trundling towards them was what looked like a blend of a carriage and a train compartment. Anja held out her hand in a signal, and a long honk came from the cable car.

It stopped right in front of them and motioned for them to climb on. In the carriage were two long, wooden benches facing each other. There was room on the right side, so Elise and Nessa sat down while Anja gave the driver a few coins and spoke quietly to him in Sundish. The passengers who were already seated were silent, either looking out the windows or reading books. Their clothing was warm and elegant, though, so Nessa assumed that, despite their calm exteriors, they were also going to the faire. Their stillness was a sharp contrast to Elise, who bounced in her seat and said, "Almost like a train, is it not?"

"Yes, I'd say—"

"Exciting as the cable car is, I cannot wait for us to arrive at the faire. I want music, food, and entertainment!"

Nessa shook her head at Elise's overexcitement and then kissed her cheek. It was soft but cold. Nessa kissed it again, making Elise coo as she leaned into the kissing.

"Overly affectionate as always, I see," Anja said, chuckling as she sat down next to them.

The cable car started up again. It was jerkier and slower than the train, but Nessa was too relieved to not have to walk or be jolted about in a horse-drawn carriage to mind.

Four stops later, Anja bumped Nessa's shoulder. "Time to... what's the word... alight. The river is just over there. Come on, get off before the cable car continues."

Nessa and Elise obeyed. They left the stillness of the car

and stepped into a world of noise and colours. Nessa knew that she was looking at a frozen river, but all she could see were vast swaths of stalls and tents, all in bright reds, yellows, greens, and gold. They were such a contrast against the dark night and the eerily white snow that it assaulted Nessa's eyes. The moon came out from the clouds and helped the street-lights that lined the river, and the torches perched outside every stall and tent, illuminate the faire.

Nessa smelled something like burnt sugar, warm dough, and spices. Was that cloves? Cardamom? She frowned when a whiff of alcohol-sharp vomit hit her. There was a man in front of them, stumbling off the ice to throw up into the trampled snow.

"Charming," Elise muttered, walking past him and onto the river. Anja and Nessa followed. The first stand they saw was selling beverages of all kinds, many of them looking alcoholic. On the makeshift bar stood glasses filled with clear liquid and tin mugs which steamed with warmth.

"Hello, good sir. What drinks do you serve?" Elise asked.

He smiled at her. "Arclidian? Welcome to Storsund and welcome to the faire. You'll love it, yes?"

"I will if I get something strong and sweet to drink," Elise countered with a smirk and a few bats of her lashes.

"Is she flirting?" Anja whispered.

Nessa shook her head. "No, not really. It's the way she socialises."

The man behind the bar pointed to the glasses and mugs already lined up. "We have vodka with pressed mint leaves. Next to them are mugs of fortified, spiced black wine. All for three coppers each, yes? If you want to spend more coin, we can make you something special. Something unique which—"

"No. Nothing 'unique.' I know how much that costs at a faire," Anja interrupted. "Ladies, cold vodka with mint juice or hot black wine?"

Elise was busy pouting, so Nessa picked. "One vodka and one wine for us, then we can try each other's."

Anja nodded and ordered in Sundish. He replied in their language, too, seeking her gaze. Anja was too busy counting out coppers to notice.

"My treat as we're celebrating," she said and placed the coins on the counter.

As she had reverted to Arclidian, the barkeep spoke in it too when he handed over the drinks. "I assume the vodka is for you, yes? You're sweet enough to not require sugary drinks."

Anja looked at him with puzzlement. "No, I'm having wine. I'm freezing my arse off because these two wished to see the faire. Honestly, young women are trouble. If they come courting you – chase them off with a stick."

A light came on in his eyes. "Aha, these two are… with you. I see. Congratulations!"

Anja frowned. "What?"

Elise started giggling, and Nessa had to elbow her before telling Anja to take her wine and come along.

As they walked off with their drinks, Nessa explained to Anja that he had been flirting with her and then mistaken her disinterest for that the three of them were in a relationship.

Anja gaped at her. "Oh, for snow's sake! People! They're hopeless. This is why I don't go out." She slurped her wine with scowl. Elise was still giggling into her glass of vodka and mint.

They were soon distracted by lights, sounds, and the hum of excitement filling the air. It was an icy cold night, but as they passed torches outside of tents or crowds of fur-clad people, gusts of heat invigorated them. Nessa and Elise tried each other's drinks and then swapped back when Elise burned her tongue on the wine. Anja was looking around, dodging people on skates whizzing past and muttering about how annoying the accordion music was.

"I know it is not snowing, but still… it smells like snow in the air," Elise said, taking Nessa's arm as they walked.

"It's winter in Skarhult, lass. It always smells of snow," Anja muttered, but she smiled at Elise as she said it.

"Where you are! I mean, there you are," a male voice boomed from behind them.

Nessa stopped the ascent of her glass up to her lips. Annoyance and recognition struck her at the same time.

Elise laughed. "Albert! Eleonora! Little Sonja! What in the name of the gods are you doing here?"

Elisandrine was bunched into a clumsy four-person hug, trying to hold her vodka out of the fray. Nessa sighed.

The Lindberg family? They can't be here. They live in Charlottenberg. Why would they be here?

Before Nessa had time to ask any questions, it was her turn to be squished into a hug. All in all, not the best one of her life. The two grownups were all fur and leather clothing, while Sonja was hugging Nessa's legs so tight that Nessa worried about falling. Still, the affection did dampen her annoyance.

Eleonora answered Elise's question. "First night of the frost faire, yes? No one wants to miss that. Besides, you said you were going to Skarhult, so we hoped to run into you. We've been keeping an eye out, haven't we, butter nose?"

Albert, clearly happy to be called *butter nose*, replied, "Yes! Fun on the ice and meeting our favourite Arclidians, too? Superb. We've not stopped talking about you since you disappeared to Skarhult in a puff of dust, I mean, smoke."

"Sonja? Maybe it is time to let go of Mrs Glass' legs now, yes? The blood flow to her feet must be cut off," Eleonora pleaded with her daughter.

Sonja looked up at Nessa. "Taste your drink? Then I let go, yes?"

"Yes? No! I mean no! It's a grownup drink. Dangerous for children," Nessa replied.

The girl's lower lip wobbled. She looked like she was either about to cry or vomit. Nessa wasn't sure which option was scarier, especially considering the girl's vice-tight grip on her legs.

"Come away from there, honey cake," Eleonora crooned.

With a grimace, Sonja obeyed. Nessa busied herself with drinking her wine. She wanted the temptation of the beverage gone from Sonja's mind. And yes, dealing with their old traveling companions would be easier with alcohol in her system. She saw Elise take another sip of her vodka, grimace, and then subtly put the drink on the counter of a booth selling roasted chestnuts. Nessa swallowed the last gulps of her wine and put the empty mug next to Elise's glass.

I drank that far too fast. Stupid. Now I'll be sloshed in five minutes.

"This is extraordinary," Elise said, scanning the faire. "Such a crowd!"

Albert followed her gaze. "Most true. It's as busy as Friday market, yes?"

Elise's brows knitted, barely visible under her bonnet-style hat. "Friday market?"

"Yes. The Skarhult Friday markets. Have you not been, child?" Eleonora asked.

Elise quickly glanced over at Anja and then back. "Oh. Um. No. We have mainly kept indoors. It has been chillingly cold."

Albert laughed. "Not *so* cold. You have a whole city of adventure waiting and you've been indoors?"

Anja scoffed. "Adventure can be having your bag stolen in broad daylight. Or being spied on by Joiners Square, looking for recruits and exploits, yes? Or throngs of people everywhere, especially pesky children who are snotty and rude."

All was quiet as Nessa tried not to look over at little Sonja who was sucking snot up her nose.

"Yes, Skarhult children can be rude, yes? I blame big city life. Charlottenberg is so much more civilised," Eleonora said, clearly clueless to the insult having been aimed at her daughter.

Nessa actually heard Elise breathe a sigh of relief.

"However, as someone who's the head clerk at the Charlottenberg Joiners Square office, I cannot agree that Joiners Square spy on people," Albert said, running his hand over his beard.

"No?" Anja asked with raised eyebrows.

Albert began to squirm and threw glances at Eleonora who looked, very pointedly, back at him.

Huh. What's going on here?

Elise broke the tension. "Where are my manners? You have yet to be formally introduced. Anja, this is the Lindberg family. Albert, Eleonora, and Sonja, this is Anja Ahlgren, our lovely hostess and patient guide. We are staying with her, and I assist her in her work."

"Aha! You are the one, yes? The one what has stolen our ladies away from us," Albert said with a big grin.

Anja looked at Nessa, who could only shrug and look apologetic.

"Oh, come now, we were not stolen. We simply desired to see Skarhult. Speaking of which, what should I make sure to see at the frost faire?" Elise said, linking her arm with Eleonora's.

"Sugar work!" Sonja screamed. She took off running and Eleonora rushed after, dragging Elise along.

Albert laughed and indicated for Nessa and Anja to lead the way in their pursuit.

As they walked, Nessa leaned in towards Anja. "Sorry if this is a silly question. But what is sugar work?"

Anja waved her hand dismissively. "All manner of things created from sugar and sugar products."

"What, like sculptures?"

Anja hummed. "Sort of, but only small things. Sugar is expensive. The murderous rates the Western Islanders charge for the stuff and for the shipping over! Although I suppose they do have to pay their workers properly for the graft. I hear it's hard work."

Nessa's mouth watered. "I tried sugar once. My friend Layden was bribed with a few sugarplums from Prince Macray's confectioner... long story. Anyway, he shared them with me. They tasted so different. Not like things using our usual sweeteners, honey and sugar pumpkin. I can see why it's costly."

Anja finished her wine. "Mm. What about Elise? Has she tried it?"

"Probably. I bet there was lots of it at court. Um, I mean around court, back in Highmere. Did I t-tell you that Elise is from Highmere? I forget. Being tired m-makes me forgetful," Nessa stammered.

Gods-cursed idiot! Don't let your guard down. That's how you end up bloody talking about court or the Queen.

Anja shrugged. "With that accent, it was obvious."

"Where'd they go? Can you see them?" Albert piped up from behind them.

"Over there," Anja said, pointing to a tent on the other side of the ice.

The tent had probably been white once. Now age and the shadows of nearby pine trees coloured it various shades of beige and grey. If the tent was underwhelming, the wares inside it were all the more astounding, much like the woman selling them. Nessa watched as the heavyset, rosy-cheeked blonde showed off her sugar creations.

Her hair is so white it makes the snow and sugar look dark. Is this one of the people from the north? What were they called? Viss?

Nessa's eyes drifted to the marvellous wares before her. Small sugar-paste figurines stood out, shaped like everything from cats to court jesters. They were so smooth, white, and decadent that they looked like frozen cream. Behind them were glass jars filled with little balls with dark centres covered in thin, semi-transparent layers of white.

"Surely they're not pure sugar?" Nessa asked the crowd in general, pointing at those jars.

"No, no, silly Arclidian girl. Let me explain. They're comfits – bits of spice or seeds covered in layers of sugar," Albert said, puffing his chest out. "The jars on the other side, the ones with round red and yellow clear things? Those are boiled sweets. And the colourful squares next to them – they're candied pieces of fruit."

Nessa bit down the sarcastic reply that even *backwards Arclidians* had heard of candied fruit.

In a tent opposite, a singer started crooning in Sundish, accompanied by a violinist. Anja, Eleonora, and Albert moved closer to listen. Nessa stayed with Sonja and Elise, marvelling at the sugar work.

"They are all so dainty and beautiful," Elise whispered. She was holding Sonja by the hand, and they were both staring at the figurines.

Reverently, Sonja said, "I want a... um... the girls that dance pretty."

Elise bent down, probably to follow the girl's gaze. "A ballerina? Good choice."

Elise turned to Nessa, raising her eyebrows in silent question. Nessa gave her the coin purse and a smile, which was returned before Elise approached the confectioner.

"Hello, madam. What a marvellous array of treats you have! May we please have three sugar ballerinas? One for me, one for the little princess here, and one for my beautiful wife."

The confectioner smiled. "Of course, miss. Three pretty ballerinas to dance on your tongue." She gently placed the figurines into a small paper bag and handed them over. "That will be six coppers."

Elise looked at the tiny sugar creations, then at the coin purse, and finally over at Nessa. "That is rather steep for a treat. Perhaps we will only purchase a ballerina for Sonja?"

Nessa's heart stung.

Bugger stressing over coin tonight. Splash out. Your cherished shouldn't have to give up all her treats because you can't stop worrying about coin. It'll be all right. You won't starve.

She smiled at Elise. "No, I think we'll have all three."

Elise tilted her head, a line between her sculpted brows.

Nessa nodded encouragingly. "It's all right, heartling. They're so special and I want you to have one. We brought enough for food and drinks tonight. Besides, it's the frost faire. This is not a place to be saving your coin."

With a flush, Elise smiled and blinked her golden eyes, setting Nessa's heart fluttering.

Anja appeared beside them. "For snow's sake! Stop looking all gooey-eyed and buy the treats. A line is forming."

The line was only one man and he seemed in no hurry, but Elise obeyed her new boss and handed over the coppers. Sonja and Elise hurried off with their treasure. Nessa followed, having to admit that she looked forward to tasting the sugar. They stopped next to the tent, the pine trees rustling gently in the wind above them.

"Go on. Try them," Eleonora prompted.

Elise handed the ballerinas out. Sonja took hers with less care and reverence than Nessa and Elise. Whether that was due to her age or because she was more likely to receive another one from her parents if she broke this one, Nessa couldn't tell.

Elise placed the ballerina in her palm and made it spin around.

Sonja laughed. "She dances! Again, again!"

Why did that child seem so much more palatable when she was with Elise? Nessa marvelled at the love of her life as she spun the little figurine again, making Sonja giggle and clap.

Then Sonja popped her ballerina into her mouth and crunched down on it, breaking the magic that Nessa had been caught up in. Elise gave the child an admonishing look, tapered down with a patient smile. Then she gently, almost tenderly, placed her own ballerina on her tongue and closed her mouth.

Nessa watched as Elise sucked on the sugar figurine with eyes as wide as her smile. It filled Nessa's belly with butterflies.

"Looks like the ballerinas are as yummy as they're pretty," Albert said with a chuckle. "I wonder how they're made. I bet the sugar arrives in big blocks, like ice or wood, yes? Then the figurines are carved in a factory, by clever machines."

Elise shook her head. "Simpler creations are made in factories. Art like this is handmade by confectioners. That, and the price of the imported sugar – cane sugar from the Western Isles or sugar beets from Arclid – is why these are expensive. It is exported in sugar loaves, millions of granules squeezed together in a cone shape," she explained around a mouthful of ballerina. "Then the confectioners, only employed by the Nobles and Royals in Arclid, break them apart and purify the dirty sugar, quite the sight! After that, it can either be melted and turned into sweets like comfits or boiled sweets, or be made into a paste, moulded, and finally dried."

Everyone stared at her after the little speech. Nessa's stomach sank. The gaiety of the night was making them both reckless.

Elise, how would you know, and have seen, all that unless you had been close to a confectioner? Which you just explained was only for Nobles and Royals. I knew it was a bad idea to make friends. Oxen-shit!

Carefree as a child, Elise laughed. "Oh, look at your confused faces. I lived in Highmere, remember? Sugar and scandals were the focus for all."

The confused tension broke.

"Ah. This explains it," Albert said to Nessa, who was still anxious.

Nessa waited until Eleonora started enthusing about the carousel before she tried her ballerina. She couldn't stand the idea of them all watching and looking for her reaction as she ate.

As the sugar figurine hit her tongue, she heard Eleonora say to Anja, "I sat on one of those painted horses backwards once. No one told me until I got off. Might have had a drop too much wine that night, yes?"

"Yes," Anja muttered.

Nessa sucked on the tongue-tingling sugar, wishing she could have more of it. Memories rushed in, of being a child with an unquenchable hunger after a day of schooling and an evening of farm work and chores. Of wanting sweet things but never being able to have more than a dollop of honey. Or a handful of berries in sugar pumpkin juice. Her parents' sad faces as they explained that they couldn't afford more. And only a walk away, at Silver Hollow Castle, that prince of theirs could have his fill, even of something as exotic as sugar. Without having worked a single minute. Suddenly, the sugar tasted less sweet.

Nessa was pulled out of her reverie by Elise taking her hand and saying, "Cherished, shall we go on the carousel? Oh, and Anja, are you coming along?"

It took Nessa a moment to remember what they were talking about, so Anja beat her to replying. "No, thank you. It makes me dizzy. I'd like to return home and finish reading my book."

Elise reached for her. "Oh no, you should stay and—"

Anja held up her hands, smiling at Elise. "None of that. No guilt or pity. The spectacle of the faire is not for me. I brought you here and you found proper, enthusiastic guides. They'll show you the sights. I'd be happier at home, reading."

Elise seemed to hesitate, then she stepped forward and kissed Anja on the cheek. "As you wish."

Nessa gave her a one-armed hug. "Travel safely and enjoy your book. We'll see you later."

Anja nodded, curtly as always. Nessa wasn't sure if it was her imagination, but she thought Anja looked embarrassed but pleased with the signs of affection from her boarders.

"Farewell, Mr and Mrs Lindberg and young…" She hesitated while looking at Sonja. "…young lady. Have a lovely night and make sure Nessa and Elise make it home safely, please."

She left with her usual confident strides. Nessa noticed a pang of concern in the pit of her stomach. Part of her safety net was leaving.

Albert clapped his hands. "Right, ladies. To the carousel."

Nessa blinked away the daze of her quickly downed wine and the buzz of sugar racing through her veins. "Wait! It… doesn't spin very fast, does it? Or cost a lot of coin?"

They all looked at her for a moment. Then Eleonora put her arm around her shoulders and said, "You really must learn to fret less, Nessa. The carousel is slow and cheap. Compose yourself and come along, yes?"

∿

A while later, they stepped off the carousel, its discordant but cheerful music ringing in their ears. Sonja rushed off towards a set of clockwork toys in a scarlet and gold tent. Albert went after her, leaving the three women to walk in peace.

Eleonora smiled. "Fun, yes?"

"Oh, rather!" Elise exclaimed.

"I wish we could ride it again tomorrow. Although maybe we shan't see you again after tonight," Eleonora said, looking as if someone had stolen all her birthdays.

Elise glanced over at Nessa, who sighed but nodded. The Lindbergs weren't completely intolerable, especially not when you weren't in close quarters with them on a ship.

Having received the go-ahead, Elise squeezed Eleonora's shoulder and said, "Shall we plan to meet up again?"

"Certainly," said Albert, returning with Sonja curled up in his arms.

The toys must not have been able to counteract the fatigue of the late hour and all the excitement, because Sonja was now leaning her head against her father's shoulder, blinking sleepily. Albert was kissing her hair and hugging her tight to his chest.

Eleonora took Nessa's hand. "If we do not see you before, we simply must meet up at the Joiners Square Fest. It is held here at the faire in… when is it, Albert?"

"Seven weeks, my sugar rabbit. One night only. Like a winter ball, yes? But on ice! No expenses spared, you Arclidians won't have seen anything so fine. We arrive on the 4.25 train and sleep at the lax… lex… luxurious Skarhult City Hotel afterwards."

"You mean there is something even more festive than the frost faire?" Elise asked, bouncing slightly on the balls of her feet.

While looking at Elise, Eleonora squeezed Nessa's hand so hard it pinched.

"Yes! Joiners Square arrange a splendid event to show their gratitude for all the support and loyalty. Right, Albert?" He nodded, and Eleonora carried on. "It's most excellent. We can spend the whole evening together! Then perhaps you can come with us back to—"

Nessa extricated her mangled hand. "Sounds lovely. We'll think about it. Until then, why don't you give Elise your address and we'll send you letters and postcards, keeping in touch that way."

"What a splendid idea!" Eleonora said. "Albert, give them one of your cards."

Albert carefully adjusted the now-sleeping Sonja, apologising to her under his breath as he did so. He reached into his inner coat pocket and produced a white card with sloping gold script. Elise held it up so she and Nessa could read it.

Albert Lindberg
Head Clerk, Charlottenburg Division
58 Krasny Street
Charlottenburg

"Thank you," Elise said. "I shall write as soon as I can. Thank you for a wonderful night." Then she kissed Eleonora and Albert on the cheek. While she leaned in to kiss Sonja's curls, Nessa gave Albert and Eleonora quick hugs.

Albert nodded at them. "Yes, now is an acceptable time for you to leave. Don't take lifts from strange men, don't walk on the cable car tracks, don't stay out in the cold all night. And don't become out-of-place."

Nessa was about to correct the last statement to "don't get lost" and then point out that they could actually manage. Luckily, Elise pulled her away just in time.

"Quite the role reversal. Me keeping you from losing your temper," Elise whispered with a giggle.

Nessa just rolled her eyes as they sauntered away from the lights and the noise.

Overbearing, pretentious man, she thought. *But very sweet to his family.*

She shook away the ache of missing her parents. And Layden, who, as well as being a wonderful friend, was also a considerate father and husband.

Nessa and Elise walked on, hand in hand, towards the cable car. It was freezing away from the fires and crowds, but the beauty of the now-cloudless night made the cold insignificant. Nessa breathed in the last whiffs of booze, roasted nuts, and sugar.

When they arrived at the lit-up cable car stop and stood there waiting, Nessa had time to really observe Elise. She nearly drowned in those deep-set, golden eyes. There was a glow to them tonight that she hadn't seen for so long. Was it ever since before the Queen waltzed back into her life in Nightport? She noted a carefree swagger in Elise's movements when she bent to re-tie her boot laces. How had she missed that this had all been gone? How had she missed that some of Elise's fire had flickered out and been replaced with... what... worry? Detachment? Sadness? Whatever it had been, it seemed to have lifted. Nessa could only pray to the gods that it was a permanent change.

It gave her pause. Had her own constant worry been eating at Elise the way it always ate at her? Or was there something else? Was it the threat of the Queen?

Biting her lip, Nessa looked up at the winter stars. They twinkled, perhaps happy to be free from the clouds. Nessa wished she could be like them.

CHAPTER 16
PURPOSE AND BELONGING

A few weeks passed, bringing evenings of walks and occasional visits to the frost faire, when they weren't staying in to read and play card games in front of the fire.

Elise felt as if the days flew by. Nessa had thrown herself into learning her craft, while she and Anja found a good system for their work. Anja would dictate to Elise in the morning and then do research in the afternoon.

That was the only time that didn't hurry by for Elise. She rattled around the house, looking for things to do. The first week she wrote in her notebook, usually addressing her writing to her father. Jotting down what she'd seen in Skarhult during their evening walks and writing about her constant dreams. Or nightmares, rather. After a week of penning the nightmare scenarios and realising that they all had one common denominator, the Queen hunting her and managing to catch her, she developed a distaste for writing in the notebook.

After that, she practised her new skills of dusting, tidying, and washing clothes. Anything to keep busy and be of use while Nessa and Anja were both busy working. But there was only so much cleaning and cuddling of the cat she could stand. Even her hair seemed to be growing listless.

One afternoon, she was dusting off the spice jars filled with the oils she and Nessa had made before she got her apprenticeship. They were acceptable in quality but not as potent as the ones Nessa's mother had made.

I bet it was because the herbs were cheap and old. All right for food but not for scented oils. And are these spice jars fit for purpose?

Elise stared at the bottles and tapped her fingers against her lips.

I know my way around Skarhult enough to go searching for materials now. And now we have income to spend.

She marched up to Anja's room, her eagerness dictating her speed.

Knocking on the door, she called out, "Anja? I am going to take the cable car into town to get some ingredients and bottles for scented oils. Would you like anything from Skarhult?"

"What? Hm. No, thank you. Take a key," Anja replied distractedly.

"Will do. See you shortly," Elise replied and hurried back downstairs.

Sitting in the chilly cable car, she pondered scents. What materials could she get? What would smell nice on the soft skin of Nessa's beautiful neck? What might Nessa like to smell on Elise? Was there a scent she could convince Anja to try? It was only when she was getting off at her stop that she realised she had not considered her own wishes and tastes.

Rose. I long for the smell of roses.

She missed a step. The smell of roses was as connected to

the court of Highmere as the Queen's cursed lavender perfume was. Why had she thought of roses? Elise growled. That horrible woman refused to fade into memory. Like an unresolved question, Queen Marianna was always in the back of Elise's mind.

Like a wound that refuses to scab over and bleeds every time it is touched.

Discomfort spread through her faster than the cold of the winter air. She tried to ignore it, busying herself with what she would buy and how much she was willing to spend.

She hurried along the street, passing people with hats pulled low and scarfs pulled up to their noses. A few nodded in greeting, which was more than she'd gotten back in Nightport. She found that she liked it here in this city of cold and blinding white. They celebrated what warmth they had and knew to be grateful for food and drink that didn't come readily from the snowy, hard ground. That was new to someone born a Noble.

This was why she adored the frost faire, it embodied the idea of taking hard living conditions and making them appear wondrous and magical. She gazed towards the river and considered going over there to see what the faire looked like in daylight. Was it even open? Would the faire seem mundane in the muted winter sunlight?

No, that had to wait. She needed glass bottles, strainers, labels, ready-made oil, or nuts to be squeezed into it, and... she tapped her gloved fingers against her thigh.

Oh! Herbs and dried flowers for scents. I saw a shop that sold scented oils, soaps, and cosmetics that first night in Skarhult when we bought clothes. Where was that?

She recalled the general direction of the shop and walked that way. After about half an hour, she found herself outside Sinclair's Scents.

Yes, this was it. A window filled with potpourri bags, soaps in all shapes, and minute bottles of scents of all kinds. A thrill rushed through her as she opened the door and stepped into a room so packed with fragrances that her head swam.

She walked straight over to a table with little glass bottles, some with ornate stoppers and some with plain corks. As she stood there, trying to figure out how much they cost, she overheard a man speaking with a woman in Arclidian. It was so uncommon to hear her language here, without it being directed at her, that she couldn't help perking her ears up.

"Genia, I am telling you... there is no obvious reason why that shop should suddenly be without customers. Everything is the same: staff, wares, and procedures. All which have made that shop flourish for years. And yet, it has been many weeks of little to no footfall."

"Perhaps customers simply want a change, yes? Or maybe more people can afford tailored clothes?" the woman replied in a thick Storsund accent. This 'Genia', Elise assumed.

The man grumbled. "Firstly, wanting a change would not keep them away this long. Secondly, my other second-hand clothing shops in Skarhult are doing well, so customers do not only want tailored clothes. No, it is *that* shop. I looked in before coming here, as it is just down the street. The shop was empty, the clothes hanging wretched and abandoned."

Elise squeezed one of the bottles in her hand. It was growing clear that this second-hand shop was the one where the Wayfarer-hating cashier had behaved so horribly towards her and Anja. This was the owner, lamenting his lack of customers. An issue she had probably caused by spreading the word of rats and moths in the shop. She chewed the inside of her cheek. Did he know of his staff's behaviour? Anja had claimed it was a common form of bigotry in the city. Perhaps he shared it.

Genia hummed. "Well, I don't know what to tell you. My

shop is doing well. You saw sales figures for this quarter, yes? We are making you a good bit of coin, Mr Sinclair."

"You are, indeed. Thank you for that and for letting me pour my complaints into your sympathetic ear. I simply cannot help but fret over that shop, as it has four employees who need to make a livelihood. I would hate to deprive them of that."

Elise put the bottle down. This man sounded like a good person. And if he wasn't, well, he still needed to know the truth. She strode towards the voices, which were coming from a curtain that parted the shop from some sort of backroom.

She cleared her throat. "Excuse me?"

A woman's head popped out from the curtain. She wore heavy amounts of cosmetics, and hair balanced on top of her head in a complicated up-do.

"Hello, miss. I will be with you shortly, yes?"

"Thank you, but it is your employer I wish to speak with. Mr Sinclair?"

The curtain was pulled aside, and a man stepped out. He was a severe-looking man, softened by kind eyes and wavy, greying brown hair and beard.

"May I help you?" he asked in a crisp Midlands accent.

"Yes. Well, as a matter of fact, I think I may be able to assist *you* with something. I could not help but overhear your discussion and can shed some light on what happened to that shop."

If he thought her eavesdropping rude, he didn't show it. "Really? If that is true, it would be most helpful."

"It is true. I know why the shop has few customers these days. I know, because I am the reason."

His dark eyebrows shot up his forehead. "Indeed?"

"Yes. Although I believe I had good cause. Do you know of your staff's prejudice towards Wayfarers?"

His eyebrows, having for a while retreated to their usual dwelling, shot back up. "No. Certainly not!"

"Well, the woman who served my wife, my friend, and me when we were there had a good helping of that frightful attitude. She served only my light-skinned and light-haired spouse, shunning me and my friend, who shares my colouring. My friend explained that she probably assumed we were Wayfarers and therefore was prejudiced towards us."

Mr Sinclair's mouth made a perfect O before the corners of his lips drew down in a deep frown. "If that is true, she has no place in my organisation. I know many people in Skarhult have that stance towards Wayfarers and the Viss, but I and those in my employ should never make anyone feel of lesser value. What did she look like?"

Elise described the woman in as much detail as she could remember.

His expression turned grim. "I know of whom you speak. Her name is Lena."

Behind him, Genia stepped forward. "Excuse me, Mr Sinclair?"

He turned. "Yes?"

"The lady bringing it up has reminded me of something, yes? Mrs Sten who runs that shop has been rude about Wayfarers and Viss in the past. When I confronted her about it, she always said they were jokes and apologised. But now, I wonder. Perhaps her opinions have trickled down onto her staff? At least on young Lena."

Mr Sinclair looked even grimmer still. "I see. It seems I must speak to them both, or possibly to the entire workforce."

"Perhaps so. The young lad who works there also tends to curse a lot, yes? In case you wish to speak to him about that," Genia added, clearly warming to the subject.

Sinclair nodded absently. Then he looked back to Elise. "May I ask how this is connected to you and the shop being abandoned? Did you tell people of the bigotry you experienced in the shop?"

Elise squirmed. "Well, yes and no. I felt furious and helpless when I understood this to be a common attitude towards a whole group of people, even though I do not actually belong to that group—"

"I thought not. Few Wayfarers have a Midlands accent," Sinclair pointed out.

Elisandrine ignored the interruption and carried on. "It angered me to the point where I had to do something. So, I did the only thing I could think of." She steeled herself. "I told customers that there were vermin in the shop and that the shop's standards had dropped. I told them to spread the news to get people to stay away. Clearly it worked. Perhaps I should have contacted you, but I do not see how I could have reached you. I was new to the city, cold and tired."

They both gawped at her. Then Sinclair began to laugh, Genia soon chiming in.

"Clever! Perhaps not the right thing to do. But clever, yes?" Genia said through chuckles.

Elise shrugged, relief flooding through her at the lack of a reprimand.

Sinclair peered at her. "So. You are clearly from the Midlands, like me. I hail from Chislehurst. May I ask where you are from?"

"I was born in Silverton but moved to Highmere. Then to," she stopped herself from mentioning Silver Hollow Castle, "Nightport and then some weeks ago I took the journey over here."

He smiled. "Well-travelled, I see. Enjoying Storsund?"

"A great deal. The people are kind and the snow is beautiful. Oh, I forgot to introduce myself! My name is Elise Glass. Pleasure to meet you."

He took her hand and kissed it. "Carlton Sinclair at your

service. Now, Mrs Glass. I should like to help you in some way, mainly because I wish to make up for your awful experience in my shop, but also to assist a fellow Arclidian here on this vast, cold continent. As you have only been here for some weeks, do you require a position?"

"A position? No, I have a job. I take dictation for a historian." She glanced at the bottles she had been perusing, an idea forming. "Although, if I were to try my hand at making something. Say... scented oils. Would you be willing to sell them?"

He rubbed the left side of his beard, silent for a few seconds. "Perhaps. It would depend upon the quality of the products."

Genia placed her hand on his arm. "You know, if they're good oils, they might come in handy. As I mentioned, we're selling splendidly, yes? Customers want more soaps, scents, and potpourris than we can supply..." She trailed off before picking up with renewed vigour. "This gives me an idea. We need more space and more products, yes?"

He ran his hand over the right side of his beard this time. "Go on."

"If we took over the second-hand shop, cleaned it out, got new signs, painted it, put new staff in and sold other products... it would wipe out the bad smell of bigotry and the rumour of vermin. And we'll have a store in which to sell more products, yes?"

Sinclair looked from Genia to Elise and then back to Genia again.

"And if this lady manages to make good scented oils..."

Genia smirked, interlocking the fingers of her clasped hands. "Then we market them as exotic Arclidian wares. Made by an actual Midlands lady." She turned to Elise. "Don't fret. I know you're not a Noble lady. What would one of those be doing here? If they even came to our continent, they'd send a servant to shop. It doesn't matter if you're *actually* a lady. It is sales talk, yes?"

Normal breathing resumed, Elise replied. "Naturally. Sound like a splendid idea. Everyone desires some luxury, clean skin, and to smell good. This city has lots of tailors and second-hand clothing shops, but not many places to buy fragrances. You should open another one, and yes, give my oils a chance."

Mr Sinclair kept running his hand over his dark beard, but more slowly, as if unaware he was doing it. "I do wish to do you a good turn, and I appear to require more merchandise now. Fine, bring me samples of your oils. If they are suitable, we shall buy some to sell here. If they are *excellent*, they will be part of the base of my new fragrance shop." He pointed a finger at her. "Now, excellent means a lovely scent, an attractive label, and long-lasting fragrance. People will not buy oils that stop giving scent after an hour."

Elise bit her lip to keep from whooping. "Certainly! Thank you. Well then, I should go back to shopping for bottles, sieves, herbs, and dried flowers."

He nodded and returned behind the curtain with Genia, leaving Elise with a shop filled with luxurious ingredients and a tingle in her stomach.

Back at the house with new ingredients and materials, she stared at the jars of already made oils in disappointment. Sure, she could bottle them and create labels to make them pretty. Perhaps even add some colour to the oil to make them stand out. It still wouldn't change that they'd been made with old, dried herbs. Neither strong in scent nor long-lasting. She squared her shoulders. She would simply have to find a way to strengthen and complicate their scent. Quickly.

She looked over at the warm bowls of oils they had managed to amass. There should be enough to fill the twenty pretty bottles she had bought at a discount. But how to improve them? Elise stared at the bowls, pondering which scents stayed longest on the skin. The answer was simple: ones mixed with alcohol. But purified alcohol was expensive and not kind on the skin. Besides, it reminded her too much of the Queen. No, Elise's scents were oil-based, that was part of the brand which was forming in her mind. Exclusive, caring, natural, rich, sweet. That meant oils and not sharp, purified alcohol.

Alcohol.

Elise stopped dead. She glanced up at the large decanter of black wine Anja always kept on the counter, next to the bread bin.

She contemplated the contents of black wine. Blackberry wine, honey, and… ebony root. A root known to always keep its black colour, thick texture, and aniseed-like smell. Perhaps it could prolong scents without the negative effects of alcohol?

She shook her head.

Surely some chemist or other scholar would have thought of that? Still, it cannot hurt to try it in a few of the bottles.

It would at least give them a unique base scent, viscosity, and colour. She took the lid off the first bowl, which contained dried winter cherries and dammon nut oil, and sieved it. Then she funnelled some into a bottle, heart pounding with excitement. She retrieved some ebony root from the spice cabinet. Fresh would have been better, but for her experiment, this would do. She topped up the bottle with the black granules, put the stopper on, and shook it. She'd have to upend it several times a day, forcing the ingredients to mix.

Biting her lip, Elise considered the ground ebony root. Moments ticked by. Then she made a decision to trust her impulse. After all, that was how she had lived her whole life.

She'd make half of the finished oils with ebony root and the rest with just oil and the scents. She had three bases, now she just had to choose what went with what. She mixed the meadowsweet with lemon rind, the watermint with the winter cherries, and the lemongrass with violet, all offsetting sweetness with freshness. She could only hope that Sinclair's customers would share her scent preferences.

She chuckled, hearing it echo in the empty kitchen.

Papa, remember how you used to laugh when I put flowers together not because of how they looked, but how they would smell together?

She closed her eyes and conjured an image of him.

You were always so proud of my peculiarly keen sense of smell. I think I can finally use that skill. To bring in coin. To be creative and to enjoy my work.

She brushed away memories, hope, and grief. That could wait for the notebook if she felt like writing in it tonight.

Now she had to focus. Had to remember that the scents would change as they infused, especially those with the added aniseed scent of the ebony root. Also, to turn them several times a day to mix them. She had to get this right. This was her chance to show that a quick-to-emotion Noble girl could do more than inspire others. Time to show that she could be the main attraction, not merely a decorative supporting act.

She got to work, and when she finished, she beamed at the bottles. Half of them were in light yellows, pinks, and greens, while the others darkened and thickened with the ebony root. She hoped the ebony root ones would work best, it could become her trademark. Arclid was known to be old and dark, she had met enough people from the other continents to know that. If her Arclid-branded oils looked dark and thick – with a hint of smoky aniseed lingering behind the more pervasive top notes – it would make her oils unique.

Anja came down, probably for more coffee.

"My. That's a lot of pretty little bottles."

Elise blew out a breath. "Yes. I am going to sell them in Skarhult."

True to form, Anja began making coffee. "Really? How do you plan to do that?"

"Is that *doubt* in your voice? Well, quash that right away. When I was in town buying materials for the oils, I ran into a man who wishes to stock my oils. Well, no, he wants to try them and then decide if he will stock them."

"In that case, I'm sure he will. Take it from someone who's had weeks to learn, if Elise Glass has decided on something, it'll happen."

Elise did a double-take. She had expected to have to defend herself further. To fight to be taken seriously.

Tentatively, she reached out a hand and rested it on Anja's shoulder. "Thank you. Even though I am aware that you were only complaining about me forcing my dictation services on you." Elise added a smirk to show that there were no hard feelings.

Anja stopped making coffee and looked at her, those bright green eyes grave. "I wasn't. I haven't known you that long, but I've picked up that you're a determined person and that you…" She hesitated. "You have that air about you. The kind that tells people that you're destined for something more. Something bigger."

Elise was speechless, a rare sensation for her. She let go of Anja's shoulder and began fidgeting with the high collar of her dress. "I… hope you are right. I should like to be able to earn decent coin. Then Nessa would not need to worry so. And I could treat us. Perhaps take you and Nessa out for fine meals in the city?"

Anja scrunched up her nose. "Why would I want to go somewhere to eat? I have a kitchen, cutlery, tables, and chairs right here."

Elise quirked an eyebrow. "Variation, perhaps?"

"Phah! I suppose I'll go if you wish. But we were talking about your oil business. Start small, work yourself to the bone, and dream big. If I hadn't dared to do that, I'd still be working at the school. Frittering my inheritance on wine and regretting never writing my book. You need to find what makes you happy, what drives you."

Elise gazed at the fogged-up window. "I have always enjoyed scents. I like how much they can change if combined. Something simple gets mixed with something plain, and together they become extraordinary. It is like magic."

Anja resumed making coffee. "There you go then. That's your dream. As I made writing this book mine, and Nessa is out there fulfilling her dreams of creating," she waved her hand around, "glass thingamabobs."

Elise laughed but stopped as Anja's words sank in.

"Huh. Nessa wants to turn sand and a few simple components into practical yet beautiful objects. You want to combine your knowledge and some paper into a book to entertain and inform. Now…" She looked around the kitchen for the right words. "I know that I want to blend aromatic items and oils into scents. Ones people can wear to drown out the foul smells and dreariness of everyday life. It is perhaps not as practical or useful as both your dreams. Maybe it is frivolous or vain. Nevertheless, it is somehow important to me."

"It'll bring people joy. Few things are more important than that, Elise." Anja inclined her head and smiled.

Filled with a new sense of purpose, Elise returned the smile before fetching Anja's favourite mug for her. Those shared smiles felt a lot like belonging.

CHAPTER 17
DON'T THINK

When Fabian handed Nessa the blowpipe, she took it with greater confidence than the first time Secilia Brownlee had handed her one back in Nightport. At least she was growing in confidence when it came to glass. She began huffing air into the blowpipe, expanding the blob of molten glass at the end. Her master cheered her on, making her grateful that the heat and exertion covered her blushing.

"Most excellent, Mrs Glass. Today we will make glass bowls. Pretty little things, to hold berries or candied fruits. You know what sort of bowls I mean, yes?"

"Yes. Dessert bowls. Ornate ones, by the sound of it?"

"Exactly. Must be pretty as a sunrise. We have an order for two dozen, for Joiners Square if you can believe it! An honour. Even if they are corrupt, power-hungry uniform monkeys."

Nessa handed him back the blowpipe. "Uniform monkeys?"

"Yes. All dressed up in those tight, woollen uniforms. You've seen them, yes? Ugly grey with silver buttons. Collar up to their chin and with little fur-blanket for the shoulders."

Nessa sniggered. "I think you call it a cape. Or cloak. Maybe a stole?"

"Whatever." He blew into the pipe to keep the glass from receding. "They're everywhere, yes? Wanting coin and to know what all citizens are doing. Kicking those who do not have a voice with steel-tipped boots. Following orders blindly, not caring about anyone. So yes, uniform monkeys."

Nessa frowned. "Everyone here talks about Joiners Square taking over everything and that the government isn't really in charge? I don't understand it. Arclid is ruled by the Queen with the help of her advisors. It is that simple. Here on the other hand—"

Fabian interrupted by clicking his tongue. "Here, not so simply. You're right. Joiners Square run the country and make us all pretend they're don't. Through bribes and threats, they make us talk about a government which is actually only puppets."

"I have had the basics explained to me. First, they formed a much-needed union, like other trades did as well. But then their leaders began growing their union into some sort of shadowy organisation, it grew in coin and prestige until they were involved in all parts of the running of Storsund. Right so far?"

"Yes."

"Next question then." Nessa scratched the back of her neck. "What is a joiner?"

Fabian huffed into the blowpipe again and picked up a tool with his free hand. "Joiners are similar to carpenters but only do certain things, yes? I can't explain better. Ask someone else. I use glass, not wood."

He paused to use the tool known as large tweezers to begin moulding the orange blob. Nessa watched intently, itching to try using the tweezers. Still, deep in her stomach lurked that old fear of failing, of disappointing her master, and as it flared up, she was glad that she was only watching for now.

Fabian switched tools and carried on speaking. "It all came from them having been so badly treated that they became aggressive, yes? They fought their employers, and when that fight was over, they simply kept fighting. Until they had fought their way to power."

"And then they grew?"

"Yes, by recruiting other trade unions first. Then the military. Our soldiers were eager to fight but had not been in a war since the last time we fought the Western Isles, about a hundred years ago, yes? All those violent, bored fighters fit in perfectly with the angry joiners." He paused to manoeuvre the glass and glanced over to Nessa.

She nodded to his unasked question. "I'm watching what you're doing *and* listening. Please carry on, master."

"Good. Where was I? Oh yes. Then they gathered the rich folk who wanted more than sitting at home eating cakes, like your Nobles do, yes? They gave them power and 'gods' to worship – the war lords which now lead the organisation." He paused to wipe his brow on his sleeve. "Then Joiners Square took over all trade, calling themselves the Storsund Trading Company and reaching their power as far into the other continents as they could, yes? After that – the schools."

"Schools? Why? What could they want with children?"

"Not children. Young adults and teachers with the sharpest new minds. Inventors, yes? Paying them to come up with steam power, gas lighting, and then things like factories and trains. That is why we have knowledge and things that the other continents do not have."

"I see. My landlady, and friend, mentioned that not everyone here supports them?"

The glass was now bowl-shaped. Fabian switched tools again. "No. But most people pretend to, yes? Joiners Square can raise our taxes, push our nation into a war, plant evidence on us, or just start killing us off for being traitors. They also reward any regular citizen who spies on their neighbours. Makes it hard to keep secrets as you never know who will sell you out to the uniform monkeys, yes?"

Nessa swallowed hard, paranoia creating a lump in her throat as well as an ache in her chest. She glanced at her master.

Surely, I can trust him? He wouldn't be talking like this if he was one of their civilian informants. Still, what have I told him about me and Elise?

She tried to listen to his words, watch his actions, and at the same time replay every conversation she had carried out with him.

He continued speaking, clearly unaware of her panic. "Some people do dare to stand up to them, like the Viss and the Wayfarers."

"Because Joiners Square believes that the Sund area and the Sundish people are the real Storsund?"

"Yes. Very stupid. Still, the Wayfarers and the Viss need to stay nonthreatening or they get… eh…"

"Persecuted?" Nessa suggested.

"Yes, persek… pers… that. So, their defiance, as well as that of any Sund people who are brave enough, stays underground. It's seen as shameful if you do not support Joiners Square. Your neighbours will whisper and glare at you, yes? People worship the top uniform monkeys as gods." He snorted. "Grand Marshall Karlberg and High Captain Nordhall – people actually pray to them. Even your Queen likes them, everyone knows they make deals together."

Nessa grimaced. "Your nickname makes sense then. I'll be careful in any dealings with them."

"Good, good. Now, less talking and more making bowls.

Time to decorate this with pretty swirls. I'll show you and then you'll do second one, yes? Ready?"

Nessa swallowed. "I suppose I'll have to be."

"You will be fine. Don't think too much, yes? Just do."

~

It was nearing midnight. Anja was upstairs, probably sound asleep. Nessa and Elise were laying on the sofa which served as Nessa's bed, cuddling while discussing Joiners Square.

As they spoke, Elise drew circles on Nessa's stomach with her fingertips. She had opened the buttons leading down to the waist of Nessa's new wool nightdress. Elise's fingers moved rhythmically around her belly, not gentle enough to tickle and not hard enough to be uncomfortable. She had learned exactly how Nessa liked to be touched.

Elise hummed. "So, Joiners Square really are pulling all the strings from the shadows?"

"Yes. Fabian said that all Storsund people know about it. But they're either too scared to act or they don't mind, as long as they make good coin, have homes with all the modern conveniences, and handsome Joiners Square soldiers making them feel safe and proud. Some people even report other's secrets and personal affairs to Joiners Square for favours or coin." She shivered at the icy tendrils of paranoia sliding down her spine. "Do you think we have to worry about that? About someone reporting us?"

Elise hummed. "I think not. We have kept our secrets, and no one here knows our faces. Furthermore, they would report to Joiners Square, not the Queen. Try not to fret so much, heartling. You will wear out your heart by making it pound this fast."

Nessa took a deep breath. "I'll try. Anyway, that's why most people here don't question Joiners Square."

"What a contrast to Arclid. If the royals even sneeze too loud we revolt."

"I know," Nessa said, absorbed by the subject. "Apparently, the Viss and the Wayfarers have tried to make Sund people see the dangers of having an organisation with its own motives controlling their nation but failed. The Sunds just keep quiet and carry on because they end up with most of the coin and land due to Joiners Square. The few that have rebelled have been imprisoned or shunned from society, forced to live underground."

It hadn't escaped Nessa's attention that Elise's fingers were tracing those circles lower now, brushing over the line of downy hairs leading from Nessa's navel down to her groin.

"Interesting, in a frightening way," Elise said. "Meanwhile, we have now covered my day and my successes with the oils. Then we spoke of your glassblowing. And now you have enlightened me regarding Storsund's strange rulers. What is next on the agenda? Hm?"

Her fingers made circles even lower, moving past the nightdress' buttons and below the fabric, into the mass of curls.

Nessa gasped and through clenched teeth whispered, "Elise! We're trying not to do that here again, remember? It's not fair on Anja or proper form to fu... have *amorous congress* here."

Elise hummed in agreement, but those fingers kept making circles in the pubic hair. Nessa stifled a thrilled giggle. "Heartling, consider how mortified she would be. Gods, think how mortified *I* would be."

Elise's fingers slipped lower, and she smiled as Nessa moaned in response. "Do you want me to stop? If so, I will cease immediately. However, considering how slick and puffed-up your petals are, I think you want me to continue."

"I do," Nessa whimpered. "Please don't stop."

Elise fingers grew more confident.

Nessa had to bite her lip to keep from moaning. "Just be quick, and if I get too loud, cover... m-my mouth with your free hand."

"Anything you want, my cherished," Elise purred and began kissing her neck.

~

It must have been twenty minutes later. Or maybe twenty-five. Nessa couldn't tell. She couldn't sense anything but her own pleasure mingling with frustration. Her struggle to climax had reared its ugly head again. Elise had tried with fingers and tongue, she had even made Nessa touch herself to see if she was missing a trick. All to no avail.

"I'm sorry," Nessa murmured, defeat weighing her down.

Elise kissed her, whispering, "No need to ever apologise, my dove. It is only because you are trying so hard to be quiet that it is not working."

Nessa sighed as quietly as she could. "You know it's not that simple. This happens every third time we make love, and it was constant before I met you. I don't know how to mend what's wrong with me."

"Heartling. Please do not see it like that. There is nothing 'wrong' with you, you are just different. We knew that you can physically manage a climax. It merely does not come easy to you, pardon the pun."

Nessa decided to ask the question she could no longer ignore. "Since it doesn't seem to be my body causing it, do you think... there's something wrong with my mind?"

Elise hummed softly. "Not *wrong*. But it is probably what is causing your issue. Do you not think?"

Nessa readjusted against the hard pillow. "You're the expert on bedding women. You tell me."

"Heartling, I have experience with women, but no expertise with this. I doubt there *is* an expert on this. Physicians do not seem to care about women's pleasure, only about if we can conceive." Elise paused to intensify their eye contact. "However, I do know that you should never apologise or feel bad about it. All it means is that I get the great joy of trying a little longer – which means touching you more – which is marvellous."

Nessa tried to smile. "Thank you. I'm so glad to be able to talk to you about it and that you want to help."

"No need to even mention it, my cherished. What is important is that it all feels good, is fun, and allows us to be intimate, right?" She paused to nuzzle Nessa's nose. "There is no obligation to end our lovemaking with an orgasm. I have often engaged in bedplay where I satisfied the other woman and that was it. Climaxes are not the be all and end all."

"R-really?" Nessa asked, unable to meet her eye.

Elise sought her gaze and finally got it. "Of course not, sweetest heart. I simply want to make you feel good and for you to sense how much I love you."

Affection seemed to spread from Nessa's heart out into every limb. "You're so lovely."

"No, merely a decent human being who loves you." Elise's face lit up. "Oh, I know what we can try! If you still want to try? Turn around and bite the pillow. It will stifle sound, and it is a good position for strong orgasms."

"All right."

Nessa got into place but couldn't help worrying about how long this was taking. She had hoped to have peaked and to be on her way to pleasing Elise by now. She sucked in a deep breath.

One more try. If it doesn't work now, I'll take her up on her offer of skipping the orgasm tonight.

Nessa lay on her front. Soon Elise mounted her, laying

down and draping herself over her like a warm blanket. A blanket with clever fingers.

Nessa bit down on the pillow, annoyed and distracted by the taste of lye soap and faint hint of the goose feathers below the pillowcase.

Elise's fingers were making circles again, but urgent, more precise circles on the little pearl which held Nessa's pleasure. Or rather withheld it at the moment.

Nessa closed her eyes and kept repeating in her mind, *Don't think. Just feel. Relax. Feel.*

Elise was licking at her ear, nibbling on her earlobe.

Nessa began moving her hips, meeting Elise's fingers and adding to the friction. It felt good, almost good enough to make her stop listening for the creak of the upstairs floor-boards which would tell her that Anja was awake and on her way down.

Suddenly Elise released the earlobe and whispered so quietly that Nessa could only hear it because it was spoken into the shell of her ear. "That's it, my naughty vixen. Lay there and let me do whatever I please with you. *I want you so badly.*"

Nessa noticed her every muscle tensing and heard her own needy, animalistic groan into the pillow.

Elise purred. "You liked that? My, you are gushing now. Ah, I think I know how to distract your overactive mind. I need to… talk to you."

Nessa nodded, hoping Elise would feel the movement of her head.

"What exactly was it that did the trick, hm? Did you like me taking charge? Did you like me calling you naughty? Did you like hearing me say how much I wanted you?"

"Taking charge," Nessa moaned, muffled by the pillow.

"Mm. Good. I will continue to take what I want then, and tell you all about it," Elise whispered. "I desire every voluptuous, magnificent part of you, but especially the one I am toying with right now. It. Is. Mine."

These last words were punctuated by deft fingers on her slick pearl. Whimpering into the pillow, Nessa nodded again. Her pleasure and need were rising, like waves threatening to crash over her. She wasn't afraid anymore. Elise would take care of everything, Elise knew what was best.

"You feel so good. I never want to stop taking you from behind like this. Your only task is to lay there and *let me have you*," Elise whispered, her usual silver bell voice now lower and dominating.

Another whimper into the pillow, this one even needier. Elise taking her was all that she wanted. There was such a pleasure in all decisions and responsibility disappearing. If Anja found them, if Nessa couldn't finish... none of that was her concern anymore. Elise would handle it. Nessa smiled and let the pillow stifle another of her moans.

Elise made a wanton purring sound before licking the outer rim of Nessa's ear. Her fingers were moving faster now, sliding easily through soaked heat as she whispered, "Shame I was not in your life earlier. You would not have had to wait so long for your first climax. I would have spent every evening sneaking into the barn with you, to seduce and take you like this. Over and over again. Mercilessly."

Hands gripping the sheet underneath, Nessa whimpered and bucked. She was so close. Anxious thoughts still struggled to break through, but Elise's words were drowning them out.

"I can feel you nearing it. Give in. Now," Elise growled.

Nessa's eyes rolled back as the orgasm took over her, making each muscle spasm and filling every nerve and vein with hot, rushing pleasure. The world faded into background noise. All she knew was sensation. After a moment or an eternity, she heard Elise croon in her ear, "Good, let it take you over. You are doing so well, my heartling.".

As Elise held her tight through the last throes of climax, Nessa's rock-stiff body morphed into softest clay. Everything was warm, comfortable, and relaxed now. When she regained the power to speak, Nessa broke her mouth free of the pillow and rasped, "Thank you."

Elise gently kissed her ear. "No need to thank me. You never need to thank me. I love you and pleasuring you is my favourite pastime. However, if you do want to show your gratitude, contract *those* muscles."

Nessa knew exactly what was expected of her and grinned. She flexed the strong muscles in her rear and felt Elise begin to slide over them, always finishing the motion over Nessa's unusually protruding tailbone. A few minutes of increasingly fast riding, and Elise climaxed, barely stifling her usual yelp when the pleasure crested.

Elisandrine slid down next to Nessa, the two of them barely fitting in the narrow space.

"I…" Elise paused to catch her breath before continuing to whisper. "I think we will have to stop there for tonight. It is getting late and I am," her eyes fluttered closed, "wearied."

"Agreed," Nessa murmured back.

Everything was still so warm and lovely. Nessa was sated, in love, and oh-so sleepy. She'd tell Elise to move back to the bed soon and go to sleep. Just a little more cuddling. Just one more minute.

Nessa woke to being kicked in the leg. She could hear laughter, hoarse but heartfelt laughter. Her eyes flew open, and she heard Elise gasp next to her. Nessa pulled the covers over them while trying to remember how to breathe properly. Then, steeling herself, she looked up.

Anja stood next to them with a cup of coffee in one hand

and a snoozing Svarte squeezed between her chest and her prosthetic arm. "Ha! Someone didn't make it back to their own bed last night, hm?"

"I am... s-so sorry. I..." Nessa trailed off.

Elise bailed her out. "We are dreadfully sorry that you had to see that. Even more sorry that we could not control ourselves while under your roof."

Anja tutted. "Oh, for snow's sake. As if I didn't expect a young couple to have some *horizontal refreshments* once in a while. I'm only amusing myself. Look at your faces! Svarte, see how embarrassed humans can get. Silly, yes?"

The cat's ears flicked at the mention of his name, but otherwise he didn't move.

"You're heavy when you sleep," Anja said and put him down clumsily. "Anyway, you two clean up, stop blushing, and then light that fire before we all freeze to death. Porridge will be done soon."

She walked away, chuckling while sipping coffee.

Nessa buried her face in her hands. "Gods-cursed oxen-shit."

Elise blew out a breath. "Well, at least she is more cheerful these days."

Nessa groaned and fell back onto the pillow.

CHAPTER 18

A CLARIFICATION, AN
OPPORTUNITY, AND AN
INTERVIEW

S tanding in the kitchen, Elise scrutinised the two scent
bottles in her hands. Or rather, their labels, which
stated what the oil was scented with and above that,
the words *Lady of Arclid* in a swirling script. Her oils had been
stocked in Sinclair's Scents for a week now and these two were
the only ones yet to sell, so she had taken them home again.
They were without the ebony root and therefore less potent
and less long-lasting.

Poor things. Oh well!

Elise sung a little under her breath as she thought of how
the ones with ebony root had flown off the shelves. The experiment had paid off! Everyone asked her what her secret ingredient was. So far, only Nessa and Anja knew.

She ran her fingers over one of the bottle labels. "Nessa, do
you mind the brand?"

Turning with a perplexed look, Nessa paused her conversation with Anja. "The brand?"

"Sorry to interrupt. I am somewhat... concerned about
the brand name of my oils. Mr Sinclair thought they would

sell better with this title, but I am aware that the one who taught me to make them was you, who in turn were taught by your mother."

Nessa smiled. "Yes. So?"

Elise fidgeted with the bottles.

I wish she would be quicker to catch up so I did not have to spell everything out.

With a tight swallow, Elise replied, "So, I could not bear you feeling that I am taking credit for something that your mother taught us. Or that I am erasing the fact that a commoner, not a lady, came up with the recipe. It would vex me greatly to know that I hurt or offended anyone, especially your family."

Nessa came closer. "Heartling, no. A lot of people make these oils. Mum doesn't have some sort of patent on squeezing nut oil. Or sticking herbs and dried flora in it. Besides, you were the one who thought to add the ebony root."

"Brilliant idea, by the way," Anja added before having a sip of coffee.

Elise softened her taut jaw. "I am glad to hear it. If you do at all mind, though, rest assured that I shall clear up any misconceptions at any given opportunity. For example, Mr Sinclair asked where I learned to make these oils."

Nessa tilted her head. "And what did you say?"

"I said I was taught the basic recipe by my mother-in-law and named her. Was that acceptable?"

Nessa gently took the bottles out of her hand and placed them on the table. "It was lovely. And I know Mum would be proud to be known as the mother-in-law of such a successful, charming woman."

Elise looked down, trying to keep her bashful smile out of view.

"Hey, come here," Nessa said and pulled her into a kiss.

Anja had her back to them, refilling her coffee. "Your

oils are popular. When people find out what's in them, where the recipe's from, and how nice the original sugar pumpkin oil is – the Clays could do well for themselves. They grow sugar pumpkins, have dammon nuts growing on their grounds, *and* make the original oils… They could rake in a fortune."

Through the kiss, Elise heard Anja sigh, snigger, and add, "But I see I'm talking to myself now. Young love is rude. You two enjoy your kissing and I'll take my coffee and join the cat by the fireplace."

～

As time passed, Elise found herself busier than ever. Her oils had been requested long after her first batch had been sold out. After that, it was a matter of waiting for the second batch to finish infusing. Thus, the following weeks rushed past in a happy blur of dictation, oil-making, and acclimatising to her new home.

After around a month of Elise using the cable car to deliver her oils in bags only to have them sell out so fast that she must hurry to make the trip again, it was decided that she should increase production. A horse and cart came for the next double-sized batch. She was frantically busy. And adoring it.

It was about midday on a day when the snow had just begun falling. Anja and Elise had finished dictating and were discussing lunch when there was a forceful knock on the door. Elisandrine went to open it and was faced with Carlton Sinclair, dressed in black fur and a velvet top hat.

"Hello, Mrs Glass. I trust I am not disturbing? I meant to pay you a visit earlier in the day, but I fear work intervened."

"Oh, not at all. Please come in, Mr Sinclair."

She offered him a seat on the sofa, which he took while brushing snowflakes off of his hat. "Thank you. I shall not be detaining you for long. I merely wanted to give you some good news and discuss an exciting idea. Well, two ideas."

"I shall be glad to hear them. May I offer you water or coffee before we start? Some leaf tea perhaps?"

"No, thank you. After this I am meeting a supplier over lunch."

Elise smoothed her skirt underneath her and sat down on the other side of the sofa. "I see. Well then, what was it you wished to discuss?"

He adjusted his sitting position so they were facing each other. "I should like to start by telling you that your oils are now outselling our other scented oils. You have even enticed some of the alcohol-based fragrance crowd to try your products."

Elise had no doubt her smile was ridiculously big. "I am thrilled to hear it! Thank you."

"No need to thank me for the truth, Mrs Glass. It seems that secret ingredient of yours has intrigued and won over the customers. Will you still not tell me what it is?"

Elise clasped her hands in her lap. "Afraid not, Mr Sinclair. I must protect my unique selling point. Let me just say that it is a mix of ingredients. Perfectly harmless but quite complicated."

Elise was facing the kitchen while Sinclair was not. Therefore, it was only she who saw Anja hold up the almost empty ebony root spice jar and make a theatrically sad face. That was the second jar Anja had needed to buy because her lodger used it all for her scented oils. Elise shot her a glare. She didn't want Sinclair seeing the jar and connecting the dots. Although she doubted anyone would believe that such a mundane article like ebony root could be her big secret.

"Ah. Well, as you please, Mrs Glass. The next step is to keep your customers while also continuing to attract new ones. One way to achieve that is to expand the range. Keep the oils you have, but add some new exotic ones as well? What do you say?"

"That sounds marvellous! Did you have any scents in mind?"

Sinclair jerked his head back. "Me? No, not at all. I am a business man, not a creator. My brain sees only opportunities and numbers. You could, however, speak to Genia. She has worked with fragrances for near thirty years."

Elise hesitated. "There are a few scents I had considered. Arclidian sugar pumpkins being one of them."

"Ah, from the original recipe, I seem to recall? How I miss having sunberry tarts with sugar pumpkin sauce. The taste of home. Do you miss the Midlands?"

Elise had a mental image of Highmere, blindingly white and pink in the sharp sun. "Some of it," she replied, clasping her hands painfully tight in her lap.

He searched her face for a moment and then cleared his throat. "Ah. Well. Yes, let us return to business."

"Yes," Elise said, faking a smile.

The wrinkle between his eyes smoothed as he sat forward. "Oh! I almost forgot the best piece of news. I have been contacted by the *Skarhult Chronicle*. Do you know that publication?"

"I am afraid not."

"It is our biggest magazine. A messenger brought me the letter from them this morning, in which they asked if the mysterious 'Arclidian Lady' of scented oil fame would be willing to do a quick interview. They have never asked to inter-view any of my other suppliers, so this is a tremendous honour."

Elise's stomach was all aflutter. "Really? They are interested in me?"

Have I truly achieved something more than charming people or getting into trouble?

He pointed at her with his top hat, all smiles. "Yes! They have yet to fill the edition which comes out the day after tomorrow and so wish to devote a small column to your oils."

Elise adjusted her hair. "Oh! Oh my. I... do not know what to say."

"Say you are interested! It would be a golden opportunity to spread the news about your new range of scents. This is how you get your oils into every home in Skarhult."

There was no denying it. Confidence was taking root in her chest and slowly blossoming, spreading little tendrils of pride throughout her.

"Yes. I shall gladly do the interview."

"Splendid!" He stood up and replaced his hat. "I shall leave you to ponder new scents while I take the cable car to my luncheon. Do contact Genia if you need advice, she has grown quite fond of you."

"I will. May I ask when the reporter will come to speak to me? And where?"

"Oh, of course. Pardon my haste. I shall tell her to come here. Unless you wish to meet at a coffeehouse or tea parlour in town? The *Chronicle*'s dreary offices are not fit for outsiders, they rarely do interviews there."

"Either will be fine."

He walked towards the door. "Right. I shall contact her today and send a messenger to you as soon as I know."

"Excellent. I hope your luncheon goes well."

"Thank you. And I wish you a splendid day, Mrs Glass."

"Same to you, Mr Sinclair." She closed the door after him and looked towards the kitchen where she could just make out Anja crouching on the floor, tickling Svarte's chin.

Elise joined them. "Did you hear all that?"

"It's not in my nature to eavesdrop," Anja replied, still scratching the cat's chin.

"But you may have picked up that I am to be in the papers?"

Anja looked up with a smile. "Yes. Congratulations! You deserve it. Seems like I might be losing my assistant soon. Not to mention all my ebony root."

Elise rolled her eyes. "I still have time to take dictation. Furthermore, I shall buy you a whole shelf of jars of ebony root. And a cake as a thank-you."

Anja scoffed. "The ebony root will do nicely. Now, food. Sandwiches or fried porridge?"

"Oh, sandwiches. Absolutely sandwiches," Elise said with a grimace which made her hostess laugh.

The next day, Elise was perched on the edge of the sofa, waiting for her interview. She had physically prepared as best she could in Anja's small mirror. Her eyes were now lined in black, cheeks blushed, and her mouth tinted a subtle red. Her hair had been combed to perfection and scented with her watermint and winter cherry oil.

She had practised her answers regarding herself and her oils, putting extra focus on how not to divulge the secret ingredient or how she was discovered by Sinclair. Not to mention the important lie about coming to Storsund with her wife for an adventure and a change of scenery. The secrecy made her head swim.

Perhaps this was a bad idea. Is it too late to cancel? Perhaps I can say I have contracted some ailment. Have I had the measles? Wait... is that an illness or a small furry animal?

She kept blinking at the door while her mind whirred. From upstairs she heard Anja pacing, as she often did when she was pondering a new chapter or trying to remember a fact from some old tome. Usually Elise found the sound soothing.

Now the steps sounded like seconds ticking away until the reporter would arrive.

A knock on the door nearly gave her a heart attack. She smoothed down her dress, breathed deep to quell her nerves, and opened the door with what she hoped was a charming smile.

A woman of her own colouring and height returned the smile. She was wearing spectacles and a simple wool coat in darkest green. "Hello. Mrs Glass, yes? My name is Sara Kvist. I'm with the *Skarhult Chronicle*. May I come in?"

"Well met. Yes, I am Elise Glass." Elise recalled her manners and stepped aside. "Naturally. Come in."

"Thank you." The reporter stomped snow off her boots before entering. "So, *Glass*. That name is not common, I think?"

"It is rather common in Arclid, where my wife and I hail from."

Sara's eyes twinkled. "Ah, my editor mentioned that you were from the little green continent, yes? Finally, a chance to practice my Arclidian!"

"I am relieved you do not wish to conduct the interview in Sundish. I have begun studying your language. Thus far I am fairly decent at understanding it but frightful at speaking it."

Sara waved the notion away. "Worry not. I need to practice my languages if I'm to fulfil my plan of travelling the orb, bringing back reports from distant lands, yes?"

"Good for you! Travelling washes the eyes and grows the soul. It will suit you." Elise breathed in, feeling some confidence settle with the air in her lungs.

You know how to play the social game, especially if you can use flirtation to oil the wheels. Only remember to keep the secrets and not flirt too much.

"I think so, too. May I sit?"

"Oh! Where are my manners? Of course. Please sit," Elise

said, indicating the sofa. "Would you like any refreshments? Drinks or something to nibble on, perhaps?"

Sara was fetching a notepad and pencil from her satchel bag. "Maybe a glass of water, yes? Long conversations go better if you keep your throat from going dry, I think."

"Agreed. I shall return with two glasses of water."

Walking to the kitchen, Elise noted more of her confidence now in place. What had she been so worried about? She really had to get back into talking to people again. Her skillset was growing rusty.

When she handed Sara her glass of water, the reporter smiled. "Many thanks. You've been told that this is only a short interview, yes? Only a little column space in this edition, I'm afraid."

Elisandrine sipped her water and placed the glass on a side table. "Yes, that is fine. I am not all that fascinating anyway."

"Oh, I'm sure that's not true."

"Well, it all depends on what you find interesting, Miss Kvist." Elise noted the low flirtatious tone in her own voice and bit her tongue.

No! Not too much. You could hurt Nessa.

Sara didn't seem to have noticed. "Where did you learn to make these oils, Mrs Glass? Mr Sinclair told me that it involves your… what's the expression … mother-in-law?"

Elise wanted to clap with joy. Such a perfect opportunity to set the record straight. *Perhaps we can send a copy of the article by ship to Arclid? Reading it, the Clays might think better of the Noble brat who took their Nessa away. Perhaps they may even like me once I have given credit where it is due.*

"Correct! My mother-in-law, Carryanne Clay, instructed Nessa, who in turn taught me. Carryanne makes the most amazing dammon nut and sugar pumpkin oil. I simply tried it with different fragrances and added the secret ingredient to increase its scent and longevity."

Sara was frantically taking notes. Elise tried to read them, but they were in Sundish and in near illegible handwriting.

Above them she heard Anja pacing again and Svarte meowing, probably wanting to be let into the study. Elise frowned at the distraction.

Sara looked up from her notebook. "I assume we're not to be told of the secret ingredient?"

Elise gave her best attempt at a wink, managing, as usual, to close both eyes. "No, I fear that must remain a secret."

Sara laughed. "Ah, no big reveal for me. Never mind, some things are better left as mysteries, yes?"

Another meow came from upstairs, they both looked to the ceiling.

"I hear you live with cats?" Sara asked with a chuckle.

"A cat. It belongs to our hostess, Anja Ahlgren. You may have heard of her, she is a famous and brilliant historian. She is writing a book at the moment. One I suggest everyone purchase when it is published," Elise threw in. Perhaps she could get into Anja's good graces as well as the Clays' with this interview.

Sara sat back. "Fine compliments, yes? Could help with sales, hm?" She gave Elise a conspiratorial grin.

Elise laughed. "Anja deserves it. Not only because it is true but because she is a good friend and landlady. We shall probably have to find a more permanent place to live, you know. However, as we always have pressing reasons to keep moving, who knows how long we will stay.

The ease the interview had lulled Elise into suddenly broke. She fidgeted with her hair.

Did I say too much again? Why do I never think before I speak?

The pencil scratched against the paper as Elise's confidence slowly ebbed back out.

After a while, Sara looked up. "Tell me, do you use your own oils?"

Back to the oils. Thank the gods!

"Yes, in fact, I am wearing the watermint and cherry oil today. I thought it fitting to wear one which is a mixture of Arclidian watermint and Storsund winter cherries."

Sara clicked her tongue. "Nice touch. I can see you put a lot of thought into your scents, yes?"

Certainly. When I do not rummage around for any old herb in Anja's kitchen.

Elise crossed her legs in her most ladylike fashion. "Scents are important. Your smell says a lot about you."

"Yes. If a person smells unpleasant, it can for example say that they're allergic to strong smells and can't wear scented oils," Sara replied, a twinkle in her eye showing that there was no harm meant.

"That is true. Out of consideration for others, I personally try not to overdose on fragrances. Which is why a scented oil can be better than an alcohol-based fragrance. It is subtler. More likely to be smelled by someone close, like a friend or a lover, than the whole town."

Sara pointed her pencil at her. "Now that will make a good quote. We're getting somewhere, yes?"

After that, a few mundane questions followed. Queries about how Elise was settling in, how she handled the change in climate, and if she had seen the frost faire. When that was all answered and jotted down, Sara packed away her notebook and pencil. She finished her water and stood up.

"I shall leave you to the rest of your day. No doubt you have oils to mix, yes? Secret ingredients to harvest." She stopped by the door. "No, wait. Not harvest, very little grows under snow. Perhaps you must mix chemical things, yes?"

Elise smirked at her. "That is for me to know and you to guess."

Sara laughed as she opened the door. "Apologies. I had to try once more. Thank you for the water and conversation. The article will be published tomorrow. With the title 'Sniff Elise Glass' Arclidian Elegance.' Not perfect, but the sort of thing our readers like, yes? Farewell."

With that, she was gone. Elise was left worrying her lower lip. She'd assumed they would keep to the custom of calling a married person by their title and surname, not their first name. Still, Elise was a common Arclidian name, Glass was a pseudonym, and neither would mean anything to people here. No one in Skarhult was searching for her.

Wait, does that title mean that the article will be posted in Arclidian? No, of course not. She merely translated for you. Stop fretting over nothing, you nervous skitter-beetle.

She straightened her back, taking a few slow breaths.

Anja walked down the stairs with Svarte in her arms. "Silly beast keeps meowing. I think he might be hungry, even though I fed him plenty this morning. I swear this cat will…" She tapered off as she looked at Elise. "You look like someone put ice in your porridge. Did the interview go badly? Was the reporter rude?"

Elise hugged her arms around herself. "No. It went well, I think. I have just had this… uneasy, haunted feeling all day. Never mind. It is probably my monthly curse approaching. I should bleed in a couple of days, that always makes my mood peculiar."

Anja looked at her, searchingly. "As long as you're sure that's all it is. This sounds more like Nessa than you."

"I am fine. Anyway, tomorrow is the Joiners Square Fest. We told the Lindbergs we would meet them there. It shall be such fun!"

Anja rolled her eyes. "Having to see people and eating trash food, all while being out in the arse-freezing cold. Yes, heaps of *fun*."

CHAPTER 19
JOINERS SQUARE FEST

The night of the Joiners Square Fest finally arrived. As Nessa stepped out onto the well-trodden ice, she was almost as excited and curious as Elise.

How do you add more extravagance and colour to something like the frost faire?

She was about to ask Anja, when Elise pointed to the confectioner's tent and hurried towards it.

Anja chuckled. "She's off then. I suppose I'll go get us all some black wine. No, you cannot have anything else, and no, I'm not letting you pay for your own."

"Thank you!" Nessa shouted after her retreating form.

On her way to join Elise, she took in the sights. The frost faire's reds, golds, and greens had all been switched out for Joiners Square's silver and pale yellow in every light and every fabric. It made the whole affair seem classier but colder. Nessa wrinkled her nose at it.

People crowded the ice, barely leaving room for those on skates to pass through. Everyone was dressed up. Anja and Nessa had complained about having to trade in their usual trousers, vests, shirts, and sweaters for pretty, bell-shaped dresses, but Elise had insisted they make an effort. She had not only gone out and spent a chunk of her newly earned gold on dresses, but also picked up new, elegant wool coats for herself and Anja. And, knowing that Nessa would not be parted from her tatty leather coat, gotten her a new fur cloak, hat, gloves, and long boots which all matched the brown coat.

They arrived at the sugar works tent. Smiling at them was the round, white-blonde confectioner who had been there last. "Hello again, madam. Back for another ballerina?"

Elise started. "You remember me?"

"With those unusual golden eyes? Of course I do, madam."

Nessa smirked as she saw Elise blink a few times extra and adjust her hair.

Anja caught up with them, balancing three mugs of hot wine. "Nessa, take one of these. And tell Miss Sugar-Addict over there to get me some rose-flavoured sweets."

Nessa took her mug. "I'll buy them for you. Elise is busy flirting with the pretty confectioner."

"I can see that. Most wives would be jealous."

Nessa almost said that they weren't married until she collected herself. "I'm sure they would, but I trust Elise. Flirting is merely her way of interacting. I think it might've been the way she was raised. To be pretty and make everyone adore her. She doesn't know that there's much more to her than that."

Anja blew on her wine, sending the steam Nessa's way. "True enough. Still, are you sure it doesn't bother you?"

Nessa shrugged, looking at the love of her life who was being shown different sugary treats. "Not with strangers. Her flirting with friends, people who see beyond her pretty surface, that worries me more." Nessa winked at Anja as she added, "Like you."

Anja nearly choked on her wine. "Me?"

"Yes, you. The two of you quickly formed some sort of bond."

"Only because she wanted to work for me and…" Anja seemed to hesitate, and when she spoke again, she was no longer meeting Nessa's eye. "Because she noticed I was lonely."

"There's more to it than that. She trusts you, likes you, and wants to impress you. Also, let's face it, you're a beautiful woman."

Noticing Anja's scepticism, Nessa said, "Remember the man in the drinks tent the first night of the frost faire? How he thought you were romantically involved with me and Elise?"

Anja gaped for a moment, a lock of her thick hair sticking to her lip. "But… but he was clearly joking. I'm older."

"So?"

"And bad-tempered."

Nessa laughed and repeated, "So?"

"I have a prosthetic arm."

Nessa frowned at her. "Oh, come now, Elise would never discard anyone as a lover because of that. Nor would I."

Anja nodded. "No, of course not. Sorry. But I'm also… dull."

"Oh, trust me, I thought myself dull when I met Elise, too. But she finds what is interesting in people and brings it out. She makes annoying people like the Lindbergs bearable. And more, um, plain and discontent people like you and I – glow brightly."

Anja sipped at her wine, deep in thought. "Well, I do not think Elise feels anything romantic towards me. I still say she merely pities me because I am lonely. Perhaps she sees me as a mother figure, but that is all."

"That's not true. If she wasn't madly in love with me, and truly making an effort to be a one-woman sort of woman, she'd be all over you. Who wouldn't?"

Nessa tasted her wine, relishing the warmth and sweetness of it. Anja stood silently, looking into her wine cup.

"Nessa?"

"Yes?"

"You're not hitting on me, are you?" she whinged.

Nessa nearly spat her wine out. "No, sweetest Anja. I do find it adorable, though, that you went from assuming that no one wanted you to now thinking both I and Elise are trying to get under your dress."

"Hold your tongue," Anja muttered. "I hate this dress. Why should I dress up for these Joiners Square buffoons? Silly idea."

Nessa chuckled and continued watching Elise picking her sweets. The pink-cheeked confectioner now nodded at her and picked up the jar of candied fruits. She put the little waxy gems robed in delicate sugar into a white paper bag, hiding them away until they got to cross Elise's scarlet lips. The sudden need to kiss those lips that were hers, and only hers, to kiss overwhelmed Nessa.

Elise turned to her, eyes twinkling and cheeks reddening with the cold and the excitement. "Heartling, you must have something! Shall I buy you one of these pink sugar hearts? They are cherry-flavoured. You love winter cherries."

"Yes, please. Buy me two and get a bag of boiled sweets for Anja, the rose ones."

As Elise was making her purchases, Nessa spotted something on the other side of the ice. The torches and lights of the faire glinted off a building on the bank.

They're reflecting off glass.

"That's new. What is it? A greenhouse?"

Anja frowned at her. "Why would there be a greenhouse by the river? And why would it be built in winter?"

"I don't know. But there is a glass building over there. Look!"

Anja followed Nessa's pointing finger. "Huh. Odd. It has the Joiners Square colours on the rooftop flags. But then, tonight everything has their colours. They seem to have bought up the whole faire, ice and all." She was nodding towards the nearest of the many Joiners Square emblems that had been carved in the surface of the thick ice.

Nessa's attention left the ice, more interested in the glass. The tall building was a narrow rectangular shape, starting on the edge of the ice and going back into the copse of pine trees which separated the riverbank from the road on the other side.

The structure was made solely of glass and steel. Most of the glass was clear except for the stained panes above the door, which showed the Joiners Square emblem in grey and yellow. The doors were wide open, allowing chatter and happy shouts to spill out into the starlit night.

Elise joined Nessa and Anja, handing them their bags of sweets. Nessa was about to pop one of her cherry sugar hearts into her mouth but was distracted by the commotion in the glass house. She peered inside and saw people in exquisite finery, men in smocks and great overcoats and women in the most extravagant furs.

"I can see a few of the leading elite of Joiners Square in there," Anja said, her voice laced with distaste. "They're the ones who are not in uniform but are also not drinking alcohol, leaving that to their dignitary guests – the ones drunk out of their skulls. All the better to con them, charm them, and whatever else it takes to make them give up their every copper."

Nessa was about to ask if they were really that bad when she was interrupted by a Joiners Square soldier brushing past her and Elise. He walked quickly and looked haughty in his stark uniform, his pale cheeks red from either cold or drink.

Elise put a gloved hand on his arm. "Excuse me. May I enquire what that impressive building is?"

"Good evening, miss. That is the new pride of Skarhult,

yes? The glass palace of Joiners Square. During the Fest, it will be a part of the frost faire, where we arrange sled rides and give out free liqueur coffees. After that, it shall be a tearoom and a hall for people looking to join our ranks."

She let go of his arm. "I see. Thank you."

"Not at all, miss." He looked her over with a wolfish grin. "If you wish to see it closer later on, I could give you a *private* viewing. Now I must fetch Grand Marshall Karlberg, but after that, I could be all yours, yes?"

Elise raised an eyebrow. "Thank you very much, but I think *my wife* and I can see it fine on our own."

He laughed, shrugged, and then hurried off to see to his task.

"She doesn't always flirt, then," Anja whispered to Nessa, her breath smelling of rose and sugar.

A pop was heard as a cork flew off a bottle inside the glass building, followed by whooping and happy cries.

Elise linked her arm with Nessa's, then looked behind them. "Anja, shall we go see what those Joiners Square people are up to? Or at least inspect that singular building of theirs? A palace of glass. Who would have dreamed of such a thing?"

Nessa looked unblinkingly at the building.

Those huge panes of glass. What would it take to create those? A daunting but esteemed task indeed.

Anja's attention was on the sleds next to the building. They were filled with furs of all kinds, and large huskies were tied to them, barking happily.

"All right. We'll go in. As long as I can have a closer look at the beautiful sled dogs when we come out. I adore those," Anja said.

"Of course. Now do come along," Elise shouted while dragging Nessa into the oblong glass building.

They stuck their bags of sweets in their pockets and pushed themselves through throngs of people. The farther in they got, the more of the people were in Joiners Square uniform. They were of all genders but all equally handsome, fair-haired, perfectly groomed, and broad-shouldered. They also all wore the same unsympathetic expressions on their pale faces.

She saw Elise shiver and leaned close to her to whisper, "Are you all right? Is it the unfriendly air in here that bothers you?"

Elise seemed to hesitate. "No. I simply have the most peculiar sensation of being watched. Or perhaps followed." Her scowl melted into a wan smile. "I am certain it is merely the hostile air in here, as you say. Ignore me."

Nessa looked about her, trying to shrug off the return of the paranoia that Fabian Smedstorp's words about civilians reporting secrets had created.

Finally, they reached a large, raised square made of yellow glass. It was being used as a table and was so clear and sparkling it looked like it was made of gemstones. On it stood huge pots of what must be the liqueur-spiked coffee. In front of those were grandiose bottles with old-looking labels in Sundish and six small, delicate glass bowls.

Nessa smiled from ear to ear. Those were the bowls she and her master made. They were filled with little, round things in light grey and creamy yellow.

"Those bowls there, I created them. Well, Fabian made the final touches, but I shaped them," she said.

Anja clapped her on the back. "Fine work. They're so pretty and thin that they look like shards of ice. What's in them? Some sort of sweets?"

Elise hurried over to the bowls, looking them over while making impressed noises. Then she took a few of the yellow and grey treats out, sniffing them. "I can only smell sugar. I wonder what they are."

"Arclidian dammon nuts, yes? Covered in fine sugar shells.

Can't you see that, foreigner?" a woman in white furs drawled before walking past them, nearly pushing Elise into the table.

Elise looked over at Nessa and Anja with raised eyebrows and a grimace. They both laughed and joined her, Nessa to try the dammon nuts and Anja to fill a mug with the boozy, sweet coffee. The complex smell of it filled the air around them. Nessa savoured the scent as she ate a nut, crunching through the brittle sugar shell and sighing happily as the taste filled her mouth.

She barely had time to enjoy the treat before she was startled by the sensation of her legs being hugged from behind. She looked down and saw Sonja Lindberg's adorable, tawny face poke out between her knees.

Sonja chirped, "Hello, Grumpy!"

"Hello," Nessa replied.

Sonja looked over to Anja. "Hello, Grumpier!"

Anja crossed her arms over her chest. "Good evening, child."

Eleonora said something in Sundish to Anja. Probably an apology, but Nessa wasn't sure. Unlike Elise, she didn't seem to be picking up this sharp, pretty language.

Sonja spotted Elise and rushed her instead, while Eleonora and Albert shook hands with Nessa and Anja.

Albert turned to bow to Elise. "You came! Eleonora was not certainness you would be here. But you are, yes?"

Elise laughed. "In the flesh. How are you three enjoying the Fest?"

"Most excellent!" Sonja shouted before standing on her tippy-toes to dive into one of the bowls of sugar-shelled nuts.

Eleonora clapped her hands in glee. "So impressive, yes? Have you gone on a sledge ride yet? Or is it sleigh ride? Either way, they seem such fun and are free!"

"They call it sled ride when it has sled dogs," Anja said wistfully, staring out towards the majestic animals.

Albert's eyes went wide. "Oh. Speaking of impressionists, no, I mean impressiveness. Sweetest Elise, I hear you were interviewed by the *Skarhult Chronicle*, yes? Marvellous! The people here should be joyed to see you, then."

Elise's brow furrowed. "Because I am… famous?"

"No. Well, yes, that as well. But because the *Chronicle* is owned and run by Joiners Square, yes? The … what's the word… editor-in-chief used to work with me back in the day. Tasty man."

Nessa cleared her throat. "Albert, you know I hate to correct your Arclidian, since I cannot even speak your language, but I think you mean that he's a *good man* or that he *has good taste*."

"Yes. Why not. That, too," Albert said with a shrug. "Anyway, the *Chronicle* is fired out by Joiners Square. In six languages, reaching all four continents, no less. This is why it's filled with news about the latest feats of the Storsund Trading Company." He whispered the last bit conspiratorially.

Eleonora put her hand on Nessa's arm. "And they say that the *Skarhult Chronicle* is read by all the continent leaders, yes? Even your Queen receives the version translated to Arclidian!"

Out of the corner of her eye, Nessa could swear she saw Elise's skin go from its healthy sandy brown to ashen grey.

Nessa put a hand to her chest, feeling her heart thump like it was trying to break through her ribcage and escape.

Anja scoffed. "Ah. The people at the *Chronicle* are known to exaggerate their rag's popularity. They'd claim the queen of the seas read it if it wasn't for the fact that their ink isn't waterproof."

Nessa's heart slowed a little.

Of course. People exaggerate. Still… I wonder if it's too late to get them to not print the article about Elise.

One look at her love's stricken face reminded Nessa that the journalist had said that it would be published in tomorrow morning's edition. Meaning it was probably being printed right now. She attempted some deep breaths, trying to to remind herself that the Queen didn't have much time and probably wouldn't read magazines concerning kingdoms that weren't hers. And that, yes, people exaggerate.

While the others were busy talking about the glass palace, Nessa whispered to her heartling, "You gave your fake name, right? Elise Glass?"

Wide-eyed, Elisandrine whispered back, "Yes. But I… mentioned your first name. And your mother's full name. I think I also said that we were staying with Anja and gave her full name. In the hope of spreading the word about her book."

"Elise!"

"I know! I am so terribly sorry. I got carried away because the reporter had such a calming air. And because Mr Sinclair said it was an important way to advertise my oils, and…" She trailed off, staring at her feet. "Because someone actually liked something I created. Also, because there was a way to give your mother credit and get in your parents' good graces, I suppose. As always, I did not think before speaking." She looked back up at Nessa. "In my defence, I assumed the *Skarhult Chronicle* was just distributed around Skarhult. Hence the name," she said, wringing her hands.

Nessa sighed. "Yes, so did I."

Elise looked like she was awaiting her execution. "I am awfully sorry, Nessa."

Nessa pulled her close and kissed her cheek. "It's all right, heartling. An easy mistake. We don't know if the Queen will read it. And if she does, who knows if she'll connect the dots? Or care about you anymore. Perhaps she has a new plaything. We'll talk about it tomorrow."

Elise gave a hesitant nod, her lips pressed into a tight line.

Anja came over and used two fingers to lift Elise's chin towards her. "Are you all right?"

"Yes, thank you. Just… lost in thought."

"Right. I'll pretend to believe that," Anja muttered with a glance in Nessa's direction. "Anyway, we should get out of this place of revolting wealth and brainwashing and go see about those sled rides. The fresh air will do you both good."

The Lindbergs came closer, too. Sonja, with a mouth full of dammon nuts, yelped, "The cute puppies, yes?"

Anja pursed her lips at the child. "They're grown dogs. But yes, they're… cute. What do you say Elise?"

Nessa put her arm around Elise's trembling shoulders and felt her straighten up before she replied, "Yes. Smashing idea."

Out in the cold air, Nessa watched the wolf-like dogs yip cheerfully at each other and their onlookers. The animals had apparently been on a break to eat and rest and were now ready to work. There was a queue, but Albert's Joiners Square connections meant their party could skip the line. A thrill whirred through Nessa at the thought of traveling the thick ice pulled along by those strong, quick animals. She wasn't even that worried about the speed. Or the thickness of the ice.

Or slipping on it.

Or any of the other things that could go horribly, terribly wrong.

She swallowed and took Elise's hand.

The long, elaborately crafted sleds were now being attached to the dogs' harnesses by female and male Joiners Square soldiers. Nessa tried not to be impressed by the striking warriors in their fitted grey uniforms with pale yellow buttons, finished with resplendent, silvery-white fur capes over their shoulders. A handsome exterior was nothing if it hid cruelty.

Finally, their two sleds were ready. The Lindberg family sat in one while Anja, Elise, and Nessa sat in the other. The sleds had six seats each, so they could have fitted in one vehicle, leaving the second one for others waiting their turn. However, that was not the Storsund way, Nessa realised. Back in Ground Hollow you used only what you needed, mended what was broken, and made do with what you had. Here, opulence and luxury were a sign not only of status but of good taste. Why have one sled when you could have two?

Wasteful. Inconsiderate. Boastful.

The words made Nessa think of the Queen of Arclid, making her stomach turn.

Nessa and Elise sat next to each other, while Anja took a seat behind them, wrapping herself in the furs that lined the sled. She threw one at Nessa's back. "Cuddle up with this, you two. I'll not have you catching a cold and making me sneeze for weeks."

"No, Anja," they replied in unison, with matching smiles.

The soldier who was to drive their sled looked back at them. "Ready? My furry little comrades run fast, so don't be brainless and stand up in the sled, yes? I cannot have you fall off. You'd hurt the ice."

Elise had that look which usually was followed by one of her quick bursts of rage, so Nessa hurried to reply, "Certainly."

With that, they were off. The soldier cracked a whip into the icy night air and the dogs barked happily before taking off running. They raced past onlookers who stood with steaming coffee cups and sugary treats, shouting their glee as the sled passed by. Nessa sat closer to Elise and pulled the furs over them as the rushing air grew colder. They sped up, the light from torches and gas lamps and the intoxicating smells enveloping them.

Giddy and drunk on excitement, Nessa glanced at her beloved and saw that Elise was beaming, her mouth slightly open and her golden eyes wide. She was so beautiful that Nessa's chest tightened. She couldn't wait any longer, she had to lean in and taste those red lips. Elise giggled into the kiss before throwing herself into it. They parted after a few blissful moments, sharing looks of love and joy.

The romance was rudely interrupted by something heavy landing in the sled. Nessa's heart skipped a beat. They all turned their heads and saw a person, bundled in furs and with a giant fur hat, plonked on the seats behind Anja. Nessa remembered Elise's fear over being watched or followed, and her heart skipped yet another beat.

With a long tirade in Sundish, Anja seemed to be asking the person what they were doing. Or perhaps cursing at them. The soldier pulled on the reins, slowing the dogs to a gradual halt. Then he began hauling abuse at the stowaway as well.

"I do sincerely apologise for barging in like this," the newcomer said. "However, I saw that you were getting farther away from the faire, and I could not risk losing Nessa and Elise when I had finally found them."

Wait… Arclidian? With a Midlands accent? I recognise that voice.

Nessa peered at the fur-clad person who was now sitting up and correcting his oversized hat.

"Hunter! What in the names of the gods are you doing here?" she exclaimed.

"You know this person, yes?" the soldier barked.

Elise gave her silver bell laugh. "Oh yes, we know him all right. Hunter Smith, the man with the uncanny knack of showing up where you least expect him. Even when he is meant to be on another continent."

The soldier scowled before grunting, "We carry on then, yes? People are waiting back at the glass palace."

"Yes, of course. Drive on," Nessa replied, trying to smile apologetically at him.

He cracked the whip in the air above the dogs and they took off running again.

Anja was staring from Hunter and back to her house-guests. Elise was still laughing incredulously. It was left for Nessa to repeat her question.

"What are you doing here, Hunter?"

He gave her his charming, sparkling smile. "Seeing my two favourite travelling ladies of course. Arclid was terribly boring without you."

Elise quirked an eyebrow at him and his smile faltered.

He coughed daintily. "Fine. I also had to escape the probing questions about you from a certain mutual acquaintance of ours. The one who played cards with Nessa? Therefore, I fancied a change of scenery and took the next steamer over. After six cold weeks at sea, I arrived this evening and headed for the faire, knowing that all of Storsund would join the Fest. I have been keeping my eyes peeled for you two all night."

Nessa shivered under the furs when she thought about the questions the Queen might have asked Hunter.

Hunter's smile returned, but it looked about as real as his overly white teeth. "Besides, my employers finally had enough of the rumours surrounding my lack of interest in that *certain human aspect*. My reputation had sunk to that of a river toad. Quite frankly, they did not deserve me."

Nessa saw Elise frown and knew that she was also thinking how unfair it was that Nightport would judge a man for his lack of interest in romance and bedplay. How could anyone assume you'd be incapable of power and ambition simply because you didn't want to bed anyone? Nessa could only hope that Hunter had been right when claiming that Storsund was more accepting of that sort of thing.

Anja scoffed. "Well, this is all very confusing. Do all Arclidians shroud themselves in secrets and riddles?"

Elise gave her a wan smile. "Not all. The three of us are

bad examples. Especially Hunter and I. Nessa merely keeps our secrets."

The last words were almost whipped away by the wind as they travelled on. They were far down the river now, the lights and sounds of the faire growing dimmer behind them. Nessa wondered how long this ride would last and how far ahead the Lindbergs' sled was. Unease niggled, making her fidget. It was as if the Queen was closer now than in the past few months. Finding out that Elise's interview could possibly reach the court, and now hearing Hunter say that only six weeks ago he escaped the Queen's questions about them… it made her recent, and still fragile, sense of safety fall away like crumbling bricks.

In pregnant silence, they journeyed through the starlit night, which now seemed colder and darker.

∾

Back at the palace, with frost-bitten cheeks and the silence still prevailing, they stepped off the sled. The soldier didn't stop to say farewell but started loading up new passengers immediately.

Anja brushed some snow off her coat. "I want more coffee. Go ahead and discuss your secrets and riddles." With that, she sauntered off.

Nessa watched her go, torn between the guilt of not telling Anja all and the awareness that Anja didn't care about people's pasts.

Would she even want to know our infected secrets?

Perhaps she deserved to know as she was housing them? Although, perhaps Anja was safer not knowing?

Hunter wasted no time. He pranced away from the crowds and further up the snowy bank of the river. When he saw that the three of them were alone, he began feverishly whispering.

"The Queen figured out that I was connected to you two. She was searching for any information about you, but quietly, so her desperate pursuit wouldn't be common knowledge, I suppose. Your rousing speech to the punters of The White Raven surely helped with that, Nessa." He gave her a conspiratorial smile. "Anyway, she took me to the castle and started asking questions. When I did not reply, a man resembling some disfigured oxen punctuated her questions with his fists to my midsection."

Elise gasped, but he held up his hands. "I am fine, heartling. I have taken worse punches than that growing up in Nightport. Anyway, when I did not reply, they left me to think it over."

"But… how did you escape?" Nessa couldn't help asking.

"You know me, I make sure people owe me favours everywhere. Like you two do, remember?" He smirked before continuing. "I waited until a guard who owed me came on duty. I reminded her about the time I saved her brother from two men in a dark alley. She agreed to open the door and say that I had knocked her out through the bars and stolen her keys. For the silver coins in my pocket, she also lent me her cloak as a disguise and suggested an escape path out of the castle. I can only hope the Queen did not kill her for it."

Elise nodded tightly, and Nessa took her hand.

"What about the others who were with us that night?" Nessa asked.

"Cai and Fyhre were interviewed long before me. They were released unharmed and went into hiding. Back to *my* story," he said with an impatient look. "I ran to 21 Miller Street to get my emergency bags, which I keep packed in my closet. Paranoia is your best friend in Nightport, after all. Then I hurried down to the docks, hoping that my bribed guard hadn't reported my escape yet."

He paused to pull his hat over his ears. "I went into the

sailors' tavern and caught the first captain I knew sailed to Storsund. I cashed in my owed favour with him, giving me not only free passage, but a place to hide until the ship sailed the next morning. I huddled in a lifeboat, hearing all the ships being searched. I overheard the Royal Guards tell the captain that they were chasing a man suspected of treason. No mention of you two. As far as I know, the Queen is still hiding what she actually wants."

Elise's pretty features twisted. "Her tinderbox-maker back," she intoned.

Hunter nodded.

Nessa patted him on the arm, remembering that this was one of the few physical touches he did not mind. "I'm so terribly sorry you had to go through that. And that you had to leave your home."

He waved it off. "Do not concern yourself. As I said, I needed to go anyway. On top of all of that, living in rented rooms in a lodging house and working two jobs was growing tiresome. I was envying you two your shiny new adventure."

Elise quirked an eyebrow. "I fear being hunted is… nothing to be envied. We have not dared to put down real roots. We have not even hired rooms despite being here for months now. We live in Anja's house, the woman you met in the sled."

"Ah. No jobs yet?"

"Those we have," Nessa said. "I've recently started an apprenticeship and Elise helps Anja write her book. Then she spends the rest of her time becoming quite famous in the fragrance business. Everyone in Storsund wants to wear her scented oils. She's recently been interviewed about it, actually."

Hunter whistled low. "Rented rooms or not, you seem to be doing well for yourselves!" He adjusted his hat, avoiding their gaze as he added, "I hope I shall be as lucky with my new life here."

Elise smiled sweetly at him. "We were fortunate enough to run into someone who could help. That is the joy of this world – if you are desperate and lost enough, you are bound to find both good and bad people noticing. Then you must gamble on which is which. Anja is certainly one of the good ones." She chuckled. "Granted, she was reticent to help us at first. But that is only because she is a loner and we were total strangers."

Nessa hummed. "Secretive, pushy strangers. But yes, Anja is a good person. If we ask her, I'm sure she'll take you in like she did us."

"Highly likely. However, with the coin coming in from my oils and your apprenticeship, we are not completely reliant on her anymore. Especially not as we are getting to know Skarhult better. If push comes to shove, we can quickly find lodgings for us three," Elise said, a hint of pride in her voice.

It warmed Nessa's heart to see Hunter look a little more cheerful. That wasn't all he was looking, though.

"Hunter. You look ridiculous in all those furs. It's below freezing, yes, but you're wearing more clothes than half of Skarhult put together. You can barely move!"

He scowled. "I think I look like a handsome ice bear tamer. Still, have no fear, I have one of my usual velvet three-piece suits underneath. You will adore it when you see it." He winked at her, just as unsuccessfully as Elise's frequent attempts. "Now, shall we go find that grumpy hostess of yours so I can work my charms on her? I think she went over there to buy coffee. Do come along, Mrs and Mrs Glass."

He took off in his usual peacock way. Except now he looked less like a bird in colourful plumage and more like a moving fur pile. Only his square-jawed face showed there was a man under there.

Nessa turned to Elise who shook her head in amusement and said, "I have missed him."

~

With the recently fetched Anja in tow, they walked back to where Hunter had left his baggage with a lad in a betting tent.

While Anja sipped her coffee and Nessa and Elise took one last look at the Joiners Square Fest, Hunter paid the boy two coppers. In return, he was handed two huge suitcases, which the boy had to drag out from the back of the tent.

Nessa's jaw dropped. "Wait. *That* is the emergency luggage you kept in case of a quick getaway? There's more packed there than I have ever owned!"

"Yes, country girl. And that is why I am better dressed, cleaner, and more prepared for anything than you have ever been," Hunter taunted.

"Cleaner? Ha! More drenched in scented oils, perhaps. I bathe more than you do. I used to live in the same lodging house as you, so I know," Nessa countered, playfully.

Elise put her gloved hands on her hips. "Enough quibbling. You are making a terrible first impression on Anja. Why would she want to host you now, Hunter?" She turned to Anja. "They are not half as annoying as this most of the time. Hunter is actually quite lovely."

Anja finished her boozy coffee while surveying him. "So. Another wayward Arclidian seeking shelter under my roof, then?"

He shifted his weight from one furry boot to the other. "Temporarily, yes. I have the coin to pay my way, and I promise to find a better solution as soon as possible. I also swear to be less trouble than these two."

Anja pursed her lips. "Well, I'm out of beds and won't have my floor littered with youngsters indefinitely. Why do I keep taking in strays now? When did I become this soft in heart and head?"

Nessa opened her mouth to answer but was stopped by

Anja holding up a hand. "Nessa, that was… how do you say it in Arclidian… a rhetorical question. Come on. Let's catch the last cable car of the night. I'm not walking all the way back with you cold-toed foreigners grumbling all the way."

They all followed without question.

CHAPTER 20
DARK EYES AND A CRUEL SMIRK

Elise was exhausted by the time they got back to Anja's house. Worrying about her mistake with the interview had taken its toll, and hearing Hunter's story hadn't helped one whit. Still, she was happy that Anja had let him stay. She hadn't even asked any questions. All she had done was mutter about trusting Elise and Nessa and something about him not making a mess of her washroom. Elise smiled to herself, proud of that trust.

Now Anja stood by the stairs with her arms crossed. "Right. I have one more pillow but no more blankets. You'll have to bunch up sheets for a mattress and to cover yourself."

"That will do. I have slept in worse circumstances," Hunter said with his charm-offensive smile.

Anja scoffed. "Why, thank you. My home and I are blushing at your enthusiastic compliments."

"Oh, I did not mean—"

She snorted at his appalled expression. "For snow's sake, I know what you meant. Come up and get your pillow and sheets."

When Hunter and Anja had gone upstairs, Elise dashed into Nessa's arms.

Nessa kissed her hair and rubbed her back gently. "It'll all work out, heartling. By the way, I assume this is about the Queen and not Hunter sleeping between us on the floor?"

Elise slapped her rear, admonishing her for the attempted joke.

Nessa jumped at the smack. "Sorry. In all seriousness, let's not panic before we're certain that she is closing in on us. She was questioning Hunter, yes. But *six weeks ago.* She's probably moved on by now. She has a nation to run and not endless time to hunt you."

"Are you only saying that to calm me?"

"I'm saying that because it makes sense. Doesn't it?"

Elise rubbed her forehead. "I suppose. I simply… cannot shake the feeling that she is breathing down our necks. I have not wanted to worry you, but I have had nightmares about her finding me. Silly, perhaps, but with Hunter's tale and the realisation that my interview might reach her, it all seems so—"

Their conversation was interrupted by Hunter and Anja returning, seemingly discussing Skarhult accommodations.

"You mean there are even *houses* around here for those reasonable amounts?" Hunter asked from somewhere under the pillow and sheets in his arms.

Anja got out of his way. "Yes. This part of town is away from the centre and mainly an industrial area, which means factory smoke and delivery carts speeding around all day. Not to mention the cable cars being filled with workers every morning and at the end of the working day." She paused to pet Svarte, who was glaring at the new house guest. "Also, the available houses and rooms for rent here are all in older, less attractive buildings. Often with old stoves and leaky roofs. This is not a sought-after part of Skarhult."

"Despite the cable car line?" Hunter asked, dropping his bedding on the floor and terrifying the cat.

Anja picked up Svarte. "As I said, the cars are always full of factory workers here. There are plenty of other places in Skarhult with accommodation *and* less busy cable cars."

Hunter gaped at Nessa and Elise. "Can you fathom such luxury? Trains for the long distances and cable cars for the short. How do the people of Skarhult not get out of shape from never walking?"

Nessa and Elise didn't get a chance to answer. Anja put the cat down and glared at Hunter. "Because we don't use the convenient travel all the time. If something is only a twenty-minute hike away, we walk. Humans need fresh air and…" She seemed to struggle to find the right words. "You know… moving their muscles about."

"Exercise?" Elise suggested before helping Hunter lay out layers of sheets as a makeshift mattress.

Anja pointed at her in triumph. "Exactly! Anyway. You're all annoying me now, I'm going to bed. Does anyone want something before I go? Some wine? Leaf tea? A glass of milk?"

They all said no, and Anja slowly nodded.

As if she were disappointed, Elise realised.

"In that case, I shall leave you young people to chat while I go to sleep." She looked down at the cat at her feet. "Sleeping in my bed tonight, little monster? Or are you going out to scare Nilsson's goats?"

He chirped in an unusually friendly way, so Anja scooped him up and headed for the stairs. "Good night, Arclidians. Sleep soundly."

"We will try. Thank you for everything today," Elise replied, wondering if there was a suitable way to get Anja to stay.

Hunter bowed to her. "Thank you again for housing me, madam. You have a kind heart and a lovely home."

She scoffed and continued up the stairs. The three friends smiled at each other.

"I really have missed you two." Hunter chuckled. "Anyway, are you on-board with the idea of us searching for a place to live together? Either a good lodging house like back in Nightport or by sharing a small house, perhaps? I know I barged in and requested that you uproot—"

"Well, no wonder, considering the trouble and pain you got into because of us," Elise interjected.

Hunter pursed his lips. "I was not finished. I was going to add that I am aware that this is all moving very fast. Things always seem to when you two are involved."

Elise glanced at Nessa who shrugged with a smile. She knew they were both more worried about who might be chasing them than who they lived with.

"Yes, I fear Nessa has picked up my habit of living on impulse. Still, before any decision is made I am sure she will have thought it all through." She looked to Nessa, who nodded reassuringly, and then continued. "Perhaps you and Anja can go look for what is available in the neighbourhood tomorrow? She likes a stroll and shall make an essential guide. After we have finished our work on the book in the morning, that is. I highly doubt she would venture out before the work is done. Storsund work ethic, you see."

Hunter fluffed up his careworn pillow. "Do you think she wants you two to leave her nest?"

Elise pondered that for a moment. "I think she feels that it is inevitable. And that she misses her alone-time. However, I believe the reason she has taken the initiative here is so that she can assure we are still close by. That we are not abandoning her, perhaps?"

"That rings true," Nessa said, sliding her arm around Elise's waist. "And we're not going to abandon her."

Elise stole a kiss, making Hunter groan. "You two have not grown tired of all that, then?"

"Kissing each other? Not even remotely close to it, mate," Nessa gushed.

"Ugh. Very well, kiss all you want, but *do* spare me from anything more strenuous. Some of us are still recovering from a long trip and need our beauty sleep," Hunter said while getting under his covers.

Elise laughed. "Naturally."

She kissed Nessa and went to wash up before bed. When she came out, Nessa was reading a book by the fading fire and Hunter was splayed out on his back. His wheat-coloured hair, complete with fancy black streak, was in a mess on the pillow, and his mouth open as he snored.

Nessa looked up at her with raised eyebrows and a glance that seemed to say, "Are you hearing this?"

Elisandrine, smiling, went over to kiss the top of her head. "Your turn to go wash up. Good night, my cherished. Let us hope for good dreams and that he stops snoring before I am forced to throw a sock at him."

Nessa grunted her reply and went to the washroom.

Elise spread her sheet across the sofa and tried her best to keep her thoughts away from a tall, imperial woman in Arclid. Dark eyes and a cruel smirk. The imagined scent of lavender and alcohol seemed to fill her nose. She remembered what her father had said, "If you try too hard not to think about blue skitter-beetles, then all you shall think of is blue skitter-beetles."

She sighed and prepared herself for a sleepless night.

The next afternoon found Elise in the kitchen, turning her latest batch of oils. The components blended dutifully as she shook the bottles. She sighed with contentment, only the cat to hear her. Nessa had, as usual, headed out to the hot shop early in the morning. Anja and Hunter were both out, too. After the morning's dictation, they had gone out in the search for nearby rooms to rent. Maybe even a small house, now that there was three of them and they had some coin to invest.

Nessa and I can have a real bed, one we can share.

Blinking away her reverie, Elise shook a scent bottle of violet and lemongrass vigorously. The ebony root wouldn't quite mix in this one. Had she got the measurements wrong? Was there something wrong with the ebony root?

There was a loud rap at the door. Elise put the errant bottle down.

Odd. Cannot be Nessa, she has a key and is still working. Hunter is with Anja, who also has a key. Besides, they only left a short while ago. Perhaps it is Mr Sinclair?

She strode to the door, smoothing down her bell-shaped dress. When she opened the door with a polite smile, she saw two strange men. One of them barged in and the other soon followed.

"Excuse me! What in the name of the gods do you think you are you doing?" Elise snapped.

The blond men in Joiners Square uniforms stood straight-backed and tight-lipped. One was fresh-faced and the other more grizzled, but both watched her with indifferent, icy blue eyes. She put her hands on her hips, about to repeat her question. Maybe even in Sundish if she could remember the words. Then the older man handed her something in a canvas bag.

Elise took it reluctantly and brought out the item she could feel inside. The breath froze in her chest when she saw what it was.

A package wrapped in midnight blue. With a white ribbon. The size of a box and heavy as metal.

"No. No. Please no," Elise whispered.

She stumbled. It was as if her world was closing in. She looked down at her hands, unsure why they were opening the package. She knew what would be inside. And yet, with shivering hands and beating heart, she tore the paper off and saw a box in white gold. It was ornate, patterned with flames around the edges. It didn't have the royal seal on it. Of course not. *She* would not be so imprudent as to leave such clear evidence. After all, rebellion was always in the air in Arclid.

Elise turned to the soldiers. "What does this mean? Is the Queen merely sending this to show me that she knows my whereabouts?"

"She is sending it as a sign of her appreciation. And how much she looks forward to seeing you soon, yes? You will come with us now. A ship awaits."

She took a step back. "What? No. I... I cannot."

The older soldier grabbed her arm, hard enough to make her wince. "Wrong. You can. Come nice and easily, yes? No violence then."

Elise jutted her chin out, hoping her eyes didn't betray how close to tears she was. "You mindless brute! Will I at least be allowed to leave a note to my loved ones?"

He shook his lined, grim face.

Elise swallowed.

My poor, poor Nessa.

"I see. What about packing?"

"No."

Elise counted to ten in her head. Her fear was morphing into pure, icy rage. She had to control herself. These men had to deliver her alive, no doubt, but they probably didn't need to worry about delivering her *unharmed*. Bruises and small cuts healed well during six weeks in a ship's cabin.

As he let go of her arm, she took a deep breath to gather herself and headed for the washroom.

"Where do you think you're going?" the younger soldier asked.

Elise gritted her teeth. "I am in the middle of my monthly bleed. So, unless you plan to sit at my feet with a bowl between my legs for the next few days, I shall require clean rags for the journey."

The two men stared at each other, the younger one wide-eyed and the older with an exhausted look.

"Fine," the older one clipped.

"Thank you. You are a marvel of gentlemanly spirit," she replied acerbically.

He grunted, and she strode with dignity to the washroom. She picked up all the rags she had washed and hung in there to dry. All while looking around for some way to alert Nessa of where she was going and to tell her that she loved her. She found nothing. Quickly, she changed her current rags, trying to focus on her basic needs to keep from crying or punching the wall. She had known the Queen was closing in. She had felt it in her bones. Why hadn't she grabbed Nessa and run? Especially after last night?

When she had finished, she heard Svarte meow at the two men. Then a quick scuffle before the cat hissed loudly. Elisandrine rushed out to make sure the brutes hadn't hurt the poor creature.

She found the two men arguing in Sundish. Then the older one kicked in Svarte's direction. The younger soldier shouted something at his colleague and bent down to check on the still-hissing cat. Svarte shunned the gentle hands of the younger soldier but didn't hiss at him. Instead, he turned and ran for the stairs, tail between his legs.

Elise made a note of that. One of her captors had a heart. She could only hope it beat for humans as well as cats.

The older soldier spotted her and stepped towards her. Elise didn't back down. Didn't hide or run. What would be the point? There were two of them, they were in better shape than she was, they knew this town better. And there was the fact that they had all of Joiners Square behind them. She had no chance. Consequently, she only lunged for the satchel by the door, put the fresh rags into it, and then grabbed her coat. The older soldier pointed to her boots, and she put them on. He grunted impatiently as she tied them and yanked her up by the arm when she had finished.

Oh, how close she came to spitting in his face then. But his eyes were cruel and his teeth bared. She swallowed another icy dose of rage and held on to her fear. For once, it might just keep her more or less unscathed.

As he pulled her out the door, she chided herself for not saying that the rags were upstairs so that she could have jumped out the window.

No. He would have come up with me.

Moreover, as she had decided before, running was pointless now. They had escaped the Queen back in Arclid because she couldn't be seen hunting them. Elise didn't have that luck here, Joiners Square did whatever they wished. She swallowed something jagged and blinked away tears as they pushed her into a carriage.

At least the tinderbox lay forgotten on Anja's floor, she realised. Elise's need for clean rags and the incident with the cat had made the soldiers forget all about it. Nessa would know what it was, and therefore who had abducted her lover. That was something at least.

Nonetheless, Elise wouldn't settle merely for the hope of rescue. As the carriage rolled into motion, she balled her hands into fists and tried to formulate an escape plan.

CHAPTER 21
THE BOX AND THE EMBASSY

Nessa had a spring in her step as she came home. She had done most of the work on an intricate vase today, and it had ended up looking almost like, well, *a vase*. She was improving and coming to understand the temperamental and delicate thing that glass work could be. The Brownlees had been teaching her things slowly, in tiny morsels, taking great care of their sparse materials. Fabian didn't have that issue. If Nessa ruined something, there were plenty more components waiting to be made into glass. She was free to fail and free to grow.

When she closed the front door behind her, her good mood morphed into confusion. She saw Anja staring perplexedly at something in her hands. Next to her was Hunter, who stopped chewing his nails to turn towards her lightning fast.

"Nessa! I... I am not sure what this means. We came home, and Elise was nowhere to be seen. There's no note from her either, but there was a wad of wrapping paper on the floor and," he pointed to the object Anja was holding, "this thing. I might be jumping to conclusions, but… it looks like a tinderbox without the contents."

There was ringing in her ears. She caught herself against the wall as her knees grew liquid. Anja stepped forward, still looking confused, and handed Nessa the object.

"Yes. It looks like a container for the contents of a tinderbox," she croaked.

Hunter rubbed at his bitten nails. "It could be something else, right? Perhaps a tin for her to keep her tiny scent bottles in? Or something she bought in town and had delivered?"

Nessa shook her head. "And she would be missing for what reason? Popped out to buy more boxes in town without leaving a note? No. *She* has her. Look at the flames decorating it… she always called Elise fire-starter or tinderbox-maker." Nessa ran her hand over her face, laughing mirthlessly. "You know, I keep thinking about that gods-cursed article that we were so worried about. It couldn't have reached the Queen yet. She must have already known."

"Perhaps she followed me?" Hunter said quietly.

Nessa shrugged. "Or perhaps she has spies here. Wouldn't surprise me."

Anja grabbed the box and smacked it down on the fireplace mantle. "Right. I don't ask questions about people's pasts. Partly because individuals don't interest me as much as history as a whole does, and partly because I'm a firm believer in minding my own business. Now, however, I'm going to have to ask for details."

Nessa tucked a few hairs that had fallen out of her braid behind her ear as she slumped on the sofa. "Of course. You deserve to know why we were so eager to get to stay with someone and why we had so little luggage. Most of all, you deserve to know why the woman you have worked with, and befriended, is now in grave danger." Her voice cracked at that last word. How could she have been so stupid to let them stay in one place? They should have run further, kept on the move. Sure, they had stayed put so Hunter could find them. The second he showed up at Joiners Square Fest, though, they could have run. *Should* have run. Her heart was racing.

That's hindsight talking. Stay calm. Stay focused. What matters now is getting her back. Safe and untouched.

She cleared her throat and began telling Anja the whole story. All the way from when she had first seen Lady Elisandrine Falk leaning out a castle window, to when they left Ground Hollow, through when she played cards with the Queen, then working her way to their voyage over and finally up to when she just walked in through the door. It was brief but still more detailed than the three-minute version Elise had given Hunter on the Nightport docks. He occasionally hummed and exclaimed as he got the full picture.

When Nessa had run out of words and sat staring at her hands, Anja hissed. "I'll tell you now, we're not letting that tapeworm you call your monarch keep Elise prisoner."

Hunter nodded emphatically. "Certainly not. And neither is Elise. She has a backbone of hardened steel. No matter where she is right now, you know she is planning her escape."

"Mm. You're both right. I… simply don't know what to do. Well, of course I know what I'm going to do – I'll take the next steamship to Arclid and then get to Highmere where I assume that the—"

"Tapeworm," Anja supplied.

Nessa nodded distractedly. "Yes, the tapeworm is keeping Elise."

"But you don't know what to do from there?" Hunter guessed.

"Exactly. I can't barge in and say that I want the love of my life back and just have Elise come sauntering down the stairs and into my arms. Violence won't work either, that castle is known to be tremendously well-guarded."

Nessa stared at her hands again. Out of the corner of her eye she saw Hunter return to chewing his nails.

"Perhaps there's a way to get into the castle without being discovered. Or at least without being immediately thrown out," Anja said, unusually hesitant.

Nessa looked up at her. Anja was gazing into the distance, her eyes glazed over and the corners of her mouth turned down. She seemed suddenly older.

That look isn't only worry over Elise, Nessa realised.

"Are you all right, Anja?"

She scowled at Nessa. "Of course I'm not. A person I'm fond of has been kidnapped."

"Yes, but…" Nessa started.

Anja held up a hand. "Fine, I may also not like the solution I am about to suggest." She blew out a long breath. "I know a person at the Viss embassy here in Skarhult."

"What is a Whiss?" asked Hunter.

"*Viss*," Anja said pointedly, "are the people who live in the north of our continent. A more peace-loving and calm people than the Sundes or my people, the Wayfarers."

Nessa stood, sensing the tiniest hint of hope in the air. "Yes. The white-haired, pale people. Like the confectioner at the faire. How can this person at the embassy help us?"

"Her name is Diinna and she is the right hand of the Viss ambassador. She… was meant to marry me a few years ago. Obviously, that didn't happen."

Nessa's cheeks grew hot. "I s-see. I'm very sorry to hear that, Anja. May I ask how she can help us?"

Anja shook, as if shedding her discomfort. "The Viss have long tried to overthrow Joiners Square who, as you know, are in an alliance with your Queen. If we're going to take up arms against *Joiners Square* kidnapping Elise for *the Queen*… Diinna is the perfect person to turn to."

"Why? Because the Viss are experts on Joiners Square and the Queen?" Nessa asked.

"Or because they want to take on both the Queen and Joiners Square and therefore we have common enemies?" Hunter suggested.

"Both. Diinna told me that Joiners Square are officially in talks with the Queen over trade deals. Unofficially, they want something answered and believe that Queen Marianna has the answer. But, the Viss think that Joiners Square *also* want to spread their... what is the word... dominion over to Arclid at some point."

"Right now, I'd almost welcome them in," Nessa muttered.

Anja carried on as if she hadn't spoken. "Meanwhile, the Viss have become more and more vocal about wanting to separate our government from Joiners Square. They're not alone in that, but for now, Joiners Square is too strong." Anja paused to run her hand through her hair. "I don't know what they're planning, all I know is that they're not friends with Joiners Square nor their co-conspirator, your Queen. And that Diinna will help me. She owes me that much."

There was venom in the last words, and Nessa shot Hunter a glance. Anja fetched her coat and began to get ready; Nessa followed her example. Hunter carefully smoothed down his hair before starting to apply his lush fur coat, fur hat, furry boots, and even a scarf lined with what looked like mink fur.

He's taking ages. And looks like he's wearing two packs of rabbits. I hope the meat was used so those animals didn't just die for human vanity.

Anja opened the door and Nessa's thoughts turned from animal deaths to her own suffocating panic. She saw flashes in her vision and reminded herself to breathe. She had always helped those who needed her, and she had always sacrificed everything for Elise. Now, she would have to find the confidence to do that again. Somehow.

～

Stepping off the cable car, Anja explained that Diinna was constantly busy and that they would probably have to wait for an appointment. All while Hunter shrieked with joy as he saw snow fall for the first time. Nessa just wanted to be on a ship. She had finally found something worse than her fear and insecurity: helplessness. Her stomach roiled and ached. She put a gloved hand on it, willing it to calm.

"It is only a few minutes ahead. You see that one building that isn't just white? The one with the mint green gables? That is the Viss embassy," Anja explained.

"Oh, look, the colours of the building match the flag up there, white with a mint green cross. I like it. Sort of winter-themed, I should say," Hunter answered, leaving Nessa to her panicked silence.

She focused on breathing and putting one foot in front of the other, meaning that she wasn't looking up into the snow-dotted sky. Because of this, she walked straight into a man who had stopped in front of her.

"Nessa? I thought that was you. Careful there, yes?"

She looked up at the man. "Master Fabian? What are you doing here?"

He beamed. "I'm on my way to a restaurant. Meeting a lady friend tonight. One who I hope will be more than a friend soon, yes?"

Nessa wiped away the snow that was landing on her eyelashes. "I see." She turned to Anja and Hunter. "Go ahead. Try and get an appointment to see Diinna. I'll meet you there as soon as I've talked to my master."

"All right. Don't delay," Anja said and trudged on. Hunter smiled at them before hurrying to follow Anja's much faster gait.

Nessa shifted her weight from foot to foot. She needed to say goodbye to Fabian. She'd be leaving soon, either to save Elise and settle down somewhere or to help Elise escape and then spend the rest of their lives running and hiding. Either way, she had to leave this life they had cobbled together, including her apprenticeship. It was a conversation she had to have now, but she wanted to hurry away, to be actively doing something to save Elise, not stand here wasting time wondering how to say goodbye. Wondering if she should be honest or tell a lie. She fidgeted with her hat.

"Nessa? You look like you have ants in your blood. Are you hurt?"

"No. N-not physically, anyway. I'm… just not sure how to handle this situation. I need to s-say goodbye to you. I m-must leave. I don't know how much I should tell you and I don't have much time to explain."

Fabian surveyed her with his head tilted. "I see. Tell me only the necessary then, yes?"

Easier said than done. Short version… think, Nessa… what is the short version?

She wrung her gloved hands. "Um, well. I n-need to go free Elise, which will anger the uniform monkeys and probably have dire consequences."

Fabian laughed as he clapped her on the shoulder. "These are decent things, I think. Go help your wife and kick those apes in their monkey nuts, yes?"

Nessa almost smiled. "I'll try."

"Not try, you *will do it*. And you'll tell them that Fabian Smedstorp says hello. Also that next time they want my services… they let me make the whole glass palace, not just the dainty bowls. Those big-time glaziers have been boasting constantly about making that palace." He snorted before adding, "I could grow my business, get machines, and employees, and I could make their glass panes, too." He scowled and spat into the snow.

For a moment Nessa could hear Elise's voice in her head. "Did he just spit in the snow? How crude and unhygienic." She chuckled sadly and then felt her whole body itch with the need to be doing something, to be helping Elise, to be closing the distance to wherever she was now.

She took Fabian's hand. "Thank you for taking me on as an apprentice and for everything you've taught me. You've increased not only my skillset but my confidence. I'm sorry I must leave before you've finished my training."

He laughed. "Don't worry about that. You're good enough to start learning on your own, yes? Now you only need to practice, practice, and practice. You will get it wrong 499 times, yes? But he 500rd time will be most excellent. You don't need me to be there for that. Just don't give up on the glass. It likes you."

Nessa had to smile at that. "Thank you. I like it, too, and I like you as well. I'll miss you."

"And I you. Open a hot shop that becomes famous all over the orb, and I'll come and visit, yes? First making sure you've steadied your hand when you open up the glass, like we've been practising. Then taking all the credit for your education, yes?"

"Ha! I think my first masters would dispute your claim. Anyway," she bit her lip, unsure of how much to say. "There might be some political rumblings around here. Take care of yourself and perhaps speak quietly of having known me."

He scoffed. "I always survive. If the uniform monkeys rule Storsund, I'll teach them not to overlook my skill again. If they're overthrown, I'll make the new government love me, support their revolt, and then make all *their* glass. I land on my paws."

"Your feet," Nessa corrected before squeezing his hand, not an easy thing to do when they were both wearing such thick gloves. Still, she hoped he felt the squeeze and the sincere sentiment attached to it.

"Thank you, good luck, and goodbye."

"Same to you, Nessa Glass. Now, we cannot say goodbye without big bear hug, yes? If you don't like hugs, better stop me now!"

In reply, she laughed and hugged him, an instant of respite from the sharp fear and impatience biting in her stomach.

Then, as he walked away, the respite was over. Her mind's eye filled with images of Elise. Angry, worried, or worse… crying, trapped, petrified. Nessa set her jaw and took off running through the falling snow, chasing Anja and Hunter into the embassy.

CHAPTER 22
THE KONSPIRATORIA

Something woke Elise. Was that a seagull's cry? Her eyes struggled to open. Her eyelids felt heavy and sluggish, slow to obey her mind's commands. Not that her mind was all that sharp, a fog of confusion and sleepiness lay thickly over it. As her eyes finally opened, the light cut Elise and worsened what promised to be a headache of epic proportions.

This is worse than the time I challenged that duke to a drinking contest in Obeha. Luckily, I do not appear to be wearing a horse racing trophy as a hat this time. Thank the gods for small favours.

She forced her eyes open a little more and instantly regretted it. Why was she feeling like this?

"Have I... been poisoned?" she whined, not realising she said it out loud until she heard the words echo around her.

"Not poisoned," a voice said. "Only given strong powders to make you sleep and be... happier to come along, yes?"

Elisandrine's eyes popped wide open now. There someone in here with her! Wait, where was *here*?

"Who are you? Where am I? This is... not right. Wait, I..." Something cleared in her mind.

Strong powders. To make me sleep.

"You beasts! How dare you slip me some sort of anaesthetic? Where was it? In the water you gave me in the carriage?"

There was a snigger. "So many questions. So much shouting."

The speaker came into view. It was the young Joiners Square soldier who had taken her, the one who had defended the cat. Elise looked around but couldn't see his older colleague.

"Answer them and I might shout less," she growled.

He grinned, his hands in the pockets of his uniform trousers. "I can answer some, yes? I'm Under Lieutenant Anders Dahl. You're in a cabin on the *Konspiratoria*, bound for Cawstone. When we have... what's the word... docked, we will travel to Highmere. You'll be delivered like a parcel. Hopefully unharmed, yes?"

"*Konspiratoria*? A ship. To Arclid. Is it a sail ship?" She asked with a glimmer of hope.

The under lieutenant snorted. "A steamship, of course. We would not travel on something as old and slow as a sail ship. Not like you backwards Arclidians, yes? Was that how you came to Storsund?"

She winced. She had hoped they were travelling slower, giving her ample time to figure out a plan before they got to Highmere.

Or perhaps a chance for Nessa to free me.

"No. I arrived on a steamship, too," she snapped, rubbing her temples to clear some of the fog and headache. "I need to use the washroom. I must change my rags."

He paled but immediately helped her up, and even handed her the satchel with a diffident bow.

Moments later, when Elise was climbing back into the bed, she said, "So, six weeks at sea together. I am glad to have a name for you then, Under Lieutenant Dahl. I would tell you my name, but I assume you know."

He avoided her gaze. "We were to fetch the woman disguised as Elise Glass. That was all I need to know. A soldier doesn't ask questions."

She quirked an eyebrow. "You were not curious? About my name? Or the reason you are taking me to Highmere?"

"We're taking you to the Queen," he answered defensively.

"Yes. However, you do not know why. Do you?"

He stood firmer, avoiding her gaze. "I don't need to know. I'm a—"

"Soldier," Elise supplied. "Yes, I know. Still, a little curiosity is simply human. Especially in someone as young and clearly intelligent as you."

A small twitch by his eye was the only reply he gave. It was enough. She knew now that he was curious. She leaned on her elbows to see him better and fought her headache enough to put a hint of flirtatious teasing into her voice. "I could answer your questions, you know? Divulge the secret of why such a big deal is being made of me. And the rush to get me to court."

That twitch appeared again. He opened and closed his mouth in a way that made him resemble a fish. "I… I don't need to know. Joiners Square gives the answers I need, nothing more and nothing less."

Curse it. He was not lured in.

In anger, Elise dropped off her elbows, regretting it the second her head hit the pillow. She peered over to the door.

He followed her gaze. "You can't escape through there. The sergeant is on the other side."

She groaned. "Of course he is. So, is he the man you were with when you kidnapped me?"

"Kidnap is an ugly word, yes? You came voluntarily."

"Only to make sure you did not batter my head in!" she screamed, rage triumphing over her headache.

He shrugged, looking down at his feet, discomfort visible in every part of his frame.

Not fond of violence. Good. I can work with that.

She rubbed her temples again. "If we are to travel together, we might as well get to know each other. You are a proud soldier of Joiners Square. Were you actually a joiner at some point?"

"No. Only the first people were joiners. Back when it was an organisation for joiners' rights at work, yes? Do you call it union?"

Elise tried to nod, but it made her head pound worse. "Yes, a workers' union."

"I was recruited a few years ago. When it had grown to a national organisation making our nation thrive and creating a, um, organised society. No more endless talk and wasted time, yes? We get things done."

He looked so proud that part of her wanted to laugh.

Under Lieutenant Dahl smoothed his short blond hair. "So. Yes. Uh, my father was a joiner and part of the organisation from the start. He wanted me by his side, so proud of me being a soldier. Now I serve in his memory."

"Your father has passed away as well, then?"

He looked up, searching her face for a second. "Yours, too?"

"Yes. My father died when I was young. He was an architect. He worked himself sick for the woman you are forcing me to go to right now."

Dahl swallowed visibly. "I'm sorry to hear that."

Elise rubbed at her forehead. "I do not expect you to apologise. You are a soldier following orders. Joiners Square knows best, right? If they say that forcing a woman into slavery to someone she abhors is the right thing to do, you must do it. Correct?"

His pale cheeks flushed red. He took a step back, as if she had slapped him. "Don't say things like that!"

The sound of his shrill voice must have alerted his sergeant. He barrelled through the door, barking questions in Sundish to his under lieutenant. Elise tried to follow the rapid conversation. The sergeant was asking what was going on and Dahl was replying something about having questions. His superior moved close to him and in a threatening hiss said something she couldn't make out.

Dahl left the room with unsure steps. Elise was left with the sergeant who was smiling at her. "Couldn't help but make things difficult, yes? They said you were trouble. They gave me this to help with that." He took out an oblong box from the pocket of his uniform jacket.

He opened it and Elise saw a vial of clear liquid and a small syringe.

"What is that?" she whispered breathlessly.

The sergeant held the already filled syringe up to the light. "A powder. Well, it was a powder but now has been mixed with liquid. Like the water we gave you in the carriage, yes?"

Then, lightning fast, he stabbed her in the neck and pushed the plunger on the syringe down before she could move away. She didn't have time to even shout until he pulled the syringe out. Then, she screamed at the top of her lungs. In fear, in pain, but most of all, in rage.

"Screech all you want, Mrs Glass. The people on this ship have been told that you're mentally ill and likely to wail and make up strange stories. Soon you will feel dizzy, yes? Then tired. I suggest you sleep. The trip will be so much nicer for us all if you only eat, sleep, and use the... what's the word... commode. Nothing else, yes?"

She bellowed with primal rage and threw a pillow at him, but he simply dodged it and continued speaking. "And no talking to Under Lieutenant Dahl. He's young and soft, you'll confuse him, yes? I said he was wrong for this mission, but they wanted him to learn. He does well on smaller tasks but is not ready for this. Still, if I keep you from talking too much to him, he should be fine."

He said something after that as well, but Elise struggled to make it out. Everything was growing dim. A panicked part of her fought the calm and drowsiness that was filling her. She fought the slowing of her heart and the relaxing of her muscles, but to no avail. Before she knew it, her eyes were closing, and everything grew black and warm.

The last thought in her mind was, *Did I tell Nessa that I loved her this morning?*

CHAPTER 23
THE VISS EMBASSY

Nessa caught up with Anja and Hunter on the steps outside the embassy.

"Gosh, the Viss have impeccable taste," Hunter whispered while admiring the round building.

Anja grunted. Then she took a deep breath and strode up the stairs. Nessa and Hunter followed her up and through to a reception area. Nessa heard her speak in a language that to her sounded more languid than Sundish.

After a brief discussion, Anja waved to them to join her in following the male receptionist.

Anja whispered, "We're being brought to Diinna's office. Apparently, she was about to go home for the day. However, the receptionist said we could go see if she'd take a meeting with us, as long as we leave without a fuss if she can't."

"Fair enough," Nessa conceded.

They walked in silence until Anja stopped dead in her tracks. She looked like she was barely breathing. Nessa followed her gaze. It was fixed on a well-dressed, short woman with a long mane of greying platinum blonde hair. As the woman turned, Nessa was met with a pale, open face boasting piercing grey eyes and a dimpled smile.

This must be Diinna. Yes, I can see why she would have an effect on Anja.

The diplomat's smile died as she spotted Anja. Something wary and troubled replaced it. She strode towards them and greeted them in near-perfect Arclidian.

"How may I help you?" she asked, clasping her hands behind her back.

Anja blinked quickly a few times and then cleared her throat. "Can we go somewhere private?"

Diinna inclined her head in agreement and led them to a room at the end of a corridor. The room was sparse but cosy, with a table and several padded chairs in the centre. On the wall next to them was a coat rack, which they all used to hang their snowy outerwear while Anja raced through the main parts of the story. She started with Elise upsetting the Queen by spurning her in Nightport and ended with the fact that they planned to rescue Elise but had no idea how.

Throughout all of it, Diinna looked Anja straight on, a wrinkle between her intense eyes. Diinna looked intelligent and reassuring to Nessa. Someone you would trust and respect. A leader.

"I see. Well, Marianna Hargraves is known for her blind determination. She is also known for assuming that everyone can and will adore her if kept in her presence long enough. My spies tell me that she claims that was how she got such a close relationship with Joiners Square. However, we both know that's not the reason, don't we, Anja?"

Anja only grunted, clearly feeling she had done her part of the speaking.

"What is that?" asked Hunter.

Diinna peered at him before replying. "They believe she has the answer to a question, one which is of great importance to them. That is why a Joiners Square delegation is at the castle now. Officially, to discuss trade. Unofficially, to get their burning question answered."

Impatience was niggling at Nessa, but she tried to keep it out of her voice. "Anja mentioned that. What is the question?"

In her own language, Diinna shot a question at Anja who replied in Arclidian, "Yes, they can be trusted."

Diinna bored her intense gaze into Nessa's. "If magic exists."

"Oh. I didn't expect that. Um, well, does it?" Nessa asked.

"And why would the Queen know the answer?" Hunter added.

Diinna smoothed the back of her dress and sat down while she answered. "Because there's always been rumours in the higher echelons of Storsund society that the Arclid monarchy had access to magic but kept it to themselves. Kept it hidden, only using it when they had to in order to maintain their power. Who knows if it's true."

Anja sat down opposite Diinna, a table between her and her former betrothed. Nessa and Hunter flanked her. While Anja scowled, and Hunter adjusted his hat-flattened hair, Nessa sat forward to ask the only important question.

"So, will you help us find a way to free Elise? Please? We can give you information on the Queen and maybe even on Joiners Square in return."

Diinna ran her hand along her jaw and up to her mouth, tapping her lips with her fingers. "I wish to help you. Not merely because you are friends of Anja and," she hesitated for a moment, "I owe her any favour she wants. But, also, because it would give us an opportunity to prove to the world that Joiners Square and your Queen are as corrupt and criminal as we've claimed. Joiners Square kidnapping a young woman and Queen Marianna holding her prisoner… now that's something people can revolt against."

Nessa's palms were sweating. "You want to use Elise as some sort of warning sign?"

"More like a match," Diinna said. "To light the fire that is so far only sparking feebly."

Hunter giggled, and Nessa stared over at him. He looked apologetic as he said, "Elise as a *match*. When everyone says she is a *fire-starter*. It is funny that she appears to have come full circle, linguistically at least."

When no one answered, he slumped into his seat. Nessa tried to smile to put him at ease, but the smile wouldn't come.

This is taking too long. I need to locate a ship over there and help Elise. Now.

Breaking the silence, Diinna said, "Back to the subject at hand. We've been wanting to oust Joiners Square, or at least to make people question the amount of power they have. If that happens, we can replace the puppets we call a government and get real leaders in. Ones that have been chosen through democratic vote and have no ties to a corrupt organisation which paints its leaders as gods."

"Real leaders. Like you?" Anja said, bitterness dripping off her voice like cold, congealed coffee.

Diinna blinked at her a few times, then quietly replied, "You know this is not about my ambition. It's about what is best for Storsund. Yes, I am one of the suggested Viss. However, there are also Wayfarer ambassadors and politicians, one that I believe to be distantly related to you. Others suggested are part of the Sund underground movement, who have bravely spurned Joiners Square's propaganda and bribery."

"A real government? Actually made up of representatives from all three groups?" Anja queried.

Diinna started at Anja's tone but still met her steely gaze. "Yes. Lately, our society has, despite Joiners Square's best efforts, taken steps towards equality. But one obstacle even bigger than Joiners Square is always there; the Sundes still have more coin, more land, and thereby more power than the Viss and the Wayfarers. If we're to start over, that issue will be addressed. Power can be redistributed fairly and used to improve life for us all."

Nessa was tapping her fingers against the table. "I applaud that idea. However, how's that relevant to our problem?"

Diinna turned to her. "Joiners Square's greed for power doesn't end with Storsund. They want to know about magic because they believe it is the ultimate tool for them to achieve world domination. They want to rule not only our continent but the entire orb. Starting with Arclid."

"I doubt the Queen would allow that," Hunter said with a scoff.

Diinna hummed. "She may not have a choice. You know better than anyone how shakily she sits on that throne. Revolts always spring up due to her new laws, strange whims, high taxations, and tendency to hold her country's development back to maintain her own power. Not to mention that her lack of heir causes some to say that the Arclid monarchy itself is in danger."

"Not only Arclidians complain," Anja murmured.

"No, her leadership is being seen with unfavourable eyes everywhere," Diinna agreed. "Ambassadors in Obeha and the Western Isles have been discussing possible replacements to lead your continent. Someone who'll negotiate without silly games. Someone that can be trusted not to start a war to soothe her own ego or because she's in a foul mood." Diinna curled her upper lip. "Thus, the Viss and the Wayfarers have reached out to lend support to that cause. Sadly, we cannot speak for all of Storsund as the Sundes follow Joiners Square's line of supporting Marianna."

"But there's no one to take her place," Nessa said, exasperated. "Arclid's revolts always die down for lack of decent options. Any government we elect starts to fight internally, all wanting absolute power. And when we try to decide on a new monarch, well, different parts of the land back different Noble candidates and wars ensue. In the end, we always end up back with the cursed Hargraves."

Diinna sat forward, some blood in her cheeks now. "Yes, but we've found a candidate. Someone we've all discarded as subdued. Listen, reclaiming power from Joiners Square will be a long process for us, requiring proof of corruption and months of arguing in court. Then elections." She pointed to Nessa and then Hunter. "You, however, can be rid of your Queen much faster. Your people want a new ruler, and there's a contender standing by. All you require is the support from the Noble families and the royal guards, then the contender can take the throne with a mere change of crests and a new royal portrait."

"Who is this person?" Nessa asked.

Diinna hesitated. "I'm not sure how much I am allowed to divulge, for the contender's safety. Considering your situation, it's important that you're aware that this person is already in Highmere, waiting in the wings, ready to step up if the Queen is taken off the board."

"Off the board? You sound like you are playing a children's game and not dealing with people's lives," Anja said, disdain in every word.

A muscle twitched in Diinna's jaw as she ground it shut and stared at Anja, who glared daggers back at her.

"Do you two wish to talk alone before we get back to rescue plans?" Hunter asked softly.

"No time for that," Anja snapped. "We need to help Elise now. She's the only reason I'm here."

Diinna bared her teeth before countering, "I'm sure she's a very worthy cause, but I must look at the bigger picture. There's a devious organisation using coin and brainwashing to control the biggest nation on the orb. And a Queen in a neigh-bouring land who bleeds her nation dry and chokes its devel-opment by spreading rumours that new inventions, like trains and steam, are dangerous. Not to mention—"

Nessa held up her hands. "Enough! You said you could use what happened to Elise to prove that Joiners Square and the Queen must be removed. So, let's focus on getting Elise back so that she can testify. Then you'll have proof for your court case against Joiners Square. And Arclid will have something solid to accuse Queen Marianna of – imprisoning a Noble. So, how do we free Elise?"

Diinna clasped her hands on the table. "Well, I should like to wait until we've contacted the other embassies and discussed if now is the time to start this process. I fear we need more proof than just Elise's testimony. We need all the details of the coup against Joiners Square ironed out. As well as the succes-sion in Arclid."

Anja banged her fist on the table. "There isn't time! We don't even have time for the bloody speeches you've been spouting these last few minutes. Elise was taken today and is probably already on a ship. In six weeks she'll be in Arclid and in the hands of the Queen. She could kill her." Anja gave the table another whack. "I, for one, won't sit here and wait while you… *iron out details*. Help us now, or we go in on our own. Probably getting ourselves killed and ruining your plans to use Elise for your revolution."

Hunter cleared his throat. "I cannot speak to what is happening here in Storsund, but Arclid is ready to rebel right now. You mentioned Arclidians being unhappy with the Queen? I heard the crew on the boat over say that people are talking about a revolt over Arclid's lack of trains. They see how trade and manufacturing blossoms in the other three conti-nents and do not want to be left behind. Now is the time, I am sure of it."

Diinna looked unconvinced and so Hunter pushed on. "Arclidians are especially irate now, because of the coin spent on Prince Macray's wedding and this secret manhunt of the Queen's. Arclidians have had enough. If you do not want to strike now to save Elise, do it to make the best of the momentum building in Arclid."

Diinna stared into space for a while. Then she sighed. "I suppose we might as well begin the process while Joiners Square are practically leaderless. They do seem quite helpless without him. All those blustering joiners, blowhard aristocrats, and old soldiers who are more used to drinking wine than making national decisions." She said the words so quietly that Nessa wasn't sure if they were meant to have heard them or not.

"Who is 'he'? This leader you mentioned?" Nessa asked.

Diinna glanced towards the door. "Naming names is not good practice. You do not need to know." She sat forward and caught Nessa's gaze. "All you need to know is that I shall contact people and make plans while you are on the ship to Arclid. I'll set all the wheels into motion and spread the news of what Marianna has done and how Joiners Square assisted. Perhaps we can even uncover the spies who found Elise and reported to the Queen."

Nessa nodded. "They must've found her pretty quickly. We've only been here a few months." Her laugh was hollow. "We were so worried that her fame from making the scented oils and that bloody interview would alert the Queen to her whereabouts. The witch was already aware and planning Elise's kidnapping."

Anja put her hand over Nessa's on the table. "You couldn't have known. You weren't even sure if she was chasing you."

There was a pause, during which Diinna glanced down at their hands. She cleared her throat. "We're all agreed, then. You're to travel to Arclid and fetch Elise back to testify about what happened to her. No passenger ships leave this late at night, but I can locate a ship that leaves first thing tomorrow morning. Your biggest problem, however, is what to do when you get there."

"Yes, Diinna. That's why we're here," Anja said through clenched teeth. "If it were simply a matter of getting on a steamer, we could've achieved that ourselves."

Diinna held up her hand. "Calm down, I hadn't finished. I was going to suggest that I find you some backup, some volunteer Viss and Sund underground rebels who look like they could be Joiners Square soldiers. Partly in—"

"Great. I'll be the too-dark-too-thin odd one out," Anja interrupted with a sneer.

Diinna threw her a glance before carrying on. "Partly in case there's violence, and partly so you can enter the castle under the guise of reinforcements for the soldiers stationed at Highmere for the talks between the Queen and Joiners Square's High Captain Nordhall. The problem is that I can't easily procure uniforms."

Hunter sat forward. "Uniforms?"

"She means Joiners Square uniforms that we and her underground rebels can disguise ourselves in," Anja answered him, her gaze still fixed on her former lover.

"Exactly. Copies are easy to get wrong and take too long to make, so that's out. I'm afraid I'm not aware of any Joiners Square staff whom I trust to betray their leaders by delivering a set of uniforms and then keep the secret," Diinna said, sounding truly apologetic.

A thought struck Nessa. One that was equal amounts amusing and terrifying. *Albert.* The pompous chatterbox, with his loud family, the man who had grated on Nessa's shy personality from day one… he might be the key to helping Elise escape.

"I think I know someone who can help," she said slowly.

She turned to Anja. "Remember Albert Lindberg? He and his family adore Elise, and he works for the Joiners Square branch in Charlottenberg."

Hunter slapped his thigh. "Superb! That is where we have to go to catch a ship to Arclid anyway."

Anja ran a hand through her unruly hair. "All right. We go to Charlottenberg tonight. We talk to Mr Lindberg and ask him if he can sneak back to work, steal some uniforms, and hand them over to us. If he can't or won't, we rent rooms for the night and then get on a ship to Arclid with the underground fighters tomorrow morning anyway, hoping to figure out a plan while we travel. Correct?"

"Anja, your Arclidian is vastly improved. Must be the company you keep these days," Diinna said with a nod to Nessa and Hunter.

Anja ignored her. "Did I get that right?"

Nessa scratched the back of her neck. "Hm. Well, before we go to Charlottenberg, we must return to your house to fetch some coin and essentials for the trip. Otherwise I think you covered it. Oh, and whether he helps us our not, I'm sure Albert will lend us a room for the night. No doubt their residence could fit the entire Arclid navy."

Hunter tapped the table with his index finger. "You both missed one thing. What if he reports us to his superiors? What if they come for us?"

Nessa swallowed. Why hadn't she thought about that? What else might she have overlooked?

"Then we hope we get enough warning to have time to run." She blew out a breath, facing the facts.

"I apologise for wasting your time, Diinna, but I have to take a moment to convince Anja and Hunter to let me go alone." She looked at her two friends. "This is sounding like a dangerous plan at best and as a suicide mission at worst. I'll locate a uniform, make the trip, blend in with the other soldiers, and try to sneak Elise out. No doubt she already has a plan that I can help with."

"No," Anja said simply.

Hunter nodded. "What she said. Nessa, I came all this way because I wanted to start my new life in the image of you and Elise, free but responsible. I will learn that by watching you. Besides," he smiled, "I want to help. You two have given me so much confidence. Confidence to leave Nightport. Confidence to admit openly that I do not engage in affairs of the heart or the genitals."

Nessa chewed the inside of her cheek. "Hunter, you were held down at Silver Hollow Castle by the Queen and some of the Royal Guards she travels with. They'll know your face."

"No, heartling. They would recognise a clean-shaven, well-fed man in pretty clothing. I am a lot skinnier now and will be wearing a uniform, like the other Joiners Square soldiers. And I will have grown a full beard on the boat over."

"Ship, not boat," Anja muttered.

Nessa disregarded the interuption. "I really can't convince you, can I?"

He beamed his full-on charmer smile. "I came all this way, in bum-freezing winter, to see you again. You certainly cannot keep me from journeying back to our balmy, green homeland with you."

Nessa smiled back, wanting to hug him but aware of his aversion to touching. "Fair enough. As long as you promise me to leave or hide if I request it. I don't want you to risk detection. Both for our sake and your own. After all, you need to come back to Anja's house to fetch those enormous suitcases when we're done."

She winked at him, and he laughed. "I am a Nightport lad. I know when to hide and when to run and I'm not ashamed to do either," he said, still chuckling.

Nessa looked to Anja, who stared back unblinkingly.

"What about you? It's different for you, Anja. You have more to lose, a home, a pet, friends, family, a reputation, and your life's work. You can't take this risk."

Anja tossed her head, sending her thick pepper-and-salt hair flying. "Don't tell me what I cannot do. Hunter isn't the only one who's had his life changed by you two. You pulled me out of my hibernation. My loneliness. You and Elise even helped my book along, not only through dictation, but by igniting my passion for the project again. Also, you made me cheer up and remember that life can be fun." She gifted Nessa a smirk before she began stretching her arms out to the sides. "Besides, it's not in a Traveller's nature to grow stale in one place. I am overdue a journey. I don't really like my friends or my family, so there's no problem there. When it comes to the cat and my work, well, I'm sure Diinna will break into my house, finish the book, and steal the cat."

Diinna opened her mouth in shock but then gave Anja a surprised, frail smile. "Svarte always hated me. But yes, I'll take him and your book on. Not that I'll need to, it takes more than a castle full of Royal Guards and a squadron of Joiners Square soldiers to even bruise a woman like you."

Anja seemed to hesitate over her answer but settled for, "True enough. Wayfarers have iron in our blood. We do not scare or die easily."

Nessa held up her hands in defeat. "All right, I see I cannot stop you. Let's just hope that Albert doesn't betray us, so we can at least make it as far as the castle and actually clap eyes on Elise."

"And that your impatience doesn't kill you on the ship," Anja muttered.

Diinna stood up. "I shall leave you to prepare for your voyage. I need to pick your team. I believe I know just the people for this. Ask this Mr Lindberg for uniforms for yourselves and seven other people. Ten souls will make a believable squadron for reinforcements for a diplomatic mission."

"What sizes for the other seven?" asked Hunter.

"Oh, I should say two women's uniforms and the rest men's. I'm picking athletic people, to ensure they look like Joiners Square soldiers, so the uniforms will fit them better than the thinnest of you three. Never mind. You'll have worse things to worry about. May nature's spirits be on your side."

With that, Nessa and Hunter bid Diinna farewell and thanked her, leaving her to the thorny task of finding and convincing skilled underground rebels to risk their lives. Nessa watched her go, not envying the fact that for the next few weeks Diinna would have to explain and defend her decisions today and fight to see the political upheaval started.

Anja didn't say a word to Diinna as they left the embassy. Nevertheless, Nessa could see her body language growing tenser with every step away from the silver-haired ambassador.

"Do you know what happened between those two?" Hunter whispered to Nessa.

"No. She doesn't. Moreover, I'm not deaf," Anja replied. "As you could probably tell, Diinna did something unforgivable. She feels guilty while I feel hurt. That's all you need to know, nosey boy."

Hunter looked stricken but said nothing. Nessa reached out to brush Anja's arm, but the older woman pulled away.

"All right. We shan't talk about it," Nessa said calmly. "We'll return home to pack the necessities for the sea voyage and subsequent carriage ride to Highmere. After that, we'll hopefully wear uniforms."

"Don't pack *too* much," Anja muttered to Hunter.

Nessa finished her thought. "After we've packed, we leave for the train to Charlottenberg. Do we know when the next train departs?"

Anja checked her pocket watch. "Unless the evening

timetable has changed, there should be one in two hours and fifteen minutes."

Nessa felt a stab in her bowels. "That long? There's nothing sooner?"

"No. But considering we all have to pack, I need to get the neighbour to feed Svarte, and then we have the journey to the station, we need that time," Anja said. "You have a six-week steamer trip, perhaps more if there's bad weather, ahead of you. Start practising your patience now, lass."

Hunter smiled at Nessa, probably trying to take some of the sting out of Anja's words. "I know it is not easy. Nevertheless, you must try. Besides, you need sustenance before we carry on," he said. "I can hear your stomach growling. You require food and drink."

Nessa was about to argue, but then she saw Anja's stern expression and shrank back. "Fine. When we're at the station waiting for the train, we shall find something to eat."

Anja took her hand. "That's more like it. You must keep strong. You know *she* is. Elise is probably fighting them with all her might and giving them a terrible time."

A glimmer of mirth crept into Nessa's heart. "That's true. She's probably ruining their day even before she's breakfasted."

The hour was late when they finally arrived in Charlottenberg. There was snow in the air, but nothing was coming of it. The weather seemed to hold its breath.

"The evening is wearing on. What if this Albert is asleep?" Hunter asked.

"Then we wake him," Nessa clipped. "He won't mind. He adores Elise and would get up at any hour to help her."

"I see," Hunter grunted.

He was struggling with his bag, not only because it was

stuffed with all that he deemed *necessities*, but because he lacked the muscle Nessa had. Anja had packed light, and if she was struggling with her bag, Nessa knew she would never complain or show it. It reminded Nessa of the people back in Ground Hollow, don't show weakness and don't whinge.

Nessa ignored the bags and concentrated on remembering the address.

What was it? Think, Nessa, you oxen-brained cretin!

She closed her eyes and tried to visualise the card Albert had given them at the first night of the frost faire. Gold, sloping letters which spelled out his name. Then his work title. Then… *58 Krasny Street, Charlottenberg.*

Nessa opened her eyes. "I've remembered the address. We need to hire a carriage."

Anja didn't waste time, she walked to the side of the road and stuck her arm out. After a moment, a carriage in the light colours of Charlottenberg stopped. Nessa told the driver the address and they entered the cold carriage. It was a silent journey with everyone lost in thought. A tense, aching silence. One that could only have been broken by someone as carefree and charming as Elise. Nessa blinked away tears.

What do I do if Joiners Square has brainwashed Albert so much that he won't betray them?

Nessa swallowed, blinking again.

I suppose if he won't… I'll have to find a way to make him. Wherever Elise is, she's fighting for her life. I must stop agonising and do whatever it takes to help her.

The carriage stopped. Nessa stepped out into the snow, which was slushier here than it had been in Skarhult. While Anja paid the driver, Nessa and Hunter looked up at a house coloured creamy yellow with silver-grey details and ivy creeping up the front.

Nessa muttered, "Great. The house is bloody well painted in Joiners Square's colours."

"This does not bode well for trying to get Albert to betray them," Hunter replied.

"No, it doesn't. Still, I'll convince him somehow. For Elise."

Nessa stiffened her spine, balled up her fists, and walked up to the front door.

CHAPTER 24
DISAPPROVAL

Marianna stood behind a pillar, a glass of sunberry wine in her hand and a wicked chuckle just barely suppressed. She was eavesdropping as High Captain Nordhall spoke to his second in command.

"These wasted months," Nordhall griped. "I am sick of the pageantry of Arclidian court. Pretty clothing, elaborate dinners, and old-fashioned customs. Phah! All I want is an honest answer to our question."

"Of course, High Captain," his second replied. "Your time is too precious to be wasted by the Queen stalling and playing games. Do you think she will reveal if magic exists?"

A muffled thump signalled that Nordhall had hit a wall.

Marianna smirked. *Both literally and figuratively,*

"She must! I deserve as much for fetching that wench for her." Nordhalls's voice deepened. "I must return home. Our associates are not strong or intelligent enough to hold off the Viss and Wayfarers, who dare challenge us openly now."

Marianna sipped her wine and enjoyed his disquiet. That faltering tone had never been in his bombastic voice when he spoke to her. Perhaps he thought himself safe right now, believing her to be in bed with her courtesans and mistakenly thinking she didn't speak Sundish.

As if a royal does not learn every language on the orb as a child. Cretin!

She took another sip as Nordhall launched into a tirade about how unreasonable Marianna was being and how they should colonize this backwards country and make the Queen spill every single secret. She laughed inwardly, knowing that she would rather burn her nation, and everyone in it, than let Joiners Square take it over. Or anyone else for that matter. It was hers. When would these oxen-brained snowmen grasp that?

When will it dawn on them that I shall not tell them anything, no matter how many favours they do me? Or how long they stay, looming and scowling in their drab uniforms and unnecessary fur stoles.

A whisper came from her side. "What are you doing?"

With a jolt, she found Adaire sneaking towards her. Those silent steps were hidden completely by the shouting Storsundian on the other side of the pillars.

"Eavesdropping on our distinguished guest. Finding out how to best use him for my own purposes," Marianna whispered back.

The sight of her queen's aide warmed her. Their animosity over the past weeks had been slowly draining, at least on her side. What Adaire was feeling wasn't relevant. Marianna put her free arm around her thin waist, pulling her close.

"Fun, is it not? It is like when we were young. Two girls sneaking around the castle listening to all the gossip," she whispered.

Adaire's pretty mouth was twisted in disapproval. "Fun, my Queen? Sometimes I find your lack of moral code unnerving."

"Unnerving but very useful, I should think. And perhaps attractive, hm?"

Marianna pulled her even closer. Her lover's breath smelled of honey cakes and Marianna kissed her, mixing that breath with her own wine-tasting one.

Adaire drew away with a patient smile. "Have you heard enough? Are you ready to retire for the night?"

Marianna listened to the Sundish behind the pillar and found that Nordhall was now complaining about the insects brought on by Arclid's mild winter.

"Yes, I seem to have heard all that could be useful."

They walked away quietly. When they were a corridor away, Adaire asked, "I assume you want me to ring for your courtesans?"

Marianna yawned. "No, I want you. Your banishment is over, you may return to the royal bed. If you like?"

Adaire seemed to hesitate, but then she leaned in and kissed Marianna before whispering, "Yes. Gods help me, but I would like that."

Marianna found she didn't even mind the negative remark. As long as she was getting what she wanted and as long as Adaire kept nuzzling so sweetly at her neck as they walked.

CHAPTER 25
58 KRASNY STREET,
CHARLOTTENBERG

I t was Eleonora Lindberg who opened the door and found Nessa standing outside it, wearing her desperation as a shield.

"Nessa? Hello! What a most charming surprise. And you brought company, yes? No Elise, though?"

"N-no. She couldn't be here. That is why I've come. M-may I speak to Albert?"

Nessa's hands balled into even tighter fists. She had tried so hard not to stutter.

Eleonora tilted her head as she inspected her. "Yes, of course. Come in and have some coffee, yes? I will fetch Albert from the games room. He and Sonja are playing Fool the Angel. The game you taught them on the ship over, yes?"

Nessa followed her in. "Yes. S-Sonja caught on very fast."

Behind her she heard the tentative footsteps of Hunter and Anja. If Albert were to blow the whistle on them, they were walking into what could become their holding cell.

"There's a coat rack over there," Eleonora said.

They took off their outerwear. A part of Nessa wanted to keep it on, in case they had to run, but it would look odd. Not to mention that they would roast in those warm clothes in this house, which seemed to be baking with log fires and gas lamps everywhere.

When they had stuffed their bags underneath their coats, their hostess led them into an elegant drawing room.

She smiled at them. "Please do sit down, yes? I shall have the coffee brought presently. And Albert fetched, of course." She surveyed Nessa's companions. "Ah, I remember the serious historian. Good evening, Anja. But who's this handsome gentleman? Wait. You were the one from the Joiners Square Fest, yes?"

He bowed and gifted her his charming, twinkling smile. "I was. That is an excellent memory you have there. As brilliant as your beauty. Hunter Smith at your service."

Eleonora tittered and then curtsied deeply. Nessa gave Hunter a look, wanting to point out that they didn't have time for his games. He shrugged, shamefaced.

Eleonora rang a bell and a maid came rushing in through the open door. She didn't even look at the three tense guests hovering behind her mistress. Eleonora reeled off a list of instructions in Sundish and the girl vanished again. The three guests took seats at the long table. Nessa saw a grandfather clock against one wall and felt as if her heart was matching the seconds ticking away so rapidly. Where was Elise right now? Was she hurt?

A booming voice was heard from outside the room. "Nessa Glass in my house? Where? Where is the fair Arclidian, hm?"

With that, Albert entered the room and clapped eyes on Nessa. She stood to greet him and was pulled into an unexpected hug.

"I'm such happiness that you took us up on our offer to visit. But what's this? You brought us guests but no Elise? Where is the golden-eyed picks?"

"Pixie," Eleonora amended.

Nessa took a deep breath before answering, "She's gone. Held against her will. By Joiners Square."

Albert's broad smile died on his face, wilting into a confused frown. "This… this is some sort of strange joke, yes?"

"No," Nessa replied in a croaked whisper. "She was taken earlier today. They kidnapped her to bring her to the Queen of Arclid."

Her voice broke at the last words and a sob escaped her. Anja took her hand and pulled her back into her seat.

"Sit down, Nessa. I shall explain," she said matter-of-factly.

Anja, with all the skill and efficiency of her profession, summarised what Nessa had told Diinna earlier.

When Anja had finished, both Albert and Eleonora were staring at her, Albert's fair skin blotching into red and Eleonora clasping the bejewelled necklace at her throat.

"But…" Albert started before gaping at his wife and then back at the guests. "But Joiners Square fight for the good of everyone. It was started by humble joiners to battle the unjust system, yes? They could not do such a thing."

Anja shook her head. "No matter what their ethos once was, they don't live by it anymore. We all used to believe in them and their cause. Storsund working conditions had to be improved, so unions have been one of the best things to happen to this nation. And the other unions still fight for good." She furrowed her brow. "As a historian, a neutral observer with some distance, Joiners Square stopped fighting for that when it was no longer about workers' rights. It became about power, coin, and making their leaders into godlike symbols. 'Good' was abandoned like a pair of worn-out shoes."

Eleonora grabbed the sleeve of her husband's smoking jacket and said something in a strangled voice. Anja leaned close to Nessa and Hunter to translate. "She's reminding him of some sort of inconsistencies he has been finding over the last year. Saying that she told him that something was wrong. She's talking about 'the missing coin and the way it has been covered up.' Apparently, just last week he was complaining about the ever-increasing secrecy coming from the top."

Albert nodded dazedly at his wife. He looked like a rabbit that has been told that he's sharing his warren with wolves. Still, Nessa could see his reluctance. If he called for a servant she'd assume he was sending a message to his superiors. She'd prepare to run. Her hands were already on the chair, about pull it out and get up.

Time ticked by. It seemed the whole room was too busy thinking to breathe. The maid brought a tray of coffee and little cakes topped with sunberries.

Albert waited until she had left. "Why... why did they take Elise, then?"

"Because the Queen of Arclid wants her. And they want a question answered. Thusly, it appears they traded Elise for the answer," Hunter said.

"Why did the Queen want... No, never mind. I know too much already." Albert rubbed his pale face. "If what you say is truthness, and I see no reason for you to lie, why tell me? I am only a worker bee, yes? I have no power over them and their decisions. I cannot get your wife back, Nessa."

Nessa swallowed down another sob. "I know. I don't need you to. I'll do that. Well, *we* will." She pointed to the other two before focusing back on Albert. "I need something else from you."

It wasn't Albert who replied, but Eleonora. "Name it. We only knew Elise for a short time, but she's impossible not to love, yes? If she's in danger, we will help any way we can. Right, husband?"

Albert nodded feebly, shock still glazing his eyes.

Nessa's tense shoulders dropped a little. "Wonderful. Thank you. What we need are some Joiners Square uniforms."

Nessa was still not sure whether to relax or prepare to run. Reading people wasn't her strong suit, she had Elise for that.

"Uniforms?" Albert spluttered.

Hunter sat forward, suddenly animated. "Yes, allowing us to disguise ourselves as Joiners Square soldiers and get into the castle. We shall have Storsund rebels with us who can maybe wheedle out where Elise is from the other soldiers. Then we sneak her out without the Queen knowing there are intruders at her court and then we get on the first ship back. Hopefully."

"You're bringing Storsund people?" Eleonora asked.

Hunter replied, "Yes, seven of them. So, we need four female and six male uniforms."

Eleonora tilted her head. "Why bring others?"

"Reinforcements," Anja explained. "If there's a fight we'll have more manpower and people who are used to scheming and fighting, unlike us. And for appearances. With seven others, we'll look like a normal, minor squadron sent to assist the delegation at court. Not like three weak civilians."

Albert was frantically tapping his fingers against his leg, eyes still glazed over.

After a pause in which they all watched him, Anja cleared her throat. "Mr Lindberg. A strong heart and solid spine come from a confident mind. Have faith."

Focus returned to Albert's eyes. "Quoting the works of Gyllenkvist? We… read her books at school, yes? That quote fits well here." He ran his hand over his beard. "Well, I don't know about this plan, but I want to help. I suppose I can go back to work, make up a reason to go down to the supply section and pick up some uniforms. It should be quiet down there this late at night."

Eleonora patted his arm proudly. "Well done, sugar badger." She turned back to her guests. "Is there anything else?"

"Well…" Nessa hesitated.

Hunter had no qualms and happily filled in, "We would be terribly grateful for lodging for the night. Our ship sails tomorrow." He paused. "Do you say 'sails' when it is a steamship? I was on a clipper once, big beautiful white sails. On that they said that we 'sailed', but is there a different steamer term? I have been wondering about that for months."

"Not relevant right now, Hunter," Nessa murmured.

He looked down. "No, of course not. Nor is where we sleep. We will find beds for the night somewhere around the Charlottenberg docks. Hopefully."

His pitiful speech worked as Eleonora clasped her necklace again and exclaimed, "Certainly not! You will stay with us, yes? We have many rooms. I'll have three guest bedrooms prepared, and Albert will go fetch uniforms. You sit there and enjoy the coffee and the sunberry tartlets, poor kittens."

With that she rushed off and Albert, confused without his wife's guidance, hummed to himself.

"I will get leaving then, yes? Yes. Hm. I need my hat and my coat. I will return late, you'll likely be asleep. So, I shall bid you goodnight. Tomorrow, I will hire a carriage and escort you to the docks with the uniforms safely in a bag, yes?"

Nessa squeezed her eyes shut, well aware that she had to ask what she didn't want to. "Albert?"

He turned while putting his top hat on. "Yes?"

"You... aren't on your way to turn us in, are you? You're not about to warn Joiners Square about our plans?"

"What?" He stepped back through the arch into the drawing room, looking taller than his short body should allow. "Child. Who do you think you're speaking to? I may not be so wonderful... I know I talk too muchly and I don't understand rules of being a social creature. But..." He banged a fist against his chest. "I am an honourable person and decent. I would never put an organisation ahead of a friend in need. Especially not a rotten organisation."

277

Nessa swallowed. "No, I'm sure you wouldn't. It's just that I d-don't know who to trust. I'm in over m-my head and I feel like I'm... drowning. I wasn't made for this."

He deflated back into his usually slouched posture, smiling slightly. "I see. If it makes you any more calmly, I swear on Sonja's head that I shan't betray you in any way. And you know there can be no oath that means more to me than that."

Nessa felt an unexpected rush of affection for this man. Right now, he seemed five times the man she had thought him to be and she regretted her annoyance at him. Well, most of it, anyway.

"Thank you. Once more, I'm sorry to have doubted you, Albert."

He smiled wider. "Think no more of it. Have cake and coffee. Or milk if you want to sleep better. Then go to bed and even if you can't sleep, try for some resting, yes?"

They all murmured their agreement and he put his coat on and left.

Anja, Nessa, and Hunter ate in silence. To Nessa, the cakes tasted like air and the milk seemed to curdle as she drank it. Nevertheless, she remembered Anja's words about eating and resting to stay strong. She forced down another mouthful of milk as she prayed to every deity she could remember, begging them to keep the love of her life safe and unharmed, pleading with them to make her strong and brave enough to save Elise.

The next morning found Nessa exhausted. She had flitted in and out of sleep for a few hours. The rest of the time she had laid there in the plush bed while her brain painted nightmare scenarios of how Elise was spending the night.

Nessa had never looked forward to a drink as much as the several mugs of coffee she was currently inhaling. She forced down some bread and salted ham with it, casting glances at Albert as she ate. After a while he noticed.

He gave her a paternal smile. "I have the uniforms and I spoke to no one while getting them. Please feel free to calm some."

She obeyed. Hunter, who was buttering his bread with as much sophistication as he could muster, was making small talk with Eleonora. He complimented her drapes, making Albert join their discussion. It evolved into a chattering mess where Albert and Eleonora talked over each other as they boasted about travelling all the way to northern Obeha to buy their drapes and cushions. Hunter happily interjected questions when he could, clearly not minding the loud, confusing, and fast speech of the Lindbergs. Nessa caught Anja scowling into her coffee, though. That scowl deepened as Sonja came in and added her chatter about waking up to find people in her house.

It was a relief to Nessa when they were finally getting ready to go to the docks and sail for the Arclidian harbour closest to Highmere, Cawstone.

As they were donning their outerwear, Anja got Nessa's attention. "I had a thought this morning. Do you remember what I was doing in Charlottenberg the day we met?"

Nessa thought for a moment. "You were picking up your earnings from your investments in the Storsund Trading Company."

"Exactly. I'll pop in there when we pass it this morning. You carry on to the docks to meet up with Diinna and the rebels. I'll meet you there. It might be good to have some extra coin. After all, we do have six weeks on the ship, then a few days travelling from the port to Highmere, then six weeks back."

Anja paused to take the gloves that Hunter handed her. "Thank you. Oh and Elise won't have any luggage. She'll borrow clothes from us and we'll just have to do our washing more often."

Nessa swallowed. "You're so sure that we'll save her and that we'll come back? All of us?"

"You'll fail unless you assume you can win. But yes, I am certain. Between my determination, Hunter's apparent skill for survival, and your unwavering loyalty to Elise, we can face down any enemy."

Nessa nodded, unconvinced and yet with tears crowding her eyes. Anja grabbed her by the shoulders. "That loyalty isn't all you have to offer, lass. You're strong and smart. You can do this. Now, I know you have a heart full of worry and a head full of doubts, so leave the mundane things to me. I'll keep us all clothed and fed."

"Thank you. I can never thank any of you enough," Nessa said, trying to conceal a sniff.

"We are not solely doing this for you, Nessa. We are doing it for Elise and for ourselves, too," Hunter said, gingerly placing his fur hat over his perfectly combed hair. "Not to mention that it is the right thing to do. No need for thanks."

"Still. Thank you," Nessa croaked. "I have never had much faith in myself and my abilities. Without you all, I would—"

"Be fine and manage to help Elise on your own," Anja finished sternly. She raised her voice. "Is everybody ready?"

They all answered yes and marched out towards two carriages waiting outside.

"Two carriages? But they seat four. Even with all the bags and the uniforms, we still only need one carriage," Nessa said.

Albert waved her concerns away. "The lad. You know, the letter child—"

"Messenger boy," Nessa, Anja, and Hunter all corrected at the same time.

"Yes, him. He accidentally got two carriages, so we thought we'd all come along and wave you off," he said.

Nessa shrugged. "All right. As long as we all keep calm and discreet when we get there."

"Of course. We'll all be quiet and subtle. That includes you, doesn't it, Sonja?" Eleonora said.

The child bounced a little on her heels. "Yes. I'm good girl for whole trip. I've promised, yes?"

Nessa tried to smile at Sonja, but her fraught nerves probably made it into a grimace. "Splendid. Let's get moving."

She, Hunter, and Anja stepped into the first carriage and got comfortable. Hunter was looking out the window, one hand lifted to rap on the roof to signify to the driver that they were ready, just as soon as the Lindbergs were in their carriage. They waited as Hunter surveyed the scene, a line forming between his eyebrows.

"Strange. They are putting something into their carriage. Playthings for Sonja perhaps? Gods, how many toys does that child need for a short journey?" he asked.

Finally, the line between his eyes smoothed, and he rapped on the roof. They took off down the slush-covered roads, and Nessa's nerves calmed a tad. Moving was good, moving was doing something.

A painfully long time later, they were at the harbour, getting out of their carriage.

Anja grabbed Nessa's arm. "I am going over to the Storsund Trading Company's office, then. Diinna is undoubtedly right where the ships are docked. She loves the sea air."

"All right. Hurry back."

"I will," she called over her shoulder as she marched away.

The Lindbergs finally spilled out of their carriage. Eleonora was struggling with a large box marked *Joiners Square Supplies*, seeming completely unaware of how indiscreet that was.

The uniforms. Good. But what's in those big bags that Albert is hauling out?

"Those aren't toys for Sonja," Nessa muttered to Hunter.

He sucked in air between his teeth. "No. Sorry, I simply assumed. I should think that is…"

"Travelling luggage," Nessa filled in. Her fatigue increased as her stomach began to ache.

Sonja leapt out, a stuffed toy under one arm and the little red bag she had been travelling with on the *Fairlight* in her other hand.

Nessa groaned. "No, wait a minute! Surely they don't mean to take Sonja along? Dash it, what are they thinking? Why would we even allow such a harebrained idea?"

Hunter winced. "Not sure. Nevertheless, you should speak to them before they start packing all that onto the ship. I doubt Diinna shall be happy with that."

"Happy with what?" a voice asked behind them. They turned and saw Diinna standing there in an elegant, white-grey coat which matched her hair.

Nessa chewed the inside of her cheek. "You'll see soon enough. First things first, good morning and thank you for coming to find us."

"Think nothing of it. The *Wave Cutter* shall be leaving for Cawstone in a little less than an hour. Plenty of time to converse and get you settled on board before she sails."

"Oh! So you *do* say 'sails' on a steamship then," Hunter exclaimed.

Diinna squinted at him. "Pardon?"

After a glance from Nessa, Hunter smiled and said, "Never mind. You were saying?"

"I was saying that the team of underground rebels are already on the ship. The people I had in mind were all willing. They've been waiting for something to do for weeks. They're eager to free Elise and bring her back here to testify about her kidnapping."

Nessa breathed a little calmer. "Excellent. I look forward to meeting them."

"Good. Now, I must point out that this is as far as the Viss can be involved. We have to lay low until the new government is ready to take control. Well, an interim government during the court case against Joiners Square, that is. After that, we hope to hold elections where everyone can vote."

Hunter clapped. "That sounds like what the Western Isles have – a democracy. That settles it, I am putting down roots here. Unless it is turns too chilly, then I may have to go to the Western Isles. Would you and Elise consider moving there, Nessa?"

Nessa gave him a sidelong glance. He held his hands up and muttered, "Not the time. Understood."

Meanwhile, Diinna was looking at Sonja, who was waving frantically at them.

"What is that child doing?" she asked.

Nessa stifled a sigh. "Yes. About that. I must speak to that child's father. We might have a… snag."

Diinna raised elegantly arched eyebrows. "A snag? It would be wise to unsnag it as soon as possible."

With that she stepped aside and let Nessa and Hunter approach Sonja and her parents.

Nessa gathered up her patience and tapped Eleonora on the shoulder. "Hello. What's all this?"

Eleonora turned and had the decency to look ashamed. For a moment. Then she smiled and blinked her long lashes at Nessa. "We're accompanying you to Cawstone, yes? We have holidayed there before, but it was years ago."

Nessa pinched the bridge of her nose. "No, you're not."

"Yes. We are. We shall help, yes?"

"No," Nessa answered.

Eleonora adjusted the box of uniforms in her arms. "Oh, I think so. I doubt you'll get these uniforms unless you allow us to help. Albert! Where did he get to? Albert, come here and explain to Nessa that we are coming along, yes?"

Nessa closed her eyes for a minute. Dragging Anja and Hunter into this, not to mention the Storsund rebels, was bad enough. But at least those people knew what they were getting themselves into. And they could be of use. The Lindbergs did not fit either those categories. A chatty socialite, a child of about six, and a hapless man who was risking his livelihood and reputation simply by being here… no, they were not coming along.

When Nessa opened her eyes again, Albert was in front of her. He was holding his top hat in his hands, nervously spinning it round and round by the brim.

She clasped his shoulder. "Albert. You three cannot come with us. It's incredibly dangerous. Besides, we have to be stealthy, quiet, and look like Joiners Square soldiers. I don't see Sonja pulling that off, I'm afraid."

"Oh, she will not arise with us to the castle. She and Eleonora will stay at a sweet, little inn we know in Cawstone. Their job will be to guard the possessions. All the clothes and things that we cannot bring to the castle. Soldiers don't carry big bags, yes?"

While that did make sense to Nessa, she still wasn't sure about the idea. Clearly it showed on her face as Albert spun the hat even faster.

"Nessa, don't be idiot. Travels are dull without children and pretty people. My wife is pretty and my Sonja is a child. They don't want to be without me for months. Especially not if I go away on a dangerous trip. Also, they are both bored."

"Like you?"

"No. I'm not bored. I am essence."

"Essential," Nessa corrected. She pinched the bridge of her nose again. "Why? Why are you essential, Albert?"

He cocked his head. "To speak to the soldiers at the castle, of course. I march up and tell them that I and my scud… *squadron* of ten soldiers were sent as… rainformations?"

"Reinforcements?"

"Yes, that. To document the talks between High Captain Nordhall and your Queen. That is a normal part of my job as a head clerk. Also, High Captain Nordhall has met me before so that means you don't have to hide, yes? You'll have a reasoning to be there and be free to run around the castle."

Nessa was about to argue when she, to her horror, realised that this made perfect sense. It would be helpful not having to skulk around an unfamiliar castle, terrified that any Joiners Square soldiers would question them. However, there was still a problem. Two if she counted Albert's tendency to put his foot in it, but that wasn't the problem she was going to bring up. She was raised on a farm, not in a barn.

She levelled her voice. "I can't put you in danger like that. Even if Eleonora and Sonja stay in Cawstone and only you travel with us to Highmere... gods only know what'll happen in the castle. What if we can't find Elise? What if we have to confront the Queen and her army of Royal Guards? What if we're discovered?"

Albert put his hat on. "That is why I'm essential, silly. With me, we can search the castle toff to toe, yes? Or head to bottom or whatever it is. Saying we're learning where everything is, yes? Or that we're taking notes to bring back to Grand Marshall Karlberg. We will find Elise and the Queen will not find us. I feel it, yes?"

"And if you're wrong?" Nessa said softly.

His upper lip trembled for a second. "If there is violence, well, it's about time I was brave. My life's been safe, but never important. I am a middle-class, middle-aged man, in middle management with a middle-sized fir... four... fortune. It's time I stand out from the middle, yes?" He planted his feet. "One day, I'll tell my daughter that I did not simply stay quietness and carry on working for a bad organisation. I can tell Sonja that I stood up to the bad."

Nessa didn't know how to argue with that. She had always believed in staying safe, but her time with Elise had taught her that risks were necessary to live life to the fullest. She rubbed her forehead. Why couldn't Elise be the one dealing with this? Nessa could be the captive and Elise could be here, planning a daring rescue and knowing what to say to keep the Lindbergs out of harm's way.

No. Elise would check that they knew the dangers and all their options. Then, if they still wanted to go, she'd let them.

Nessa tried one last tactic. "But what about your job? If this Nordhall knows you and sees you there, if we give your name... they will know you betrayed them."

He stared at her as if she was stupid. "I am obviously leaving my job quickeningly. It was tricky working for them when I knew they hid coin and kept secrets. But when they kidnap and push people, ones who came to Storsund as a shelter, into danger? I won't work for them. And, maybe when tales are told of me helping you, I might get a job with the new government."

He grinned as if he had just found a bar of gold on the street. Nessa knew when she was beaten. She turned to Hunter and Diinna, who had walked over with Anja just behind them.

"Ambassador, Hunter, Anja... Did you all hear that?" she asked.

Hunter nodded. "It is your decision."

Anja adjusted a new bag over her shoulder. "Well, we need the uniforms and he's right when he says he can be useful. Also, I think squadrons *do* usually have a higher-ranking person with them. Right, Diinna?"

Diinna had crossed her arms over her chest. "Yes, I believe so. Besides, we don't have time to argue. You must get settled on the ship. I'd let them come along."

It doesn't matter to you, Nessa thought bitterly. *Because if we all die, it plays even better for you to use us as rallying points for your cause.*

She immediately regretted the unkind thoughts. Moreover, Diinna needed at least Elise alive to testify, which brought something else to the forefront of her mind. "Oh, and if we come back…"

"*When* we come back," Anja interjected.

Nessa rolled her eyes. "Fine, *when* we come back, Albert would be a superb additional witness in the Joiners Square trial. Not only regarding this kidnaping but also embezzlement."

Diinna's head shot towards him. "Is this true?"

Albert puffed his chest out. "Yes. I know things. I also have notes from the last year, with dates and names of who signed off on what. They are in mine home on 58 Krasny Street. Just in case I do not survive, yes? You'll find them in my office on the second floor."

Diiinna pointed to him. "You! Make sure that you came back safe and sound. Storsund needs you."

"Of course, ambassador!" He puffed himself up even more, standing as tall as his short stature would allow. Nessa found herself feeling not only affection but pride towards him. Elise would have liked this, she would've been hugging him and saying that she knew he had it in him.

Elise.

There was a painful throb in Nessa's chest, as if her heart was beating incorrectly.

She mumbled, "We need to get on the ship."

CHAPTER 26
FORCED BACK

Elisandrine woke up frequently during the sea voyage, but it all mingled into a haze. She remembered eating meals with the help of Under Lieutenant Dahl. There were also recurrent memories of the two soldiers outside the washroom door when she cleaned herself or used the commode. Other than that, her journey seemed to have been made up of sleeping and of dazed walks on deck, where all she noticed was endless water and biting cold.

The rare times the sedative was out of her system enough for coherent thought, she was furious. The fact that they were taking six weeks of her life by making her mostly unconscious kept popping up. She knew she should be angrier about the kidnapping, her helpless state, and what the Queen would do to her. Nevertheless, what permeated her foggy mind was anger at missing a part of her life. Her father's death had taught her that life could be short and having to miss a part of her own enraged her.

Her father's death was one of the few things that she could use to her advantage. One of her few memories of a conversation on that ship was about his death. It must have been late evening or night, as she could faintly recall the porthole showing nothing but black. The cabin had smelled faintly of sea salt but more of the stuffiness of a room rarely opened. Dahl had been feeding her vegetable soup as her own grip was weak, making her likely to spill.

Fighting drowsiness, she swallowed a mouthful of soup and surveyed Dahl. "May I ask you something? Do you still think about your father every day? I seem to have stopped doing that, which makes me feel wretchedly guilty."

He glanced at the door then. Outside it stood the sergeant, probably chatting to the other passengers as usual.

"No. Not every day. I did for the first couple of years, yes? He was my hero and so... how do you say... closely tied to Joiners Square, that the first year it was hard to come to work. Now he mainly crosses my mind when I see something he'd like. Or dislike. Or something brings back a special memory."

Elise hummed. "Precisely."

"It is a strange thing, yes? To lose someone you love so much. Someone you need so much. The hole in your heart... it never heals," Dahl whispered.

"No. It does not. Neither does the guilt of surviving and living your life when he could not."

Dahl sighed and looked up at the ceiling. The spoon slowly drooped, until it landed in the bowl. "You're right. And as you said before, there's also the guilt of not always missing him, yes? Not constantly thinking about him."

Elise decided to test their burgeoning bond. "I carry him with me in all that I do, even if he is no longer at the forefront of my mind. My sweetest papa. You know, it is such a shame."

"What is?"

"My father always excelled at seeing things coming. Perhaps if I had been channelling him before my abduction, I might have foreseen my capture. Escaped in time. It was silly to try to settle down, to assume that the Queen would let me go."

"Why… why hasn't she?" His voice was low, clearly aware that he wasn't meant to be asking questions.

"Pride, I think. It started with that she found me diverting and a good lover. Now, however, I can only assume that it is her pride and her hatred of rejection that makes her obsess over me. Why else hunt me when I am so insignificant and bringing me back takes so much time and coin?"

He had blushed at the word 'lover' but now he paled. "What does she plan to do with you?"

Elise had shivered then, unsure if it was the chemicals in her system or the question sparking it. "I am not certain. Torture as a punishment? Murder me to keep me from telling people I disobeyed her?"

"I don't think so. Our orders were clear. You should arrive undamaged, that's why we were given the powders to keep you safely sleeping, yes? If she wanted you dead, she would have asked us to kill you and send her your head, yes?"

Elisandrine gritted her teeth. "Unless she wanted me brought to her, pristine and unharmed, so she could kill me herself. Or perhaps she still plans to, well, conquer my body."

"By f-force? No, she's a woman."

"Oh, women can violate, too. However, luckily for me, the Queen finds rape beneath her. Too crude, too easy. While she does not much care about others' wishes, she is terribly vain and cannot stand the idea of someone not wanting her. This is a game to her and I wager that the only way to win is to either make me come crawling back or to kill me so no one else can have me."

Elise looked away. She was plagued by memories of unwanted desire creeping into her fear of the Queen. It shamed her to the core. A part of her had always desired that callous woman. Perhaps for her power and the danger of her?

Not this time. No matter how she coaxed and pushed. No matter how she made Elise feel or if she kept her locked up for the rest of her life. It was death or freedom.

Her thoughts were interrupted by Dahl. "So, you believe she wants to end your life?"

Elise grabbed fistfuls of her blanket and blinked repeatedly, but tears still fell. They seemed to upset Dahl more than anything that had been said. He moved closer, his brow knitted.

Elise swiftly wiped her eyes. "I am not certain. Perhaps she intends to keep me around as a pet, make me a slave? Arclidians tend to have a strong distaste for slavery, so her people would not look kindly upon that. However, that viper does not seem to care what anyone thinks anymore, so who can say."

In silence, Elise looked at the food while she made her decision. She blinked away fresh tears and met Dahl's eyes. "I do not know what she wants with me, but I can tell you this, it will be nothing more than pure horror and I… will not simply accept that fate!"

Then she had pushed the bowl of hot soup onto his lap. It burned him enough that he hissed and moved out of the way. She rushed for the door, pointlessly, of course, because where could she go? The sergeant was outside, and the ship was far out at sea with nowhere to swim. She couldn't even swim. Nevertheless, she had to run. She must *try*.

She screamed as Dahl caught her and shushed her while pushing her back towards the bed. He had not been unkind or gripped her harshly.

"Shh. Don't let him hear you struggling, yes? He'll sedate you before you've finished your food. The soup is gone now, but you still have a bread roll and the winterberry juice. You do not want to keep missing meals. Not good for you, yes?"

She had glared at him through tear-misted eyes. That was

when he leaned in and whispered, "Also, Mrs Glass. If you're going to keep fighting you must save your strength until you are on dry land, yes? Use this time. Sleep, eat, and plan. I'll keep you safe until we're in Arclid. After that, who knows what'll happen."

She had wiped her hot, wet cheeks and nodded, letting him hand her the juice to drink.

No matter the drugged haze and the constant rage, in her heart she kept that conversation. Both the idea of preserving her strength and the fact that Dahl had made it sound as if he was on her side.

CHAPTER 27

ICE

S tanding on deck, a few days into their journey, Nessa ignored Hunter droning on about how impressive Anja was to give the approaching ship's captain her full attention. He was scowling in a way which made her skin prickle.

The captain cleared his throat. "Good morning. I'm afraid ice floes have been blown in from the north and are blocking our way, yes? We must travel around them, meaning a longer voyage. I have explained this to all your traveling companions and understood that this is unusually bad news for you?"

Hunter gasped. "I should say so. We are in great haste!"

The captain winced. "Not much I can do, yes? The sea is the sea and ice is ice. 'Tis the season for slow travel. My apologies for this trouble."

Nessa felt her nostrils flaring. "How long will this delay us?"

"I cannot say. A week? Maybe more, yes?" He nodded his farewell, mumbling, "May the winds be with us."

The sea wasn't the only thing besieged by ice now. Nessa

had the sensation of hoarfrost lining her heart, freezing her where she stood.

So much could happen to Elise while I'm stuck out here. Thrale, grant us quicker passage over your seas.

She shivered. Praying no longer gave comfort. To think that not long ago she had worried about things like having to lie about being married, finding an apprenticeship, or about being in a foreign place. It all paled in comparison to what she was facing now.

Hunter dragged a hand across his face. "I cannot believe it. We managed to make such good time in procuring a ship. We were only a little more than a day behind her. Now... Oh, what do we do, Nessa?"

She looked at him, trying to find something reassuring to tell him. His face showed the frustration and panic that she felt, and she wanted to relieve his worry despite not being able to relieve her own. But the words wouldn't come.

I wish he didn't hate being touched. I need to be held. I need to cry and let this out.

"I d-don't know, Hunter. I'm going to check if they require assistance in the engine room. I must keep moving or my thinking will drive me mad. Go talk to Anja. I have to go."

With that she ran, wishing she could run to Arclid instead of only to the engine room.

CHAPTER 28
MOMENTS OF LUCIDITY

E lise surfaced from the depths of foggy slumber. She assumed it was morning judging by the bright light hitting her eyes. There was no rolling or churning of the sea. Nor was she in her cabin aboard the *Konspiratoria*. She was sitting in what appeared to be a stationary carriage with tiny windows. Somewhere horses were whinnying. She rubbed her forehead, wishing the headache from the sedative would give her a single minute of peace. Her usual rage made her pound her fist against the carriage door, but this made the headache grow exponentially.

Calm down. Collect your thoughts. You are finally alone, use that!

Just as she had decided to get out and run, even though her drugged mind and tired body wouldn't get her far, one of the doors was flung open. Her two Joiners Square guards clambered into the carriage. The Sergeant looked as furious as Elise felt.

"I can't believe this old, silly country. No trains! Madness! The trip from here to Highmere will take days, yes? My spine will be crooked, and my arse will be broken." He finished with a few words that Elise knew to be particularly vile Sundish curse words.

Under Lieutenant Dahl looked her up and down. "Good morning. I hope you don't mind that I carried you here. You were sleeping deep with the powders, yes? The ship's captain said goodbye to you." Dahl looked down at his hands before adding, "And wished you a speedy recovery."

Elise scoffed loudly, only to be met with another tirade of curses from Dahl's surly superior. She sunk back into her silence, continuing to rub her forehead.

There was the sound of horses whinnying again, and then the carriage began to move.

"May I… have something to drink? And perhaps to eat?" Elise asked.

Dahl's face lit up. "You *want* to eat? That is best news, yes? Wait a moment."

He rummaged around an army satchel and produced a canteen and three rectangles covered in pale yellow icing sugar. "They're wafers. I've been saving them. But now that we're on land and I can have foreign treats, you're welcome to them. You can use some sugar to stay awake," he said, clearly trying to make his voice sound neutral.

His superior took one look at the wafers and harrumphed before looking out through the small window. Elise accepted the meagre meal with a gracious nod. As she took the iced wafers she noticed Joiners Square emblem in grey icing. "Ha! Look at that. Even in your sugary treats…" Despite herself, she hummed in amusement. "Joiners Square truly does get involved in everything it can reach."

Dahl shrugged, a smile barely visible on his chapped lips.

She drank as much of the water as she could stomach and handed the canteen back to him half-full. Then she began to nibble on the wafers. They tasted far too sweet and were dry as sand. Still, she was hungry. If the sugar could help her with her headache, she would eat a raw sugar beet at this point.

Outside the carriage, the landscape rushed past. She spotted familiar trees and fields. The sight of her homeland should be comforting, but all it did was constrict her throat and form an icy grip on her heart. It was as if Highmere, and the court within it, were rushing to meet her. Rushing to imprison her.

Elise abandoned her second wafer, half-eaten. For once, she longed for when they would sedate her again. She couldn't stand feeling like this, and right now, planning for her escape seemed as impossible as eating another bite.

～

The next time she woke to complete lucidity, the light was different, beaming through big windows. Pure, butter-yellow sunshine reflected off Centurian marble walls. She blinked away sleep grit and sat up. The bed under her was comfortable with luxurious bedding. There was a whiff of roses and lavender in the air.

Highmere. I have arrived. Gods curse it. I have been drugged too heavily throughout the ride to formulate a plan. Or even stay awake.

She sniffed, tears breaking through, doubling her headache and despair. She sat up and slapped herself, making her cheek sting. It was bracing, so she did it again.

Get a hold of yourself! You shall formulate your plan now, and it will be even better because you will learn what exactly it is the Queen wants with you.

Elise breathed deep, replacing anguish with controlled rage, and then rang the little bell by her bed, summoning a servant.

A young waif of a man entered and bowed. "Milady rang?"

"Yes. Good morning. I require something light to break my fast. Poached eggs, leaf tea, and fruit. Perhaps some toasted oats?"

"A small selection shall be brought to you presently, milady."

She tried to keep her voice calm, to keep the control. "I also require a hot bath to be drawn, with a mountain-sized soap." She rubbed at her forehead. "Then I suppose I must dress. I assume that the manipulative, rotten viper has left me whatever clothing she fancies me in?"

The servant nodded reluctantly, his eyes huge at her words.

Elise crossed her arms over her chest. "Calm yourself, she cannot hear you. I daresay she treats you monstrously, so she deserves none of your loyalty. Return with breakfast and the clothing as soon as you can. And get someone to draw the cursed bath. Stop staring, boy! Fetch me what I require!"

He bowed and scurried to the door.

Elise groaned. "Wait. Before you go… I apologise for shouting. It is not you I am angry with, and you should not have to bear the brunt of my ire. Please forgive me."

Was that a smile that flashed past the young man's lips?

"No need to apologise, milady. I… understand. Thank you, milady." He bowed again and took his leave.

Elise ran her fingers through her sleep-mussed hair. It had grown far out of its perfect length. How long had it been since her last haircut? That had been in Storsund, with her blossoming career, her agreeable new home, her new friend, and… her cherished Nessa. The longing for her was an acute ache in Elise's already bruised heart. She bit back tears and let her rage fuel her again. She just had to remember to aim that rage in the right direction.

Elise got up and pulled her travel-worn clothes off. It amazed her that the Queen had spared her the shame of having someone undress her. But then, changing into clean clothes when her skin was dirty would've been pointless. She glanced over at the bed which must be filled with road dust and her sweat.

I shall have to ask for clean sheets.

There would be no end to how much the Queen would mock her if she didn't smell completely fresh. A pet should be adequately groomed, after all.

Elise gritted her teeth, calming herself by imagining the look on the Queen's face when she, one day soon, would find her tinderbox-maker escaped.

It girded her spine.

It made her smile.

~

An hour later, Elise felt human again. She was clean, dressed, and fed. Most of all, she had drunk two pots of leaf tea to flush the sedative from her system. She could only hope that was working. Either way, she was much improved. The headache, from the medication and the large amounts of sleep on the ship, still throbbed away, but it had faded to something manageable.

Breakfasting had certainly helped. She had requested something light, thinking herself too upset and pained to eat. She'd been wrong.

The Queen had remembered her every favourite dish and had either made sure it was served now or that it had been made into a morning meal version. Like her beloved roast beef with sugared parsnips, which had been on one of the breakfast trays in the form of sweet parsnip bread with slices of roast beef. The vast array of food wasn't a shock, everything was over the top at court. What was shocking was that the Queen had noticed what food Elise liked and had made sure it was all served. And how Elise had wolfed it all down.

EMMA STERNER-RADLEY

There was another knock on the door, this one without an ounce of politeness. Nor did the knocker wait until told to enter, informing Elise who it was before she even saw the Queen. She stood and steeled herself.

The door banged close. "Ah, Lady Elisandrine Falk. Good morning, my pretty little runaway. I trust you slept well," the Queen purred.

Elise stood quiet, waiting. But the Queen merely smiled at her. Golden eyes challenged dusky blue. The silence reigned until Elise gave up and asked, "Where is the rest of it?"

The Queen clasped her hands, still smiling. "Pardon?"

"Where is the mocking? The triumph? The cruel comments?"

The smell of purified alcohol and lavender filled the room, spreading from the haughty woman in front of her like mist. The Queen stayed still. So still it was impossible to even spot her breathing.

"Sweetest Elise, I did not spend all this time and coin to hunt and find you only to *mock you*. If that was what I wanted, I would simply have sent you a letter and been done with it."

"Then what do you want?"

"You know, I picked out that dress for you because it was said to be comfortable and I believed it would suit your light-brown skin, but now I am unsure. Perhaps something in cream would have been better?"

Elise stomped her foot. "Answer the question, curse you!"

The Queen raised her eyebrows. "Now, now. Do not get agitated. You must feel terrible after all those sedatives those cruel Northmen injected you with. I will send my chemist up to give you something pure and natural to help you. Some dried white shrooms perhaps?"

Elise remembered her mother giving her those when she had a cold. They soothed aches, but most of all they made you

300

happier and calmer. The effect wasn't huge, but right now, she would take what she could get.

"Yes, I should like that."

The Queen gave her a subtle look and Elise kept herself from rolling her eyes as she amended it to, "Yes, please, I should like that, Your Majesty."

"Splendid. I shall have him come to your room after our little conversation."

"Thank you. Will you at any point answer my question?"

The throbbing, pulsing of Elise's rage was simmering just under her control. But for how long?

The Queen took a step forward, towering over Elise. "I want to start over. I want what I asked you for that night in the dreadful tavern in Nightport. For you to come here and stay with me." Another step closer, filling Elise's nostrils with lavender. "I overdid it that evening, fire-starter. The talk of making you a courtesan was in bad taste. I should not have assumed that you wanted to bed me again... like you so often used to."

A shiver ran down Elise's spine, but she made an effort to remain unmoved.

"Well, I am here now. What exactly do you expect of me, Your Majesty?"

"You only have to stay, recover, and... converse with me. I have missed your company. Your, shall we say, *unique* way of seeing things. Highmere was dim and dreary after you left, you know," she said softly.

Elise was confused and not only due to the chemicals still poisoning her blood. The Queen was never this nice, not even when she wanted something. Even if she was clearly lying, she was still being too gentle. Too considerate.

The clouds in Elise's mind cleared.

Oh. She wants me to like her again. Just as I said to Dahl, she intends to win by making me want and need her. Perhaps even love her. Surely, she does not believe all it will take is my favourite foods and some kind words? What mind games does she have in store?

Dahl – that reminded her. "My Queen, if you plan to have guards outside my door, may I request the young Joiners Square soldier? You can have one of your usual Royal Guards present to keep an eye on him. I should like to keep him close. He was in the middle of telling me a story."

The Queen raised her thin eyebrows again. "A story?"

"Yes, about trolls and forest beasts. You know, tales from the north."

The Queen seemed to contemplate it. Elise prepared herself for a no.

"I cannot see a reason to deny you that. I am sure you would not try to use him to… leave again. And if you were to commit such a rude and witless act, the castle is filled with Royal Guards and Joiners Square soldiers. You would not get far. What is his name?"

"Under Lieutenant Anders Dahl."

"Then he shall be on duty as soon as he is located. Anything else you wish to request, my pretty little tinderbox-maker?"

The Queen's smile was familiar. It was the intimate smile one only saw after bedplay, in a sated glow and still buzzing with pleasure. Elise ignored the unwelcome tingle that ran through her.

"No, thank you, Your Majesty."

The Queen took another step closer, so near now that Elise could feel the heat from her body. "No? Not even some fragrance oil? The soldiers who accompanied you here informed me that you have begun making your own. Creating quite a name for yourself in Storsund. If you wish, I can have some raw materials brought to you and you can thrill the court with your wares?"

"No." Elise hesitated. "Well, not right now, anyway."

Perhaps I can use that later as a diversion? Or use some of the materials in my escape.

The Queen smiled again. "As you please. Well, I have meeting with my councillors regarding taxes. How unbelievably dreary. I wish you could join me and spice the whole affair up somewhat."

She reached out a hand as if to touch Elise's face, but then slowly pulled it back. Instead she said, "I am glad to have you here and to see you looking so well. Despite your ordeal, you are as stunning as ever. I shall send the chemist up to cure the worst of what ails you and return to visit you later in the day."

With that, she turned and walked out.

Elise stood frozen in place. Her heart was pounding.

How disturbing to see her so kind. As disturbing as her belief that she can beguile me to stay of my own accord.

Elise looked up at the ceiling.

She assumes I am still the insecure girl needing someone strong and powerful to want me, needing it so much that I will not mind being used. She will not like the outcome of this.

Her temples throbbed, the headache returning to full strength. As if summoned by her pain, there was a knock on the door. After she called "enter," a small man with thick spectacles came in. Elise recognised the chemist. In conjunction with the court physician, he saw to the Queen's health, preparing any medication or digestive aid that the monarch required.

He greeted her before handing her a small bowl filled with shards of dried shrooms. Craving the pain to go away and for her mood to lift, she ate them.

He smiled kindly at her, like a proud grandfather. "Well done, milady. They were dipped in honey before being dried so they should have a more pleasant taste. Especially the tree shrooms."

Elise jolted. "Tree shrooms? But those were white shrooms?"

"Most of them, yes. I added some tree shrooms, to heighten the effect. They are perfectly harmless and natural. Do not fret, the Queen would not hurt you. She merely wants you relaxed when she is not here."

Right. She is going to give me mood enhancers while I am alone. Keep me happy and drowsy so I do not plan my escape. Why does everyone want to alter my mind by force? What have I done to deserve that?

"I see," Elisandrine said with effort. Her lips seemed to disobey her and want to move in their own way. She giggled at the idea of them running off and starting a new life without her.

The chemist nodded at her. "Very good, child. Now you are enjoying your stay here. That is what we want, a happy and relaxed young lady." He adjusted his spectacles. "Now, you have books over on the shelf and you can always call the servants if you desire something to eat. Enjoy your day, milady."

With that he took his leave. Elise ambled around the room, her heart light from the shrooms and her mind gliding from subject to subject. She looked out the window and saw one of the castle's turrets. Lining it were carved fantastical beasts, all made out of the same pink-streaked Centurian marble as the castle itself. Facing her was a gargoyle with a gruesome but comical face, big, clawed paws, and a snake-like tail hanging down. Elise squinted at it, giggling because she was sure it had moved. Just then, the statue turned its face to her and grinned.

Elise smiled back. "Hello, Mr Gargoyle. Want to help me plan my escape?" she whispered.

There was no need to whisper as she was far from the door

now and could not be overheard. But she was going to be ever so careful and clever.

The gargoyle nodded its marble head and its sharp-toothed grin grew even bigger.

Elise pointed at him. "Excellent, Mr Gargoyle. Let us begin with acquiring thicker socks. These floors are cold, and you may scratch them with your claws. I am not sure I have socks to fit you, we shall see."

With that she went to fetch thicker socks from a drawer. Her languid mind considered plans just beneath the crazed thoughts about socks for statues.

"Trust me, Mr Gargoyle," she said with confidence. "It will take more than shrooms to keep Elisandrine Falk in check."

CHAPTER 29
SUBMISSION

Marianna sat at her desk tapping her steepled fingers against her chin. She reminded herself not to frown, the last thing she needed now was more premature wrinkles.

Elisandrine Falk had been in the castle for weeks. To absolutely no avail. She showed no sign of weakening her resistance or of ceasing her coolly civil behaviour. They danced around each other, both pleasant and accommodating. Marianna saw the temper under Elise's politeness, but it never broke out. And Elise's resistance never broke down.

Where was the impulsive and passionate creature that had floated around court, tempting and causing trouble? Always willing to trade a caress for some attention. Always putting fun ahead of sense.

Marianna splayed her hands on the desk and took deep breaths through her nose.

Why does nothing I do work? Not kind words. Not displays of power. Not invitations to dance. Not even the offer of bathing naked in the castle's fountain at midnight.

Her tinderbox-maker had never been able to say no to

that. Now, however… Elise stayed untouched in her bed, growing paler and more closed off by the day. Perhaps it was the shrooms? Maybe she was pining for her farm wench or merely being difficult because returning to Arclid hadn't been her idea. As if that mattered to a girl like her. Marianna couldn't understand it, and it vexed her.

Adaire was right, the light-eyed slattern was not worth the effort. She is not even as beautiful as I remembered.

Marianna leaned back, gazing into the looking glass on the wall and smoothing away that stubborn frown.

Nevertheless, I worked hard to get her here. I am not going to simply allow her to stroll out of the castle.

What if this disgraceful affair got out? Besides, everyone Marianna wanted fell for her in the end. She had had a life-time of lovers who had either fallen for her charm or for her position in life. Or in some unsavoury cases, her wealth. But they all fell for her. They all became hers in the end.

Marianna sniffed, sitting up straight. Elise was turning into an unwanted distraction. She should be focusing on the Storsund problem. Joiners Square grew stronger and more predatory by the second. But also more volatile. It wasn't tenable to have such a big organisation so badly run. It was filled with ambitious but clueless workers, many of them joiners of course, but also rich wasters and boorish soldiers. All Storsund's actual rulers and politicians had either been bribed into obedience or mysteriously disappeared when they did not support Joiners Square.

Still, this union-turned-syndicate had the great unwashed masses of Storsund behind them, believing that their uniform-clad maniacs would conquer all four continents. They were supporting Joiners Square with vast amounts of coin, allowing them to stockpile weapons and produce all those cursed new inventions. She shook her head.

These people are dangerous and unpredictable. No land should be run by an organisation, especially not one without any experienced rulers.

Marianna sighed. She may not be a loved leader, but she benefitted from generations of advice on how to govern. Tips and tricks learned by trial and error for the four hundred years since the fateful War of Thorns. One important rule was to never bite off more than you could chew.

Joiners Square ignored this, rushing forward, growing ever larger, like one of their steam trains picking up carriages at every stop. Racing towards disaster. And now they wanted to bite off another mouthful of the orb and swallow Arclid. Well, that was certainly more than they could chew. More than that, if they stuck their pointy teeth into her land, she would end their pitifully short rule. It would be so easy, a fractured nation like Storsund with only a sprawling, badly run organisation in charge... Sow discontent and Joiners Square would quickly wither on the vine.

Until then, she could keep toying with Nordhall and his desire to learn about magic. And she could keep toying with Elise's mind. Soon the isolation, boredom, and need for more shrooms would make her more pliable. Then she would submit to her Queen.

They will all submit to me in the end.

CHAPTER 30
HEART-TO-HEART

One morning, a few weeks into her captivity, Elise woke up with a mind cleared of shrooms but, because of that, once more brimming with anger and helplessness.

She had asked the maid to open the windows, and now she breathed in the fresh, chilly morning air. She purposely ignored the scent of roses and lavender and focused on the fact that the air here didn't hurt her lungs as it had in Storsund.

I would happily exchange this comfortable climate to be in Skarhult again. At least there I was free. Besides, winter is nearing its final weeks now.

She massaged her temples.

It has been a long, cold season this year. Literally and metaphorically. Too bad it is not over yet.

A familiar voice, complete with terrible Arclidian, could be heard from outside the door. Under Lieutenant Anders Dahl was on duty again today. She was glad that he never managed to keep his voice down, that way she knew when he was there.

He seemed to like her but was still wary. Guilty as she was about using his friendship, she intended to bind him closer to her. To do to him what the Queen was trying to do to her: win affection and trust against all odds. The difference was that the Queen was convinced no one could resist her for long, while Elise was well aware that the real world didn't always go her way.

Oh, and my motive is less morally bankrupt. That is an important difference.

She looked out her window, to the statues lining the turret. The gargoyle was there, ever grinning. She wasn't sure why she had hallucinated about that particular statue coming to life. Perhaps because the others were so pretty and harmless. If she was to come out of this with her sanity intact, she needed to awaken the beast in herself. Not to rage, but to be cunning.

Her gargoyle served her well there. It suggested that she bide her time, make the Queen think she was being docile but not won over, all to keep the Queen preoccupied with wooing her. It had also suggested making Dahl like and pity her enough to free her. Its third bit of useful advice had been to charm the servants in case she needed their aid or maybe even to escape dressed as one of them. She had no coin to bribe anyone, like Hunter had when the Queen was interrogating him, but she had her likeable personality. Hopefully that would be enough.

Elise rubbed her throbbing temples in wider circles. Yes, she had plans brewing, but she needed to find the perfect time to enact them. She needed the castle to be as empty as possible when she escaped.

Finding out when that might be would be easier if my mind was not muddled by the cursed shrooms and this hunger!

The shrooms had made her too distracted. She would be planning or eavesdropping, and then she would be distracted by how cold the floor was, or how her gargoyle friend was flirting with the unicorn statue next to him on the turret. It was most vexing.

Even more vexing was the fact that when she had turned down the shrooms, they had begun sneaking them into her food. The shrooms were usually ground down and mixed into every course she was offered. They were invisible to the naked eye, but the taste came through, no matter how they tried to hide it with spices or honey. Thus, to stick to her plan, she only ate when she absolutely had to.

Which meant her delirium was caused as much by hunger as the shrooms, but at least the hunger kept her angry. And focused. They could take away her freedom, but they couldn't take her mind.

She rang the bell and waited for a servant to bring clothes and breakfast. Her empty stomach cramped. She would allow herself about half of the food today, then throw the rest out the window. The blasted gargoyle could eat it.

~

Later, when she was cleaned, partly fed, and dressed, she called for Dahl. He opened the door and stepped into her bedchamber, smiling at her with brotherly affection.

"Hello. Gotten some sleep, yes?"

She beamed at him. "Some. Now, let us not waste time. Tell me a fairy tale before the shrooms kick in and my mind wanders."

His brow knitted. "I wish they'd stop giving them to you. There's no need. You shan't run away."

"I wish they would stop, too. The shrooms make it increasingly hard to know what is real and they make me feel plain dreadful. Nothing I can do about it, however."

Not yet anyway, she added to herself.

She saw Dahl's lower lip wobble. Then he composed himself. "I'm sure the Queen will stop giving you those when she gets what she wants."

EMMA STERNER-RADLEY

"Yes, although I believe myself to be too strong to give in to unreasonable demands. I think you are the same. Our fathers taught us that before they were taken from us, would you not say?"

Using their grief to win Dahl over didn't sit right with her, but if no else played fair, neither would she. He had to let go of his blind faith and loyalty to Joiners Square. He had to do the right thing and help her escape.

He was fidgeting with his sleeve while his eyes flitted to the door.

Quick, make him comfortable before he finds an excuse to leave again!

"Oh, I meant to enquire, Under Lieutenant. Did you manage to ask the other soldiers how the Queen found me? She refuses to tell me."

This was a small but important test. Would he go against the Queen's, and by extension his superiors', wishes and answer her? Had he even asked around on her behalf?

His eyes lit up. "I did, Miss Elise! Apparently, the Queen got all the passenger lists from all Nightport ships for the night you left. She had staff reading them until all names similar to yours were found, yes?" He looked so excited now, like a child recounting the story of a treasure hunt. "Then she had people hunt down every name. Elise Glass was in Charlottenberg, so she sent letters to her spies there and they began looking for you. After a long search, they found you in Skarhult, yes? Don't know how. Perhaps it was one of the civilian spies who informed that two strangers were in this woman's house and Joiners Square connected the dots? Bad luck, yes?"

"Yes," she murmured.

"Perhaps you should have hidden more. Gone farther into the country or kept on the move. Maybe having a different name, leaving the name 'Elise' behind, yes?"

Elisandrine hung her head. As she suspected, her own

overconfidence and panicked impulsivity had caught her out. She remembered a conversation with her captor three weeks ago.

"Your Majesty, may I ask how exactly you found me?"

"Ha! Is that not obvious? I have power, sway, and reach. While you, sweet Elise, you are too recognisable, too exuberant, and too impetuous to hide well."

Elise had been forced to press her nails into her palms to keep her fury under control then, but now, she was resigned to it being true. She swallowed hard and then smiled at Dahl, as warmly as she could manage.

"I see. Thank you for telling me. Now, how about that fairy tale?"

He pulled up a chair and began to tell the story about the troll princess who married a human. He'd already told her this one last week, but she liked it and didn't mention his error. Instead she laid back and let the fairy tale world take her away from her situation for a while, hoping the shrooms from her half-eaten breakfast would be enough to dim her regret.

~

Hours later, Elise was alone in her room. The shrooms had made her warm, relaxed, and giddy.

Now you know. Half the breakfast is enough to have this effect. Unless they have increased the amount of shrooms?

She shrugged to herself and stored the information for later. Now she was too pacified to care. It was so peculiar to not be able to detect any trace of her usual fits of anger. She stood by the window, watching the last rays of the afternoon sun hit the turret outside.

The gargoyle rested its gruesome head in its hands. "Let us talk of the Queen."

Elise made a disgusted noise. "No, thank you."

"Now, now, she is crucial for any planning, you know that. What is she thinking? What is she going to do next? And most of all, how can you use it to your advantage?"

Elisandrine sighed. "Fine, Mr Gargoyle. We shall talk about the Queen."

"Splendid!" the statue said, licking its sharp teeth before carrying on. "So, what is her next play to win your affection? She has been serving you your favourite foods, playing the board games you two used to play, spoken of your favourite books, and, of course, massaging oil into your hands in that way you like."

"Yes, the only time she has touched me so far. Good thing, too, my temper would not stand for anything more intimate."

"No. You would explode."

"Mm. Anyway, I am not certain what is next. She has tried being kind."

The gargoyle swung its tail. "Yes."

Elise began to pace back and forth past the window. "And, as you pointed out, attentive. Remembering my favourite treats and pastimes."

"Without fail."

"The shrooms are clearly to keep me docile and happy."

"Yes, yes. No need to cover what we already know. What weapons does she have left in her arsenal?"

"Continuing to play on my insecurities and faults. At some point, she will ramp this up from simple mind games to… brainwashing."

"Well, yes, obviously," it agreed.

Elise paced faster. "Perhaps using my past?"

"Ah! Now we are talking. Do you think she will use the loss of your father? Or perhaps bring your mother to the castle to talk sense into you?"

Elise stopped cold in her tracks, looking at the gargoyle. "Do you think the Queen would do that?"

"Yes. Unless she has told everyone that you are dead. Then it would be hard to let your mother see you."

Elise pointed to the statue. "Right! There is no way my mother would buy that she could speak to me if I were dead."

"No. Very discriminate, your mother. Only speaks to living humans. Not like you who has so kindly befriended me."

Elise scrunched up her nose. "Well, I mean to say, that might have something to do with the hallucinogenic shrooms."

The gargoyle shrugged what little shoulders it had. "Still, you picked me to have a heart-to-heart with. Out of all of those statues. You could have chosen the pretty unicorn or the proud gryphon. You chose me, I am very happy about that."

Elise returned to pacing. "I am glad to hear it."

The gargoyle dipped its head. "I am glad you are glad."

There were voices outside of Elise's door again, the ever-loud Under Lieutenant was speaking to someone. But it wasn't in Arclidian.

"Not Dahl's fellow guard, then," Elise whispered to the gargoyle. "I am going to move closer, meaning I cannot speak to you anymore. Go back to being an inanimate object."

It stared at her with pupil-less eyes. "Well, I mean, I never actually stopped."

Elise waved at it, annoyed. "You know what I mean. Shush!"

She snuck to the door and listened. It was definitely Sundish. She concentrated, clearing the shroom-fog as much as she could, trying to remember her Sundish lessons with Anja. Her ears pricked up when she heard who Dahl was addressing, High Captain Nordhall, the man Elise had come to know as the visiting Joiners Square emissary. Throughout her weeks here, Elise had picked up that he was staying here indefinitely, trying to get something from the Queen, who was being unaccommodating.

No surprise there.

When Elise had mentioned Nordhall and Joiners Square to the Queen, she had scoffed and muttered, "Frost-trolls. Ice in their heads, hearts, and between their legs. No fun at all!"

Now Nordhall was outside her door and she heard his voice for the first time. It was clear and demanding. She translated it in her head as much as she could.

"Dahl. I want you to stay close to this girl. She might still be the key to making the Queen tell us about..." Then there was a word Elise didn't know.

She heard Dahl reply, "Of course. I believe she can be an asset. She is not like the others Arclidians. She is not backwards, gossiping, lazy, or only interested in bedplay and fun. She has depth. She can be of use to our nation." He paused, allowing Elise a moment of pride at his words. When he picked up again, his voice was shaky. "Perhaps... when we have what we want from the Queen, we should bring her back to Storsund? The people of Skarhult will miss her scented oils. Moreover, her creativity, ambition, and sharp mind can be used to further Joiners Square's goals."

Elise wasn't sure that the last word really meant 'goals', but she thought it a likely assumption. She was squinting her eyes closed, hoping with all her might that Nordhall would say yes.

Please agree. Come on, taking me away with you would be a slap in the face to the Queen, showing your power.

She knew it would be easier to escape there than try to outfox both Joiners Square and the Queen in this castle. Or at least she would find it easier because she was close to Nessa there. And their friends. She wouldn't be stuck here, behind enemy lines with nothing more than an imaginary statue to rely on.

FOCUS, ELISANDRINE! She shook off the distracting thoughts and listened closer.

After a few sentences regarding their squadron and clothing supplies, she heard High Captain Nordhall scold

Dahl for not attending last week's Visitors Dinner, a dinner that the Queen apparently threw for Nordhall and his soldiers every week.

"It's the one break you're allowed from guarding the Queen's feral pet. The nerve of having my scarce soldiers stationed outside her unwilling courtesan's bedchamber!" There was a bang. Perhaps from a fist against a wall or a boot against the floor? "What's even more galling is that she only invites us all to a feast when she can spare nearly all her Royal Guards to watch us. To keep all us 'violent Northmen' from assassinating her over the winterberry pie," Nordhall spat.

Elise's heart was racing. If she had translated all that correctly, most of the Royal Guards and all the Joiners Square soldiers were in the castle's vast dining hall on the same evening every week. An unmissable opportunity! She had to try to plan her escape for one of those nights.

As long as the Queen does not stop having the dinners before I have won Dahl over enough for him to help me.

Nordhall muttered something else that she missed, then he said farewell. Dahl replied and thanked him.

Elise, wobbling slightly from the shrooms, snuck back to the window. She looked out at her gargoyle and whispered, "Did you hear all that?"

The statue raised his imaginary eyebrows. "No. My ears are made of marble. But you did, so yes, I suppose we can claim I did."

"Excellent! Now, we have a weekly event during which we must stage the escape. And we have Dahl and the servants to recruit. So, we have the *when* and the *whom*. Now we need the *how*. Any thoughts on methods?"

The gargoyle shrugged. "You thought about dressing as a servant and sneaking out before."

"Yes, clever of me. That is a viable option. What else?"

"Well, you could ask Dahl for a long rope and climb out the window and down the castle wall?"

Elise slumped onto the bed, staring at her hands.

The gargoyle winced. "Ah. Too reminiscent of your escape from Silver Hollow Castle when you and Nessa first met. Clumsy of me, must be the marble brain. Please accept my apologies."

Elise sighed. "It is fine. It is only that I… miss her so much. I never knew how much strength she gave me. She always needs me to be brave and bold. That in combination with her infinite faith in me makes me able to achieve anything."

"Then *achieve* this escape and return to her. After that, if I were you – and I am – I would sit down and ask myself why I keep being locked up in the top floors of castles."

Elise scoffed. "Easily answered. In Silver Hollow Castle, Prince Macray had me locked up on the instructions of his sister, the Queen. This time, she has done it herself. Well, given the order at least."

"Mm. Well, you might want to ensure that royalty stops imprisoning you in castles. The lady-awaiting-rescue look does not suit you."

"Stop being rude."

"Make me."

"Ha! That appears impossible. If I could shut your stony mouth up, I would have done so a long time ago."

"No. That would leave you all alone. You do terribly with being alone, the Queen is counting on that to break you. Little did she know that your shroom-addled mind would invent me. Would you like me to keep you awake by singing lewd songs about busty women again tonight?"

Elise glared at the statue. "No!"

"Suit yourself. Where did you learn that song anyway?"

Elise stood up to walk away. "The groundskeeper I lost my

maidenhood to. Gods, she was stunning, strong, and beautiful. But with the decorum of a mud-covered toad."

"Ah, yes. I can see that in your memories now. Oh my, you allowed her to take quite a few liberties there!"

"Oh, shush. I will not be shamed for my sexual exploits by my imaginary friend, I get enough of that from society. Anyway, we are meant to be planning my escape."

They were silent for a while.

Then the gargoyle hummed pensively before saying, "Was that bit in the winterberry bushes really sanitary? Had she washed that thing first?"

Elise growled, slapped her own head to make him shut up, and went to pour herself some of the brandy she had been allowed.

She had to sleep, and tomorrow she would not allow herself any of the laced breakfast. Preferably not the midday meal or supper either, if it could be done. She had to try to come up with other escape plans than the two she had thought out. She needed options and meticulous planning. There was no Nessa to help her this time. No Hunter with useful connections. No Anja with her practicality. Elisandrine was alone and had to rely on only herself. And for that, she would certainly need a clear mind.

CHAPTER 31
TINDERBOX UNDER WINTER STARS

Nessa stood on the deck, looking up at the twinkling winter stars. She wore two layers of clothes, stretching her leather coat to the maximum, and had her fur over her shoulders. Despite all that, she was shivering, and her teeth clattered. She still preferred it to being inside. Inside they were laughing and chatting, getting on with life.

It made more sense to be out here, turning the tinderbox over in her frozen, gloved hands.

Does it even count as a tinderbox if it doesn't have tinder material in it? I bet Elise would know.

Nessa let her tears fall. She shoved the box in the pocket of her leather coat and wiped hot tears off her cold cheeks. She looked out at the black sea. The crescent moon reflected in the water, bringing a line of light across the dark waves. Normally it would've looked like a ray of hope to Nessa, but tonight there was nothing hopeful to be ignited in her.

She blinked to clear her eyes. The ocean was so vast and dark, the ship so foreign and cold. She didn't even know if they were back on their usual course towards Cawstone yet.

She blew out a shaky breath, scrambling for anything resembling safety. All she found was fear, fretful impatience, the hole in her heart from Elise's absence, and… doubt. She was not built for rescue missions. She could not come up with plans, lead people, scheme, or even fight.

Am I leading these people to their deaths? All to find that Elise might already be dead? Have I already failed?

She wiped away more tears as she heard voices through an opening door. Soon, the flamboyantly dressed Hunter appeared.

"I really do not see why you are so grumpy, Anja. He was only flirting. The captain flirts with me, too, and despite not being interested in romance, I flirt back. To be polite."

Anja growled as she followed him towards where Nessa stood. "If I wish to be polite, I'll hand him the salt when he asks for it at dinner. I'll not flirt back only to inflate that already oversized male ego. I have more important things to do."

Hunter beamed. "Of course. You are busy being brilliant."

Anja snorted. "I was more thinking like *checking on Nessa*, which is why we came out here to this freezing deck, remember?"

"True." Hunter turned to Nessa. "Are you all right, heartling?"

Nessa winced at being called any term of endearment. That was only for Elise.

"I'm fine. I'd like to be alone."

Anja sniffed. "Of course, you do, misery. You want to brood, grieve, and make your gloom that much deeper by burrowing further into it. That's not healthy. We all know you're anxious. But what you need is what I keep recommending – staying strong, mentally as well as physically."

Annoyance prickled Nessa. "Well, that sounds easy when you say it, but I'm not quite sure how I'm meant to achieve it."

Anja looked incredulous. "This from the woman who passed the glassblower's test?"

"That was about knowing about glassblowing and moving heavy things. Not comparable."

Hunter took a step closer. "Come inside with us? We are dancing and telling stories. The captain is treating us to samples of his personal collection of vodkas. One is ice-flavoured!"

Anja adjusted her hat with a look of disdain. "Ice-flavoured, my arse. It's strong vodka with a bit of salt and pieces of watermint leaves. You have to come inside with me, Nessa. These people are all as stupid as hot water bottles in a desert."

Nessa almost smiled.

Maybe they're right. I'm no use to Elise out here.

"If I come in with you, will you promise not to squabble the whole time?"

Anja and Hunter looked at each other in shock. "We do not squabble! I agree with all she says because I adore her," Hunter blurted.

"And I adore him back. He's just like my beloved Svarte, vain, pretty, unpredictable, and usually useless."

"What? Excuse me!" Hunter said with hands on hips.

Anja playfully tugged on his beard. Nessa noticed it had grown quite a bit, allowing Anja to pull on the strands which were the same wheat colour as his long hair.

"Don't be like that, man-child. I said I adored you, be happy about that."

He smirked and puffed out his chest. "Of course you do. People of great taste, like you, cannot hate Hunter Smith."

Anja ignored him and linked arms with Nessa. "Come in to the warmth and lift your spirits. You will be more use in there than out here. If you befriend your team, they'll serve you better when we get to the castle."

"You reckon?" Nessa asked.

Anja rubbed her arm. "Without fail. Furthermore, they all feel sorry for you and that's not a situation I think you like. Come show them what strong stuff a Ground Hollow woman is made of."

"And demonstrate how much you can drink before you get inebriated. They are Northmen, they will be impressed by that and follow you into any battle," Hunter added.

"It's hardly *battle* we're going into," Nessa muttered.

Anja cackled. "Obviously you haven't seen how I deal with those who cross my friends."

She took Nessa by the arm and they all headed for the door.

CHAPTER 32
NIGHT VISION

E lise shivered, not from cold as her luxurious bedding kept her warm enough, but from hunger and fatigue. She peered at the grandfather clock in the corner and tried to make out the time with only moonlight for illumination. Three in the morning. Had she slept at all? It didn't feel like it. She'd managed the whole day with only a bite or two of her shroom-laced food, giving her hours of relative clarity where she took the chance to endear herself to the servants and surreptitiously make enquiries. Consequently, she'd managed to store up information she could use if the circumstances were right, but she was now suffering from hunger pangs and shroom withdrawal.

Everything appeared so bleak. How had she thought she could manage this all on her own? Where was Nessa? Was she coming for her? Had Joiners Square caught her, too? Perhaps the Queen had ordered her death.

No, no. Do not start this line of thinking. You will only deepen your despair. Sleep. Tomorrow you can have breakfast. Then, shrooms allowing, you can continue planning your escape and return to Nessa. Things will appear cheerier then.

She squeezed her eyes shut. Her stomach no longer growled or had hunger spasms. Instead it had a continuous, gnawing ache, as if it were trying to eat itself from the inside. Her head pounded, and her skin had developed a disconcerting crawling sensation. She curled herself into a foetal position and tried to count back from a hundred, like her father had always told her to do when she couldn't sleep as a child.

She got to seventy before her eyes opened and squinted towards the cup on the dressing table. The tea. They always provided her with a small cup of herbal tea before bed. Undoubtedly the *herbs* in it were mainly shrooms. She always left it or poured it out the window in the morning. But now… its temptation was breaking her resolve. It wasn't food, but it was something to fill her stomach, and the shrooms would make her feel a little better. Perhaps she could even sleep?

You do not need a clear head tonight. Stop being so obstinate. Drink it.

She stood up, far too quickly, and then stumbled towards the cup. She downed the tepid liquid in one go. Then she held on to the dressing table, waiting for the sensation of nails being pounded into her temples to ease enough so she could return to bed. To add to her discomfort, her stomach lurched at the sudden appearance of the tea.

When the queasiness and throbbing had abated, she dragged herself back into bed. She lay there, gently rocking back and forth. Using all her strength not to cry.

Not true. You are using it to make sure you do not give in. Oh, but it would be so simple. You still have desire for the Queen, even though that makes you a vile person. And being at her mercy was not all bad, was it? There were good times.

Elise growled at herself, but the propositions kept pecking away at her.

You could simply surrender. Get peace, untampered with and delicious food, the freedom to come and go. You could attend balls again and sit and gossip with the other courtiers. No more loneliness, pain, or fear.

Elise picked up a pillow and put it over her head, trying to drown out the thoughts.

Stop. No. I fought for my freedom. I am not to be owned and kept as a pet. I may not deserve better than what the Queen is offering me, but Nessa does. She wants to lead her life with me. She wants me to stay with her and love her and by all the gods – I shall.

"Yes. Still, you should not only keep fighting for Nessa's sake. You deserve better than this golden cage the Queen is offering you."

Elise lay absolutely still. There was no one in her room. There couldn't be. And yet, she had heard a male voice.

She relaxed. It must be the gargoyle again. The shrooms had clearly taken effect. She removed the pillow to find someone sitting at the end of her bed. It wasn't the gargoyle.

Elisandrine perched herself on her elbows. "Papa?"

"Yes, my cherished girl. Or, well, at least your anaesthetised mind's memory of me."

She wet her dry lips. "Why… are you here?"

Even in the moonlit darkness, she could see him smile. "Perchance because this is not a conversation you could have with your gargoyle friend?"

"Of course," she mumbled, looking down. "How silly of me."

"No need to be ashamed. You are doing what you need to survive, keep sane, and find a way out. That is what I would want you to do, we both know that."

"Yes, Papa."

He sought her gaze and held it. "Hence my appearance to remind you to *never* give in. My cherished girl is the sort who, if she cannot swim to safety, keeps treading water until she finds a way to swim. Prove to me that this has not changed."

Elise raised her chin. "I will, Papa. I shall eat only when I must, so that I can continue gathering information, and bonding with people who can assist me."

"That is my brave fighter."

Elise put her hand to her forehead. "I am suddenly lightheaded."

"Understandable. You have had no food or sleep, and now the shrooms are doing their worst. You must close your eyes and rest."

"Papa, will you leave if I sleep?"

"I fear so, my cherished. But I shall see you in your dreams. That is where I live now. In your dreams and in your memory."

Elise blinked heavy eyelids. "I will start writing to you again. In my notebook."

"If you wish. You do not need to, though. All you must do is think of me as you see things. Experience things. And learn things. Through your senses, you will share it all with me."

His voice was growing fainter. Elise strained to hear, fought to stay awake long enough to say farewell to him. As she had as a child when his eyes had closed for the last time.

"I see. Thank you. Good night, Papa."

"Good night, my cherished. I shall see you in your dreams. We will again play in the gardens back in Silverton or read books by the fire in our house here in Highmere."

His voice came from far away. Elise wanted to reply, but slumber was pulling her down into warm depths of oblivion. She let go and slept.

CHAPTER 33
COMPANIONS

For better or worse, Nessa was now inside with the others. The warmth and the smell of grog and bread welcomed her. Anja was leading her to a long table. Around it sat the four Sundes and three Viss from the underground, shoulder to shoulder with the Lindbergs and the senior staff of the ship.

Smaller tables lined the walls, filled with people she didn't know. There were plenty of other passengers on board, many more than there'd been when Nessa took this journey the other way. Apparently, now that the worst of winter was passing, and the ocean was less ice-riddled, balmy Arclid tempted the Storsund people.

Nessa sat down, and one of the Viss, she really had to learn their names, handed her a shot glass filled with clear liquid. The white-haired woman said something in Viss, and Anja quickly translated. "Ten-year-old vodka. Made with water from the River Orla."

Nessa noticed that the chatter at the table had died down and everyone was looking at her. She should've spent more time with them. They were two weeks into the journey and these people were getting to know each other, while she had foolishly kept to herself and her fears. She had to make up for lost time.

A good place to start seemed to be this shot. She downed it in one gulp and tried not to grimace as it burned its way down her throat. Everyone cheered, well, everyone except for Sonja, who was asleep in her mother's arms.

A man whom Nessa thought might be the ship's chief engineer took out a mandolin and began to play. Soon someone else found a flute of some kind and upbeat music filled the air. Eleonora snuck out, probably to put Sonja to bed. Albert and the ship's officers gathered around the players to clap and holler along to the sea chanties. Nessa stopped the seven pretend-soldiers from joining them. With Anja translating for the two Sundes who didn't speak Arclidian very well, Nessa first apologised for being distant and then for leading them into danger without an exact plan.

One of them, a heavily built man who looked well into his fifties, spoke up.

"Not to worry, lass. If someone had taken the person I love, I would've been without speech and plan too, yes? We can't make much of a plan yet anyway. Not until we know what it's like in the castle. We must get there, fit in, find out where your ladylove is. Then we can plan, yes?"

A red-haired woman sitting opposite added, "Don't fret. We've all been fighting Joiners Square for years. Sabotaging and protesting any way we could, yes? This has made us all brave and ready to think on our legs."

"The expression is 'think on our feet', actually," Hunter corrected. Everyone looked at him. He grinned, adding, "Not that this is important in the middle of a rousing speech, of course."

A younger man with a wiry beard leaned in closer and whispered, "I know we have the uniforms, but what about weapons? Joiners Square soldiers carry standard-issue knives and, if they're guarding or attacking, flintlock pistols or even blunderbusses, yes? We have neither."

Albert sat down with a thump, clumsy from the vodka. "Weeeeell, we have the knives," he slurred.

Everyone's gaze went to him. "We do?" Nessa asked.

Albert hiccupped. "Yes. Knives of the onic… unique white steel of Storsund. With the correct, little symbols on them. As the man says, they're part of the uniform, yes?" Another hiccup. "And I was asked to get full uniforms. In that supply box are the uniforms, hats, and knives. No pistols, I'm afraid. You need… what is word… special access to get them."

"Right, that's a start. But what if things go wrong and they start shooting at us, yes?" the redhead asked.

Knots twisted Nessa's stomach. "Um, well, we're meant to use stealth. Not violence."

The man with the wiry beard ran his hand through it. "Sure. But we were brought along partly to make up the ten of a squadron, but also to be muscle in case of conflict, yes?"

Anja slammed her glass down, loud enough to break through the noise of the instruments. "Well then. You should've brought weapons. You knew you were coming on a mission with inexperienced people who had to set this up with a moment's notice. Luckily for all of you, I picked up a few things at the Storsund Trading Office. There's always shady merchants there, swigging bad coffee and making new connections."

Something dawned on Nessa. "Oh, so that was the bag you had over your shoulder when you came back? I thought it was empty but for whatever coin you managed to pick up."

"No, full of firepower. Sadly, I had to part with most of the coin I'd collected from the Trading Company. The bugger even charged me for the bag," Anja said with a frown.

"You said 'a few things'. What things exactly?" asked Hunter.

"Four flintlock pistols and a blunderbuss, which has been upgraded with a sight and a mechanism for easier reloading."

"We will not all be armed, then," Hunter said with a sigh.

"You didn't expect to go in there with anything other than your pecker to point at them a moment ago! Now you'll have a knife and know that good marksmen from your group can protect you. Don't complain," Anja growled at him.

Instead of looking cowed he beamed at her. Nessa wasn't sure what their strange friendship was all about, but as long as they were happy, she was happy.

Albert hiccupped again and started poking at a tattoo peeking up at the top of the shoulder of the heavily built man who had first spoken. He closed his eyes and put up with it. When Nessa stared at them, the man who looked and sounded like a Sund explained. "When he gets drunk, he loves everyone's tattoo, yes?"

Albert looked at Nessa with exaggerated gravity. "Joiners Square personnel aren't allowed talt... tattoos. The higher ranks say it looks messy. But now I can say bugger that, yes? When we get back, I'm getting Sonja's face tattooed on my back."

"I... see. Well, if you're certain that's what you want," Nessa replied with concern.

"Don't worry about mine, yes? The uniform is high-collared and will hide it when we sneak into the castle," the big man said.

Albert dragged a vodka bottle across the table and poured some into every glass he could see. "Now, we drink vodka and discuss tattoos, yes?"

"Define *we*," Anja said with a snort.

"Oh, come now, allow the man some fun now that he is

about to escape the strict restraints of Joiners Square," Hunter said.

Albert appeared to shiver. "Yes. Strict. Very tight. I regret working for them, yes? But it was a desired and well-paid job. I got it to impress Eleonora. Everything I do is to impress her. She's too good for me. Too smart. Too sweet. Too pretty." He quaffed his vodka. "I needed good job to deserve her. Then I started seeing problems, yes? Much many problems. Coin going missing and things being swept under floors. Dark whispers and…" He paused to hiccup. "And things that did not make sense. Eleonora said that Joiners Square was bad. She told me to be careful and to look for other jobs, yes? How right she was. Always right. Always right and… and… and pretty. Yes, pretty. Long, slender arms and legs. Skin as smooth and dark as Wayfarers' hats."

"Wayfarers' hats?" Nessa whispered to Anja.

Anja leaned closer. "My ancestors wore broad-brimmed hats which were made of chestnut-brown velvet."

Nessa patted her arm. "Ah, thanks."

Albert was about to hiccup but burped instead, taking himself by surprise and distracting him from his rambling. "Oh. Oh my. Pardon that. Where was me? I mean, where was I?"

"Your wife being pretty?" the redhead suggested.

He peered at her. "You sound, uh, what's the word… spectacle? Are you sek…scek… sceptical about my wife's beauty, madam?"

He had shouted the last words, and the redhead's eyes went wide. Then she laughed. "No, she's very fine-looking." Albert kept peering at her, as if doubting her sincerity. She cleared her throat and added, "Had she been single, I would've courted her. Even if I don't have an impressive job, yes?"

There were genial chuckles around the table. Albert's face split into a wide grin.

"Good. Good. She is a princess amongst dogs. She told me that Joiners Square was growing rotten."

"And right she was," the big man said. "More and more people notice. But no one says anything, yes? No one wants to court trouble. Everybody wants to be loyal, to stay in their favour. All to be safe, getting better jobs, and more coin."

"Better houses, too," Anja added. "Joiners Square can do a lot for you as long as you don't question them. That's why I've had to tiptoe with my book. If I'm too openly critical of Joiners Square – *boom* – my house gets vandalised or the publisher for my book withdraws her offer."

The man with the wiry beard pointed to her. "Aye! People are seeing that now, they're starting to question them, yes? We in the underground found each other and then allies in the Viss. The Wayfarers, too, but they're hard to find since they never stay in one place. There are people who'll bring Joiners Square down. People who'll fight no matter how impossible the battle looks, yes? The little critter can fight the big monster, if it just tries its best and gets help."

Everyone cheered, and someone appeared to make a toast. Nessa didn't quite hear it. She kept mulling those last words over in her mind.

Can it be that simple? Can I take on more if I simply dare to… try? Surely not.

She looked at her hands. Calloused and small. Not the hands of a hero. But the hands of someone who had always tried, in the end. Those hands had gotten her this far. Furthermore — she looked around the table – she had help.

Albert banged his glass on the table. "Yes! I can do anything, even if I'm a small man. I'll get a job with the new gov-tent… government. They'll employ me, praise me, write songs about me. Then I'll get tattoos and, after that, my Eleonora will be unable to ever keep her hands off me!"

There was another cheer. Everyone seemed to indulge

Albert, but Nessa noticed that the Viss, who had not spoken, stared at him as if he was from another world.

Makes sense. They're Viss and he used to be Joiners Square. Also, he's Albert.

She had seen the Viss rebels around the ship, always helping the crew when they could. Quiet but generous.

She had avoided them all, she realised. Not just because she'd been brooding but because without Elise, she'd reverted to avoiding people. Back to her own shy, people-fearing ways. She needed to learn to be braver and practice her social skills without Elise. She had to learn a lot of things if this was to go well.

Eleonora came back without Sonja and launched straight into a dance when she heard the music. Albert abandoned his vodka and threw himself at his wife shouting about "dancing with the sweetest girl on the steamer."

Nessa was happy to see how thrilled Eleonora looked with the compliment. Those two only had eyes for each other, even after so many years of marriage. Would she and Elise be afforded that luxury?

Clearly Anja was pondering their marriage, too. "Strange to imagine being so happy for so long. It was what I always wanted. What I, for a while, thought I had."

"With Diinna?" Nessa ventured.

Anja said nothing for a while, then she nodded slowly, eyes fixed on the dancing couple.

Nessa looked down at the vodka Albert had poured for her. "May I ask what happened between you two?"

Anja swallowed visibly and then got up and walked out.

Nessa was left sitting there, watching Anja with concern churning in her stomach.

A short man with the telltale white hair of the Viss leaned over the table to be heard over the music. "I was there, you know. I worked with Diinna back when they were together."

As with Diinna, his Arclidian was exceptional. Nessa wondered if the Viss were always better at Arclidian than the Wayfarers and Sundes.

Hunter jolted forwards. "Oh! Bjorn, is it not? Can you tell us what happened? Or is it a secret?"

The short man mumbled, "It's *Björn*, actually." He hummed uncertainly. "Well, everyone who was there knew about it, so it's not really a secret. Anja and Diinna were together for years. They met at an equal rights rally, when Anja still worked at the school and Diinna had recently arrived for her post at the embassy. She, I, and Ravna over there," he pointed to a woman opposite, "arrived together, actually, since we came from the same area. Diinna was ambitious even then. Pleasant but addicted to work."

Nessa smiled. "Sounds like she would get along well with Anja."

He shrugged. "Storsund work ethic, nothing special about that trait. But yes, they shared it. They also shared a thirst for knowledge. And the fight for equal rights for Sundes, Viss, and the Wayfarers."

"Subsequently, they met, found they had things in common, and were together for years. We are up to speed now. Then what? What happened that was so horrible that it broke Anja like this?" Hunter asked, real concern in his voice.

Björn looked down, scratching his neck. "Their relationship was always fraught. But there was one occasion which marked the end." He lowered his voice, now barely audible in the noisy room. "On the day of her mother's funeral, Anja found Diinna in a compromising situation in the bathroom. With Anja's friend, Matthias."

Hunter hissed as if in pain.

Nessa gaped. "The man who died in the accident where Anja lost her arm?"

"Exactly. Their mountain climb was a year later, so obviously Anja forgave him. But not Diinna. Actually, the funeral wasn't the first time Anja caught Matthias and Diinna together. Anja and Diinna were known for cheating on each other. Then they'd confess, fight about it, and get back together."

"So, it was not the cheating Anja could not forgive?" Hunter asked.

"No. It was the timing and how publicly Diinna did it. It must've been to punish Anja for something? For two private people, their stormy relationship was always very public. They simply weren't good together."

"It certainly doesn't sound like it," Nessa agreed.

Björn sat back, clearly saddened by the memories. Hunter upended his glass, looking at the door through which Anja had left.

The two ship's officers launched into a new song, this one a ballad. Everyone watched them for a moment. Then the Viss began speaking amongst themselves in their own language.

Hunter poured Nessa another shot and shoved a bowl of dried sunberries over. "Have some of these, apparently they keep seafaring folk from getting scurvy."

"Hunter, we're not in the olden days. People eat varied diets. They don't get scurvy," Nessa said patiently. She still ate some berries to soak up the alcohol.

Hunter tapped his fingers on the table in time with the music. "Are you all right?

Nessa looked down while searching for an answer. "No. But... maybe I will be."

"You will. You are so much more capable than you think. Anyway, sad to hear about Anja and Diinna. Bad form, that."

"Very sad and very bad," Nessa agreed. Despite the unhappy tale, the alcohol and the company were having a pleasant effect. Muscles popped in her tight jaw and her shoulders dropped from up by her ears.

Hunter frowned. "Speaking of Diinna. Do you remember when she mentioned that there was someone waiting in the wings at court, ready to take the throne if we finally ousted the Queen?"

Nessa swallowed down her vodka. "Yes, I remember."

"Do you happen to know who that person is?" Hunter shouted, to be heard over the upbeat song that now started.

"No. Do you?"

He bit his lip. "I have a guess. If I am remembering my schooling properly. Sadly, I did not attend many lessons before I had to quit to help my fathers at work."

There was a crash against the table as Albert and Eleonora danced into it.

As Eleonora started to apologise, she stopped herself and exclaimed, "You two! You're not dancing. Such crime, yes? Albert, dance with one of them and I'll dance with the other. They're too young and sweet to sit here and drink in unhappiness."

With that, both Hunter and Nessa were pulled up on the dance floor and conversation was lost in an evening of vodka, music, and trying to chase away the destiny that awaited them on the distant shore.

CHAPTER 34
ELISANDRINE AND MARIANNA

Elise woke with a start and blinked into the darkness. The door handle had slowly been pulled down, that was what had awoken her. Or had she imagined it? Was it the shrooms playing tricks with her mind again? The door began to open, letting in a shaft of frail light.

Not imagined, then. Surely, it must be the middle of the night. Who would come in here now? Why have the guards not stopped them?

Striding into the room was the Queen. Of course. Her Royal Highness could come and go as she pleased. Elisandrine watched the figure in an elaborate nightdress, and holding an equally elaborate candelabra, close the door behind her.

"My Queen. To what do I owe this late-night visit?" she whispered, not sure why she didn't speak in normal tones.

"Late night or early morning? Are you so sure what time of day it is, sweet fire-starter?"

"Stop trying to confuse me. Your shrooms do enough of that already." Elise realised her anger was showing and that she was meant to keep the Queen sweet. She added a smile and the words, "I believe it to be night. Am I incorrect, Your Majesty?"

"No. It is twenty minutes past two."

"I see. Trouble sleeping, Your Majesty?"

"Not exactly. More along the lines of… boredom. I thought I would come see how my guest was before returning to bed."

Elise inwardly scoffed.

Fine. We shall pretend that you are not here because of your frustration at my lack of submission.

"How can I assist with that, Your Royal Highness? I would suggest a midnight picnic, but sadly, I am confined to this room."

The Queen grimaced, but Elise couldn't find it in herself to regret her words.

Queen Marianna strode towards her, stopping at the foot of the bed. "There are ways of entertaining me in your room, sweetest Elise."

The silence in the room was deafening. Elise weighed her options.

She examined the figure still looming at the end of the bed. Marianna Hargraves was as tall, as high-cheekboned, and as strikingly *imperial* as always. But the latter seemed affected, no longer an obvious trait but something she had to fight to uphold. She wasn't even as beautiful as Elise had remembered. Her selfishness and cruel deeds seemed to show in her callous face and her cold, pale body.

Elise searched herself for a trace of the unwelcome arousal she had felt in the past. Then she searched for the feeling that the Queen saw right though her and could control her. She found none.

I am done with her. Done with unwanted desire. Done with being frightened of her. Done feeling anything but pity towards her.

339

Elise kept examining the woman in front of her. All the glamour was falling away, revealing cold, hard facts. This selfish creature had taken advantage of her low self-esteem. And the loneliness which Elise's mother's neglect and the loss of her father had instilled in her. That was all over now. Elise was a different person, she had seen what other lives there were out there. Real lives outside of court, which had strife and trouble, but were free. Free from manipulation, from being beholden, and certainly from frequent imprisonment.

Elise smiled to herself.

I no longer need her validation. I have learned that I am a good life partner, an attentive friend, a world-wise traveller, and I made the best scented oils in Storsund.

Truth bred truth and with a lump in her throat, Elise understood what she had never been able to puzzle out before.

Validation, that was all it was. Never love or admiration. Not even desire, that was merely me punishing myself. I believed the only worth I could have was as an ornament or a lover to be used. I am so much more.

In response to Elise's silence, the Queen said, "I know you have needs. And I know that you have treated me kindly, if somewhat aloofly, during your time here. Why not simply give in and allow us both what we want? Pull away the covers, open your legs, and beg for me to come to you. You know I can make everything right."

Elise bit her tongue. She knew what she wanted to reply, but she also knew that she didn't want to be tortured in the morning. The old Elisandrine would have given in, of course. But then, the old Elisandrine would have given in the second she realised that someone wanted her as much as the Queen seemed to. That Elisandrine didn't exist anymore.

Elise sat up straighter. "No, thank you. I know I have been saying no in the vaguest ways possible up to this point. Therefore, let me be clear now. No. Absolutely not. Never again. Not even if my life depends upon it."

The Queen – *no, Marianna. Her name is Marianna. She is just a person* – Marianna stomped her bare foot on the marble floor in a way which must have hurt horribly.

"No! I found you. I brought you all this gods-cursed way! You *will* beg for me. You *will* want me. You will pray to be my favourite again," she hissed.

Elise pretended to consider this. "Are you talking about me desiring you or loving you? Or perhaps fearing you? Do you even know the difference, Your Majesty?"

"You cursed, dreadful little harlot," Marianna bellowed, spitting as she did. "I shall keep you here for the rest of your life. In time, need and your denied love for me will make you plead. And when it does... oh, I will make you beg on your knees for what you want, humiliate yourself for it, and I shall make you wait... until the need nearly kills you."

"I think not. However, it sounds like we will have a long time to find out which one of us is right. Which is fine. I am in no hurry. I do not have a nation to run or a throne to defend. Nor enemies around every corner." Elise smiled. "I have plenty of time and effort to put into merely continuing to not want or love you. You, however... well, I would not deign to assume what time and effort you have to spare."

Marianna threw her candelabra against the wall with a roar. It clanked deafeningly while the candles all smashed, spraying melted wax everywhere before their flames went out.

"Careful, my Queen. You would not want to *start a fire*," Elise said.

The next thing she heard was the door being slammed and bare feet stomping away down the hall. Elise smiled to herself in the dark, and for the first time since her capture, nestled into her bed and fell into deep, restoring sleep.

CHAPTER 35
THE QUESTION OF MAGIC

Marianna looked at the missive she had just signed and felt that vein in her temple pulse. The last three letters of her signature tilted the wrong way. It was a small thing, but it mattered. Everything mattered. Especially anything which could be seen as weakness or distraction. That was what one learned if one had subjects who frequently rebelled.

"Adaire?"

She looked up from where she had been refilling Marianna's second fountain pen. "Yes, my Queen?"

"How is the mood of the people?"

"Stable, I believe," Adaire replied.

"Really? I thought I heard an uproar outside Highmere's gates when I was riding yesterday."

"I shall look into that, Your Majesty."

"Yes, do. Could… there be lingering resentment regarding my hunt for Elise?"

Adaire handed her the refilled pen, her elegant features blank as usual. "They knew you were distracted when hunting someone and that the hunt is now over. They do not know that you are holding someone at the castle. Perhaps any uproar is due to raised taxes and the decline in trade with the other nations? Both have hit your people hard, my Queen."

Marianna observed Adaire. This was the first time that the chase for Elise hadn't made Adaire purse her lips and talk about how "misguided" the whole affair was.

Strange. Is she no longer jealous? Or was it never jealousy to begin with? Could she have considered my distraction bad for my rule, as she claimed?

Marianna shook her head. She shouldn't second-guess herself like this.

Adaire spoke again. "There *have* been rumblings about the Joiners Square soldiers being here, although that is mainly from the Nobles, the courtiers to be exact, who have chosen to do their luxuriating and trading in gems and gossip elsewhere."

"That explains why the castle has been so quiet," Marianna said with a wink.

Adaire looked stern. "Nevertheless, you must make court hospitable for the Nobles again, my Queen. You need them on your side. When will the talks with Nordhall be done and they all return to Storsund?"

"Oh, who can say? Officially, he stays because our trade agreements are not finished. In truth, he stays in the hope that I will reveal the secret of magic now that he has handed me Elise."

"Yes, I gathered as much. It has been many weeks since Elise came here. Is he not getting impatient to get his end of the bargain?"

"Oh, certainly. You know those letters and books I have had you deliver to him? They are all documents which hint at the existence of magic but never quite prove anything. Every time, he thinks I am giving him what he wants. He scours the text and then comes in here shouting in disappointment."

"Surely that trick cannot work for long, Your Majesty?"

Marianna sighed. "No, it cannot. In fact, it is wearing thin."

"Then tell him what he wants to know. Or inform him that you shall never tell him."

"Tell him? Ha! I would tell him to go learn how to fly off a cliff, but I think that would start a war. And that would endanger my position on the throne, giving the peasants another silly reason to revolt."

Adaire adjusted a stack of papers. "Well, they would be the ones dying in the war."

"Whose side are you on, my cherished?" Marianna snarled.

"Yours, my Queen. So, what are you going to do? Answer his question?"

"I believe it may be too late for that. He wants more than my word, hence the texts I have had you deliver. He wants historic documents from my ancestors, either denying or confirming if magic is real and if we have used it. He no longer trusts me."

Adaire looked up, but if she was about to say "I wonder why" or something of that ilk, she stopped herself.

Good. I should be loath to punish her. Well, no, not if it was the fun sort of punishment.

"Then I suggest manufacturing such a book, my Queen."

"Pardon?"

"Create a book which says what you want it to, order your papermakers to make the book look old and tatty, and ensure it is dated a hundred years ago. Give him that and send him back to the cold."

"That could be an idea. Clever woman. Let me think about that for a while."

"Of course, my Queen."

Marianna observed her again. "You really want them gone."

"Yes, my Queen."

344

"Why the rush?"

"Joiners Square cannot be trusted. And as you said, it is only a matter of time until they self-destruct. Arclid should not be caught up in that."

"That is not all, Adaire. I can see it in those dark blue eyes of yours."

Adaire sniffed. "I told you, the Nobles became uncomfortable amongst all the severe uniforms and the feel of conflict in the air. I am trying to protect your position. If you have the people against you, that can be handled. If the Nobles turn against you…"

"They might search out another Queen?"

"Or worse. They might be inspired by Storsund and eliminate monarchy all together."

"Ah. That would not happen. I have made them fear the progress, including the political mayhem of Storsund and the complicated democracy of the Western Isles. Age-old monarchy, like in Obeha and Arclid, looks safe and stable."

"As you say," Adaire said, her placid demeanour showing the tiniest hint of disbelief. "Just get rid of the Northmen, Your Majesty."

Marianna bristled at the near-order. "In time. For now, they entertain me, keep the castle safe, and help guard my little… guest up there."

"As you say, my Queen," Adaire repeated.

CHAPTER 36

FROM CAWSTONE TO HIGHMERE
CASTLE

Shifting her weight from foot to foot, Nessa squinted in the direction she'd been told Arclid *finally* was. The dread in her veins made her even colder than the wintry morning did, but the dread was trumped by the relief of soon being able to *do something*. That relief was taking on her feelings of inadequacy, and she could swear it was winning.

The ship's captain appeared at her elbow. "A slow trip, yes? Almost two weeks longer than the usual journey-time. Again, my apologies for the trick the seas played on us. Still, we should now see Cawstone in under three days."

She thanked him, and he walked on to speak to more talkative passengers.

Hunter and Anja joined Nessa. Hunter was smiling at Anja and chirped, "You were right. You said at breakfast that we were close to shore. How clever you are!"

Anja cackled. "Take your nose out of my bottom, manchild." She switched her gaze to Nessa. "Are you all right?"

"No, but I shall be when I can see that bloody castle. Because I'll either leave it with Elise or die in it. Either way, the waiting will be over. And I'll be with Elise."

Anja patted her shoulder. "Yes, lass. And she'll be thrilled to see you. I'll have no talk of dying, though. Come get some coffee when you're ready."

They left Nessa to gaze out at sea, looking for the sliver of land and failing without any binoculars. She prayed to Ioene, the moon goddess that she had thanked for bringing Elise to her. She prayed until her head hurt and then focused towards the direction of Arclid, her hands clenching into fists and her resolve firming.

~

Cawstone. The barren ground was still frozen here, but oh-so welcome under Nessa's feet. She'd never been here, but she knew it was close to Highmere. She frowned at the thought. When the ship's other passengers had milled away to the local taverns, inns, and lodgings, Nessa gathered her group.

"Right. We need some carriages to take us to Highmere. I should think the journey will take a few days." She turned to her fellow Arclidian, and Hunter nodded his agreement.

Albert groaned. "No trains? No cable cars? Not even for some of the way?"

Nessa crossed her arms over her chest. "No. The Queen has warned us off those things, remember? We've been told that they're dangerous and prohibitively expensive."

"Yes. The newspapers are full of those 'facts.' Positively absurd," Hunter said.

Björn, the short Viss man, tutted. "Shame. I hear you have the sort of land where coal mines are aplenty."

"Odd that you've allowed her to keep you in the dark like this, yes? You live almost like animals," Albert said with a scrunched-up nose.

Before she could stop herself, Nessa channelled her old master and whispered "spoiled uniform monkey" under her breath. The comment wasn't only due to Albert having worked for Joiners Square, but also in regard to the uniforms they'd all changed into before leaving the steamer. If the ship's crew or their fellow passengers had noticed, they hadn't said anything.

The Viss woman who seemed so in charge, Ravna, shrugged off her standard-issue fur cloak. "At least it's warm here."

"It is freezing, heartling. You Storsundians are so used to the air being half ice that you think anything that does not give you frostbite is balmy!" Hunter said with a sneer.

"You didn't complain about the cold when it allowed you all those pretty furs," Anja said, grinning.

He ignored her and adjusted his ponytail while looking around. "Nessa, there is an inn with a carriage hall over there. I can go procure some carriages at a good price. You know my excellent haggling skills."

"That would be splendid, thank you, Hunter."

Nessa examined her brave, motley team of rescuers. Albert was kissing Sonja on the head, it was only then that Nessa remembered that she and her mother were staying here.

After some hesitance, Nessa went to embrace Eleonora. "Thank you for letting your husband risk his life for Elise," she whispered.

Eleonora pulled away so they were eye to eye. "Not only for Elise, sweet Nessa. Albert is doing it because it's the right thing to do."

"And to fetch a good job when the dust settles, yes?" Albert added with a snigger.

Nessa laughed. "Of course." She gave Sonja a farewell hug, too. "Well, while you three go find this fancy inn you've previously stayed in, we shall follow Hunter and try to get ourselves some ale and something to eat, I think."

"I'll meet you there, yes? Just be careful, people here are not so fond of *us* Joiners Square soldiers."

The way he said *us* was a clear reminder and warning, they had to act their parts now. The carriage drivers had to think they were with Joiners Square or they might give away the ruse when they arrived in Highmere. Everyone from now on must think them to be disciplined, unfriendly foreign soldiers.

Nessa nodded to him, then turned and grabbed Anja by the arm. "You and the other Storsundians do the talking since you have the right accents." A thought struck her. "In fact, I've no idea how Hunter is getting along with his fake Highmere Noble dialect in the inn right now."

Anja laughed. "The way he gets away with anything. Lies, charm, and that blinding smile. He's a talented rat, our sweet boy."

Nessa shook her head. "As I say, you do have the strangest friendship."

Anja looked at her boots as they walked. "You cannot help but love him. He needs affection and belonging more than most."

"Agreed," Nessa said, rubbing Anja's arm tenderly before letting it go. She wasn't sure just how much Joiners Square soldiers walked arm in arm.

They all headed for the inn, still getting used to their new boots, the starchy uniforms, and the knives chafing at their sides. Nessa prayed again, this time that their deception would work. She'd have to learn to pray for one thing at a time, lest she drowned the moon goddess in demands.

Four days later, at the break of dawn, Nessa awoke to her carriage bumping over something. It jolted her awake and made Albert, who'd been snoring on her shoulder, mumble in his sleep. Then he returned to snoring. Nessa glanced down at him.

Why does he sleep on me? Probably the same reason he keeps telling me bad jokes and asking me to explain Arclidian things he finds idiotic – he thinks we're friends.

She smiled to herself.

Well, annoying as he is, I could do worse when it comes to friends.

She thought ahead to their destination, imagining the Queen with the Joiners Square emissary and all those cruel Noble courtiers who treated Elise so badly.

Yes, I could do much worse.

She moved her shoulder to be a better height for Albert to sleep on.

Now wide awake, Nessa gazed out the window. The fields were covered in low mist, which she knew was heat escaping the fertile ground. Her father always said it was fairies dancing, though. Her heart stung. It was odd to be on the same continent as her parents again, and yet so far from them. She hoped they were safe and happy, and not worrying too much about her.

She thought again about the marriage lie she and Elise had told when they created their new personas. The lying had grated on her conscience, but the idea of being married to Elise had felt true. It had seemed right and natural. As natural as her parents' marriage had always seemed.

Something in the distance caught her eye. A collection of bright buildings. They were high and even from this distance looked fancy.

Highmere.

It had to be. The fields they were passing must be the royal grounds that Elise had talked about. The fields stopped reminding Nessa of home and began to look menacing.

She took a deep breath. She was so close to her heartling now. In her yearning, she almost felt she could smell her skin, her hair. If she got Elise back, she would never let her out of her sight again. She closed her eyes tight, willing the white and pink city closer. She daydreamed about storming in, picking Elise up, and running far away with her in her arms.

The next time she opened her eyes, the dawn light was a tad brighter and the carriages appeared to have stopped. They got out, all hesitant.

Are they as frightened as I am?

Nessa found new things to fret over every second. As they unpacked their bags, she wondered if it was customary to have different luggage or if they should all have standard-issue Joiners Square bags. As Hunter walked next to her, she wondered if they might recognise him despite his beard. When they all strode towards the white iron gates, she wondered if they should be marching. And when Albert was speaking to the guard at the gates, she worried that he would not be able to keep up the ruse.

Keep fretting like this, and you'll be a wreck before you even get the chance to be killed.

They all waited, trying to look normal. Tricky, considering how hard Nessa was tensing her whole body. There was no turning back now. They were at the castle, in their disguises, and about to either be let in or discovered.

She breathed through her nose, trying not to hyperventilate. Her heart pounded out the seconds. The wind blew right at them. As she felt a warm breeze caress strands of hair away from her face, her heartbeat calmed. In her mind she heard the words Albert had said back in Charlottenberg, "Well, it's about time I was brave."

Now is my time to be brave. I think I might be able to manage it.

She was finally doing something. Not hiding. Not worrying. Not planning. She was taking action. Somehow being here, even if it got them all killed, made the mission feel possible. The safety she had sought by hiding from danger she was

---

somehow finding here. In herself. In this moment of utter danger.

Now was the time to be brave, and Nessa Clay was ready to try. Try in the same way she did with her master's cart in the glassblower's test, one step at a time. She squared her shoulders, looked around at the others and gave her team a reassuring smile.

All of a sudden, the guard opened the high gates and asked them to follow him. Nessa took the lead after Albert and marched through the courtyard with her squadron in tow. She wasn't praying. Or fretting. A strange sort of calm warmed her from the inside. What would happen would happen. All she could do was try her best.

The guard escorted them to High Captain Nordhall, who welcomed Albert in Sundish, seeming happy enough to see him. It was hard to tell with Nordhall's face appearing so stern and cold that it could've been cut from the same marble as the castle around them. After a while, Nordhall slapped Albert on the back and walked away to converse with some of his soldiers.

Albert stepped back to Nessa and the team behind her. "He's happiness to have more troops, yes? He didn't seem as happy to hear that I'd be taking notes during the talks with the Queen. He said there were... hmm... things best kept out of written logs."

"Ha! I wager there is," Ravna said.

Albert frowned. "Anyway, he asked us to go wash all road dust off and catch up with the soldiers who were off-duty. Apparently, they're in the left, I mean *east* wing."

Nessa clapped him on the shoulder. "Good job. We now know where to start. I suggest that when we get there we pretend to be settling in. Then those who speak Sundish can make small talk with the soldiers and try to figure out where Elise is being held."

The rebels all nodded and mumbled agreements.

"Good planning," Albert said, adjusting his tight collar nervously. "Nordhall pointed in that direction so I am thinking that is where the east wing is."

"Yes, I rather think the east wing will be to the east," Anja muttered.

"Be nice to Albert," Nessa said, trying not to smile.

As they walked towards the east wing, Albert filled them in on how Nordhall was Joiners Square's golden child but that no one knew what he actually did.

Albert was wide-eyed when he said, "Nordhall's known to be... what's the word... robeless."

They all paused, some probably thinking about what word Albert wanted and the others dealing with mental images of High Captain Nordhall without a robe.

"Ruthless?" Björn suggested.

"Yes, *ruthless* and filled to the ears with secrets," Albert added.

They all let the ear comment pass and kept walking. Whenever they passed servants or any Royal Guards, they were glared at.

"Are they staring at us because they recognise us?" Nessa whispered to Hunter.

He ran his hand over his thick beard as he watched a guard stare openly. When they were out of earshot, Hunter shook his head, making his ponytail dance. "No, I think not. I believe it is merely distaste. From what I have heard, everyone resents that Joiners Square are here. People are suspicious of these powerful, rude, and meddling foreigners. Yet another way the Queen has angered her people. Good for us, bad for her."

When they arrived in the part of the east wing which had been altered into posh barracks for the soldiers, they found a few of the Northmen lingering there. Some sitting on the beds, smoking pipes and chatting. A couple of them were cleaning their weaponry. One male soldier was trying to get the attention of one of the Queen's passing footmen, who seemed uninterested in stopping to flirt.

The soldier turned to the newcomers and said something. The redheaded rebel replied and made him laugh. Anja held her hand over her mouth in a faked cough and whispered, "He's complaining that he hasn't slept with any of the staff lately. Saying that in the first months they were here, all the Arclidians wanted to bed the newcomers. Now they're just hostile."

There was more Sundish spoken, and Anja again found ways to subtly translate. "She asked him if he'd bedded the mysterious Storsund prisoner that she's heard so much about."

"Was that when he laughed?" Nessa snarled.

"Yes. Then he said that that no one bedded her. Only the Queen, servants, and someone called Under Lieutenant Anders Dahl are allowed in her room." Anja paused to listen to the rest. "Oh, and apparently a chemist, too. He gives her some sort of shrooms to keep her docile and to connect this place with happiness? That's apparently the rumour; that the Queen is making the prisoner like it here. To make her *want* to stay."

"Oxen-shit," Nessa growled. "Did he say where her room is?"

"No," Anja whispered. "Let me get involved and see if I can figure it out. You two act like you're relaxing after a long voyage. And don't speak!"

With that, Anja stepped forward and joined the conversation. Her tone was light, betraying none of her usual grumpiness. Nessa was impressed. It almost distracted her from the itching sensation under her skin. Was it the starched uniform? Or her nerves?

Maybe it's being so close to Elise and yet so bloody far away.

A few minutes later, the conversation ended. The soldier

turned to accept a pipe from a comrade while the redheaded rebel and Anja returned to Nessa and Hunter.

Anja leaned in to whisper, "She's held in a room three floors up, overlooking the northern turret. He also said that her room is the only one always protected by two guards, that should help us find it."

"Apparently, it's usually guarded by a Royal Guard and this Under Lieutenant Dahl that the soldier spoke of, yes? Unless Dahl is off-duty in which case it's two Royal Guards," the redhead added.

Nessa nodded, wishing she'd learnt this woman's name.

Anja was biting her lower lip. "The involvement of this Dahl confuses me. It seems he's one of the soldiers who kidnapped Elise. So, she struck up a rapport with him and wanted him to be one of her jailers? Peculiar."

Nessa chuckled. "Not if she's grooming him to free her. Knowing Elise, she's probably been charming him ever since he abducted her. He probably eats out of her hand by now."

"Possible," Anja agreed with a new light in her eyes. "Well, we shouldn't waste time. If we amble towards the stairs, the team should notice and subtly follow us."

"Good thinking," Nessa said.

She scanned the room, catching the eye of some of the others in their troop. Then she, Hunter, Anja, and the redhead walked towards the staircase. Soon she heard the clumsy steps of Albert Lindberg behind them. By the time they were one flight of stairs up, all eleven of the group were there.

Anja filled them in as they hurried up the stairs, making her as out of breath as Albert and Hunter. The rest of them, more used to athletic endeavours, took the lead without having to pause for breath. Nessa only stopped when she saw two people outside a door in the corridor ahead. One was a young man in a Joiners Square uniform and the other was a tall woman from the Royal Guards.

"There," Nessa whispered to her followers. "Now we need to get past them."

"Should we knock them unconscious?" Hunter panted.

"No," said the big Sund man. "There's too many people walking through the corridor who could see. Or who'd miss the guards when they were no longer on their post, yes? Also, they might hear thuds and shouts of pain."

"Precisely. We need to convince the guards to let us in," Ravna agreed.

"Leave it to me," Albert said between wheezes.

He took a few deep breaths and then strode towards the door. "Greetings. I'm Albert Lindberg, head clerk at the Charlottenberg branch. I've been sent here to document the situation and report back to the head office. Grand Marshall Karlberg wants a decree... a deb..."

Nessa turned her head, unable to watch. *No, no, no. He was doing so well, sounding so commanding.*

The Royal Guard quietly ventured, "A *debrief*, sir?"

"Exactly, a debrief of this prisoner. My squadron and I need access straightaway," Albert stated.

The soldier, presumably this Dahl, peered at him while swallowing visibly. "Pardon me, head clerk, does your entire squadron need to come in for that? My orders are to limit the people who enter the prisoner's – I mean the guest's – room, yes?"

Albert barked something in Sundish at him. The only word Nessa could make out was "Nordhall." The young soldier stood to attention and opened the door for Albert, who turned and beckoned to them. They followed him in, Nessa trying to look as military and calm as she could.

When the door closed behind her, Nessa's world crumbled. Every minute of the past

months, she had been waiting to see Elise. Needing her

like air. Now she took in the sight of the woman who had changed her world and found herself breathless and dizzy.

Elise got up from the bed she'd been sitting on and took a few stumbling steps towards Nessa. All the others moved to the side in quiet unison. Nessa didn't care what they did or what was happening around her. She was busy assessing Elise and her sluggish movements.

She's so pale. How did that glowing, sand-coloured skin turn so grey? And her eyes are as unfocused as her movements. Wait, did Anja did say that they gave her shrooms?

"My cherished. Are you quite all right?" Nessa breathed.

"No," Elise said in a sob. She threw herself at Nessa, pulling her close in clumsy, violent movements. Nessa matched the ferocity and held her tight, willing her own strength into Elise. Nessa's heart hammered with anger at how her heartling had been treated. She conducted a quick check-up.

She's much thinner, but all body parts are present and accounted for. No bruises unless they're under the long dress. Energy low. Mind and body clearly affected by the shrooms, but she remembers me and has the strength to stand and to hold me.

The relief of embracing Elise was intoxicating. Nessa breathed in the scent of her skin, distantly wondering if she was crying as Elise was.

"You're going to be all right now. I'm here and I won't let anyone hurt you or take you away ever again. You're safe," she said in a cracking voice.

She kissed Elise's thick, soft hair and mumbled "I love you" and "I've missed you so much" over and over again.

Elise was still sobbing, holding on for dear life and spilling hot tears on Nessa's neck and shoulder.

Distant alarm bells were going off in Nessa's head, telling her they had to move soon. But she couldn't listen. She had to hold Elise for just a few more seconds. To make sure she was alive and knew how loved she was. To allow her own heart and mind a chance to slowly come off the precipice of constant fear and guilt. If she was killed or captured now, at least she would be with Elise. Nothing seemed more important in that moment.

She noticed that she had begun gently rocking Elise while still kissing her hair. Elise clambered even closer and whispered, "You came for me."

"Of course, heartling. It was time for me to learn to be brave and bold. Just like you."

CHAPTER 37

THE GUARD AND THE SOLDIER

At first Elise had thought it another hallucination. After all, if there was one thing her mind would wish to conjure up, it'd be Nessa. However, if her brain was going to create a calming, wonderful fantasy, it would have made Nessa appear healthy and well-rested. She'd have been alone… and probably scantily dressed. What Elise saw when that door opened was a group of people in uniforms, ones which stuck out because they appeared newly washed and starched. In the group was a careworn, pallid version of Nessa. Consequently, no hallucination. That assumption was confirmed when Nessa melted into Elise's embrace, solid, warm, and eagerly whispering that she loved her.

There was no holding back her tears, Elise let herself sob like a child onto Nessa's shoulder.

As lost as she was in emotion, it was impossible to ignore that there was a risk in Nessa being here. If they were caught, Nessa would be hurt, punished, or even killed. Perhaps all three. And yet, Elise had to confess that if death was in the cards for them, she was glad they were together.

Ah! What is this defeatist drivel? We shall jolly well not be caught, we are going to escape and that is that. Pull yourself together!

Elise sniffed and wiped her tears away. Then, about to speak, she saw Nessa's worried face and couldn't help but kiss her. The kiss was like sunshine after a long, dark winter.

Someone cleared their throat. "Come on, ladies, we must go. The guards will no doubt have heard the sobbing and become suspicious."

Elise recognised Anja's serious, gravelly voice. She broke away from the kiss and lurched over to hug Anja. Soon she noticed that Hunter was hugging them both. She allowed it to carry on for another second and then pushed them away.

"I am ready. What is your plan? How do we escape a castle full of guards, servants, courtiers, and Joiners Square soldiers?" Elise asked before fishing out a handkerchief to blow her nose.

She saw Anja look to Nessa, who looked to Hunter, who looked to Albert, who looked to the people they'd brought. Who all peered down at their shoes.

Elise dropped her handkerchief, staring from face to face. "Do you mean to tell me that you arrived without a strategy?"

Nessa kept her eyes downcast. "There wasn't m-much time to plan, heartling."

"Oh my, and they call *me* impetuous. No time to plan? Did you not have a six-week voyage over here?"

"Actually, we were delayed by ice floats that we had to circumnavigate. Thus, it took about *eight* weeks," Hunter mumbled.

Elise was spared raising her eyebrows at him by a man with a wiry beard, who stepped forward. "We did not have any information, yes? So, we came in Joiners Square uniforms. That, combined with Mr Lindberg giving us a sound reason to be here, means we've been able to simply walk in. Now, we walk out, yes?"

Elise smiled, regretting her reprimand. "Ah, so you do have

a plan of sorts. It has a flaw, however. You can simply 'walk out'. I cannot. I have no uniform and all of court knows my face."

"Right. Um. Well, we can't alter your face since you can't grow a beard like him." Nessa pointed at Hunter. "But we can get you a uniform."

Elise took Nessa's hand and ran her thumb over the back of it. To ground herself in the here and now, and not slip into the shroom-haze.

This rescue is real. Nessa is real.

Elise cleared her throat. "All right. Where and how will you get this uniform?"

Nessa looked towards the door. "Hm. There's a male Joiners Square soldier outside and a female Royal Guard. You would blend in better with us in his uniform, but it wouldn't fit your slender, girlish physique."

"I shall take that as a compliment," Elise said with a smile, squeezing Nessa's hand.

Nessa, momentarily distracted, smiled back. It struck Elise like a pleasant lightning bolt.

That smile is exactly as stunning as I remember. Thank the gods I got to see it again.

"Oh, for snow's sake!" Anja said. "We don't have time for romance. Guards and soldiers probably walk together all the time in this castle, so just pick the woman's uniform. Let's get them both in here and knock them out as quietly as possible. Then you steal her uniform and hurry out, hoping no one looks at your face or sees your room unguarded."

Elise took her eyes off Nessa for a moment. "Wait. The soldier outside, I have been building a relationship with him and gained his sympathy. I wager I can convince him to create a distraction. To ensure fewer people will notice us escaping."

"Fine," Anja murmured. "Let's just get on with it before

the Queen decides to check on her pet. Or Nordhall comes to speak to Albert."

Nessa licked her lips. "Right. Albert, order the guard and soldier to come in. Say that something's wrong in here and they need to take a look."

Albert had been cowering by the wall but now scurried back to the doorway. He stood tall and attempted to pull the trousers up over his belly before opening the door.

"Soldier. Guard. Come in here and explain why the prisoner is foaming at the tongue… I mean, mouth."

In a flash, they were both inside, the guard looking grim while Anders Dahl appeared more worried. When they saw Elise, hale and healthy, they both frowned.

The guard stepped forward, putting her hand to the pistol at her side. "What is going o—"

She didn't have time to finish her sentence as Anja thwacked the back of her head with her prosthetic arm. The guard fell to her knees, holding her head but still conscious. Anja struck again, now with more momentum. This time the blow was hard enough to knock the guard out.

"What? W-what if her brain broke? What if she's killed?" Albert spluttered.

Anja tried to wipe some blood off her sleeve. "She's still breathing. The state of her brain cannot be our problem. She might've shot us all dead a moment ago."

"That thing is more weapon than limb," Nessa said shakily. "That's the second person you've floored with it since I met you."

Anja shrugged. "You have to use what life gave you. Good or bad."

"That was marvellous! Just… Boom, thump!" Hunter exclaimed, thrilled like a little boy.

"Less admiring of the violence and more explaining, yes?"

The words came from behind them. The voice was rife

with panic, but Elise still recognised it as Dahl's. He was backing up, heading for the door with his pistol pointed in their direction. He shook so hard the flintlock pistol rattled.

Elise held up her hands, maintaining eye contact. "Take it easy. Do not leave until you hear us out. You want explanations? Then stay and listen to me. Please, Anders."

Reluctantly, he stopped.

Elise tried for a smile. "Good. Thank you. Well, I think you see the situation. My friends and some reinforcements have come to rescue me. The man who called you in here? He really is with Joiners Square, high up in the ranks. You can trust him to steer you right."

His gaze flitted from Elise to Albert, who nodded and in Sundish said, "She's right. I'm with Joiners Square, and I'm here to rescue her. This isn't right. She's done no wrong and you can't imprison innocent persons. You know that, don't you, son?"

Elise was pretty sure that had been the word for "son," if only because of how it made Dahl freeze and stare at Albert. She knew that look.

Missing a father figure.

Elise put a gentle hand on Dahl's arm. "I do not want to cause trouble. I merely wish to be free." He swallowed visibly, and she carried on. "I know you want to help me, you have shown it in so many ways, but you cannot disobey orders. Well, here is a high-ranking member of Joiners Square telling you to let me go."

Dahl let his weapon drop to the side but was still silent. Elise saw his gaze move to the two Viss who were undressing the unconscious Royal Guard.

One of them, a capable-looking woman, caught him staring. "We're only taking these off so that Elise can wear them. The Queen will not let her go, so she must disguise herself."

The explanation seemed to calm him a little, and he nodded.

With her hands up in a surrendering gesture, Elise moved over to the two women and the clothes they had piled on the floor.

"I am just going to get into these clothes while you reason this out. No harm in that, right? You still hold all the power and you have a while to make your mind up," she said calmly.

He nodded again. Elise was quickly helped out of her dress by Nessa. She pulled on the guard's uniform. It was a little big but would sustain the illusion as long as no one looked closely. At least, it fit better than that uniform did on Albert, folded trouser legs and all.

When she was dressed, she looked back to Dahl. He was glancing between her and Albert, looking like a little boy unsure of whom to trust.

Elise took a deep breath. "Under Lieutenant Anders Dahl."

His snapped to attention, focusing on her.

She made her voice as commanding as she could. "I know your father would have wanted you to do the right thing. And to follow orders. Do what Albert says and you will achieve both."

"All right," Dahl whispered.

"Good. And besides… you have to report the fire."

He frowned. "The fire?"

"Yes," Elise stated simply. She walked over to the fireplace and grabbed a poker. She used it to push two burning logs out onto the large woven rug. It started to smoke and sizzle right away. Elise heard people gasp and whisper to each other.

She cupped Dahl's chin and caught his eye. "You must take the unconscious guard, run out and down the main stairs, screaming that there is a fire. But for my sake, and to live up to your father's expectation of doing what a *good* person does, you must wait until you are a few stairs down to say *where* the fire is. That will give us time to escape and you a cover for why you were not guarding me."

Dahl broke the eye contact to look at the rug, which was increasingly catching fire. Then his eyes went to Albert.

In Sundish, Albert said, "She's right, boy. There's a fire! Warn people, but don't say where the fire is until you're downstairs. Run!"

Dahl pulled his face out of Elise's grip and put his pistol away. "Good luck, Elise. May you be free and make your own father proud." With that, he began to run towards the main stairs with the guard slumped over his shoulder.

The fire was spreading fast, now covering the rug and climbing up the curtains. Elise saw a spark shoot out to the ornately woven runner lining the corridor floor. These threadbare, musty fabrics were just begging for the flames.

Elise coughed and began running away from the smoke and flames. "Quickly, we must take the servants' stairs on the other side of the corridor!"

As the others followed, she heard Hunter whisper, "Thank the gods you knew of another staircase."

Elise smiled as she started taking the steps two at a time. "That is the joy of having spent weeks befriending servants – you learn of passages and rooms you never would have known otherwise."

They ran on light feet, trying for that illusive mix of speed and discretion needed for any escape. Screams about fires and the need for buckets of water echoed between the marble walls. Elise was barely breathing, terrified that they'd meet someone on the stairs or that people would run out with them in fear of the fire. Luckily, no courtiers could be seen, and all the staff, guards, and Joiners Square soldiers were busy panicking. Elise heard shouts about "needing more blankets" and "why no one manages to keep proper amounts of water up here."

Here is a lesson for the Queen about refusing to spend coin on fire-fighting equipment. Not all new inventions are bad, Your Majesty.

Elise led them out a side door, and soon they were running across the courtyard. The gleaming, golden gates beamed at her from the distance. She was almost free.

But then a shout rang out.

"Stop right there, girl!"

Elise shivered. *Not the Queen. But almost as bad. Adaire.*

She turned and saw the queen's aide running effortlessly towards them, immaculate features locked in a severe frown.

Why did it have to be her? Why not a servant we could have bribed or scared off?

"I ordered you to stop, Lady Falk." Adaire shouted.

"Bugger tha' for a start," Hunter grunted, slipping into his native Nightport dialect.

Elise was about to agree and pick up the speed when she looked ahead and saw the gates closing. In front of them stood the Queen and one of the head Royal Guards.

Elise allowed herself a muttered "oxen-shit." If ever there was a time to break her habit of not cursing, it was now.

The whole group halted in front of the massive gates as they banged shut. The courtyard seemed to shrink while the surrounding walls and gates closed in further.

The Queen smirked. "Well. That was rather rotten luck, tinderbox-maker. I have been down to inspect the royal stables. I sent Adaire back early, and, when I heard her shouts, I had the guards lock the gate." She sniggered. "You know, your rescuers really should have come at a more convenient time. It all comes down to research and planning. Something I doubt your *farm wench* is capable of."

"I'm capable of planning ten different ways of cutting your air supply, goat-face," Nessa snapped.

The Queen bared her teeth. "Not only are you missing the

point, you seem to have been infected with Elise's rash temper. Such a shame. Now, who are all these people in what I assume are stolen uniforms?"

Björn stepped forward but was pushed away by Ravna.

"My name is Ravna Sten. I worked for the Viss Embassy as a contact for Joiners Square. Well, until they decided that they no longer needed to communicate or negotiate with the Viss or the Wayfarers, that is. You know, about the same time they chose to bribe the Sund-filled government and make them into puppets? Now I do whatever I can to oppose Joiners Square and those who cooperate with them."

The Queen raised her eyebrows. "Lovely speech. Thank you for filling me, in but I am well aware of all Joiners Square has done over on that barren block of ice you call a continent. Better get to the point before the guards and courtiers come out to see what the commotion is."

"Oh, I think you'll find they're busy with a rapidly spreading fire," Anja said, crossing her arms over her chest. "It's just us here, Your Royal Tapeworm."

The Queen stared up at the castle and the tendrils of smoke escaping all the windows on the floor where Elise had been kept.

Please run up there to check on everything. Please be distracted.

The Queen turned to Elise, her face contorted in a snarl. "What. Have. You. Done."

Elise tried to stand tall, not letting the death glare in those dark, regal eyes make her shrink. "I merely thought my room could do with a bigger fireplace. As the daughter of a royal architect, I should be allowed to make one or two improvements, surely?"

"I will have you strung up by the ankles for a week for this," Queen Marianna said, her gaze flitting back and forth between Elise and the windows.

Adaire was only examining the rescuers. "Others will be extinguishing the fire, I am more interested in who these people are and to learn their plans." She eyed Hunter, who stood closest to her. "Not just anyone can get their hands on those uniforms. Even if you could get a seamstress to make replicas, those specifically engraved white steel knives would be near impossible to recreate. Not to mention how you got free reign to move about the castle."

Anja pointed a finger in Adaire's face. "Well, if your rude monarch had let Ravna finish, she would've known that we're a group made up of Viss, rebelling Sundes, and these three Arclidians you've been terrorising. Oh, and me. Who represents the Wayfarers, I suppose." She turned and spat at the Queen's feet. "Although I mainly represent people who think you should stop hunting down innocent individuals, like my friend Elise, and spend that time ruling your nation properly, Your Majestic Pain in the Arse."

The Queen stepped forward, raising her hand as if to slap Anja, but she was distracted by Adaire speaking again. "I see. Consequently, I gather that you, Nessa, and the young man – Hunter, if I recall correctly from your time here – have arrived to free Elise. Fair enough. Why are the rest of you here? It appears your quarrel is with Joiners Square."

Ravna chuckled mirthlessly. "It is. We'll use the testimony of this young woman to prove that Joiners Square is a corrupt, violent organisation. When she's spoken out against them, others will dare to follow."

The Queen scoffed, making Ravna raise her voice. "Our plan will be helped by the fact that their best strategist and leader is here. Nordhall is below Grand Marshall Karlberg in rank, but in truth, he runs much of Joiners Square. With him still here, or on a ship back, it'll be easier to begin to reveal and utilize the weaknesses in their organisation. Our goal is bigger than simply freeing this lady." Ravna drew her blunderbuss and pointed it at the Queen before stating, "So, please step aside so we can leave, or we'll take you hostage and *force* your guards to open the gates."

Björn placed his hand on the blunderbuss. "Kidnapping the Queen isn't necessary. After all, she won't be on the throne for long."

Everyone looked at him with confused expressions.

"What?" Ravna hissed.

Björn smiled at her. "Surely you've heard the rumours going around Viss circles? That the reign of the Arclidian Queen will end soon? I think the plan was that after the fall of Joiners Square, Storsund would team up with the other two continents and force the current queen to abdicate." He paused to allow the Queen to growl and the others to gasp. "Then they'd place the natural replacement on the throne instead. Instead of bothering with violence and kidnapping, perhaps we should simply speed up that plan?"

The Queen, Adaire, and the Royal Guards looked as if the ground was crumbling beneath them. Elise heard Nessa whisper, "Hunter, remember what Diinna said about a contender waiting in the wings?"

The shouts inside the castle got louder, and the smoke now billowed out of even more windows. And yet, the attention in the courtyard was primarily on Björn's words.

His smile grew triumphant as he added, "Perhaps the next Queen of Arclid should like to claim the birthright which was taken from her around four hundred years ago? See, I know the history of your violent nation. I've read about the War of the Rose and the Thistle."

With a start Elise remembered that part of Arclidian history, too. Anyone who had been at court would know it in detail. *The War of Thorns.* Two houses, fighting for decades over who would rule. The Hargraves with their crest of a thorny rose bush and the Aldershires with theirs portraying a long-stemmed thistle bush. The Hargraves had won and a deal had been struck. The Aldershires would rule with them, but always as monarch's aides or advisors. Never as spouses or equals. Kept in their place to humiliate them enough not to face the outside world, but in indispensable positions, to make them feel important and loyal.

Odd how long that worked. Even odder that no one in our generation questioned the arrangement.

Thinking about it, the Aldershires had been monarchs once, too. They'd be in line for the throne if all the Hargraves were ousted. Elise blinked rapidly. Arclid could have a new queen without battles and endless arguments over which Noble house would take up the crown. They'd all grumble and want their house on the throne, but in the end, no one had a better claim than the Aldershires.

Elise gaped at Marianna, who stood with her hands balled into fists at her sides and her face turned to her queen's aide, who, in turn, sighed and intently stared at the ground.

CHAPTER 38
BETRAYAL

Marianna's heart was thudding hard against her breastbone. "What plans to oust me? This is a ploy to distract and sow discontent, is it not? Adaire... answer me!"

Adaire wouldn't meet her gaze, could only stare at the ground between them. "My Qu... Marianna. This is not how I wanted you to find out. You must understand that this is for the best. For Arclid."

"For Arclid? What are you saying? And why are you saying it in front of these mud-dwellers?"

"Excuse me! I keep as far away from mud as I can. Impossible to get out of velvet," the pretty boy behind Elise said.

Marianna remembered him. The man who had aided Elise and her farm wench in escaping Arclid that evening in Nightport. Had Adaire said his name was Hubert? He would be dealt with later. They would all be dealt with later. These Northmen, these traitors, and that damned fire. All a matter for later.

Right now, right here, Marianna only cared about the actions of the woman she relied on most. The girl she had grown up with, knowing that Adaire, with her serious eyes and her soft tawny skin, would always be there. By her side on the throne, by her side in the bed. And now, these people were saying that she was going to usurp her.

And Adaire wasn't denying it.

"Answer me, woman! What do you mean by 'for Arclid'?" Marianna heard her voice turn to a whine and hated it.

Adaire shifted her jaw back and forth, as if chewing on the question. Her gaze was glued to the ground between them. "I was raised by parents who taught me the Aldershire role at court: to guide and assist the monarch but never step out of bounds. If you did, only beheading and disgrace awaited." She sighed. "But behind closed doors, my parents whispered of past monarchs with thistles on their shields. I have lived my life knowing my place but also aware of the royal blood hiding in my veins."

She took a shaky breath and then raised her head, meeting Marianna's eyes squarely. The bottom fell out of Marianna's world and her stomach roiled. She had seen it before, that look of utter determination. There was no changing Adaire's mind when that look came into those intelligent eyes.

"I have loved you dearly, Marianna. I was raised to, and while we grew up, I found the task easy. Our different personalities work well together. Your passion with my patience, your drive with my care, your fire with my ice. We complimented each other, and I adored you. Although, at times, I also loathed you."

Something appeared stuck in Marianna's throat, swallowing would not clear it.

Why are there so many eyes on me? Stop staring!

"Ha! You loathed me?" Marianna had aimed for a carefree, mocking tone, but it came out sounding false. Uncertain. Frightened.

"Yes. I was by your side, watching you steer your nation,

our nation, awry. Standing in the way of progress and stopping trade deals to control your subjects. To keep them ignorant, frightened, and beholden to you."

Marianna scoffed, but Adaire just continued. "Yet they still planned rebellions, because deep down, they knew that you did not want what was best for them. They saw you claim that taxes had to be raised for the infrastructure, only to spend all the coin on royal weddings, clothes, art, and feasts." Adaire laughed a hollow laugh, looking to the smoke-filled sky. "And that ridiculous hunt for someone they were told was a traitor. Someone I knew to be a symbol of your vanity and need for validation. You spent night and day trying to find, and then win back, a mere *lady-in-waiting*," Adaire spat out the last words.

Marianna was about to interrupt, but Adaire held up a hand. "No. Let me finish. You chased after an old lover who, while she did not want you, was everything you say you want – high-tempered, passionate, and merry. Everything I am not. You knew that, and you rubbed my nose in it. You made me help you find her and woo her."

"Petty jealousy, really?" Marianna asked. "While that could be reason for you to refuse to bed me or to slap my face, I hardly think it is reason to take my throne."

Adaire looked her straight in the eye again. "Marianna... My Queen, you are not listening. This is not about *Elise*. The way you rule – for sport and for self-promotion – *that* is why I agreed to consider the Viss' and West Islanders' suggestion of bearing the crown."

Marianna hissed. Again, Adaire ignored her and spoke on. "They told me how they desired to increase trade with Arclid and how you had curtailed that, trading only enough to keep coin in your coffers but not enough to start real alliances. Not enough for our nation to need railways and steam-powered machines for agriculture. Or even more industrial cities. That is why, months ago, I agreed to take the throne."

Marianna put her full force into looking scornful and amused. "You and what army, heartling? I only see a handful of Viss and other Storsund outcasts here. No soldiers. Not a single West Islander. I have a whole army. A whole nation of subjects behind me. You do not have a single cannon."

"Exactly. I cannot, like other contenders for the throne, attempt to take it by force. However, I will not need to. As queen's aide, I have heard what the masses shout and what the Nobles whisper. At court, I have subtly suggested myself as leader and gotten positive responses."

"*What?*"

Adaire once more acted as if Marianna had not spoken. "The people want a fair ruler and the Noble families want a reliable contender with an indisputable claim to the throne. Arclid deserves care and respect. I may not be a perfect leader, but I can at least provide that. Unlike you, my cherished."

The ill feeling in Marianna's stomach worsened. "I have heard enough. I have these miscreants to punish and a fire to put out. I have no more time for your backstabbing. Guard, seize her!"

The Royal Guard, a senior man of stern aspect, bowed his head. "I fear I cannot. The queen's aide is right. Everyone at court wants a change. I do not believe any of the guards have been sounded out on the idea of a dethroning, but as one of the highest ranks, I approve. I am sorry, I have served you for decades. Nevertheless, the key thing is that *I serve at the pleasure of the queen.* And I believe Adaire Aldershire to be the queen Arclid needs."

Marianna watched him stand to attention. Then, with gentle hands, he took a solid hold of her wrists. Her bowels turned to water. This was real. This was happening. How could this be happening? Everything had been fine just five minutes ago. Hadn't it?

The guard looked to Adaire. "Now what, my Queen?"

Adaire winced. "Do not call me that yet. We must still deliberate with the troublesome Noble families and announce it to the people, hoping they will not rebel. Then there can be a coronation. To answer your question, find a room far away from the fire and confine her there. Double set of guards. Ones not too loyal to her."

The guard took a tighter hold on Marianna's wrists. "That should not be hard. The Royal Guards' living expenses and housing have been cut to a pittance over the last decade. They have been riotous for years."

Adaire nodded, looking down again. Marianna wanted to scream.

Face me. Look at me and say that this is merely a jest. Or some elaborate plan your clever mind has concocted to best our enemies. My enemies. Look at me! I love you. Look at me and tell me you are not taking my crown.

"What of Prince Macray?" the guard asked.

Adaire cleared her throat. "Macray and his wife can go into exile or remain here if they give up their claim to the throne."

Her gaze rose slowly to meet Marianna's. "Know this, no matter what happens, you are safe. I will not execute you, although I know that is what you would do. I shall keep you in the most luxurious of prisons and visit you frequently. And, if my plan to be queen somehow fails, I will go into exile. Or allow you to kill me if you prefer," she said quietly.

Marianna's eyes burned with tears she would never let fall. Adaire reached out a hand and ran her thumb across her cheek. She had always claimed to "love those sharp cheek-bones." As that cold but gentle digit brushed along Marianna's skin, the betraying tears fell, meeting the thumb and coating it.

"I am sorry, my cherished," Adaire whispered.

"Not sorry enough," Marianna growled. "But that will change. When the people spurn you and I get my hands on you, then you shall be achingly sorry. I will cut you open, drain you of blood, and drink it while the nation watches."

Marianna spat on her face, wanting to mar the calm, sad beauty of those features. The spittle ran down Adaire's cheek just as more unwanted tears ran down her own.

Shock was making Marianna shiver. Anyone else contesting her she could fight, but Adaire…

It is like being maimed by your faithful lap dog.

The truth hit her like a surge of cold water. It was all over. No one would choose her over the conscientious, caring, and logical Adaire. Marianna squeezed her jaw shut tight. She was born to rule. Genuine royalty. Arclid would be nothing without the drive and passion of the Hargraves. Without them and their hot, red blood fuelling it, this island was just a bland, little pale-green continent. Impotent and lacklustre.

"Do you realise that without me, this nation will lose all its drama, power, and flare?" Marianna snarled.

Adaire wiped her cheek and then reached out and wiped Marianna's. "We will find out. Together. The same way we have done everything since we were children." She turned to the guard. "Take her away before she breaks what is left of my heart."

As Marianna was dragged away, she heard that wretched farm wench ask Adaire if they could help each other. "If you can detain Nordhall for a while," Nessa said, "giving us a head start to Storsund, we promise to mention you in the trials, complimenting you and pointing out that you support a new Storsund government. We'll even draw attention to your assistance in beating Joiners Square by letting us go and stalling Nordhall."

The last thing Marianna heard before she was pulled into

the castle with its shouts about the fire, was Adaire replying, "Sounds acceptable. I shall keep him here, leaving Joiners Square without information or their strongest player. In return, you plead my case to my future trade partners, and of course... take that wretched tinderbox-maker out of my sight."

Marianna bit her tongue. How different things could've been if she'd let Elise go. How different they could've been if she'd kept Adaire happy. She wouldn't have fretted about the running of the country and the treatment of the subjects then. Right?

Surely not. Why would anyone care about peasants and silly Nobles?

The guard tugged on her arm. "Stop dragging your feet, Your Majes... I mean, Milady. The sooner we can get you in a room, the sooner we can put that fire out and then prepare to place a real queen on the throne."

CHAPTER 39
LEAVING IT BEHIND

Nessa felt light as air as she took long, purpose-filled strides out of the courtyard.

I did it. I had help, but, in the end, I managed to actually get through with this without my fear buggering it up.

She hurried her steps. They had to escape Highmere's court quickly, making the gap between their departure and Nordhall's as large as possible. The group arrived in Highmere proper and hired the first carriages they could find for their trip to Cawstone.

Nessa made sure she sat next to Elise, one arm around her slender shoulders, peppering her hair and face with kisses. It began to drizzle, and the skies grew grey, but it did nothing to weigh down Nessa's light heart.

After about thirty minutes journeying in the comfortable four-seated carriage, the affectionate reunion was interrupted by speech. Elise was leaning her head on Nessa's shoulder. Opposite them sat Hunter and Anja. Hunter, a frown line between his meticulously shaped eyebrows, was the first to break the silence. "Elise. Are you all right, heartling? Did she... did anyone hurt you?"

Elisandrine laughed dryly. "That depends on what you call hurting someone. I would say no, but my body, having been filled with sedatives and shrooms for weeks on end, might disagree." She put on a brave smile. "Nevertheless, it could have been worse. So much worse. Luckily, the Queen has a combination of needing adoration and a belief that anyone who spends time with her will love her, which kept me relatively safe. She was trying to win me back, if you can believe it."

She paused, her hands fidgeting with Nessa's top uniform button. "From what I overheard, the Queen was either aiming to make me her eager courtesan for life or to break my heart when I finally became infatuated with, or at least dependent on, her again. Either way, her aim was to *win over me by winning me over*, so to speak. Proving that I had been wrong to abandon and disobey her."

Anja huffed. "That woman is a mess."

"A self-absorbed, vain, power-crazed mess," Nessa agreed. "Still, lucky for us that the fiend didn't want you back to kill or hurt you. Or to make you her lover by force," she snarled.

She felt Elise shiver in her arms. "Yes. I was lucky."

Hunter was smoothing his perfect hair, his gaze on Elise. "If you permit me, I would not call it lucky to have been kept prisoner by the royal family *twice*. You are allowed to complain and to be angry. Just because it could have been worse does not mean it was acceptable."

Elise gave him a weak smile. "Thank you. I have spent so much time trying to keep my mind clear enough from chemicals and emotions to be able to plan that I have not allowed myself to feel much self-pity."

"Go on and pity yourself something rotten! Gods know *we* all do," Hunter said.

"I don't," Anja grumbled. "I pity all the servants who no

doubt had to deal with your temper. Not to mention your need for posh face paint and fragrances."

"Be nice," Elisandrine said while slapping Anja's knee. While the others laughed, Nessa sighed in relief.

Finally, she's getting some of her usual vigour back.

"I will have you know that I have made some improvement with holding my temper. And cultivating my patience. So, there is a silver lining," Elise added.

The word *silver* reminded Nessa. "Oh, I almost forgot." She took out an object wrapped in sack cloth and handed it to Elise. "I took this with me to throw at the Que – I mean, *Marianna's* – face, but I forgot. I don't know what you want to do with it."

Elise unwrapped the tinderbox. She shivered, then scoffed. Without a word, she threw it out of the window. Nessa saw it land in the middle in a field.

"Ah! That'll be covered in mud an' rain now! It were silver. Ye could 'ave sold that for good coin," Hunter said, shock replacing his usual fake Midlands accent with his original Nightport one.

Elise shook her head. "White gold, actually. Nevertheless, I want nothing to do with that thing or the person who sent it. I am leaving all that behind. We have a complicated present and a long future ahead of us, there is no room for a painful past."

"You're such a silly arse, Hunter. She doesn't want the coin from something which'll remind her of getting kidnapped," Anja said, elbowing him.

He grinned at her. "Silly arse? That is a step up from 'annoying man-child', is it not?"

Anja peered at him, a smile tugging at her lips. "Aye. A small one, mind you. But yes, a step up."

The carriages trundled on towards Cawstone docks. Albert had taken one of the horses and ridden ahead. Together with Eleonora he would look for the next ship and ensure that they got tickets. Nessa had concerns about him finding a ship, if they would make good time, and about how the trials would go. Not to mention the issue of Adaire possibly not being crowned Queen, meaning Elise and Nessa would be back to having Marianna Hargraves on their heels.

Still, all these worries, which normally would have taken all her energy and paralysed her, were now background noise. They were subdued by a new security. The knowledge that whatever problems awaited them, whatever drama they would face, Nessa was able to step up. Even if she had no plan, even if she had responsibility for others, she *could* do it.

"You look miles away," Elise said to her.

"Thinking about our future, which looks so different now. This experience has taught me a lot."

Elise took her hand. "May I ask what?"

"Of course, heartling." She squeezed Elise's hand. "I was thinking about safety. Remember how you said I was addicted to safety when we fought back in Nightport?"

"Please do not remind me of that terrible quarrel. But yes, I do."

Nessa took a moment to gather her thoughts. "I suppose this experience has taught me about the safety I need. It doesn't exist in a certain place. Or in being away from my problems because problems follow you. Marianna proved that."

Anja chuckled. "For once, you're making sense."

Nessa smiled at her before addressing Elise again. "While you'll always be my prime source of safety, I need to have confidence even when you're not around. I cannot rely on my family, Layden, you, or even the gods. I have to be able to stay calm and believe in myself. I somehow managed that during this rescue."

"Yes, you did, didn't you? You strode into that castle like you owned it. I was impressed," Anja said with a nod.

Nessa chuckled. "Why, thank you."

Elise took her chin, turning her face back to her own. "So am I. Where did you find that confidence? Or safety, whatever you wish to call it."

Nessa chewed the inside of her cheek as she considered.

"In trying, I think. I realised that I don't have to get things right on the first attempt, I only have to try. If I don't try, if I sit and worry about things like coin, decisions, and..." She had been about to add *climaxing*, as she'd realised that she'd only been able to orgasm when leaving all control in Elise's hands, otherwise worrying so much that it kept her from simply trusting herself to *try*. But she held back as they were in company. "...and so on, I will freeze up and not dare to do anything. If I'm forced to act, if I force myself to just try, I can avoid a lot of fretting. The safety lies in, well, in no longer searching so hard for safety."

"Not sure I understand, but I am overjoyed you feel better," Hunter said, scratching at his beard. "Personally, I shall feel better when I shave off this shrubbery. It hides my handsome features!"

Anja grinned and elbowed him again, to his great delight.

Elise smothered a yawn. "I apologise, this has been a tiring ordeal. You spoke about the future, heartling. What happens now?"

"We'll get you to Storsund. You and Albert will testify against Joiners Square. We'll pass on that Adaire has claimed the throne and is willing to work with the new Storsund government. After that, we can do what we wish." She planted a kiss on Elise's head. "If Adaire fails and Marianna takes back the crown, we either move somewhere with better leadership or come back to Arclid to fight her. Either way, we'll settle where we wish. No more running. I'll make glass, and you will do whatever you choose."

"Make scented oils," Elise stated before nuzzling into Nessa's neck.

"That's decided then." Nessa kissed her hair again before looking at the two people opposite. "What about you two? What are you going to do?"

Hunter looked to Anja, who smiled at him. "Believe it or not, I'm taking the chatty pretty boy with me." She turned to Elise. "I'm relieved to hear that you plan to focus on your oils. Means I don't have to choose between you and Hunter as my assistant. He told me on the ship that he wished to help with my book, both in regard to selling it to a wide audience and writing it. He seems to believe that if we add more fiction and suspense to the story, it'll sell like hot coffee on a snowy—"

"Better than that! It can sell you straight into fortune and a golden reputation amongst your colleagues," Hunter exclaimed.

Anja grimaced at him.

He held up his hands. "Right. No interrupting. I forgot rule number thirteen."

Anja smirked at him and then carried on explaining. "Through these weeks we've realised that we get along well. He's a Wayfarer at heart, curious, tenacious, never settling for one thing, and always ready for a challenge. He has reminded me of that part of myself, although he's more annoying than any Wayfarer could be." She bumped his shoulder and then carried on. "We argue and still enjoy each other's company. Like family. So, with you having your own career now, Elise, I think Hunter and I'll focus on this book and the others that'll follow. I'll research and write them while he transcribes and sells them."

Hunter sat forward. "If you two move into a lodging house or something, I can take over the spare bed. I can have the new start I always wanted. And I get to do what I do best – charm people while I sell a product I actually believe in." He put a finger in the air. "A brilliant product that I will help to create by transcribing Anja's words, no less. All while living with someone who accepts me for who I am and will never pressure me to change or hide."

Anja scowled. "Course not. And if anyone tries to do that to you, I'll knock them senseless."

Hunter beamed at her, his eyes twinkling in a way which made Anja frown.

"As long as Svarte puts up with you, man-child. If the cat doesn't want you around, you're out on your ear," she said with a sniff.

"Oh, I can charm anyone and anything. That cat will soon be eating yellowfish out of my hand," he countered with his sparkling salesman's smile.

Elise reached over and took Anja's hand. She nodded to Hunter while saying, "Thank you both. For coming to help me."

Anja writhed in her seat. "Hm. You didn't need it. You'd have gotten out of there on your own soon enough."

"Possibly. But you both – nay, *you all* – made sure I did not have to, saving me time and suffering. Well, other than this wretched headache. I shall probably suffer withdrawal from the sedatives and shrooms for some while. Anyway, I can never thank you all enough."

"Thank her," Hunter said, pointing to Nessa. "She would have broken through every castle wall on the orb until she had you in her arms."

"Yes, and probably gotten herself killed in the process," Anja muttered. A smile took the sting out of her words.

Nessa chuckled. "True. Anyway, I can only echo Elise's words. Thank you. For helping us, for holding me up when I fell apart, and for not letting me wallow. You helped me find what I needed."

"You did that yourself, sweetest lass," Anja said quietly.

"We were only there to believe in you until you learned to believe in yourself. Repay us by not doubting yourself again!"

"I'll try. If you two ever need a favour in this nice-sounding new life you're planning, never hesitate to ask."

"Agreed. Anything you need," Elise added.

Anja waved the topic away. "Oh, for snow's sake! Enough of this sappy chitchat. We've a long journey to Cawstone and the rain patter on the carriage roof is irritating. Distract us with your story, Elise. We know they came to take you, apparently with that cursed tinderbox in tow. What then?"

Elise sat up and began to tell all. She made them rage at how she'd been treated, then chuckle at her tales of her gargoyle friend. After that, Nessa and Hunter took turns filling Elise in on their hunt for helpers, Albert's heroic part in the story, and what was happening behind the curtain in the political mayhem that was Storsund.

The drizzle finally stopped, but the conversation carried on, Elise begging for no silence. She had had her fill of that through her captivity.

~

Two and a half months later, Nessa watched Elise step out of a Skarhult courtroom. She looked prim and dignified in her grey, high-collared dress.

Nessa walked up to meet her. "How did it go?"

Elise ran a hand over her brow. "Well enough, I should think. There was a lot of repetition. Near five times I had to, in different ways, explain that it was without a doubt Joiners Square who abducted me and delivered me to the former Queen."

"Albert said the same thing. Apparently, they made him repeat his accusations and present his proof over and over again. I suppose they need to be thorough. This isn't an individual on trial, it's an organisation which has spread its roots into every part of Storsund."

"Yes, of course. Still, incredibly tiring," Elise said with a faint smile.

"Well, now that you've done your part, we're free to leave, I think. The authorities will be busy interviewing everyone who's suddenly crawled out of the woodwork. So, now what? I know we decided that I'd carry on with glassblowing and you want to continue making your wonderful oils—"

"And we are obviously staying together," Elise interrupted with an unsuccessful wink.

"Obviously," Nessa agreed, affection rushing through her. "But where? Here in Storsund or back to Arclid? Adaire Aldershire has evidently been crowned queen, and while we promised to keep you out of her sight, we didn't promise to stay out of her queendom."

"True. We have options now. Perhaps we wish to try one of the other two continents? Although, with summer approaching in a few months, both Obeha and the Western Isles might be too hot."

Nessa hummed her agreement. "It would be fun to see a new place, but now is not the time. Wait until next autumn, I think."

Elise inspected her with an incredulous look. "My, you really have changed. My old Nessa would have fretted something awful about the idea of having to adjust to a new continent."

Nessa shrugged. "There are worse things to have to adjust to. After all, trouble finds you everywhere, so staying where you believe yourself safe won't keep trouble at bay."

"Wherever we go, as long as we are together, it will be the perfect place."

"Agreed. However, we do have others to consider. Anja and

Hunter will be in Skarhult while my family will be in Ground Hollow."

"And your best friend," Elise added pensively. She was staring into space, probably weighing their options.

"You're my best friend. But yes, Layden is there, too. So is... your family. Your uncles, cousins, and your mother," Nessa ventured.

Elise looked suddenly stricken. "I know. I sent a letter to her after we left Highmere."

"Oh! That was what you gave that messenger boy in Cawstone harbour? A letter for your mother?"

"Yes."

Nessa took her hand. "And?"

"I received a reply yesterday morning."

"And you didn't tell me?"

"I could not stand to speak of it. Actually, I have yet to dare open it. I fear she is disappointed. She wanted me to be Princess of Arclid. She worked hard to achieve that through alliances and flattering the right people. I threw that all away when I left Prince Macray. And now, to make things worse, I had Macray's family overthrown."

Nessa squeezed the quivering hand in hers. "You don't know that's what she's thinking. Most Noble families were tired of Marianna's behaviour, right? Perhaps your mother thinks you a hero for getting someone worthier on the throne. Perhaps she's proud of her daughter for being instrumental in such a major part of Arclid's history."

"Unlikely. Mother never wanted a rebel or a freedom fighter. She wanted a princess, with pretty dresses and even prettier children."

"I'm sorry. Do you want me to open the letter?"

Elise cleared her throat. "No. Leave that for later. What is important now is deciding where we live. For us, not for everyone else. Taking our loved ones out of the picture, where do you *want* to settle?"

Nessa looked down. Her thumb was rubbing the back of Elise's hand as she allowed herself to really consider it. The question had been in the back of her mind, but with the Joiners Square trials, finding a lodging house, and trying to make up for lost time with her lover, she'd not decided where home was.

"Ground Hollow would still constrict me. I wasn't made for village life. But Skarhult and Charlottenberg feel too... foreign. Although, I suppose with time that could change. Still..." She trailed off, trying to put words to her unease.

Elise brought Nessa's hand up to her mouth and kissed it softly. "What about Nightport?"

"Nightport?"

"Yes. You dreamed of that city as a child and we both enjoyed living there. Up until the fight and the arrival of the tinderbox parts, that is. Perhaps we should give it another chance?"

Nessa let the image of Nightport fill her mind. Dark, busy streets, rowdy taverns. Not very safe.

Safety be damned.

"You're right. We should try Nightport again. It's close enough to Ground Hollow that I can visit my family."

"Precisely. There are also steamers travelling to Storsund if we want to visit Anja and Hunter," Elise pointed out.

"And ships to the other continents if we get restless."

Elise beamed at her. "Exactly, my cherished."

Nessa leaned in for kiss, drawing attention from two court clerks walking past.

"Nightport it is," she whispered against Elise's lips. Her next words were kissed away by the woman with the golden eyes and the softest lips Nessa had tasted.

CHAPTER 40
TO GROUND HOLLOW

The late spring sunlight flooded the road towards Ground Hollow. Elise blinked up at it through the window of the rickety but roomy carriage which was taking them to Nessa's parents' farm. Next to her, as always, was Nessa. The other passengers were busy telling her stories of what had happened in Nightport since they'd been away. Cai, Fyhre, Jac, and Sanjero had all met up with them on their first night back in Nightport. When they had heard that Elise and Nessa were visiting Ground Hollow, they had all devoted their only free day of the week to come along and see the small farming village where Nessa had grown up.

Elise saw Fyhre look out at the endless, tranquil greenery of the passing landscape with the same scepticism as she had the first time she saw it. Now Elise found herself enjoying the stillness and the beauty. She knew that Nessa would never want to move back and was pretty certain that after a few years the novelty of the countryside would wear on her, too. But right now, this place, so far away from political storms in Skarhult and royal intrigue in Highmere, seemed close to perfect.

She wished she had her notebook to write to her father of the way the landscape and the houses looked.

No, you were right, Papa… I must let the past be in the past.

Sanjero suddenly laughed. "Ye know, it's funny. We 'ave often spoken about ye both. Wonderin' what ye were gettin' up to. But our wildest guesses weren't even close to what ye were doin'. It all sounds like one of them fancy tales that Hunter used to spin."

Nessa snorted. "I wish it were one of Hunter's stories. I prefer his tales over reality, they have tidier endings."

"I 'ear he's writin' his stories down these days?" Cai asked.

"In a matter of speaking. He is helping our friend Anja pen the collected history of Storsund. They both promised me letters to let me know how the work progresses," Elise explained.

"You know what, when they start the next book," Nessa added with a grin, "I'll wager they'll spend most of their days fighting over how much fiction Hunter is allowed to sneak into the books. Anja will want them completely factual while Hunter will strive to make them juicier with his usual 'embellishments' of the truth."

Elise laughed. "Mm, not to mention how he will oversell the drama of the contents when it is time to sell the book. Oh, and the ensuing fights about Hunter aspiring to fame and fortune while Anja only wants to do her research alone in her quiet house."

Still grinning, Nessa said, "Still, it warms the heart to see two good people find someone to cure their loneliness and lack of belonging."

Jac nodded. "Aye, good to see. Maybe they'll write books 'bout Arclid one day. Gods know our former Queen an' her family would make for good readin'. Storsund might have political intrigue, but we 'ave the saucy scandals."

"Truer words were never spoken," Elise said. "Speaking of

Arclid monarchy, I am glad to hear that our new queen has started her reign well. I understand taxes are being lowered while new schools and prisons are being built."

Fyhre grunted her agreement. "Aye, an' railroad tracks bein' laid, an' all!"

"We'll catch up to the rest of the orb soon enough, just ye watch," Cai said.

"I certainly shall," Elise replied.

She looked out the window. The fields were now accompanied by farms. A few more minutes of watching the landscape in silence, then they stopped at a coach house in a dusty square.

"Ground Hollow," Nessa said under her breath.

Half an hour later, they were drinking leaf tea on a blanket outside the family farm. Jon and Carryanne Clay had prepared a picnic and invited Layden and his family to join them. Carryanne kept throwing glances at Elise. At first Elise pretended not to notice, but that grew harder as the glances became more frequent.

Is she angry because I took her daughter away? Or because she feels I put Nessa in harm's way? Maybe she finds me weak for having been captured. Again.

"Is something the matter, Mrs Clay?" she asked, keeping a carefree smile on her features.

"No. Nothing wrong. I've just been wanting to say something to you."

The chatter around the blanket fell silent.

Elise continued smiling as best as she could. "Oh, yes. What is that?"

Carryanne's thoughtful, grey eyes, so like Nessa's, were fixed on Elise. "We get newspapers out here, you know. At

391

least when there's something in them of importance. Layden here, he's a good boy, he gets us a paper if he thinks we need to read something in it."

Elise was too well-raised to show her confusion as a guest. Her smile stayed in place. "I see."

"I'm not one for sentiment. Nessa'll tell you that. But I must say, when I read you giving me credit and thanking me for the recipe for the scented oils in that Storsund paper, I was mighty proud. Wasn't I, Jon?"

He swallowed a bite of eggy bread. "She was. We both were. It's not often a Noble thanks us commoners. It's nice to know that our lass found herself a mate who knows her manners and doesn't act superior."

Elise shut her gaping mouth in embarrassment and cleared her throat. How did she reply in kind without making them uncomfortable by getting too emotional?

"I see. Well, my father raised me to give credit where it was due. You taught Nessa how to make the oil, how to press the dammon nuts, how long to leave it to settle and all that. Then she taught me, and without that base, I could not have made my own oils. So, thank you for that. Oh, and I am glad that my acknowledgment was well received."

Nessa wrapped her arm around Elisandrine's shoulder. "Elise has none of the usual snobberies of the Nobles. Her family is not as stable and loving as ours, therefore, she truly wanted to make you like her and welcome her into the family."

Carryanne looked surprised. "She makes you happy and treats others with respect, she's obviously welcome and liked here."

Jon refilled Elise's cup. "Sorry to hear your kin are… disagreeable. Still, they must be relieved that you're back in Arclid, safe and free."

There was something in Elise's pocket which called to her

then. The letter from her mother. She had forced herself to open it this morning. It had been hard to read, but it certainly had not taken long, as it was only a few lines.

Thank you for your correspondence.

Regretfully, I must inform you that it has reached the wrong recipient. I no longer have a daughter. She passed away many months ago, before she could marry Prince Macray and be mother of the next heir to the throne.

Cordial regards,

Lady Carolyne Falk

Elise shook the words out of her mind as best she could and replied, "Sadly, no. I have been informed by my mother that I am no longer a member of the Falk family."

There was a weighted silence. Sanjero reached out to take Elise's hand while Nessa pulled her closer to her.

Carryanne put down her cup and huffed. "That is the silliest thing I've ever heard. What sort of parent does that?" She waved a calloused hand as if chasing away a fly. "Never you mind. You're a Clay now, that's all the family you'll need. When we go back inside, remind me to show you where I hung the clipping from the newspaper."

"Put it in the kitchen she did, pride of place above the spice rack," Layden said. "I offered to have it framed for her but apparently I was being 'silly' and should 'focus on framing my own daughter's achievements'. Or something like that."

Layden's daughter Hanne waved a bit of sugar pumpkin at him. "I did a castle this morning. Frame that, Papa."

"*Drew* a castle," her mother Isobel corrected with a smile.

"See, that's how it starts. One day they're little girls drawing castles for you. The next, their spouses become famous and thank you in big newspapers," Carryanne said, nodding sagely.

Blushing was usually Nessa's reaction of choice but, right

now, Elise's cheeks burned. She didn't trust herself to speak, worried that she might cry.

Nessa said, "She's not my spouse yet, Mum. Although we really should see to that. I simply don't know... quite how to ask her."

Shocked, Elise was about to blurt out that she pretty much just did, when Nessa spoke again. "I suppose I could've hidden a ring in Elise's coat pocket for her to find. But then, she might be busy with meeting-the-in-laws nerves and horrible letters to notice. Hrm."

Everyone's eyes darted to Elise. With shaking hands, she checked her coat pockets. One had the letter. The other one... contained something hard. She pulled out a tiny pewter tin. Elise opened it and found that, resting on a sliver of red velvet, was a ring. A gold ring with intricate filigree framing a dazzling yellow stone.

Elise stared at it, her free hand at her chest. Cai began to cheer, and the others joined in.

Layden held up a hand. "I don't think Nessa's finished speaking. Even she can't propose without saying *something* romantic."

Nessa stuck her tongue out at him, but then, for the first time during this conversation, turned to Elise. She swallowed. "Right. I've memorised what I want to say, so please don't interrupt or I'll lose my flow."

Elise nodded.

Nessa took her hand and gazed down at it. "While we pretended to be wed, I thought a lot about marriage. How much it means to me. And how right it felt to say that I was your wife. How much I wanted it to be true. So... here goes." She bit her lip and then looked up from Elise's hand, right into her eyes.

"Heartling, you were Lady Elisandrine Falk when I met you. You unnerved me but also impressed and charmed me.

394

Then you changed into Elise Aelin and you went from a friend to a lover. After that you were Elise Glass, and you became my safety and joy. Now, I'm asking you to be Elisandrine, *or Elise*, Clay, my companion and worshipped wife for the rest of our lives."

Nessa's voice trembled and cracked. She cleared her throat. "That was it. But I'd like to add that I want anyone who sees you to know by the ring on your finger that you belong with someone. That someone needs and loves you so very much. Marianna thought she could win back your affection with the snap of her fingers. Maybe a wedding ring would've made her think twice? It symbolises that what you and I have is not a brief romance – it's for life."

Elise found herself trembling. "Never mind others, I am more interested in the ring reminding *me* that someone loves and needs me. That wonderful Nessa Clay is not a daydream, but the woman who actually married me. And you being equally reminded when you see the ring which I shall buy you soon." She kissed Nessa before adding, "In truth, I was planning to propose to you when we were reunited in Highmere. But I had no ring, and, more importantly, I worried that since you are the sensible one, you would feel it was too soon. We have only been together for about two years."

Nessa's eyes twinkled. "True. However, I've learnt to trust in us. And to remember that life is a fragile, short thing. Let's be happy now and we can be sensible later. I just want to blow glass, drink in taverns with this lot," she pointed to Cai, Fyhre, Jac, and Sanjero, "and visit Ground Hollow. However, all that would lose its appeal if I couldn't do it with you."

Elise blew out a shaky breath, clutching the box with the ring tightly. "Then it's settled! Put me down for all of that. Except the glassblowing, I have oils to make. And what better place to source ingredients than Ground Hollow with its remarkable apothecary?" She bowed to Layden and Isobel.

"And its lovely natural ingredients," she added while nodding to Carryanne and Jon.

"An' then sell the oils in Nightport where I s'pose they can be transported to places all over the orb?" Cai asked.

"Exactly," Elise said.

She leaned back in Nessa's arms while carefully putting the band on her ring finger.

"It fits," Sanjero said breathlessly.

"Aye, an' its a lovely little stone. Topaz, I reckon," Jac added.

"Exactly. Golden yellow. Like your eyes," Nessa whispered into Elise's ear.

Elise snuggled deeper into Nessa's embrace as they watched the band and its stone glimmer in the sunlight. The ring seemed to steady Elise and to radiate bliss throughout her. The anguish and stress of the past months was melting away. Even the pain of her mother's letter dulled to a distant ache.

"I love you with all my heart, Nessa Clay."

"I love you right back, Elisandrine Clay."

Elise could hear Anja's voice in her head. *Clay? That's a bit premature. Still, congratulations and all that. Now, stop being sappy for snow's sake. Light the fire and I'll put coffee on.* She couldn't wait to tell her and Hunter.

A warm breeze blew through, ruffling their hair as the others congratulated them and toasted them in tea and juice. Elise thanked them distractedly. Her focus was on Nessa's warm embrace and on that ring, which seemed to have become a part of her immediately.

Closing her eyes to take it all in for a moment, she thought to herself, *Now this… this is true magic.*

CHAPTER 41

MARIANNA AND MAGIC

There were sounds of skittering animals outside her window. Her barred window. Marianna huffed under her breath. If she was to be kept prisoner indefinitely, she could at least have been allowed to keep her usual bedchamber. This dilapidated two-room cottage deep in the castle grounds was too remote, too quiet. It had *animals* outside. And dirt. Not to mention that the lack of courtiers' watchful eyes made her guards foul-mouthed and vulgar. She was quite certain that the man and woman guarding the door were bedding each other, sometimes while on duty. And the one at the back, currently calling to whatever animals had been skittering around in the bushes, seemed too dense to even notice. What was worse, not a single one of them had responded to her flirtations. Neither had their replacements for the night shift. Adaire must have chosen them well, picking guards with terrible taste.

She heard the shuffling of guards' heavy boots outside the door and then the words, "Good evening, Your Majesty. Have you come to see the prisoner?"

Marianna huffed again.

397

"Your Majesty." Ha! And imagine asking if she has come to see the prisoner. No, she came to steal the roof shingles, you oxen-brained muscle mountain.

"Yes. Unchain the door, please."

Adaire's voice was clear and crisp, as always. It caused a knot in Marianna's stomach. As the procedure with the locks took place, she prepared herself for the horrible mix of longing and loathing that always overtook her when she saw the betraying bitch she had loved. Still *did* love, in her own way.

The door opened and closed behind the thin woman in white and mauve, shades which suited her colourings so beautifully it forced Marianna to stare in admiration.

Adaire inclined her head. "Marianna."

She nodded back. "Betraying pond-dweller."

If the insult hurt Adaire, she hid it well. She merely clasped her hands in front of herself and asked, "Are you well? You look somewhat pallid."

"Being locked up indoors will do that to a person."

"Fair enough. Still, you get more light and air here than you would down in the dungeons."

There seemed to be true concern in those intelligent eyes. For a moment Marianna wanted to fall into her arms and complain about life's unfairness, like she had done so many times. Nevertheless, she steeled herself, recalling that this unfairness was created by the very woman from whom she wanted comfort.

Adaire's face was blank. "Curb your self-pity. You brought this upon yourself."

"Leave."

"No. Not until I have visited you for a while. You grow maudlin when you do not get any social interaction."

"I grow maudlin when I am forced away from my birthright and hid in a mouldy, tiny cottage!"

Adaire held out her hands in a soothing gesture. "Calm

yourself, that vein at your temple is throbbing so badly I can see it from here. I will remain until we have talked, you cannot stop me."

Marianna snorted but said nothing.

"Now, I bring news. Your brother and Kelene have had their first child. A healthy daughter, I am told. They have settled in Obeha, apparently enjoying the heat. You know how Kelene dislikes the cold."

Marianna scoffed. "She is thinner than a piece of paper, she would be freezing while sitting in a flaming pyre."

"Let us not be unkind. Her body shape is none of our business. Rejoice that they are thriving. Macray has been given a post at the Arclid consulate in Obeha. Which brings him purpose and coin." The corners of Adaire's mouth turned down. "Also, I can have someone keep an eye on him. I am told he is so busy working now that he has little time to cheat on his wife. Another piece of good news."

Marianna glared at her. "Are we done? Are you leaving now?"

Adaire was silent for a spell.

Then she sighed. "I do not think you actually want me to leave. You must loathe me, but I believe you also miss me. I know that look in your eyes. Besides, I should think it breaks up the tedium of the day." She peered at the desk in the corner. "I see you have been writing today. Still working on your memoirs?"

"Yes, I am calling them *The One True Queen*. The finished book will be obligatory reading in all schools when the people tire of your dull reign and return me to the throne."

Adaire closed her eyes for a moment. She looked so tired. Or perhaps that was resignation? Guilt? Marianna had never been good at reading people's emotions. It bored her.

"Let us change the topic for a short while. Do you think we can do that, Marianna?"

"*We* are not doing anything. I am merely an unwilling audience to this monologue of yours. By the way, you need to have that dress tightened in the waist, it is not as flattering as it could be."

The ghost of a smile came and went on Adaire's pale lips. "I shall not thank you for the advice, as my reign is more focused on my abilities as a leader than my desirability." Her voice quieted as she added, "However, it gladdens me to find you eyeing my figure and still remembering it so well. Despite everything, that makes my heart beat faster."

"What! Your heart still beats? I was beginning to think it never had, you cold-blooded, gods-cursed betrayer!" Marianna's screams sounded even louder than usual in this quiet place.

Good, let them echo in her head for all eternity.

She considered spitting at Adaire's feet but did not want to dirty up her two measly rooms even further. The dust was bad enough. Someone should clean. Someone else, naturally. She was not going to stoop that low.

Adaire sighed once more. "You are even more ill-tempered today than usual. I shall leave you to it as soon as I have asked you one final question."

"If it makes you leave faster, I shall answer anything," Marianna growled.

Adaire stepped over to the cottage's only table and single chair. She sat down carefully.

"I have scoured all the books and annals of the Hargraves, even the ones you held back from Nordhall–"

Marianna cackled. "Nordhall. The *stalwart soldier and strategist*. Ha! I heard my guards say that he now languishes in prison, tried and convicted for seven crimes against Storsund. He shall never know whether magic is real or not now. All he shall know is his cell and that his name is besmirched for all of history."

Adaire closed her eyes. "Anyway. Most of the books mention magic in passing, but they either do not determine if it exists or give conflicting information. One saying that magic exists here because of our location on the orb, another saying that magic cannot exist because of the cease in the quakes of the landmasses. I cannot get a clear answer."

"Good. You do not deserve answers."

"Marianna, put your fury aside for a mere moment! As someone who has lived with me, ruled with me, mourned with me, and spent hours coupling with me… just speak plainly."

Marianna laughed derisively. "Why should I? Out of some form of loyalty? Nostalgia?"

"I suppose there is no point in asking you to tell me so that I may rule Arclid better?"

Marianna raised her eyebrows.

"Fine. Let us bargain," Adaire said wearily. "I hasten to say that I do not *need* to know this. Joiners Square is dissolved so not in a state to search for secrets anymore. The authorities of Storsund, Obeha, and the Western Isles do not seem to want to know, out of fear or naivety, I'm not sure. This curiosity is my own. So, do not even consider trying to bargain for your freedom. I am not *that* curious."

Marianna pursed her lips. "All right. What will you offer me?"

"You can have all the books from your old bedchambers, your adored clockwork monkeys, more writing materials, and boxes of candied fruits every day."

"I want those things and one more."

"Name it."

"I want your weekly visits changed."

Adaire rubbed at her forehead. "Fine. Would you prefer monthly?"

"Daily." The word came out quieter than Marianna would have liked, but she stood tall, keeping the power in her body.

Adaire's brows knitted. "You wish for me to visit every day? You want to have this fight, or your stubborn silences, every day?"

"Yes. That will be your punishment. Besides, as you say, it breaks up the day."

That was better. You sounded nonchalant. Now, just keep your face still. She cannot see your need for her in your eyes, she only claims to be able to. Stay still. Stay strong.

"As you wish. I shall bring the objects with me when I visit tomorrow."

Marianna gave a curt nod. Not trusting her voice not to waiver if she spoke now.

Adaire sat back in the chair. "So, with that settled, tell me the truth. Does magic exist?"

Marianna walked to the table, extending her strides so that the outline of her long legs could be seen through the dress' material. Adaire had always loved her legs.

Marianna huffed. "Silly woman. If magic existed, do you think I would still be here? Do you not think I would have magicked myself back in that castle and you into this dusty cage?"

"Perhaps. However, you might need ingredients for a potion, or require a wand. Or perhaps you still wish to hide your abilities. Maybe *you* do not possess magic, but there are those who do. The possibilities are endless."

She put one finger under Adaire's chin and raised it so that their eyes met. "Magic does not exist. My family kept pretending it did to have a bargaining chip and to make themselves appear to be superior. To keep us feared," she drawled. "There. Satisfied, my beautiful?"

She saw Adaire swallow, but her eyes showed no sign of submission. "Yes. Satisfied."

They looked at each other for a while. There was so much

history and conflicting emotion between them that the air seemed to thrum with it.

Slowly, Adaire reached up. Then she slapped away Marianna's finger from her chin. The gesture, so defiant and yet playful, made Marianna smile. It brought back memories.

Adaire stood up. "I shall take my leave. I will return tomorrow with your things."

Marianna crossed her arms over her chest. "Can I trust that?"

"I have always kept my promises to you," Adaire said softly. Then she knocked on the door to inform the guards that she wished to leave.

"True. You have never outright lied to me. Schemed, yes. But never lied when asked a clear question."

Adaire nodded to her as she left. The door was slammed shut and the chains replaced.

Marianna smiled to herself, feeling the small but important victory warm her through.

No, you have never lied when asked a clear question, my sweetest Adaire. I, however, have no problem doing that. I will lie to anyone I wish and they always believe me.

It is like... magic. Is it not?

White sparks of light, like miniature winter stars, appeared at her fingers. They crackled, danced, and then fizzled out.

GLOSSARY

LOCATIONS

The Orb
The small planet on which our story takes place in.
Arclid
A continent. (See map for further details)
Obeha
A continent. (See map for further details.)
Western Isles
A mass of islands making up a continent. (See map for further details.)
Storsund
A continent. (See map for further details.)
Sund
The southern part of Storsund. Highly urbanized and affluent.
Vitevall
The northern part of Storsund. Rich in natural reserves. Few cities, mainly forest, fjords and ice.
Orla
River which runs through most of the continent

Skarhult

Sund's largest city with many industries, amenities, and the orb's only cable car system.

Charlottenberg

Harbour city. Location of a large Joiners Square branch and the Storsund Trading Company.

Cawstone

Harbour town. The closest port to Highmere.

Highmere

Capital of Arclid. The Queen's castle is in the centre of Highmere and the city is mainly based around the royal court. Inhabited by Nobles as well as some commoners who are servants or soldiers.

Ground Hollow

A small farming village. Its only fame is that it borders Silver Hollow Castle. Home of Nessa Clay.

Silver Hollow Castle

Royal castle. Old and not well maintained. Residence of Prince Macray (next in line to the throne after his sister, the Queen.)

Little Hollow

Tiny, farming village neighbouring Ground Hollow. The two villages are
connected through a man-made canal.

Nightport

A vast harbour city with a bad reputation but is experiencing a renaissance due to the invention of steam power and following progress

Silverton

Affluent town mainly inhabited by Nobles. Surrounded by a lake. This is where Elisandrine Falk was born.

PEOPLE/GROUPS

Joiners Square

Began as a union for joiners but soon grew to a shadowy, morally corrupt organisation striving for power over all of Storsund.

Viss
A people/creed who reside in Vitevall, the northern part of Storsund,

Wayfarers
A people/creed who live all over Storsund and have an ambulatory lifestyle

Sundes
A people/creed who reside in Sund, the southern part of Storsund

Nobles
The richest and most influential people (after the royal family) in Arclid.

LANGUAGES

Vissian
Language spoken in Vitevall, the northern part of Storsund
Sundish
Language spoken in Sund, the southern part of Storsund
Arclidian
Language spoken in Arclid.

MISCELLANEOUS

Joiners Square Fest
Yearly festivity on the frozen ice of the river Orla, held by Joiners Square.
The War of Thorns
Historic event. A feud between two royal families in Arclid.
Centurian marble

Marble, expensive building material known for its pink striation in white stone

New Dawning
Architecture style invented by royal architects in Highmere, Arclid.

Leaf tea
Tea made with whatever herbs and edible leaves are around.

FLORA AND FAUNA

Sugar pumpkins
A small pumpkin that is incredibly sweet. Indigenous to Arclid. Often used instead of honey or sugar in food, as it is cheaper and more readily available.

Winter cherries –Darkly purple cherries which grow only in Storsund. More tart and fragrant than usual cherries

Ebony root
A root known to keep its black colour and thick texture no matter what it is mixed with. Component of black wine. Has an aniseed-like scent.

Black wine
Storsund speciality. A viscous wine made with blackberries, ebony root and then mixed with honey

Gullveig root
A root which when ground up is often used as pain medication in Storsund. Unpalatable taste and a tendency to intoxicate.

Green veined cheese
A strong cheese. Like blue-veined cheeses but with a more fruity flavour.

Ice-eel
Eels which survive in low tempered water. Frequent in the river Orla.

Ice bear
Twice the size of an average bear. Lives only in the coldest

parts of Vitevall but are famous around the world as the most ferocious predator on the orb. White fur and grey eyes.

White shrooms

A mushroom that when dried can sooth aches. Main use is that it improves moods and calms. Mild effect.

Tree shrooms

Similar to White shrooms but twice as potent and may cause hallucinations.

Lux beetles

Large insects that glow in the dark. Their appearance is somewhere between our butterfly and our firefly.

Marrow-oxen

Similar to our bovine creatures but slightly larger and more muscular. Often used in rural areas.

Skitter beetle

Fast, black beetles with wide backs and many small legs. Sometimes has white markings on the back, especially on the females.

Sunberry

Big, sweet, yellow berries. The flavour is similar to a mix of our strawberries and cloudberries. Together with water and honey, it makes Sunberry juice. Frequently used in the making of various kinds of alcohol.

Winterberry

Small, tart, red berries. Tastes like a mix of our cranberries and blackcurrants. Often used to make brandy but also mixed with water and honey to make juice.

Dammon nuts

Small, sweet, and oily nuts. Tastes like almonds but are softer, thereby easier to smash for food and to make oils. Common all over Arclid.

Yellowfish The most common fish in Arclid. Looks and tastes a bit like cod, but has a creamy yellow colour.

Milk cabbage A sort of flavourless but very nutritious white cabbage that is common in the midlands and exported to the rest of Arclid.

ARCLID'S GODS

Thrale
One of Arclid's main three deities. God of the sea. Usually depicted as an old, strong, weathered man with white skin and a blue beard. Traits: Indifferent to human suffering but will listen to the prayers of those who live a wholesome and healthy life. Wise and with a sense of humour.

Harmana
One of Arclid's main three deities. Goddess of the land (the ground/the soil). Usually depicted as a voluptuous, brown-skinned, large woman of great beauty with green eyes. Traits: patient, promiscuous, quiet and caring.

Aeonh
One of Arclid's main three deities. God of the sky. Depicted as a handsome, gaunt, tall man. Skin tone varies with times of day. Traits: Usually kind, unless he becomes jealous or suffers unrequited love.

Ioene
A minor Arclidian goddess. Goddess of the moon. In love with the goddess Sarine but forced apart from her by Aeonh. Usually depicted as a small, pale, timid but beautiful woman.

Sarine
A minor Arclidian goddess. Goddess of the sun. In love with the goddess Ioene but forced apart from her by Aeonh. Usually depicted as a yellow-skinned, curvy, radiant woman.

Sauq
A minor Arclidian god/goddess. God/goddess of death. Has no gender. Usually depicted as a pitch-black cat-like creature but much larger than any human or any of the other gods.

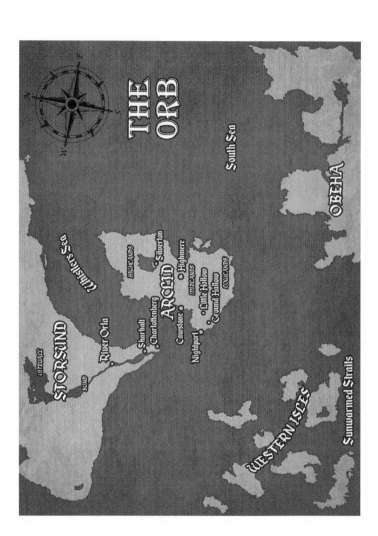

Reviews are essential for authors, especially in small genres like lesbian fiction. Regardless of quality, books without reviews quickly fall down the charts and into obscurity.

That's why authors need ARC Reviewers. These are people who are willing to provide an honest review in exchange for an early, free copy of a book.

If you would like to be an ARC Reviewer for me, please click the link below:

http://tiny.cc/emmaarc

Emma Sterner-Radley spent far too much time hopping from subject to subject at university, back in her native country of Sweden. One day, she finally emerged with a degree in Library and Information Science. She thought libraries was her thing, because she wanted to work with books, and being an author was just an impossible dream, right? Wrong. She's now a writer and a publisher. (But still a librarian at heart, too.)

She lives with her wife and two cats in England. There is no point in saying which city, as they move about once a year. She spends her free time writing, reading, daydreaming, working out, and watching whichever television show has the most lesbian subtext at the time.

Her tastes in most things usually lean towards the quirky and she loves genres like urban fantasy, magic realism, and steampunk.

Emma is also a hopeless sap for any small chubby creature with tiny legs, and can often be found making heart-eyes at things like guinea pigs, wombats, marmots, and human toddlers.

Connect with Emma
www.emmasternerradley.com

Published by Heartsome Publishing
Staffordshire
United Kingdom
www.heartsomebooks.com

Also available in paperback.
ISBN: 9781912684083

First Heartsome edition: April 2018

This is a work of fiction. Names, places and incidents are either products of the author's imagination or used fictitiously. Any resemblance to actual persons, living or dead (except for satirical purposes), is entirely coincidental.

Emma Sterner-Radley asserts the moral right to be identified as the author of this work.

Copyright © 2018 Emma Sterner-Radley

40959077R00250